THE MAN
in the
BLEACHERS

E. J. Bridgwater

BREWED INK
PUBLISHING

The Man in the Bleachers
Copyright © 2020 by E. J. Bridgwater

All rights reserved. This book or any portion thereof may not be reproduced or used in any manner whatsoever without the express written permission of the publisher except for the use of brief quotations in a book review or similar communication. Thank you for your support of the author's rights.

Published by Brewed Ink Publishing

ISBN: 978-0-9920885-3-8 (paperback)
ISBN: 978-0-9920885-4-5 (ebook)

Cover Design by Robin E. Vuchnich
Formatting by Maureen Cutajar

Printed in the United States of America

For Ian

The problem with revenge is that it never evens the score.
It ties both the injured and the injurer to an escalator of pain.
Both are stuck on the escalator as long as parity is demanded,
and the escalator never stops.

—Lewis B. Smedes

August 16, 1920
Polo Grounds
Manhattan, New York

Chapter 1

The man in the bleachers looked down at the field below and blinked. Twice. Then grunted. His attention had briefly wavered, causing him to miss a critical two seconds of action. There'd been a sudden loud crack, like a tree branch snapping. And when he'd looked up again, the Cleveland batter, who only seconds before had stood poised and upright at the plate, now lay sprawled in a heap on the ground, the crowd around him looking on, open-mouthed in stunned silence.

Missing what had triggered this unsettling turn of events annoyed the man. Almost as much as not being able to retrieve the tiny treasure he knew lay hidden within the sticky clusters of popcorn and peanuts in the box of Cracker Jack clutched in his lap.

Down on the field, a group of uniformed men anxiously surrounded the batter, unsure of what to do next, then settled on searching for a pulse. One of the men, dressed head to toe in black, pushed the others out of the way and bent down. He placed two fingers on the man's neck. Stood up. Shrugged. Shook his head.

This made the man in the bleachers smile. While he'd had nothing to do with the man laying spread-eagle on the ground, he appreciated the irony of it all. How life promised one thing and then delivered the unpredictable.

"Yes, indeed!" he chuckled softly to himself. *Always the unexpected!*

Pulling a pristine handkerchief from his blazer pocket, the man carefully unfolded it, then wiped away the late summer grime that had settled into the creases of his deeply weathered face, unconsciously avoiding the ragged scar that ran down his right cheek to just below his chin. His dark, impatient eyes furtively scanned the crowd around him. No one seemed the least bit interested in either him or his Cracker Jack. He tucked the handkerchief away, took off his hat, and ran a scarred but carefully scrubbed hand through his thick dark hair. Then he replaced his hat and shifted awkwardly in his seat, trying to ease the pain in his battered left leg. A pain and a limp that reminded him every day of the deep injustice he had sworn to avenge. At whatever cost.

"Jesus—!" blurted the man to his left. "Did ya see that?"

"I did see that," the man lied. *Well, not really. But any fool could guess what happened.* Giving the Cracker Jack box a little shake, he turned his attention back to what he'd been doing before the interruption and thrust his hand into the red, white, and blue rectangular package once again, probing for the toy he knew lay deep within. As he dug into the contents, his jacket sleeve rode up his arm, revealing a thinly sketched tattoo. A simple blue outline. A turtle, its outstretched legs propelling it forward. An imprudent souvenir from having sailed across the equator. Now, a signal buoy in the currents of destiny, guiding his every step forward.

"No, but did you—" the other man continued, having jumped to his feet to get a better look along with most of the crowd. "One minute he's standing there, the next—bam! Flat on his back."

The man in the bleachers frowned once again, shaking the Cracker Jack box back and forth as he peered deep inside. "Mm. Yes. That's what I saw," he said absently. Still focused on the task before him, he groped once again for the prize, tantalizingly just out of reach. "I expect he's dead," he added.

The man to his right chimed in. "Dead? Ya think so? I've never seen that before."

"Sounded like a gunshot from here," the man with the Cracker Jack box added, more to himself than as an attempt to be part of the discussion.

The crowd on all sides judged the remark an invitation to offer their own insights, and voices pitched in from all sides.

"Gunshot? Nah. He got hit is all. But hit good."

"I don't think that's ever happened before."

"I come here a lot. Can't says I've *ever* seen it," offered a third.

"I seen it once. Not much came of it," said a man in wire-rimmed glasses, his dirty gray overalls and workman's flat cap in sharp contrast to the others in their white and beige summer suits.

"Yeah, well, I've seen it before," declared yet another. "But not so's someone's out cold like that. I don't think he's gettin' up. Ya know what I mean? I think he's out. For good."

"I seen lots of guys get hit, but no one's ever…died," said the first voice. "Ya think he's dead? I don't think I seen anyone ever died."

The man in the bleachers sighed and rolled his eyes. "Almost certainly dead," he repeated, then immediately added, "Ha!" and leapt to his feet. "Got it!" Extracting the prize from the box, he stared at it closely, his face revealing a satisfied smile.

A rooster.

Indistinct features. Soft, dull-gray tin. Didn't suggest much of anything, really.

Except to the man in the bleachers.

He looked around, but no one seemed interested in his achievement. Everyone was still focused on the man on the ground.

Sitting back down, the man twirled the flat, miniature sculpture between his fingers.

A rooster.

He cocked his head. What could it mean? It had a meaning, of that he was certain.

Every box held a prize. Every prize a prophecy.

It only needed to be realized. He pinched his brow, trying to squeeze some clarity into his thinking.

A few ideas emerged.

Morning. Rise up. Farm. Barnyard. A new day?

Ah, yes, that could be it. He smiled.

What luck! Yes, a new day indeed! A day to mark the beginning. A day to begin setting things right.

He nodded to himself, satisfied with the interpretation.

Most of the crowd had now returned to their seats, when down on the field below, the man on the ground suddenly twitched and rolled onto his side, prompting everyone to jump up again.

"Hey, look!" shouted the man on the left, leaping to his feet along with the rest of the crowd. "Look here! He's gettin' up! He's okay!" And in that split second of spontaneous celebration, he flung his arms wide, bumping the man still seated next to him and sending his treasured box of Cracker Jack flying.

"Whoa! Look out!" shouted a few of the others, dodging sticky bits of popcorn and peanuts.

The man in the bleachers sat perfectly still, eyes ablaze, lips stretched taut, the artery in his neck pulsing violently, the tiny toy rooster squeezed tightly between thumb and fingers.

"Oh, hey, sorry, pal," said the offender. "I just…well…," he stammered, pointing to the field below. "The guy there was gettin' up and—and that's good, right? And, jeez! I know it's not real charitable or anything, but…ya see…ya see, I thought maybe he'd died. And no one's ever died before bein' hit by a baseball! Not ever! Not one single person! And, so…I was just thinkin'…ya know…this could be my lucky day! This'd be a first! And I was here to see it! That'd be somethin', huh? Bein' a witness, and all?"

The man in the bleachers said nothing.

"It'd be somethin' to tell my gran' kids, that's for sure!" the man continued. "First person ever killed by a pitch? Yep, that'd be somethin'!"

The man squeezed the rooster harder and continued to stare straight ahead. Finally, with great care, he tucked the prize into his vest pocket. "Indeed," he allowed. "That would be something."

"So, yeah…like I said, sorry about those Cracker Jacks, Mr.…uh… Say, what's your name, pal?"

Arthur Trystan Maddocks looked up at the man to his left. Then blinked twice. A thin smile leaked across his face. "Do you, yourself, come here very often, Mr....?"

"Buster Markle...uh-huh! Pleased," the man said, thrusting his hand forward in greeting, his smile bursting with self-confidence. When no hand came back to him, he lowered his own, then tried again. "You're not from around here, are you?"

"No. I am...not from around here."

"I could tell!" cackled Markle. "The accent's kinda—! You're—"

And before the man could venture a guess, Maddocks interrupted. "I take it you're quite fond of baseball, Mr. Markle."

"Sure am! I can get pretty worked up about it. I mean, I guess I did, huh?" A giddy grin pumped at his cheeks. "But I know a lot about it, that's for sure!"

"Do you?"

"More'n most people. And that's by a long shot! All sorts of things, even. Like..." The man paused for a moment to think. "Like, uh...who was it had the only...uh...jeez, what d'ya call it?" he stumbled, momentarily lost. "Oh...oh yeah...the only unassisted triple play?" The words came out like a newspaper headline, his face a mixture of anticipation and smugness.

Maddocks knew nothing about baseball, let alone this triple play thing. Nor did he care. He'd only come to the ballgame to clear his mind and reassess the intricate plan he'd been assembling for the past three years. And maybe have some Cracker Jack.

"Tell me."

"Neal Ball, Cleveland Naps shortstop, July 19, 1909." The man slapped his thigh in delight as he awaited a congratulatory response. "That'd be somethin', right? A triple play?"

Maddocks nodded, raising the rooster up to the sky for closer examination. "You do indeed seem to know quite a lot about baseball, Mr. Markle."

"Well," said the man, feigning modesty, "not everything. But yeah, I *do* know a lot."

"Mm. I see. Well…tell you what," said Maddocks, wiping the last bits of Cracker Jack from his lap. "After this game is over, perhaps you and I could take in some…refreshment together. And you could tell me…all about baseball."

"Say, that's very hospitable of you! Sure, I'd like that. Like I said, not many know more about the game than me."

Maddocks stared at the man called Markle, his own smile now vanished.

"Perfect," he said, turning back to watch as the game started up again. "I'd love to pick your brain."

August 17, 1920
Bronx, New York

Chapter 2

The smell of freshly brewed coffee and minutes-ago-baked biscuits filled the air at Aleta Jean's Sun's Up Coffee Shop. Like most days, the restaurant hummed with the usual early morning clamor as orders were shouted back and forth, dishes deposited here and there, and a steady stream of people shuffled in and out. The bell over the door greeted every customer with the same cheerful equanimity, regardless of what mood traipsed in with them.

Lucas Blaine sat at the back of the coffee shop in booth number nine, buried deep in his morning edition of the *New York Tribune*. Bright sea-green eyes, a handsomely sculpted, clean-shaven face and a square, no-nonsense jaw, together with a carefully Brilliantined and perfectly parted full head of dark brown hair, projected a look of confidence and strength. A look that disguised the fact he'd seen too much world in too little time, much of it abhorrent.

Absently, he brushed away a few non-existent crumbs from the lapels of his vaguely gray gabardine suit. Beneath the suit, a thin black tie hung nonchalantly down the front of a nearly pressed white shirt. A slightly crushed felt fedora rested on the chair next to him.

Lucas was aware of the disparity between his wardrobe and his physical presence and knew that if not for his lean, well-muscled body and ramrod-straight posture, he could easily be mistaken for someone in need.

But the notion didn't bother him.

Fashion was never his forte, as he long ago had decided that integrity was fashion enough.

Besides, he was simply more comfortable in a uniform.

Preferably one with a number on the back.

And as owner and manager of the Bronx Bulldogs, a popular and respected minor league baseball team, he'd be putting one on again within the hour.

For the third time that morning, he glanced up from his paper, hoping to determine why his eggs were still incarcerated somewhere in the kitchen instead of sitting on the table in front of him. It was already seven-thirty.

Not like I've never been here before, he mused. *Same booth. Same order.*

Yet he wasn't upset. The army had taught him patience. And the war had taught him gratitude. It was just that…well, he had a job to do and barely a month left to do it. And like every morning during baseball season, he was anxious to get on with it.

As usual, he sat facing the door.

As usual, he wasn't alone.

Sitting across from him, engrossed in his own newspaper, was the man responsible for Lucas still being alive.

Zacharia V. Tucker.

At six-three, 238 pounds, muscles that begged to be liberated from his checkered tweed suit, and a coarse fringe of red beard that rambled recklessly along a chiseled jawline, Zach looked like a lumberjack in need of a tree to fell. A weathered, indurate sculpture ripped from a stubborn chunk of granite.

But looks are never a complete narrative.

And what Lucas saw was something else.

Reliability. Honesty. Tolerance. Discretion. A friend you could call on when your own world was crumbling to pieces. The kind of friend too few people had.

Abruptly, Zach leaned forward. "Son of a bitch!"

Lucas smiled. Zach had a reliable way of summing up pretty much everything with the same four words. Frustrated, excited, confused, forlorn, surprised, angry at times—it really didn't matter. "Son of a bitch" was the way he tallied up the world. A world that, more often than not, revolved around baseball. Which wasn't all that surprising, considering his self-appointed role as the Bulldogs' assistant manager.

"Son of a bitch," Zach repeated, laying more emphasis this time on the "son" than the "bitch."

Lucas assumed this particular "son of a bitch" must have something to do with the Yankees. It almost always did. But before Lucas could question the reason for the outburst, Zach thrust his coffee cup aloft, and without looking up, yelled over his shoulder.

"Aleta!"

On the far side of the restaurant, a sturdy woman in her mid-fifties with a no-nonsense bun of gray hair pulled tight to the back of her head glanced up from the conversation she was having with another customer and looked right over at Zach. An all-encompassing look that did not include rushing right over.

"I don't think she's coming," Lucas observed, chancing a quick look in the direction of the kitchen, his eggs still nowhere to be seen.

"You'd think she'd be better at service," Zach grumbled. "Bein' the owner of this here place and all!" He lowered his cup to the table. "Woman's got attitude, Lucas! That's what she's got."

"Yep. Got the coffee, too, Zach."

Zach grunted acknowledgement, and a few more moments passed before he spoke again. "Damn, Lucas! Right in the head!" He looked up briefly to make sure he had Lucas's attention. "He's in the St. Lawrence. Up on 163rd, near Edgecombe."

"That hospital near the Polo Grounds?"

"That's the one."

"Okay. So. Who's in St. Lawrence?"

"Ray Chapman. Shortstop for the Cleveland Indians."

"Zach, I know who Ray Chapman is. What happened?"

"Got clobbered in yesterday's game. Pitch to the head."

"Christ! In the head? Who beaned him? It was Mays, right?"

"Yeah, Mays," nodded Zach.

Lucas knew all about the notorious Carl Mays. Even now, he could see him bent over on the mound, ready to throw his often terrifying and always deceptive spitball, a wobbly, unpredictable pitch that regularly sent players flailing to the ground. In fact, Mays was routinely accused of hitting batters on purpose, just to keep them off balance.

"Says here," Zach continued, eyes squinting, "'the player was placed on the operating table at midnight after a conference in which five phys—physicians took place.'" He looked across the table. "Son of a bitch, Lucas. Five docs. Must be bad."

"Mm," Lucas agreed. *Definitely not good. Or good for the game.*

Only last year, the Chicago White Sox had been accused of intentionally throwing the World Series. And that was just the start. Talk really got heated after Hugh Fullerton's article in the *Evening World* claimed the whole sport had become a victim of pervasive gambling.

In the end, it wasn't the gambling that got people upset. Gambling, after all, was just another sport.

It was the *cheating* that made people's blood boil. Cheating. Now *that* was un-American.

"Baseball could use some good news," Lucas reflected.

"Could do. But yer Yankees're lookin' after that, Lucas. The Babe's already hit forty-two. Still a month and a half to go!" Zach reached for his cup, realized it was still empty. "What the—? Damn that—!" He jumped up from in his seat, waving his cup high above his head. "Aleta!" he demanded, looking about.

Finally allowing that she wasn't anywhere in sight, he scowled and sat back down. "Damn! And all her relations, too!" he spat. "Where is that woman?"

"Could be fifty," Lucas interrupted.

"She's well on fifty, Lucas, and just as ornery as a—"

"The Babe, I was sayin'. Might hit fifty."

"What? Oh." Zach brightened. "Fifty! Hell, yeah! Near double what he hit last year? That'd be somethin'!" Zach's momentary enthusiasm faded as he turned back to his paper. "Won't be much of a celebration, though, if Chapman doesn't make it."

Lucas started to reply when he spotted Aleta's niece coming out of the kitchen. Willa May Pierce wove her way between the tables and across the room, a platter of scrambled eggs held aloft in one hand, a cup of coffee in the other. At five-foot-eleven, she was taller than many of her male customers, and few failed to notice her youthful beauty blossoming out in all directions. Sunflower-blonde hair, dazzling blue eyes, and a mischievous smile all colluded to make men wish they were someone they weren't, achieving things that they couldn't. But Lucas had succeeded in winning her heart from the day they'd first met, and they'd been discovering each other's likes and dislikes, and a great deal more, ever since.

"There you go, Mr. Tucker," she said, setting down the coffee. Zach grunted.

"And breakfast for you, Mr. Blaine," she said impishly, setting down a platter of eggs and bacon in front of Lucas. For Aleta's sake, the two had vowed to keep any overt displays of affection out of the coffee shop, but their emotions didn't always cooperate. "Sorry about that," she added. "A little mix-up in the kitchen." Her face worked a polite smile to conceal any telltale emotion.

"I was beginning to wonder," Lucas said, burying his own smile, "if maybe all your hens had just stopped layin'."

"Well, as you know, Mr. Blaine," Willa said, her voice dropping to a whisper as she leaned into his face, close enough for him to smell her perfumed neck, "our hens are very particular and only lay for people of good character. As a result...," she added, looking around, "...there was some debate as to whether *you* could be accommodated." She gave a quick glance over her shoulder to ensure that Aleta still had her back to the booth, then gave Lucas a quick kiss. "As it turns out," she added, abruptly straightening up, "we decided—or, at least, I decided—you're pretty fair fowl!"

"Well, as it turns out," he replied, "you and your hens have pretty good taste."

"Speakin' of taste," Zach interrupted, his eyes never leaving his paper, "could you two not do that while I'm still eatin'?"

"You just drink your coffee and stop minding other people's business," chided Willa. Then she bent down, sticking her face nearly into his. "Vernon!" she chirped, as if that would settle it. Like most people, she had no idea what the "V" in Zach's name stood for, but it never stopped her from trying to find out.

"Not even close," Zach smirked.

"And just how would anyone ever know is what I want to know," she pouted, tipping her dimpled chin at him.

"Those who need to already know."

"So you say. Well, I intend to be one of those people!" She threw Lucas a wink. "One day!" Wasting no more time, she stepped off to wait on another table.

Lucas watched her go, then dragged his eyes back to address his breakfast. Before he'd even lifted his fork, Zach started up again.

"Doc says it's serious, but not fatal." Sighing, he shook his head in disbelief, then rubbed a napkin across his face and beard, catching most of the egg entangled there. "Think I'll go over to the Ansonia. See what I can find out."

Lucas knew Zach would have no trouble running into a few of the Cleveland players at the Ansonia Hotel who would be eager to provide him with all of the gossip and most of the facts regarding yesterday's game.

"What about your coffee?" asked Lucas, as Zach stood up to leave.

Zach looked down at the steaming cup. "Yeah. That." He

grabbed his hat and started for the door. "Maybe tomorrow. I'll meet you up later." Without another word, he was gone.

Lucas went back to his paper and started in on his breakfast. A few bites in, a news headline so small it barely deserved the designation drew his attention.

Icepick Murder at Uptown Subway

Interest piqued, Lucas read the article.

> *A man aged thirty to thirty-five was found dead on the steps of the 168th street subway station shortly after ten o'clock last night. Police located an icepick covered in blood lying nearby. No identification was found on the victim and only a small metal rooster was recovered from the man's pockets. "Just a cheap tin toy, like something you might find in a box of Cracker Jack," Detective Arlo Barker asserted. "Most probably a robbery gone wrong." No witnesses have yet come forward.*

Icepick, thought Lucas. *Curious. But not so unusual. Not for New York, anyway.*

Plenty of gangs used an icepick to settle their grievances.

But, a rooster?

Now that was different.

Why would a grown man have a toy rooster stuffed in his pocket? A present for his kid, maybe? A good luck charm? A childhood keepsake? None of those ideas were satisfying. None of those ideas worked hard enough to dismiss his curiosity.

And for no other reason than to satisfy that curiosity, he wondered aloud. "Why a rooster?"

"Probably on the lookout for one very pretty chicken," answered Willa as she appeared at the side of his booth, coffeepot in hand, standing closer than Aleta would have liked. "More?"

"Of you? Always! But I gotta skip the coffee for now. I need to get to the clubhouse. See you after the game?"

Willa's cheeks dimpled. "Are you asking me for a date, Mr. Blaine?"

"I was thinking about it."

"Well, don't think about it too long," she huffed. "Some other handsome guy might come along and make me a better offer!"

Lucas stood up, leaned over, and gave Willa a quick peck on the cheek. "It'll be the last one he ever makes, you can be sure of that!" He grabbed his hat and headed for the door.

The rooster would have to wait.

Chapter 3

Tommy Marshall sat on a wooden crate just outside the clubhouse door throwing pebbles at an empty barrel while he waited for Lucas to arrive. As official bat boy and unofficial mascot for the Bronx Bulldogs, he deemed it his responsibility to be the first at the park for every practice as well as every game. Tall for his fourteen years, he had gentle, guileless, brown eyes and a soft, freckled face, topped by an exuberant burst of sandy-brown hair that rambled out from beneath a dirty, well-worn baseball cap. With long, gangly limbs that appeared to wander about aimlessly in all directions, he had the look of an awkward, but affable, ragdoll. But once a game was underway, he had no trouble chasing down foul balls or running to the batter's box to replace a broken bat. He knew every player's frustration limit. When to approach and when to stay away. He also knew most of the obscure rules of baseball and often quietly challenged an umpire's calls. When a call was too egregious, the challenge wasn't always so quiet.

But beyond this limited sphere of comprehension, Tommy often lacked insight into how the world worked or the ability to adjust to it. That didn't bother the players, though. Most everyone on the team liked the lad's gentle spirit and arcane game knowledge and appreciated his attentiveness to their individual quirks, outrageous tantrums, and inviolable superstitions.

The early morning air was still cool as Tommy aimed another pebble at the nearby barrel. He paid little attention to where it landed, focusing more on the carrot he was holding for the mound of caramel-colored fur that rested in his lap. The rabbit was as much a mascot as Tommy, and few players failed to stroke the animal's long, floppy ears before stroking their bat on the way to the plate. There was only so much bad luck a player could afford to attract, and those who failed to abide by the ritual were loudly castigated when the needed hit didn't show up.

Despite the early morning quiet, Tommy didn't hear the man come around the side of the clubhouse and sidle up next to where he was sitting.

"You're busy."

Tommy jumped to his feet, quickly wrapping both arms around the rabbit.

"Yes, sir."

"It's early for being at the ballpark. Are you part of the team?"

"Yes, sir. Well, no, sir, not official-like."

"Hmm. So, unofficially, we might say."

"Yes, sir. I think you could say."

"And what is it you're protecting with such…diligence…if I may ask?"

"I—I—with what, sir?"

"What have you got in your arms?"

"Oh, uh, that's Bear."

"Bear? A bit small for a bear, wouldn't you agree?"

Tommy looked at the ground and tugged at his jersey. Then back up at the man and smiled. "Oh, uh-huh. Yeah," he said, shaking his head. No, sir, it's—it's not a bear at all. No, sir. This here's my rabbit."

"Oh. So...not a bear." The man's eyes didn't participate in his smile.

"Oh, yes, sir. That's because his *name* is Bear." Tommy grinned and gave the animal a reassuring hug.

"Ah—well, that explains it, then. May I hold...Bear...for just a moment?"

Tommy jumped back a step and turned his face quickly to the ground. "Uh, well, no, sir. I mean, well, no, sir. He don't like being held by anyone else but me. I'm his—I'm his—I takes care of him, and so, well, no, sir. That is, Bear, he wouldn't want that. Uh-uh, not at all."

Twenty seconds passed. Then thirty. "So...," the man said finally, reaching into his jacket and pulling out a slightly dirty envelope. "I thought at this early hour I might have to break into the clubhouse to leave this for your Mr. Blaine myself, but I can tell that you will be a conscientious and...careful emissary of this important transmission. Therefore, I will depend upon you to deliver it posthaste into your manager's hands. Once he has arrived, of course."

Tommy looked up but was reluctant to take the envelope, as he wasn't entirely sure what some of the man's words meant.

"Give it only to Mr. Blaine. And as soon as he gets in. No one else. Clear?" He pushed the envelope further in the boy's direction.

Tommy hesitated, then snatched the envelope and quickly took a step back, retuning his gaze to the ground.

"No one else, yes?"

"Yes, sir. I—I mean, no, sir. No one else."

The man stood staring, considering. "Are you sure I couldn't just..." He shrugged his shoulders, as if to propose only a minor imposition. "...hold your pet for...one brief moment?"

Tommy looked at the ground.

"All right, then," said the man, absently stroking the scar that ran down his right cheek. "Perhaps another time." He took two steps back and then turned and limped away. "Yes, another time," he said to no one in particular. "I think we may depend on it."

Chapter 4

What with all the horse carts, push carts, motor vehicles, streetcars, buses, and bicycles—and Lucas stopping to applaud the numerous lines of women winding their way up Broadway waving their placards in favor of the Nineteenth Amendment guaranteeing women the right to vote—getting from Aleta Jean's Sun's Up Coffee Shop to the ballpark took twice as long as he'd counted on.

The Nineteenth was the second most contentious piece of legislation that Congress had entertained in the past twelve months, the first being the Volstead Act prohibiting the manufacture and sale of alcoholic beverages. Volstead had kicked off the year, and Lucas figured the Nineteenth might be ratified in the next day or so.

The difference between the two laws was stark. Volstead was largely ignored if not brazenly flaunted. Alcohol was readily available in thousands of venues, and a great many people considered the legal restriction nothing more than a minor nuisance. But the suffrage movement was something else again. For longer than anyone cared to admit, women had been denied the right to vote. But now, twenty-seven million voices were adamant that ignorance would no longer be bliss. Lucas wished them well but couldn't fathom how women were going to do a better job governing than men had done for centuries. Provided you didn't count an endless succession of apocalyptic wars and crippling national bankruptcies.

With the Great War almost two years in the past, the world was ready for change. And in no place was that feeling more palpable than America. Lucas had sensed it almost immediately upon returning from overseas. In business. In politics. In culture. In anything and everything that had once depended on an all-consuming and near universally respected code of conduct, people were now yearning for a new kind of freedom and a desire to celebrate just being alive.

As far as Lucas was concerned, the only thing that hadn't much changed was baseball. And most every waking moment of his life was consumed with the thought of it. Like the Yankees, his Bulldogs were figuring into a three-way pennant race, with enough games left to rally into first. And Lucas was intent on getting there. So when he stepped into the locker room that morning, he wasn't expecting to have to deal with the periphery of management minutiae before he'd even gotten around to the more important work of penciling in the day's lineup.

And yet, there it was.

A small but not insignificant puddle of water where water had no place being.

The clubhouse icebox, which had knocked around from team to team and was clearly arthritic even before it had finally made its way onto the Bulldogs' doorstep about two years prior, was leaking even worse than when Lucas had left it the day before. The wooden cabinet had rotted through in several places, making the drip pan all but irrelevant. His hopes that it would last out the season were leaking across the floor.

And right alongside that problem, mused Lucas, *looks like I've got another one.* Phil Dooley, the Bulldogs' swivel-footed third baseman. Hell of a ballplayer, Lucas had to acknowledge. But the brains of a corned beef sandwich.

Phil sat with one foot wrapped in a towel propped up on Lucas's desk, smoking the last four inches of a hand-rolled J. C. Newman's Judge Wright. Cigars were a ritual for many ballplayers and attracted stubborn loyalties based on little more than a cultured dislike of a brand favored by an uncultured opponent. Considering the hundreds of cigar makers that had inundated the country since the end of the war, the fact that Julius Caesar Newman had been able to keep his company thriving since its founding in 1895 was as much a testament to his marketing acumen as to the quality of his hand-rolled product. Lucas didn't mind the smoke, but he wasn't happy about Phil's foot. Or its being on his desk.

"Okay, Phil. What happened?"

"Stepped on a bat. My ankle fell over and kinda swole up."

"How swole up? One game? Five games?" Lucas was already starting to shuffle the deck for the next player card.

"Hmph. Can't really say. It's sore right now, but…I dunno." He reached down to tentatively stroke the bruise. "Probably just a game or two."

Lucas figured that, like most athletes, Dooley was wishing more than calculating. Twisted ankles were generally bad for a couple of weeks. But the wrong kind of twist meant his season was over. With a .286 average and a pivot that would shame an Egyptian belly dancer, Phil Dooley was probably not going to step on third or any other base until next spring.

"Okay, so, I need your locker. And your bats." Lucas knew he needed to move forward. The club wasn't broke, but like most minor league teams, Lucas had to manage a lot of expectations with a limited amount of money. More winning, more gate receipts, more flexibility. And the Bulldogs *had* been winning. But they needed every edge they could get. Personal equipment got a whole lot less personal when someone wasn't playing.

"What the fuck?" Dooley stood up, one hand clutching the chair he'd been sitting in for balance, his damaged foot perched in the air. "Those bats got my prints on 'em. I'm not goin' anywhere. I'll be fine by tomorrow. Day after, worst."

"Yeah, well, until you can make it from home to first in under five seconds, you're on the bench. And as for the bats, there's no way they can be stacked in the dugout while we wait for you to recover. Give 'em to Tommy before you leave the clubhouse."

"Fuck." It was all Phil could conjure. The stogie jiggled up and down between his teeth as he stood stewing at Lucas, trying to think of something to argue. "Fuck," he repeated, with a little less energy. Further words failing, he grabbed a bat from beside the desk and, using it as a cane, hobbled toward the door.

"You'll see," he said.

Lucas was pretty sure he wouldn't.

As Phil left the office, Tommy Marshall stepped into the doorway. One arm dangled by his side, something clutched between his fingers that Lucas couldn't make out. Bear was perched in the crook of his other arm.

"Yeah?" Lucas asked without enthusiasm, one eye on the pile of papers on his desk.

Tommy shuffled in the doorway. Lucas could see he was trying to figure out whether he should be following Phil to the locker room or handing over what he had clutched in his hands.

"Tommy, you got something for me?"

"Yes, sir." Tommy looked a little shaken. "Man dropped it by this morning. Said give it to you directly." Tommy didn't move an inch.

"Well then, son, maybe that'd be a good idea. Given that that's what the man said."

Lucas sat down at his desk and started to disassemble the mess of papers that comprised the coming week's work. Without looking up, he gestured to the envelope that Tommy was strangling. "From one of the other managers, huh? Carter Flinn, maybe?" Managers often exchanged notes before games advising of lineup changes and other incidentals, so Lucas had no other expectation. Flinn's Sentinels were the opposing team that afternoon, and Lucas figured for sure it must be from him.

"No, sir, it weren't him. I know Mr. Flinn." Tommy still hadn't moved from the doorway. Always a little on the shy side, he looked more frightened than reticent.

"Okay, kid. Look, I've got a game coming up here. You going to massage that letter 'til it's got nothing to say, or maybe I could just have it, yeah?"

Tommy edged into the room and made his way over to Lucas's desk. He placed the envelope down like it was fine crystal, then bolted back to the door.

"Hold it! Right there." Tommy turned back to face the manager, but his face didn't want to play along and stayed fixed on the floor. "Now, you want to tell me what's on your mind? Because something's not right. Right?"

"Yes, sir." Tommy looked up. "That man—the one that came with the envelope? It's just he—that man...the man who give it to me, he was—he was kinda mean-like."

"Mean? You mean—what? Like he yelled at you?"

"No, sir, it wasn't that. He was smilin'."

"Smiling? Smiling don't usually mean mean, Tommy."

"No, sir. I mean, yes, sir. But, it *was* mean. The kinda smile that says, 'I ain't smilin'.'"

"But...he was smiling?"

"Yes, sir. But I could tell he don't mean it. And then he said..." Tommy looked down at the floor again.

"Then he said...?"

"He says, 'Don't give this letter to no one else.' And be sure you was alone. And—and be sure and give it to you as soon as you come in." Tommy shifted the rabbit to his other arm. "He was tryin' to take Bear."

"Trying to—hold on." Lucas stood up and came around the desk to where Tommy was standing. "What did this man look like? Have you seen him around the clubhouse before? Out on the field?"

"No, sir. He was new to me," he snuffled. "Not too tall, dressed real good. His hands was all sorta cut up. Real clean, though. And he had that kinda...mean face, you know? A big crease right across here." He dragged his fingers deep across his right cheek all the way under his chin in an effort to help Lucas picture what he meant.

"Crease." Lucas thought about that for a moment. "You mean a scar?"

"Yes, sir, a scar. A big one. And he said he wanted to hold Bear. But I wouldn't let him on accounta he looked mean. Smilin' and all." The words ran out of energy and trickled down to the floor.

Lucas's eyes were staring right at Tommy, but his brain was searching its own creases for a memory of someone who might fit the boy's description. Or anyone else who might want to send him a message. No one came to mind. No player. No fan. No manager. No angry father insisting his coddled and grown-up son get more playing time. No thug. No bookie trying to cut a deal. No anybody. In fact, it didn't ring any bells at all, warning or otherwise. Lucas could only put it down to Tommy being a sensitive kid. Which he was.

"Okay, look, Tommy, so this guy comes up to you and gives you this letter…that letter you just put on my desk, yeah? And then he asks you if he can hold Bear."

"Uh-huh."

"But he didn't try and grab your rabbit, is that right?"

"No. I mean, yes, he didn't try that. But he was mean."

"Well, okay, look," said Lucas, running his hand through his hair, trying to make some sense of what Tommy was saying. "Some guys just look mean. It's not their fault. Just like some guys look stupid, or ugly, or…or something, you know? It's not their fault. But he didn't try and take Bear or grab you or anything like that, yeah? So, let's just say this. Maybe he's not a bad guy. Maybe he just likes rabbits. And he doesn't know how to act nice. But…I'll tell you what. You see him again, you come get me right away. Okay?" Satisfied that he'd lowered the alarm, Lucas turned back to the mess on his desk.

Tommy stroked the animal's soft fur, head still to the ground. "I'm gonna put Bear in his pen."

"Yeah, that's it. And if you see this guy again, you come see me. In the meantime, you've got a game to get ready for, too."

Tommy turned to the door just as Zach stepped into the room. "Bear don't like other people holding him," the boy mumbled, pushing past Zach.

"Which I know," Zach said, standing aside as Tommy shuffled out the door. He turned to Lucas. "Rabbit problems?"

Lucas was about to provide clarification but Zach carried on. "Chapman's dead, Lucas. Went last night." He took off his hat and flung it on the chair that Dooley had recently vacated, stuck his hands on his hips. "Son of a bitch! Good player like Chapman. Nice guy, too. I don't think that's ever happened before." He thought about it for a few brief seconds, screwed up his face, and nodded his head. "Yep. Never happened. I tell you, the Cleveland guys are distressed, you can say that for sure."

Then, as if he'd said all that could be said about the recently deceased Cleveland shortstop, he abruptly changed topics.

"An' what about those damn amendment ladies, too! Marchin' all the way up here from the park, cloggin' the streets an' blockin' the subway! Never seen so damn many yellow roses! I was tippin' my hat, 'pardon me, ma'am,' all mornin,' like it was on a rubber band! You think that amendment's gonna pass, Lucas? Ladies gonna get the vote?"

"Already got it in nineteen of our forty-eight states, Zach. Right? Bound to happen."

"Son of a bitch!" Zach plucked his hat off the chair where he'd thrown it and sat down. "So, what's the lineup?"

"Working on it." Lucas picked up the envelope and held it up for Zach to see. "Somebody gave Tommy this envelope to give to me. Kinda scared the kid, this guy."

"One of the other managers?" guessed Zach. "Call 'em up," he added, pointing to the phone on Lucas's desk. "Call 'em up and ask."

"Maybe," thought Lucas, looking at the phone he'd only ever reluctantly used.

"Or, you could open it up," Zach added, pointing to the envelope. "There's that. People that send letters...mostly sign their name. And people that *get* letters..." His face cracked a smile.

"Yeah," said Lucas. "I get it. Look, Zach, do me a favor, would you? Go walk around the park, the clubhouse—out by the grandstand. See if there's anybody out there we don't know."

"We don't know lots of people."

"Yeah, but we know the others. So look for the ones we don't know that look like they don't want us to know 'em, and just see what you see. Looking for a guy that might be a bit rough."

Zach snorted. "This is a baseball park, boss. Won't have to look far."

"Got a scar, too. Big one. Right cheek, I think. But dressed pretty good. Just go have a look for me, would you? Someone that doesn't belong."

"Yeah, sure. Rough-lookin'. Scar. Dressed good. Anything else?"

"That's all I know right now."

Zacharia grabbed his hat and was out the door.

Lucas leaned back in his chair, and for the first time really looked at the envelope that Tommy had brought him. No delivery address. No return address. Nothing stood out. Just Lucas' name on the front of an ordinary envelope.

He looked back at the pool of water on the floor and tried to figure out the next best step, opting to postpone any hasty decisions. The ice man would know. He'd ask him when he came around with the delivery that afternoon. If he saw him.

Picking up the envelope in one hand, he grabbed his letter opener in the other, slid it under the flap, and sliced it clean across the top.

He could feel something inside. Something not quite…expected. Something more than a letter.

He rubbed the envelope between two fingers, trying to discern what it was. It was small, hard, but Lucas couldn't guess what. He tipped the envelope up and poured the contents out into his hand.

A miniature shovel.

Metallic. Vague detail.

Simple.

Like something you might give a child.

Like something you'd find in a Cracker Jack box.

Chapter 5

With one out in the bottom of the ninth, Chip Mavers, the Bulldogs' catcher, was extending his lead off first base just a little too far for Lucas's liking. More walrus than gazelle, and the score tied 4-4, Lucas didn't want him taking disproportionate chances on getting thrown out. Particularly with shortstop and go-ahead run Geoff Canwell stretching out an equally large lead off third. The Sentinels' pitcher was not known for his pick-off talent, and Lucas wasn't anxious to afford him an easy opportunity to improve his percentage.

Canwell was fast. Lucas wasn't worried about him being able to get back to third to tag up if necessary. But Mavers was a whole other story. He was only one for eight in steal attempts on the season and had been reminded on several regrettable occasions how imagination and reality could not be counted on to play on the same team.

Lucas guessed Mavers was thinking that by stealing second he could avoid the double play, should the batter smack a groundball.

Or, at least draw a throw on a sloppy pitch and give Canwell a chance to steal home. He also guessed Mavers wouldn't succeed.

Zacharia was pacing back and forth behind the bench, trying to wave the Bulldogs' catcher back to within striking distance of first base, but Mavers just grinned, implying he was ready to make a run for it.

"That idiot never learns," spat Zach. "He's one for eight. Tell me he's not."

Lucas smiled. He knew that Zach wasn't really talking to him. He was just talking. Just keeping the nerves at bay and the hope alive.

It was another muggy August afternoon. The temperature was pressing eighty degrees, and the humidity seemed to be sapping everyone's focus. Without permission, Lucas's thoughts began leaking back to his misbehaving icebox. Something needed to be done. A new icebox? Could the iceman fix it? Had he arrived during the game? Had he even noticed the leak?

Thoughts of his icebox were making Lucas thirsty. And notwithstanding the restrictions brought on by the Volstead Act, he was looking forward to a cold beer after the game. Numerous people in the crowd weren't waiting. Throughout the stands, Lucas could see glints of sunlight reflecting off silver-plated flasks being indiscriminately lifted to the sky. Despite the law. And despite the many turned-up noses of those who insisted the time had come to root out this reprehensible habit.

But sometimes, thought Lucas, *good people craft bad laws, forcing a whole lot of other good people to take the law into their own hands. And eventually break it. Usually, with unfortunate circumstances.*

Being arrested was only one potentially unlucky outcome of violating the Volstead Act. If the alcohol wasn't properly distilled, a person could end up blind. Or on a slab in the morgue. Which happened way too often.

Like millions of his fellow citizens, Lucas was all in favor of rooting out crime, corruption, and various social problems, the likes of which Prohibition was supposed to address. But in the long run, he didn't have much faith in the remedy. Which, at the moment, left him on the wrong side of the law, a place he wasn't comfortable being.

Everyone chooses their own morality, thought Lucas. *And on this issue, I'm gonna have to stay flexible.*

A small chorus of loud voices was now clamoring for the players to get on with the game.

The pitcher, weighing his chances, stared hard at Mavers, who was inching his way further off the first base bag, but after a good long look, decided to postpone a pick-off attempt and returned his attention to the batter.

At the plate, the Bulldogs newly ordained third baseman, Alex Conway, was looking to build on an already impressive outing, having gone two-for-three with a sharply hit single past the shortstop and a stand-up double to left center. The bat sat perched on his shoulder, his hands bobbing up and down, a steady rhythm of confidence and concentration.

Winding up in a way that would have dislodged any normal shoulder, the pitcher let go a ball high and outside, but Conway wasn't biting. Mavers had already moved several feet to his right, but when the catcher jumped to his feet to make a throw to first, he scrambled back to the bag.

Lucas liked the way Conway stood at the plate. In many ways, it reminded him of his temporarily disabled third baseman, Phil Dooley. *Phil Dooley*. His mind drifted back to their conversation in the clubhouse earlier that day, Dooley's irritation at having to sit out an indefinite number of games matching Lucas's own frustration at losing a starting player. Especially one who played as well and as aggressively as Dooley. Managers never relished having to rely on luck. But luck was now in control, with Dooley out and Conway in, and Lucas prayed that whomever or whatever it was that determined the outcome in these types of situations would be sympathetic enough not to deal him a losing hand.

Low and inside, Conway sliced waist-high above the pitch and almost lost his footing.

The umpire threw his hand out to the side. "Stee-rike-a!"

Conway stepped out of the batter's box to put some time between himself and the pitcher and re-assess his game plan.

Lucas's thoughts drifted back to Dooley hobbling out the door of his office and Tommy Marshall standing there looking perplexed and frightened. Who was it that had scared the boy? Zach hadn't found anyone loitering around the ballpark to haul into the office for questioning, so Lucas still had no new insight into who might have given Tommy the envelope. And what about that toy, the shovel? What was that all about? Again, he tried to imagine what a shovel could mean, but other than the obvious association with digging, no ideas came to his rescue.

Looking up into the stands, Lucas wondered again about the crowd. He scanned the faces of those closest to him, looking for a clue. Was someone out there paying a little too much attention to him instead of to the game? Someone having a little laugh at his expense? Or was it something more sinister, something that he hadn't yet been able to imagine? Hundreds of faces stared down onto the playing field. A couple of people looked like they might be staring his way, but there was no way of telling for sure. He decided to let it slide.

A sudden ruckus in the crowd brought Lucas back to the game. Mavers had taken an exaggerated lead off first, and this time the pitcher did more than just eyeball him. He'd momentarily gone back to his set position, then whirled and threw a strike to the first baseman. Mavers had leapt back to the base, arms outstretched, fingers grasping for the fifteen inches of scuffed canvas.

The call was close. Too close for about half the crowd when the umpire called him safe. The pitcher smirked as the ball was returned to his glove, and Mavers returned the favor, adding a not-so-polite gesture for good measure. The pitcher turned his attention back to the batter, and the crowd mumbled their way back into their seats.

With one ball, one strike, and one close call, Lucas could see that Conway was itching to swing at just about anything. Which was never a good feeling for a manager. The pitcher fired, and the ball came in low and inside again, and again Conway's bat flew over top of it. *Nothing if not consistent,* Lucas thought.

"Stee-rike-a!"

"Same again," said Zacharia. "He's not thinkin'! But the kid's gonna get it. You watch."

Mavers had once again stretched off first way beyond his athletic gifts, and was about to try and steal second, when something unexpected happened. The kind of thing that happens with such regularity that it shouldn't actually be deemed unexpected. And yet…it always is.

In his eagerness to pick off Mavers at first, the pitcher turned just a little too sharply and caught his spikes on the pitching slab.

As Mavers dove back to the bag, the pitcher's throw to first sailed over the first baseman's head and spun across the grass to the grandstand. Stevens made a dash home from third, scoring the winning run.

Both sides of the crowd went crazy. Just for different reasons.

The Bulldogs leapt off the bench and rushed to celebrate with Stevens as he crossed home plate. The winning run having scored, Mavers trotted across the field, grinning like a kid who'd just found a nickel on the ground in front of a candy store.

"Told ya I could do it!" he chortled. "Had his number all the way!" He shuffled off to join the other players, leaving Lucas to wonder just what it was that determined life's outcomes.

That says it all, he thought. *Expect the unexpected.*

It wasn't a pretty win. But a win it was. And with the playoffs less than a month away, Lucas wasn't about to argue.

Chapter 6

The Bulldogs' 5-4 win over the Sentinels put some pep into Lucas's step as he climbed up the subway stairs and out onto the street on his way to his apartment.

His new third baseman, Alex Conway, had given Lucas lots to get excited about on his way home. Pennant-winning excitement. The thought was gaining traction. The young replacement had gone three-for-four with no errors in what was only his fifth appearance all season. If this kept up, Phil Dooley could quickly become a distant memory.

Daylight was rapidly waning as Lucas approached Zaslaw Prusinowski's newsstand, where the lights were on at both ends. That meant he could still get a copy of the evening paper. It almost certainly meant a brief harangue from Zaslaw on some worldly event making headlines that day. Indeed, there were precious few days when the man deemed his observations and analysis unnecessary. But Lucas didn't mind. The old man had a memorable way of expressing his opinions. Opinions that frequently made perfect sense of situations that made no sense at all. Opinions voiced in a strong Polish accent that made most everything sound cheerless. Which invariably made Lucas smile.

Zaslaw saw Lucas coming and didn't hesitate.

"He's out!" yelled Zaslaw, skipping any pretense of an introduction.

"Who's out, Zaslaw?"

"This is what I say. Should be out."

"Okay. Who should be out?"

"That bastard! Throws with his hand sideways. Underhand, too. Very sneaky—creeps up on players. Like a rattlesnake!" His eyes bulged, and he paused for emphasis. "He should be out."

Lucas nodded.

Must be referring to Carl Mays, thought Lucas. *Lots of people feeling the same way. Wanting Mays out of the league.*

And with Ray Chapman now dead, there was a real possibility it could actually happen. "Yep, definitely deserves some thought, Zaslaw."

"I give plenty of thought. This is what I do here. I think. You suppose I do nothing all day but sell newspapers? God does not give me brains only to spread ink on my hands. He tells me: think! So, this is what I do." He turned and pulled down a copy of the *Evening World* and passed it over to Lucas. "Three cents. Not more. Same as yesterday. Should be same tomorrow unless government is getting involved. You think government is going to fix? Same *idioci* that give us this…what do you say? Pro—?" He searched for the word. "Prohibition! This is working? No. Is not! People now *die* from bad vodka! Before," he shrugged, "they are just drunk. No one is hurt."

A man in a neatly tailored suit hustled by, grabbing a *New York Times* as he went. Lucas glimpsed the outline of something peeking out from under the man's jacket as he flipped Zaslaw a nickel. Without hesitating, the man continued on down the street, a slight limp to his step.

Zaslaw called after him. "Hey! Mister! Change!" he yelled, holding out a pair of pennies.

The man gave a quick glance back over his shoulder, the light from the newsstand too weak to illuminate his face peeking out from under the workman's cap. Lucas thought he caught a faint smile, but it all happened too fast to say for sure. And then the man was gone. Lucas didn't recognize him, and he guessed Zaslaw didn't either.

For a few moments, Zaslaw stared at the coins in his hand, then tossed them into a box next to the cash. "America. Tonight I am getting rich. So…what do I say? Ah, yes. He should be out of league, but no—no, no, this *idiota*, this Colonel, this Ruppert, he says—what did he say?" Zaslaw pulled back the corner of the paper Lucas was holding to point at the headline.

Players Move to Banish Mays from Baseball

"Here, I am needing glasses," he continued. "You read. Right here, down to bottom. Here," he repeated, pointing to the column. "What this Colonel Ruppert says."

Lucas didn't actually expect the Yankees owner, Colonel Jacob Ruppert, Jr., to inculpate one of his star players, but he was still curious to discover what the man would have to say about the Chapman-Mays incident. A quick scan of the article led Lucas to the relevant content, about three-quarters into the story.

Lucas started to read it to himself.

Col. Jacob Ruppert, on being shown the above dispatch here today said—

"Not read to you, Mr. Manager!" Zaslaw interrupted testily. "Read out loud! I cannot hear you read in your head!"

Zaslaw muttered to himself as if to suggest a doorstop might be an improvement on Lucas's meager offering of a brain.

Lucas started to read: "'Many players get hurt in baseball and I don't see how they can hold Mays responsible for yesterday's unfortunate accident. There is no ground for any belief that Mays hit Chapman intentionally.'"

"So." Zaslaw shrugged, his palms upward and eyebrows raised. An obvious conclusion.

"Colonel Ruppert doesn't seem to think Mays did it on purpose," Lucas offered hopefully.

Zaslaw's face remained blank.

"Well, he *is* the Yankees owner, Zaslaw. You really can't expect him to accuse his own player of intentionally hitting another team's player."

"Yes." Zaslaw exhaled, exasperated. Lucas sensed he was batting a thousand in the obvious department. "Three cents, please." He stuck out a disinterested hand to receive the money.

Lucas pulled the coins out of his pocket and handed them over the counter, tucking the paper under his arm and started toward his apartment. "Thanks, Zaslaw. See you tomorrow."

"Wait, wait. Page three, another story. I can tell you something—"

"Sorry, Zaslaw, not tonight."

Lucas gave him a perfunctory wave and headed off down the street. Moments later he was up the steps to his apartment, about to go in the front door. But before he'd even finished opening it, something niggled at him. There was something about the man who'd rushed by Zaslaw's newsstand. Something in Lucas's gut that was trying to make a connection. And his army training had taught him to always pay attention to his gut. Even when it really just wanted nothing more than a good beef sandwich and an ice-cold lemonade. *Something about that man…,* thought Lucas. But when he looked back over his shoulder, that something wasn't there.

He stepped into the hall and closed the door. As he did, he could hear Mozart's piano concerto No. 20 drifting out from his neighbor's ground-floor flat. The neighbor played it most nights, filling in the orchestral sections with just a simple one-finger interpretation of the gentle, lyrical melody.

It was the second movement, one that Lucas himself used to play. Once. A long time ago.

People who knew music had described his playing as "promising," though he knew he was no prodigy. Once the war intervened and he'd enlisted, Lucas gave up thinking about anything except staying alive. Then, on a sour gray day in November 1917, a German infantryman clambered over the edge of a mortar hole where Lucas had taken cover and put his bayonet through Lucas's left hand. If it hadn't been for the timely arrival of one Zacharia V. Tucker of the Canadian Light Infantry, who immediately put a bullet through the German's skull, Lucas would not have come home at all.

Just over a year later, on the eleventh hour of the eleventh day of the eleventh month, Lucas was able once again to think about his future. Playing piano was out of the question, as his mangled hand ensured that his music career was permanently tuned to a minor key, and images of ballrooms shaking with thunderous applause that had once occupied his fantasies had quickly withered.

Returning stateside, he refocused on his other passion. Baseball. Not as a player; he wasn't that good. But managing a team was tempting.

The Bulldogs had been struggling back then, both on the field and at the bank, and Charlie Tuttle, the team's owner and manager, was looking for a way to hang up his miserable twenty-year track record before his miserable sixty-eight-year-old body gave out for good. They cut a deal, and Lucas took over. From that day forward, he rarely had time for anything else.

As he climbed the stairs to his flat, the piano concerto began to come undone, as it did most nights, dissonance creeping into the melody. Maybe fatigue, maybe frustration, maybe a lingering sorrow. Lucas couldn't say, as he rarely saw or spoke with his neighbor. But sooner or later, the music would fragment into unhinged scraps of discordant anguish, getting louder and louder until Lucas banged a broom handle on his parlor floor or stomped on it with his foot and the music would stop.

The key wriggled its way into the lock with the usual amount of objection, and before Lucas could reach for the handle, the door flew open. Willa stood there smiling, and he stood there staring. She was draped in the most gorgeous, peach-colored satin pajamas he could ever imagine. And there wasn't much of that needed, as the soft, lustrous garment was unbuttoned almost to her navel, struggling to cover her breasts.

"Mr. Blaine. I wasn't sure I could wait any longer."

Lucas was certain he couldn't.

"You look..." He struggled to get a grip on just the right words but came up empty-handed. "Well, you look...great. And I'm glad you did wait." He stepped into the room, putting his arms around Willa as he did. "Did Aleta move to New Mexico?"

"Don't be exhausting. You know she's very fond of you. Generally speaking. And besides, she knows exactly where I am and daren't say anything. Otherwise, I'd quit and become a circus performer."

"And leave me to fend off Aleta the lion? That's a terrifying thought." He reached into his pocket to unload the day's incidentals, his fingers resting on the little metal shovel that had been delivered in the envelope. He pulled it out and threw it on the table. "How long's he been playing downstairs?"

"Just a couple of hours." Willa raised her eyebrows. "Over and over 'til I could strangle him." She picked up the shovel and examined it at close range.

"What's this?"

"Not sure. Somebody gave it to Tommy to give to me. No note or anything, just that. Probably a joke or something. I don't know. Scared Tommy a little."

Willa threw the little metal toy back onto the table and snaked her arms around Lucas's waist, her eyes widening.

"Well, it doesn't scare me, mister. And here's something that's not a joke. If you don't follow me into that bedroom in the next sixty seconds, I guarantee you it will be no laughing matter."

Lucas looked deep into Willa's eyes and his skin started to tingle.

He stomped on the floor, and the music stopped.

Chapter 7

Opening the door to his underground hideaway, Maddocks stepped through the opening seconds before the rattling subway cars rushed by. The cool air of the abandoned utility room was a welcome respite from the soggy August heat. His leg was still aching from having sat in that cramped seat at the ballpark all afternoon the previous day. But it had been worth it. The toy rooster had been an inspiration, despite his having lost half the box of Cracker Jack when that clumsy oaf had bumped into him. No matter. He'd taken care of that.

He reached for the cord dangling above his head, giving it a quick yank. With reluctance, the room brightened as the single yellow bulb hanging down from the ceiling turned on. Snapping the padlock that he'd removed from the outside of the door onto the safety hasps screwed to the inside doorframe, he gave the door a tug to see that it was securely locked. Before taking another step, he rubbed his leg again and then carefully surveyed the room. Table unmoved, a box of tools beneath untouched. Bedcovers just how he'd left them. Bible on the table still perfectly placed. Three more hooks of clothes hung perfectly straight. The barely noticeable thread across the door of the cupboard where he stored his treasures remained unbroken. All appeared as it should. A cautious smile crept across his face, the scar on his right cheek rising in approval. Although the room had not been used for several years, and was unlikely to be put back into service anytime soon, Maddocks was careful enough not to rely on probabilities.

His years as a miner digging coal in the Rhonda Valley in Wales, and later as an engineer and explosives expert with one of the tunnelling companies in the British Expeditionary Force on the Western Front, had taught him how to look for small exceptions that might indicate vulnerability. How to move quietly, how to be persistent, how to be patient. How to see things as they might be, not just as they were.

And now he was able to put it all to use once again. And he would. He must.

Pulling off his workman's cap, he sat down at the small table and thought about how far he'd come. He'd spent almost three years thinking, planning…hating. And now, he would have it. Revenge. Revenge for the monumental errors—errors that weren't his fault—that had trapped him under a mountain of dirt at the end of a tunnel and left him for dead. A tunnel that had been nearly finished and would have devastated the German troops above if only…if only. He silenced the thought from his mind. Only on rare occasions did he allow it to take over and ignite the demons inside. Only when he could control the outcome, and only when it wouldn't interfere with his precious plan.

A small gray rat poked about in the corner of the room. Its presence didn't bother the man. He'd spent years in tunnels, and rats were commonplace—though he'd learned to be cautious about what he left where, as the wretched rodents could chew through just about anything to get what they wanted.

"So, how did you get in, friend? One of the cracks in the walls of this old room, I suspect. Well, you won't find anything to satisfy your curiosity in here. Or your stomach. Unless you've learned how to open cupboards."

It had been a successful day. Delivery of item number one: complete. The boy had been frightened, but Maddocks had watched from the visitor's clubhouse and was satisfied that his instructions had been carried out. He concluded that the boy might be useful in the days ahead.

His most ambitious project, the tunnel, had also advanced. Several feet more of dirt had been removed, which brought him closer to his target. He smiled when he thought about digging a tunnel right in the middle of New York City. Not as good as the ones he'd dug during the war. But then he didn't need to create such a massive result. His target was only protected by dirt, a few pieces of furniture, and a layer of timber flooring, making the blast that much more effective.

Then there was the newsstand. Blaine had given no sign of interest, even after the involuntary smile. Of course, why would he? They'd never actually met. Still, it was an unfortunate slip, and he chided himself for his sloppiness. It would be unfortunate if Blaine were to take note of anything that might lead him to arrive at the obvious conclusion too early. Before Maddocks could spring his trap and fully enjoy the divine and ironic justice that was even now unfolding.

Foolish pride, nothing more, he thought. Like the man he'd dispatched in the subway. All because of the spilled box of Cracker Jack. And yet, it had been that very moment when'd he'd gotten the idea for leaving the prizes as clues. Almost spoiled by that stupid, clumsy man who knew a lot about baseball and nothing at all about revenge. Until after the game. He knew all about revenge now, lying somewhere under a sheet in a cold, dark morgue.

He'd later regretted leaving the rooster on the dead man. Yet he relished the intriguing dimension that it now added to *his* game. And he relished the anticipation, which would build and build until finally…finally, he would be ready to deliver the ultimate stroke.

Of course, it wouldn't always be a secret. At some point, Blaine would realize his mistake, realize that he'd had a choice to make that day after the tunnel collapsed deep under the Western Front. And that leaving Maddocks buried under a massive pile of dirt and rubble after the explosion had been the *wrong* choice. *Very* wrong! He could have rescued Maddocks, ordered his men to claw their way through the debris and find him. But he'd left. Abandoned Maddocks.

Which was why Blaine was now the target. And sooner or later, he'd realize that the Cracker Jack toys *weren't* just some game or amusement, a joke between friends. He'd suddenly realize they were a threat. Of course, at first, he'd think them just a curiosity. A mystery. But then, a feeling of danger would come over him. A sense of fear. And ultimately, panic. All semblance of being able to defuse the situation would vanish. And finally, the encounter. The horrifying realization that there could be only one outcome. One that would satisfy the wrongs that had been done, the errors that had been made, the ignorance that had been shown.

Yes, thought Maddocks. *Blaine was his target, trapped in a tunnel of growing despair.*

He glanced at the tattoo on his wrist. A turtle, its legs flung out like wings, looking like it wanted to scramble up his arm. He held it up and called out to the rat still scratching about in the corner.

"See this, friend?" he said, indicating the tattoo. "Two years in the Merchant Navy. Two years! Know what I got for it? Ha! More than this lifeless scrawl on my arm, I can assure you!"

Stealthily, he picked up a wrench from the box of tools underneath the table and stared at the rat. "What I received…" He thought about it for a moment. Then blinked. Twice. "What I received was…divine guidance." He nodded to himself. "Indeed! *Divine* guidance that would enable me to deliver…divine justice!"

Without another word, he heaved the wrench at the rat, which leapt into the air before scurrying off through a hole in the wall. Maddocks smirked. "Which is exactly what you will get the next time you trespass here!" he added.

He inhaled deeply, the fatigue of the day beginning to calm the excitement in his brain. Pulling a gold cigarette case from his vest pocket, he examined the inscription, just as he did every morning and night. *Yes*, he thought, *these words are my guide. My moral compass. They have led me from tragedy to necessity to opportunity. And morality can go to hell.*

Though he had little feeling in his stubby, scarred fingers, he ran them over the cigarette case again and again, comforted by the passage from the Bible inscribed there. A passage from Romans. And though he understood full well the intent of the passage, he chose to interpret it from a different perspective, to interpret it in a way that would bring fire and brimstone down on Lucas Blaine in one magnificent, final conflagration.

He snapped the case open, pulling a cigarette from its resting place. From the same case, a match. He struck the match on the side of the table, lit the cigarette, and inhaled deeply until the lit end glowed a dark orange.

"Burning coals, Mr. Blaine," he muttered aloud. "That, I can promise."

He finished the cigarette and headed off toward his makeshift bed.

AUGUST 20, 1920

Chapter 8

Considering that it was already after eight, Lucas was surprised to find the Sun's Up Coffee Shop much busier than he'd expected. He was even more surprised to see that someone was sitting in booth number nine—the booth he considered to be his reserved spot. Ordinarily, both Aleta Jean and Willa were quick to discourage newcomers from sitting there, and most of the coffee shop regulars, many of them Bulldogs fans, allowed Lucas and Zach to treat it like their permanent residence.

Willa saw Lucas come in and quick-stepped over to the door.

"Sorry, I know," she blurted out before Lucas could say anything. "That guy came in and just helped himself. It's been so busy, I couldn't get over there and ask him to swap seats. Look at this place," she added, marveling at the crowd in the coffee shop. "You'd think the president was in town!"

"Does the president usually come here when he's in town?" quipped Lucas, peering over her shoulder, trying to get a look at the interloper. He gave her a quick smile to let her know he was just teasing. She managed a smile back, but it came out more tolerant than jovial. Lucas didn't detect the difference, still busy trying to figure out who had usurped his booth.

The bell over the door jangled, breaking the spell, and Lucas turned, expecting Zach. It wasn't him.

"Morning, Lucas."

"Morning, Orville. You're up early."

In town to play three games against the Bulldogs, Orville Simpson was the Capitals manager and someone Lucas respected. Sixty-four years old and just a lick over five-foot-six, with neatly trimmed graying hair, hazel eyes, and a boxer's build, Simpson was a fierce competitor in the ballpark, but a smart, even-tempered, fun-loving guy off the field.

"I was hopin' I'd catch you here, Lucas." Simpson replied. "I heard the Bulldogs are looking for a new manager. Might be something I could help with."

Lucas resisted the urge to look over his shoulder at the man sitting in his booth, and stayed focused on his competitor. "Understandable you might think that," he said, responding to the obvious provocation. "Considering how poorly your own team is doing this year, getting a new club might be your best bet!" The Capitals were snapping at the Bulldogs' heels and just one more team they were outpacing by a slim margin.

"Yeah, and speaking of bets, don't forget our little World Series wager," said Simpson. "If I recall, your dough's on the pinstripes. You want to just pay me now and be done with it?" Notwithstanding his role as the Capitals' manager, Simpson was from Cleveland, an ardent Indians fan, and always ready to put his money where his loyalties were.

"I'm already counting on that dinner at Delmonico's, Orville. Just don't go runnin' back home before I can collect!"

"If you're stickin' with the Yanks, Lucas, you can count on eatin' steak and lasagne at Guardino's in Cleveland!"

Lucas tipped his hat and Simpson returned the salute. When he turned back to the room, the booth that he thought of as his was now empty. He looked around, but the man who had taken his seat moments earlier was no longer there. Customers had come and gone since Simpson's arrival, and Lucas hadn't been paying attention to who they were. In any event, the booth was empty once again, and Lucas strode over and sat down. Aleta Jean was fast on his heels with a cup and saucer in hand.

"Giving my booth away to just anyone who strolls in here, Aleta?"

"Your booth now, is it?" She placed the saucer down on the table with a little extra gusto. "And here I imagined it was *my* booth," she added, following up with the cup. "And *my* restaurant. Just goes to show how one's imagination can run away with itself. I suppose you want coffee to go with that attitude?"

"Just a cup or two. And maybe some eggs and bacon too," he said. Aleta cocked her head and looked at Lucas but didn't move. It took him a couple more seconds, but then he remembered. "Please."

"Well, bless my stars and whiskers, civility makes an appearance." With that, she turned and headed toward the counter. Lucas hoped it would be for a pot of coffee.

A few moments later, Willa appeared with coffee in hand and filled his cup.

"Thanks. I was beginning to think I might have to eat standing up."

"Like I said, it was as if—"

"As if the president was in town," Lucas cut in. "By the way, the guy that was sitting here this morning. Did you know him?"

"Never seen him before. He asked if anyone was sitting in this booth, and I said, 'There will be presently, if you don't mind.' And he said, 'Oh, I don't mind. Just a coffee, please, if *you* don't mind.' But it didn't sound like he was trying to be smart. More polite, I think. Well, anyway, you weren't here, so I couldn't exactly say no. He was neatly dressed, I remember that."

"Yeah, I noticed. Did you see him leave?"

"Nope."

"Will I see you tonight? Maybe we could go out somewhere?"

"Really?"

"I'll come by after the game."

At that moment, Aleta arrived with a plate of eggs and gave Willa a back-to-work nod just as Zach walked through the door and made his way over to where Lucas was sitting.

"Ruth knocked his forty-third yesterday," he said, sitting down across from Lucas. "Wasn't enough, though. Cleveland took it, 3-2. I heard old Baker was there to watch...."

Lucas was trying to stay focused on what Zach was saying when he noticed a Western Union delivery boy ride up outside on his bicycle and lean it against the building. The kid looked about fifteen but all brass and business in his military-cut uniform. Reaching into his leather pouch, he pulled out the customary yellow envelope. The bell over the door rang him into the coffee shop, and as he made his way through the crowd, he called out a name. Lucas's name.

"Telegram, Mr. Lucas Blaine. Telegram for Mr. Blaine."

"Over here, boy." Puzzled, Lucas took the envelope from the

messenger's hands without any idea of who it could be from or what the message might be.

"If that's some sorta love letter, I suggest you don't show Willa," smirked Zach.

"If it's a love letter and it's not from her, I'd better think about leavin' town!"

Lucas pulled the telegram out of the envelope and looked at the date. August 20, 1920. Addressed to him, care of Aleta Jean's Coffee Shop, The Bronx. Which made no sense.

Who would send me a telegram here? Why not to the clubhouse?

Just ten words long, the brevity didn't help make the message any clearer.

Lucas stared at the words, willing them to reveal their meaning. Nothing came.

LOOK FOR ME AT BALLPARK. STOP. YOU WON'T SEE ME.

"What's it say, boss?"

Lucas handed Zach the telegram. "See if you can make some sense of it."

The messenger boy shuffled his feet, eager to be on his way. "Will there be a reply, sir?"

"No reply, son." Lucas pulled a nickel from his vest pocket and handed it to the boy who was out the door and on his bike in a matter of seconds.

Aleta came by with coffee and refilled Lucas's cup.

"Thanks, I'd love a cup," said Zach without looking up from the telegram Lucas had just handed him.

"I'll drop everything," said Aleta as she went off to serve another customer.

Zach's attention remained fixed on the telegram. Lucas could tell by the look on his face that it made no sense to him either.

"'Look for me at ballpark?'" said Zach, echoing the words on the page. "Has to be someone you know. Someone who knows you come here, too." He glanced at the message again. "'You won't see me?' Sorry, boss. Makes no sense to me either."

He slid the paper back across the table.

Who is it I'm supposed to look for? wondered Lucas. *And why won't I see him?*

Lucas didn't have the answers.

But he had a lot of questions.

Chapter 9

A fifty-pound block of ice slid out of the new liquid ammonia-chilled freezing can at O'Farrell's Ice Making Company, thundered down the big rattling conveyer, and came to rest knee-high in front of where Cian Nolan stood waiting. At five-foot-eleven, 134 pounds, and a physique that could best be described as skin and bones, Cian stared at the cube and wondered if he had the strength to move yet another block of ice. He'd worked at O'Farrell's for three years now and had nothing to show for it beyond a herniated disk and two sore, swollen hands, both of which he now used to push his thin, greasy blond hair back over his ears, though the effort did nothing to rescue his thirty-seven-year-old face from giving one the impression of a wounded ferret.

Slapping his ice tongs around the giant cube, he dragged it across the floor and lifted it onto a second conveyor, which carried it down to street level, where it was loaded onto a horse-drawn cart for delivery to businesses and residences around the city.

The ice had a near crystal-like quality about it, perfectly clear right from one side almost through to the other. Not like the old days, Cian thought. Not like when he'd had to saw two hundred-pound blocks of ice out of Miller's Pond upstate, or later, right out of the Hudson River. Those blocks had had noticeable impurities. Some of which were not very healthy. And people started getting sick. Or, at least, claimed the ice was making them sick, which eventually led to his previous employer, Jenkins Ice Company, shuttering for good.

But lake ice was rare in the city these days. New, more modern companies, such as O'Farrell's, had taken over with mechanical ice-making equipment that turned out block after block of clean, mostly uncontaminated ice all day long.

Pulling a soiled handkerchief from his back pocket, Cian sat down on a barrel covered in piles of rough burlap and wiped his forehead and the back of his neck. It was barely 1:30 in the afternoon, and he was already exhausted from slinging the blocks off the first conveyor and onto the second. He'd already done one delivery circuit that morning, starting at 6 a.m., when the cooler morning air made it just a little more bearable. But now, with the sun high in the sky, it would be another long, hot August afternoon.

"So, it's your fuckin' day off, is it, Nolan?"

Cian was halfway to his feet before he recognized Fergal Mullan standing in the open doorway, wiping his hands on his own grimy rag, grinning like a fox. Yet, despite the smile, there was nothing about him that was inviting. He weighed nearly 250 pounds and stood over six-foot-four, all muscle and malevolence.

Short black hair bristled atop a head that might generously be described as gigantic, and a large, protruding brow and chin, small, dark, recessed eyes, and a long, deep scar that ran across his right cheek completed a face that couldn't be generously described at all.

"Jesus Murphy, Mullan, you sounded just like O'Farrell."

"So's it coulda been, ya fuckin' ice monger. And he'd love to catch you sittin' there so's he could shove those fuckin' tongs up yer ass before tossing ya out to the curb. For Chrissakes, Cian, it's barely 11:30. Break's not another hour."

"I know what time it is. I need a break now."

"Suit yerself, but if O'Farrell catches ya, he'll freeze ya out faster'n 'at block o' ice."

"Not before I put this fuckin' pick through the center of his head," scowled Cian, slamming his icepick into the block of ice. "Just like that, doncha know."

"Ah, and wouldn't you like to. But if anyone's gonna pick O'Farrell, it's gonna be me, sure. You ain't got the guts! You show him the shiny end of that pick, you'll be gone faster'n a silver clam at a hooker's New Year's Eve party."

Cian rubbed his chin and looked off to the side, his temper subsiding. "Yeah, well…if people keep buying them electric iceboxes, he won't have to do me in. We'll all be at the curb."

"Refrigerators you're talkin' about? Ain't gonna happen. Who can afford 'em? You? Me? I'd bet a fly could swallow 'is arsehole before we all have one of them fuckin' contraptions runnin'. Where you headed this afternoon?"

"Harlem. You?"

"Sand lots. Who you doin' goin' up to Harlem?"

"Queen Rosie and about."

For years, Clarissa Rose Washington, known by most everyone as Queen Rosie, had run a booming numbers racket in Harlem, catering mostly to a white clientele—politicians, celebrities, police. Anybody with a dollar and no place to spend it.

"You deliverin' up to them niggers, eh? I don't trust 'em. Why don't another nigger do that?"

"Queen Rosie don't like colored deliverin' her ice."

Ever since Harlem had begun enjoying a kind of cultural rebirth, Cian had delivered ice to a select few residents there willing to pay a certain price for the privilege—and prestige—of having that ice delivered by a white man. Queen Rosie was one of them. And while Cian understood the relationship, he never considered himself disrespected. In fact, not only did he enjoy the easy comradery with many of the tenants and shopkeepers in the neighborhood, it gave him easy access to the bookmakers and bootleggers who ran Harlem and helped Cian build his own little side business.

"Ahh—you're playin' them numbers, then," grinned Mullan.

"Not me. Puttin' some on with Queen Rosie for some other fellas. We got a deal, her and me."

Rosie was Cian's foremost connection. And though he'd never dealt with her in person, she'd allowed him to pick up bets from some of his customers along his route, getting paid for two jobs at the same time.

"Here, then," said Mullan, reaching behind his apron and pulling out a handful of grimy bills from a pants pocket. "Take this for me. I got this guy knows his horses."

Cian stared at the money that Mullan was holding. "You got a guy, but you got no brains, Mullan," he said, standing up, ready to grab another block of ice that had just rattled down the conveyor. "A whole week's pay? On the numbers? There's no winnin' with numbers."

"And I know that, so. But it ain't numbers I'm pickin'. You put that fifty down on number six in the third at Saratoga, Tuesday's race. I got it for good, that nag'll be singin' all the way down that track. And that's for sure," he added, thrusting the dirty bills at Cian.

Cian took the money and turned it over slowly, wondering if it might find a better use. "Number six?"

"In the third. She'll be off with big odds, that one, and it'll be a nice payday, sure. So, don't go thinkin' how's you could be tradin' that for a few bottles of whiskey that've made their way down from our kindly neighbors to the north. You don't put that money in the right place, you won't be worryin' about O'Farrell. I'll pick yer brains meself!"

"Aye, will ya? I'll be sure to make a note."

Fifty dollars. Cian's mind wandered just a little further than it should. "Yeah, I got it. Number six in the third." He stuffed the money into his pocket. "Good luck to ya."

Mullan smiled. "If it were all about luck, Cainy boy, them bookmakers'd be diggin' themselves a place to hide!"

Chapter 10

While the Babe continued hitting them out of the park, the Bulldogs continued their win streak. They'd taken three of four from the Sentinels, pretty well ensuring that particular competitor wasn't headed to the postseason, and were looking forward to taking a win from Simpson's Capitals that afternoon.

It looked like Carl Mays would be exonerated from all wrongdoing, although the public remained split on the issue of guilt. Those relenting were swayed by Mays' apparent devastation over the death of Ray Chapman. Those who wanted reform on the mound lobbied for more stringent application of the rule that had been introduced during the previous winter season banning the use of spitballs or any other type of pitch involving a physical alteration. Though well-intended, the rule included a critical exception. Each team would be allowed two pitchers who could continue to throw a spitball provided they threw no other marred ball. Like the pitch itself, the law wobbled.

Lucas leaned toward the forgiveness crowd. Pitching was as much an art as it was a science, often resulting in the ball going places the pitcher never intended. So while it was easy to imagine that striking the batter was Mays' full intention, believing that he had deliberately aimed for Chapman's head was more than Lucas could bring himself to believe.

Things in the clubhouse were back to normal. Tommy Marshall had had no further unexpected visitors, and Bear seemed unconcerned with anything more distressing than a late delivery of his daily carrot. No mysterious letters or packages had shown up on Lucas's desk, and the icebox still leaked.

It was the eighth inning in the first of three games with the Capitals, and the Bulldogs' ace, Warren Howard, had set down the last three batters in a row. He was now working on the second out of the inning and Lucas was starting to bank on a win.

"You need a new refrigerator, boss," Zacharia offered out of the blue.

"Icebox," Lucas countered without looking over. He'd always preferred the term to the more modern name. It was, after all, nothing more than a box that held ice.

"Icebox, refrigerator. Don't really matter what you call it, one or both of 'ems leakin'. Bad."

The two fingers on Lucas's left hand did a little dance up and down. The pitcher, who had been looking over in his direction, acknowledged with a barely noticeable nod.

Zach looked over at Lucas. "Curve?"

"We'll see," Lucas nodded.

Howard accommodated, and the pitch arced in over the plate like a rainbow aiming to drop a pot of gold.

The umpire, belly folded over his belt, bent down, thrust his right arm up toward the heavens, and yelled something that everyone concluded meant "strike."

"Curve," confirmed Zach, his eyes fixed firmly on the pitcher. "The guy that looked at your..." He hesitated for a split second. "...icebox. What'd he say? Something about zinc, right?"

"Perforated," Lucas replied. "He said it was perforated. In more than one spot. Little holes in the zinc lining. Then the smell of food gets into the insulation, and that's what causes the smell."

Zach waited for another pitch before speaking. "Like I was sayin', best get a new one."

But Lucas wasn't ready to concede defeat. The appliance was barely twenty years old and Lucas was hoping it would make it through another season.

They sure don't make 'em like they used to, Lucas mused in disappointment.

A flash of light from somewhere in the stands stabbed Lucas in the eye and he instinctively jerked back on the bench.

"What?" Zach kept one eye on the playing field, catching Lucas's reaction but not wanting to lose focus on what the pitcher was doing lest a sudden foul ball came whirring their way.

"Nothing. Flash of light—I'm not sure. Up in the stands somewhere. Probably off a flask." Lucas didn't want to award it any more significance than it deserved, which was almost none. In truth, the idea that the flash had come from a flask seemed a remote possibility, but he couldn't really think of another. Fans were known to bring small mirrors to the game to try and flash sunlight into a player's eyes, but he'd never heard of a manager or coach being targeted.

A fastball at eighty-five miles per hour was enough to prompt the umpire into his dance, sending the batter to the dugout, cursing the pitcher, the ball, his bat, the crowd, and everything else in the park as he went.

Then another flash. But this time longer. This time intentional. Lucas jumped up, peering out into the stands at what felt like the general point of origination. Nothing suspicious peered back, but he knew now he wasn't imagining things.

"Son of a bitch. Another flash?" This time Zach did look at Lucas, a bit of concern from someone who made a habit of leaving that to others.

"Definitely. Someone aiming for me. But I can't see him." Lucas scanned the lower-level seating behind the first base dugout, then the seats above. No one standing up, and nothing standing out. He stayed on his feet for another few seconds and then settled back down onto the bench, glancing back toward the bleachers.

"I thought there was only so much stupid to go around, but I've underestimated this crowd. Some kind of stunt. One of the Capitals' fans is my guess. Won't change the outcome, though," Lucas said, sitting back down. "We're takin' this game."

"Boss, you want me to go take a look?" Zach was now staring over at the stands, his focus on the game all but vanished.

"Let's wait. He's got my attention now and he knows it. Let's see if that's enough."

It wasn't.

Before Lucas could get his head back where it belonged, another glint of light was in his face, and he was on his feet with the intention of putting an end to this.

But whoever was responsible had no intention of backing

down. Lucas could see someone in the stands, flicking light in his eyes with what Lucas concluded must indeed be a mirror. He looked about average height and was wearing a dark brown suit and what looked like a newsboy-style cap. With the temperature testing the low eighties, the dark suit was out of place in a field of white and cream-colored linen and cotton. The hat, too, seemed out of place.

Zach had also leapt up, ready to do his part, but before he could propose anything, Lucas grabbed his arm and pressed him back onto the bench.

"Keep an eye on the game for me, yeah? I'm gonna find out who this guy is and what's his point." He stepped over the bench, ran to the waist wall bordering the field, and climbed over into the stands. Clearing the wall, he looked up to see if his agitator was still there, and was rewarded with another flash of sunlight in his eyes.

With a batter still at the plate, the crowd was mostly in their seats and Lucas ran unhindered up the steps to the walkway above the ground-level seating. The man with the mirror was making his way toward the back of the stands, gauging his time and moving no faster than he had to in order to keep the distance between himself and Lucas from shrinking too rapidly.

From the direction he was going, Lucas thought he could head him off by exiting through the center gates of the park, and he made an abrupt turn to his right, plowing into someone who had tried a zig to Lucas's zag and they both ended up on the ground, a bag of popcorn exploding into the air and raining down around them. Lucas grabbed the near-empty bag and thrust it into a disoriented face that promised to turn angry if he gave it half a chance.

"I'll be back, don't worry," Lucas shouted, leaping to his feet and heading once more up the aisle. "I'll get you another!"

The man on the ground said something that didn't sound complimentary, but Lucas was already too far away to hear. He pushed through a handful of people making their way out the gate and came to a stop at the edge of the park grounds.

At first, it seemed he'd lost the man. The street and sidewalk gurgled with people and motorcars. A group of young boys off to his right were standing lookout for pickpocketing opportunities, and an accordion player was doing his best to woo customers over to a booth selling cotton candy.

No man. No mirror.

But then, across the street, Lucas spotted him.

He stood staring, as if waiting for Lucas to catch up. Lucas ran into the street, weaving his way through the cars, horse-carts, and people, and burst out on the other side just as the man was turning the corner. He thought for certain he could catch him now.

Rounding the corner, he spotted the man standing at the entrance to the subway station. A smug smile said he was enjoying Lucas' frustration. Certain now that Lucas was still in pursuit, the man strode down the steps with Lucas a short distance behind.

At the bottom of the steps, once again, the man seemed to have disappeared. Lucas cursed the man's seeming ability to vanish at will, and racing over to the ticket window, he pointed urgently toward no one in particular and yelled to the attendant on duty. "He's got my ticket! I'll be back!"

He jumped over the turnstile, ran over to the tracks, and looked down the platform to the left, then to the right. It was crowded with chattering baseball fans and disgruntled shift workers, but the man with the mirror was still nowhere to be seen. Lucas decided to try his luck up the left run of the platform and elbowed his way through the crowd, checking behind pillars and into corners as he went.

A growing cacophony of squeaks and clangs announced the imminent arrival of a string of subway cars, and Lucas stopped and looked back down the platform from where he'd just come. Still no sight of the man. He was gone. But where or how, Lucas had no idea.

The train came to a stop, the doors shuttled open, and people stepped off as others stepped on. The doors closed and the subway started up, heading down the tracks to where Lucas stood near the end of the platform. Passing windows yielded no glimpse of his tormentor until the second to last car. As the train rattled by, slowly picking up speed, a tattooed arm snaked out of a small conductor's window and flung something onto the ground.

Instinctively, Lucas jumped back.

A mirror exploded into a hundred glittering fragments at his feet.

WESTERN FRONT
November 1917

Chapter 11

The heliographic operator methodically angled his mirror hoping to capture a few glimmering rays of early morning sunlight. As he started to flash his warning message, a German artillery shell exploded less than ten yards away, sending a thousand metal fragments in every direction and slicing the man in two. Instinctively, First Lieutenant Lucas Blaine jumped back from the trench periscope he'd been peering through and let out a sharp gasp. War was nothing like he'd expected.

The New York Times *had described it differently. Very differently. And though it wasn't the only newspaper to run a front page story on February 4, 1917, describing the sinking of the U.S. cargo ship* Housatonic *by a German U-boat, it was the one that prompted private citizen Lucas Blaine to stop thinking about the war as an abstract concept and start thinking about how he could play a meaningful role in it. He didn't have to think about it for very long.*

On April 6, Congress granted President Woodrow Wilson's

request for a declaration of war against Germany, and America began readying itself for battle in earnest. With a standing army of just 200,000 soldiers, the country was in dire need of qualified officers. Blaine saw his chance. By May of that year, he had enrolled in one of the hastily assembled ninety-day officer training camps. By August, he was a commissioned officer.

With an abundance of courage and a dearth of experience, he was on a boat to France later that month. By October, he was standing ankle-deep in gray-green slime in a trench on the Western Front. Heading up a platoon of about forty men, most of whom were as green as Blaine himself, he was part of the four U.S. divisions sent to bolster the British Expeditionary Force in Belgium.

For the past two and a half hours, the BEF's Ordnance BL 9.2-inch howitzers had been laying down a steady rain of shells on enemy trenches about four hundred yards away. The Germans had been returning the favor with their own Feldhaubitze 13 howitzers, routinely dropping shells about twenty yards out in front of the trench where Blaine and his men huddled. On more than one occasion, an enemy shell exceeded its expected range and landed directly on soldiers huddled in their trenches, flinging body parts, weapons, and a tangle of gear in all directions.

Both sides knew what was coming. An infantry assault that would ensure hundreds, possibly thousands, of Allied troops would forever be calling Belgium home from this day forward. For those lucky enough to survive the attack, it would be their job to ensure that an equal number of soldiers from Germany, Bulgaria, and Austria-Hungary would also be denied a future.

It was all enough to drive a man crazy, and frequently did, sending one's imagination whirling down an unchartered tunnel of terrifying hallucinations that came without warning and left without apology.

Blaine had experienced the terror himself and shuddered at the recollection. He was determined not to let it take control.

A Fullerphone sat quietly in the mud next to his sodden feet, refusing to ring its two-minute warning. Blaine stepped out of the puddle and onto a broken piece of duckboard, pulled a cigarette from his pocket, and checked his watch, steeling himself for the impending attack. Though the weather had improved enough to dry up the worst of what the August storms had delivered, the ground was still a blackened, swampy terrain. Nowhere across the landscape could he see a fully grown tree. Just masses of splintered stumps poking up from the ground like dirty, menacing stalagmites, ensnared in a bloody, pock-marked field of mud and ruin. Broken artillery pieces and overturned carts marked a multitude of previous advances and retreats by both armies, and the yet to be recovered bodies of the dead and wounded littered the field between the two trenches.

Blaine returned the cigarette to his pocket and checked his watch once again.

Just when he felt he could no longer stand the noise, the Fullerphone rang. He picked it up only long enough to hear the message. Two minutes to go. He slammed the phone handset back down and pulled his Acme Thunderer from the pouch on his cross strap. He gave it a quick slap to ensure that the cork ball inside was free and the whistle would work when needed. His men were already at the ladders waiting for the signal, their eyes a vast jumble of emotions. Eagerness, fear, anger, bewilderment, resolution. He was on the alert for the one man silently signalling that he would not go forward on command. The one man whose will or nerve or conscience would fail him at the crucial moment and cripple the launch of the attack.

He prayed that one man wouldn't be him.

Chapter 12

Melting ice dripped a trail of water most of the way up the street. If it hadn't been for the many brownstones casting shadows across the roadway, and the burlap and straw insulating the floor and sides of Cian's cart, the trail would have looked more like a small stream. As the horse picked its way cautiously around the various fruit and vegetable stands and between unpacked crates of dry goods and rotting piles of manure, Cian kept thinking about his conversation with Mullan.

Maybe he'd place a bet on the same horse. What was it he'd said? Six in the third? Or three in the sixth? No, six in the third. Yes, that sounded right. Mullan had claimed he had a tip and Cian wondered just how good the tip might be. Was there a fix? Jockeys, trainers, owners, veterinarians, mobsters, all sorts of horseracing regulars were routinely implicated in fixing races. And while doping was the most common approach, there were loads of other possibilities. Like ensuring a loose horseshoe or stuffing a sponge up a horse's nostrils, making it harder for the animal to breathe. With individual bets in the thousands, and sometimes hundreds of thousands of dollars, a fix was a good possibility.

But a fix was no guarantee, he reminded himself. In which case, that fifty dollars would mean more in his pocket than as a number in some bookie's notebook. So what were the odds? "Big odds," Mullan had said. And big odds meant a big payoff. But it also meant little chance of winning. Didn't it? Unless—there was a fix.

Cian felt like his brain was leading his thoughts around in circles. The heat, the clacking of cart wheels on the cobblestones, street vendors shouting to their customers, it was giving him a headache. But he couldn't stop thinking about the money. *No guarantee,* he repeated to himself.

"Queen Rosie, she ain't at home," a man shouted from the steps of one of the brownstones.

"No matter to me," Cian yelled back, flicking the reins at his exhausted horse. "I don't expect to see her." It seemed like everyone in the neighborhood knew about Rosie's comings and goings.

Pulling his cart over to the sidewalk, Cian stepped down to the ground and grabbed the tongs that were hooked onto the back of the cart. With a tremendous heave, he pulled a block of ice out and onto the ground, then surveyed the twelve steps leading up to the brownstone's front door.

"Shit," he said, the impending climb threatening to drain the last trace of energy from his body. He dragged the ice up one step at a time, then banged on the door.

Footsteps from inside the building approached the entrance. Heavy footsteps. Cian knew that this would be Skinny Taylor, one of Rosie's collectors. The door swung open to reveal a very tall, very large black man standing just inside dressed in overalls and a collarless shirt.

He tipped his chin at Cian. "You want?" he sneered.

"Got some ice here for ya, Mr. Skinny. And a coupla bets, too. You want me to take it into the kitchen?"

"I take it. You wait here." The big man reached down and picked up the block of ice in both hands, then rubbed it across his face. His eyes rolled upward, savoring the coolness. As he finished, he stuck his tongue out and licked the surface like it was an ice cream cone. "You wait here," he repeated. He turned his back to Cian and kicked the door closed.

Cian pulled out his handkerchief and wiped the sweat from his face. He still couldn't decide what to do with Mullan's bet. The easy thing to do, the smart thing, was to place the bet the way Mullan had asked. But the money was calling to him, its siren song whispering sweetly to his subconscious. He reached into his pocket and pulled out the fifty dollars, then quickly stuffed it back in before it could be noticed by people hanging about on the various tenement stoops. Exhibiting greater caution, he reached into his other pocket and peeked down to be sure his own ten-dollar bill was still safely tucked away.

More footsteps from inside, and once again the door swung open, but this time it was a different man, shorter, with a boxer's build and neatly cropped black hair, wearing light tan trousers and a white t-shirt. He stood staring at Cian, who hesitated, then spoke.

"I brung you some ice."

"I seen that, fool. You got bets to place is what I hear."

"I do, Chester, yeah." Both men knew each other well, but Chester always made Cian feel like a first-time visitor. "Got two bets here I wanna place with Ms. Rosie."

"Queen Rosie to you. She's the queen here and you best not forget it."

"Oh, I don't, Chester. I surely don't. *Queen* Rosie."

"What bets you got, then?"

"Tuesday at Saratoga."

Chester stood staring at Cian, looking like he was waiting for further clarification. When nothing was forthcoming, he reached behind and pulled out a small, black leather notebook that had been tucked into the back of his pants at the belt. "Numbers," he said. There was no question involved. Just direction.

"No numbers, Chester. I'm lookin' to place a bet on a horse to win in the sixth race." Cian grabbed his still-pounding head, the heat conjuring its dizzying spell. "No, wait, hold on a second." *Not the sixth. It was the third, wasn't it? Yes, yes, the third.* "I mean the third…Tuesday at Saratoga." That felt right.

Chester let out a long sigh, the notebook hanging by his side, unopened. Bettors often had misgivings just before putting their money in play. Cian was no different.

"What's it gonna be? Sixth or third?"

"Third." He nodded to give the decision added weight. "Yeah, that's for sure. The third. So."

"Uh-huh. Don't want no cryin' on this doorstep come next Wednesday."

"I'm sure. Third race at Saratoga. Tuesday. Fifty dollars on number six in the third."

A thin smile crept across Chester's face. "Where you get fifty dollas?"

"I got it right here, don't you worry. This is my fifty dollars and that's my bet."

Chester's smile stayed where it was. "Okay. Cian." His tongue worked its way around the inside of his lower lip. "You say number six in the third, yeah?"

Cian nodded vigorously, checking again over his shoulder to make sure he wasn't attracting unnecessary attention. Transactions at the front door usually took under thirty seconds.

Opening his notebook, Chester scanned through a few pages to see what odds he had for that race. When he found what he was looking for, his eyebrows momentarily revealed his surprise. It was a situation that needed some levelling, odds that required some protection. "Six in the third. That's what you said, six in the third?"

Cian just stood on the steps and stared at Chester, no words forming.

"That can't be right, Cian. You sure that's right? 'Cause that horse got big odds. You know what I mean? *Big*…odds." He made sure to lay some extra emphasis on the *big*. "That horse ain't gonna win nothin' Tuesday 'cept a trip to the glue factory. Number three is gonna run that race, Cian. That's the horse you want."

Cian felt disoriented. The heat and headache felt like his ice tongs were clamped around his skull. "No, no. Number six. Number six, that's the one I want," he muttered, his voice losing conviction.

"Cian. Now here, listen good. That horse ain't nothin' but a hide with four legs. Ain't no way he can win nothin'. You go with number three now."

"I—I... Hold on, I—I'm not sure. I—this number three, what makes you think it can win?"

Chester pulled the notebook up close to his face. "What I'm seein' here...that horse meant to win. Let me see that fifty."

Cian's hand crept into his pocket, feeling the bills between his fingers. If he bet on three and it won... The odds weren't as good, but the winnings would be all his. On the other hand, if he lost... "Number—number three," he stammered.

Chester cocked his head to one side. "You bettin' or no? 'Cause people startin' to wonder what we doin' out here on this stoop."

Cian quickly checked over his shoulder. A couple of men at the bottom of the steps were staring at him, hesitating, looking like they wanted to come up. A group of kids were all over the back of his cart. "Hey, get the hell outta there, you little bastards!" he yelled.

"Okay now, we done here," said Chester as he started to close the door.

"Wait, wait now." Cian rubbed both hands through his hair. "Okay, yeah, uh..." He shook his head, trying to make sense of it all. He needed a winner. And surely Chester would know which one was the better bet. Wouldn't he? He'd know which one to choose. "Okay, number three. Yeah, okay. That's it." He paused. "You sure that's it?"

"Your bet, you choose." Chester seemed to have lost interest in the whole transaction.

Cian took in a deep breath and let it out slowly, then pulled the fifty dollars from his pocket and thrust it into Chester's hand. "Number three. Number three in the third. Like you said."

"I didn't say nothin'," Chester sniffed, reaching for the money and stuffing it into his pants. "Customer got a right to his own ideas." He pulled up his notebook and a pencil that was sandwiched between the pages and started to make a note. "Name?" he scowled.

Puzzled, Cian looked around and then back at Chester, an awkward smile searching for reassurance. "You know my name, Chester."

"You got that dumbass name that don't look like it sounds. Spell it for me again."

Cian hesitated. "C-I-A-N," he mumbled. "Same as always. Sounds like Keane." It sounded like a snarl when Cian pronounced it. "It's Irish."

Chester glared at him. "Your momma coulda done better." He started to put the notebook away. "All right. I got that."

"Wait, wait," said Cian, reaching into his other pocket, pulling out his own ten dollars and pressing it into Chester's hands. "Ten more on three in the third."

Chester stared at him. Then raised his eyebrows and expelled a quick snort. "My, my. A man what got conviction," he said finally, jotting down the transaction in his notebook. "You might be president one day."

Taking the money from Cian's outstretched hand, he slammed the door in his face.

Chapter 13

By the time Lucas had talked his way out of getting arrested for jumping the barrier in the subway and arrived back at the ballpark, the game was over. Despite his absence, the Bulldogs had maintained their winning spirit and were now in sole possession of second place. His own spirit, though, had been thoroughly crushed after he'd failed to get his hands on whoever it was that had so cleverly and annoyingly tried to get his attention at the ballpark. But for what purpose? Some sort of stupid joke? An unsatisfied grudge? Or was something going on that warranted a whole hell of a lot more of his attention? It was annoying, to be certain. But was it threatening? He had no idea.

He'd all but forgotten about the little tin Cracker Jack-like toy that had been delivered to his office, but now he wondered if the two incidents could somehow be related. A toy shovel and a cracked mirror. Went together like—well, that was the point. They didn't go together at all as far as he could tell.

He decided that he was trying to produce a pattern where one didn't exist, where his mind was encouraging two separate and unrelated events to conspire and look like they somehow fit. It was that wartime vigilance insinuating itself into his peacetime life. Determined not to see shadows, he elected to set the whole thing aside for the time being. The shovel? It was nothing more than a child's toy. A ballplayer's joke on a preoccupied manager. *Maybe even one of my own players,* he figured. The mirror? An unhappy fan. Or maybe a player whose playing time had expired. He'd routinely had to contend with players who had high opinions of themselves but without the talent to match. Now that he thought about it, that seemed a convincing possibility.

There'd been one very capable player in the spring season who'd had enough attitude for an entire team, and as a result, hadn't made the cut. He was pretty unhappy with Lucas's decision to say the least, and hadn't been shy about sharing his opinion with anyone who would listen. And a great many who wouldn't. There were curses, threats, but in the end, he took his leave and Lucas forgot about him. Until now.

Frankie Miller. That was his name. A product of the urban street gangs that grew up in and ran Hell's Kitchen, Miller was talented and mouthy in equal parts. A deep scar across his right cheek left by a rival gang member during a fight over protection money added weight to his fierce reputation. For a short while, many who knew him thought Miller, with genuinely outstanding baseball abilities, had discovered the golden escape clause from a life of petty crime and near-certain early death. So, it was easy enough for Lucas to imagine the man dwelling on the bitterness of failing to make the team and the need to exact some sort of revenge. In fact, an incident involving the clubhouse being trashed and some equipment being stolen earlier in the season remained unsolved, but had kept Miller high on Lucas's suspect list long after he'd left the club. He'd pretty much forgotten about the whole thing until now and began to think maybe it hadn't all blown over. The question was, how far would Miller go? Only his formidable talent with a baseball might prevent him from going one step too far.

Lucas decided to make Frankie Miller a future consideration and get back to managing the team.

The clubhouse buzzed with the usual post-game activity as players traded highlight moments, each insistent that their personal performance had clinched the game, notwithstanding that the score had never been very close. Tommy Marshall was busy picking up bats, balls, and the occasional wayward glove and returning them to their rightful owners.

The catcher, Frosty Stevens, having just come out of the shower, was walking around in nothing more than his birthday suit singing "Take Me Out to the Ballgame" and snapping a wet towel at inattentive teammates to punctuate the end of each line.

At the same time, Marty Walsh, the first baseman, stumbled about trying to balance an upright bat in the palm of each hand. Most of the others, still enjoying the win, tolerated the nonsense, but Lucas was still struggling to get his head back into the season. He had a job to do, and he couldn't afford to let silly pranks distract him.

"Zach," Lucas yelled. "I need your help."

Zach was busy half a locker room away putting some of the equipment back into a cupboard. He turned and tipped his chin up to indicate he'd heard the call. A minute later, he was standing by Lucas's side.

"Sure, boss. What's up?"

"You remember that guy, Frankie Miller, tried out with us last spring?"

"Mr. Big Mouth? Trouble from the start, boss."

"Yeah, and I don't think…well, I've been wondering. You know where he went?"

"You mean did another team pick him up?"

"Yeah."

"He went looking around, spoke to a bunch of clubs. I think maybe he ended up with the Hornets." The Hornets had a reputation for taking in stray dogs. The strayer the better, and Miller had plenty of qualifications. Lucas often wondered if the Hornets saw baseball as their primary objective or whether making life difficult for every other team was more satisfying.

"Figures. They'd take any mutt with a spiked collar. But you haven't seen him, right?"

"He wasn't on the roster when we played them in June, and I don't recall hearing anyone mention his name. Doesn't mean he isn't around. You thinkin' he's got something to do with those shenanigans today?"

"That, and maybe the little toy shovel I showed you. I dunno. It's a long shot. But it's the best one I've got at the moment. He's the only one I can figure for this. See if you can find out where he ended up. Maybe we can straighten him out. Assuming it's him."

"Yeah, sure thing, boss. I'll see if I can meet up with Marty Majors tonight, find out where Miller mighta got to."

Marty was the Hornets manager and loved to mix things up. *He might have even encouraged Miller to make trouble with me,* thought Lucas.

"Good. Thanks. No changes for tomorrow's lineup?"

"I'm good if you are."

Zach left and Lucas stood looking around the clubhouse. Most of the players had gone, but Tommy was still milling about.

"Hey, Tommy, why don't you head off? You can finish the rest in the morning."

A broad smile overtook Tommy's face. "I'm just gonna feed Bear and then I'll leave." For a kid who moved at the speed of treacle anywhere but on the playing field, he couldn't get out the door fast enough.

The team's right fielder, Eddy Briggs, closed his cupboard and walked toward the clubhouse door. "See ya, Chief."

"Yeah, Eddie. See ya."

Lucas waved goodbye and turned to go to his office. It was then that he noticed that the door was open. Players didn't ordinarily go in there without an invitation, and Zach was always fastidious about closing the door after himself anytime he needed to go in. Tommy wasn't even a consideration.

Lucas walked across the room and poked his head in the door. A pungent odor from the icebox greeted him, but nothing else caught his attention. Until he spotted an envelope propped up next to the phone on his desk. The same kind and color of envelope that the toy shovel had arrived in. A sudden feeling of anxiety plucked at his throat.

Lucas yelled in the direction of where his bat boy had just disappeared.

"Hey, Tommy!"

No answer.

"Tommy?" Lucas quickly stepped back into the clubhouse, his eyes darting to the four corners of the room. No one in sight as he headed for the equipment room. "Tommy? Hey, Tommy, where the heck—"

Lucas had just about reached the equipment room when Tommy lunged out the door with Bear in his arms, nearly bumping into him. "Oh," he said, his nerves settling. "Okay, yeah—you're—you're okay." He felt foolish, wondering if his imagination now had the upper hand.

"Yes, sir," said Tommy, taking no notice of Lucas's concern. "I heard you, but I didn't want to yell and scare Bear. He was hungry."

Lucas could see now that Tommy's rabbit was happily chewing away on a small piece of carrot.

"Yeah, okay. So, so, listen, Tommy, you remember that man came around with a letter for me? The one who wanted to hold Bear?"

Tommy turned away and looked at the ground. Silence.

"Did he come back? Did you see him around here today?"

"No, sir. He wasn't here. I don't want to see him here."

Lucas empathized. He wasn't eager to see the man either except to get some answers. But it still didn't solve how a second envelope had ended up on his desk.

"All right, well, don't worry about it, Tommy. I don't think we'll see him again. You go on home now, yeah?"

Tommy didn't need further encouragement. He dashed into the equipment room, and as Lucas walked back to his office he could hear the sound of metal banging on metal. Bear being put into his cage. He heard the clubhouse door slam shut and then silence. He had the place to himself.

Back in his office, Lucas picked up the envelope and shook it. His heart skipped. There was definitely something inside. His imagination might have been fully stoked, but it wasn't yet running off the track. He opened the desk drawer and looked at his Colt Pocket Hammerless sitting there. He'd carried one during the war, when it was known as the "General Officer's Pistol." It wasn't the most powerful or the most recent model, but it was reliable and easy to carry. And could put a man down with authority if needed.

Will I need it? Too early to tell.

He left the gun where it was and pulled out his letter opener instead. Sliding it under the envelope flap, he wondered what it would be this time. He tipped the envelope upside down.

Out slid a small tin replica of a cat. A black cat. With glowing red eyes.

Why a cat? wondered Lucas, turning the object over in his hand to see if there were any other distinguishing markings.

And why a black cat?

A warning?

A threat?

Was it in any way connected to the shattered mirror?

Lucas couldn't help but feel his luck was about to change.

And not in a good way.

Chapter 14

Zach climbed down the subway steps, handed his ticket to the ticket chopper attendant, and strode out onto the platform. He wasn't at all sure he'd be able to track down Frankie Miller, given the number of minor league teams that Miller might have approached, but if it was important to Lucas, it was important to him. He'd met up with the Hornets' manager, Marty Majors, who'd told Zach where Miller liked to hang out. "It's a rough little speakeasy west of 10th," he'd said. Zach knew the area, and could picture the place tucked away between the factories, slaughterhouses, lumberyards, and tenements of Hell's Kitchen. Just the sort of place Miller would feel at home.

With the sun now setting and the temperature receding from the day's highs, Zach waited for the approaching train. As it came to a complete stop, the doors opened and a dozen passengers trundled out. Zach climbed aboard and fell into the first empty seat he could find. He arranged himself as best he could, maneuvering to get his body to sink further into a seat that no one would ever describe as comfortable. He gave up trying and accepted his position. He opened up the newspaper he'd bought that morning but hadn't finished and turned to the sports section.

He hadn't gotten very far before deciding to just set the paper down in his lap and let his mind drift. He was tired after sitting in the sun at the ballpark all afternoon and was looking forward to a beer at the speakeasy where he was hoping to spot Frankie Miller.

The train rocked back and forth, lulling him into a mild stupor, occasionally jerking him back to attention when it would hit some spot where the tracks didn't quite join up with precision.

"Fifty-eighth Street station is next! Broadway and 58th Street!"

The conductor walked past Zach and into the next car, but his piercing voice hung in the air, seeming out of place with the lulling sound of the wheels as they chased along the rails beneath the rocking train carriage.

Zacharia shut his eyes again. As the train pulled into the station, he lifted his eyelids and looked lazily out at the passengers waiting to board. He was ready to shut his eyes again when a movement outside caught his attention. He jerked forward and stared hard out the window.

"Son of a bitch!" he mumbled under his breath.

One of the passengers getting on the train in the next car looked a lot like Frankie Miller.

Rubbing his eyes, Zach stood up slowly and walked toward the car he thought Miller had just boarded. He pushed through the doors separating the two cars and took a tentative step into the next one.

Miller stood at the far end of the train car, holding on to an overhead strap, his back toward Zach. He was dressed in street clothes, oblivious to everything and everybody in the train. Zach pulled his newspaper up in front of his face and slid down into an empty seat.

The train lurched forward, continuing on its way downtown. Zach kept close watch on Miller out of the side of his eye.

When Miller stepped off the train, Zach waited until the doors were about to shut, then leapt out of the subway car. Miller was about twenty steps ahead of him. Pulling his hat down low over his face, Zach headed in the same direction.

At the first intersection, Miller turned right and headed toward the Hudson River. Zach followed, keeping to the opposite side of the street.

The streets were still busy with carts and people. A few automobiles headed both east and west along the roadway, a handful of kids were playing hopscotch on the sidewalk, and two boys looped a wooden wheel down the sidewalk, two dogs fast at their heels. Just past 10th Avenue, a horse-drawn cart pulled up, blocking Zach's view of Miller. When the cart had cleared Zach's field of vision, Miller was gone.

Sidestepping a steaming pile of horse manure, Zach rushed across the street. Once on the far side, he slipped between a Model T and a pushcart, frantically looking to catch a glimpse of Miller, but the man was nowhere to be seen. He walked a few paces past where he had last spotted him. Still nothing. He was about to abandon his quest when he saw Miller not ten feet away at a newsstand, his back toward Zach.

Cursing his carelessness, Zach quickly turned his back. He tried nonchalantly to stroll away but had managed only a few paces when he saw Miller coming in his direction, his face already buried in a newspaper. Again, Zach turned away and Miller continued walking right past him.

Breathing a sigh of relief, he waited for Miller to put some distance between them and then took up the pursuit again.

Another minute and two dozen buildings later, Miller turned down a flight of stairs and disappeared.

When Zach caught up to where Miller had left the street level, he could see that the underground location was probably a speakeasy. It wasn't one Zach knew, but with a couple thousand already having sprung up in the city since Prohibition had come into force, it didn't come as a surprise.

Without a password, he knew his chances of getting in were slim. He'd have to wait. It was almost dark, and he expected the multitude of dockworkers who toiled along the wharves to be leaving work soon and looking for a place to quench their thirst. He knew if he waited long enough, someone would facilitate his entrance. With a little luck, he'd just slip in on someone else's coattails.

He didn't have to wait long. Two men who looked like they might have just come off a shift at the nearby docks ambled up to the door. Talking loudly and slapping each other on the back, it was clear they'd already stopped in at some other speakeasy along the way.

They banged on the door.

"Kelly, boy, open 'er up, would ya? It's two of County Cork's smartest and best lookin'!"

This seemed to amuse them and they both burst out laughing. Zach sensed this was his chance. Feigning inebriation, he stumbled out from behind his hiding place and moved up a few steps behind them.

The door opened a crack. "You two fools," said a voice from inside in obvious recognition. "If you haven't got the brains between yas to remember the password, go on some place more fittin'."

"Oh, now, Kelly, boy," said the taller one, his thumbs thrust into his black cotton vest, "you knowed it was us, right? And we knows the secret password. Don't we, Donegal?"

"Course we knows it, you dumb fuck. But we can't tell ya."

"Ah," said the voice behind the door. "So's you can't tell me, yeah? And why is that then?"

"'Cause it's a secret!"

The two exploded in laughter and Zach edged a step closer.

"And who's yer friend?" said the voice, eyeing Zach from behind the door. "I don't recognize that one."

Both men turned to look at Zach, a stew of confusion and suspicion spreading across their faces. The shorter one squinted hard at Zach and rubbed his chin. Zach gave them a wink and mimed lifting a glass to his lips and raising his eyebrows by way of invitation. After too long a wait, they seemed to catch his meaning, grinned, and turned back to the door.

"That there's me brother, so. All the way from Ringaskiddy, that one. Works the docks there, like us here, he does."

Zach chose the moment to strengthen his hand and slipped into his best brogue. "Aye…that I do. And I could use a drink to wash away that sea passage, sure."

The two other men burst out laughing again. Zach wasn't certain if it was his accent or just the general mood they were in. Either way, he figured it was best to join in and slapped the shorter man on the shoulder.

That gave the shorter man pause. He stared hard at Zach for a few seconds. "Cat's Cradle," he finally said, without turning to look back at the man at the door.

"That's it, sure," said the taller one, recalling the password at the other man's prompt. "Cat's Cradle it is!"

"Aye, Cat's Cradle," added Zach, hoping his charade wasn't too flimsy.

The door slammed shut. Both dockworkers grinned at Zach.

"Don't you worry," smiled the taller one. "That's the password for sure."

"Aye," added the shorter one. "And don't be forgettin' us now once yer inside."

Zach tipped his hat and winked at the two of them. "I never forget a friend—friend."

The taller man grinned again and rubbed his hands together.

Zach could hear some rattling inside, probably chains being removed, and then the door swung open.

As the man at the door stood aside, the three men ambled into the dimly lit chamber and headed straight for the bar.

Zach exhaled a sigh of relief.

Chapter 15

It wasn't much of a park. Not like Central Park or Prospect Park. More like a small but jaunty collection of carelessly plotted trees and loosely disciplined shrubs, divided into two unequal halves by a dirt path that rambled languidly from one corner to the other, punctuated here and there by neat clumps of beebalm, calamint, and evening primrose that served to lightly perfume the August evening, the entirety working to present itself as both liberated yet contained and offering a brief respite from the chaos of the city to those few having both the good fortune to happen upon it and the time to enjoy its gifts. Few people were so blessed.

But it was the one spot in the city that Lucas and Willa felt had sought them out, the one spot that was just theirs, regardless of how many other people were around. It was the place where their souls had first become entwined. Ending up here hand in hand on their third date, they'd wandered through the park on an evening just like this one without noticing much of anything but each other's heartbeat. For Lucas, it was just like the day he'd first stumbled into Aleta Jean's Sun's Up Coffee Shop hoping for nothing more than a respectable breakfast of bacon and eggs and ending up with a spinning head and a thundering pulse.

Though the night had kept them out late, they felt no anxiety walking through the park. A few other people ambled about but there was nothing that felt menacing. Lovers stealing a kiss behind an agreeable tree; a man on a solitary bench staring wistfully up at the waxing crescent moon; another in overalls, head down, quietly humming a tune and happily swinging his dinner bucket, seemingly headed off to a late night shift.

As they strolled hand in hand, Lucas's face fell into darkness. He wondered about Zach and whether he'd been able to track down Frankie Miller. Even more troubling, he was thinking about what had caused him to lose focus with what Willa had just said. Now he felt he might be on the verge of spoiling the evening altogether. Quickly, he stole a glance to see if she'd noticed.

She had.

"The girl? Number 29?" Willa repeated, somewhat accusingly. "Don't tell me you don't remember."

Lucas tried to wrestle his memory into surrender, but it kept wriggling out of his grip. "Well, let's see…," he started, but then faltered.

"Really? That's all you have to say! You don't remember her in that apartment? I seem to remember you thinking she was rather pretty!" Willa added, a noticeable pout pursing her lips.

"Number 29?" Lucas strained harder. He couldn't picture the apartment, let alone a girl. Either way, he knew he was treading on patchy ground. The wrong attempt at justification or good-natured humor, even a single ill-chosen word, could stifle the high spirits they'd been in just minutes before. Having discussed and dispensed with the incident involving the mirror at the ballpark earlier that day, they'd gone out for dinner, taken a long stroll, and were on their way back to the apartment Willa shared with Aleta.

But over the last block or two, Lucas had lost track of the conversation, unwittingly allowing his mind to wander back to the mystery of the Cracker Jack prizes. And now the evening threatened to unravel.

"Lucas! The girl! Don't you remember?"

Lucas slammed the door on his own intruding thoughts and jerked his attention back to what Willa was saying.

"Right. Yes. The girl."

There *had* been another woman, right after the war. But it hadn't lasted for very long, and Lucas could barely remember the time he'd spent with her. And he certainly had no memory of her apartment. Could it have been number twenty-nine?

Stealing another peek at Willa, he marveled at the female ability to extract obscure and irrelevant scenarios from the remotest pages of absolutely any relationship and drag them into conversations that had no passing acquaintance with the subject at hand, and then mobilize those recollections in a way that reduced men to feeling awkward, blindsided, cornered, and unprotected from all things emotional. A bit like Lucas felt right now.

"In fact," continued Willa, "I distinctly remember you saying she looks rather like Theda Bara." To a nearby tree she added under her breath, "Though why he'd think that seductress looks pretty is simply beyond me!"

Lucas couldn't picture Theda Bara or any other woman right at that moment, but felt like he had better apologize anyway for letting his attention stray to another woman when it should have been firmly fixed on Willa. He was about to plead for mercy when it suddenly hit him.

"The movie!" he blurted out in abrupt relief.

Willa stopped and turned to him. "Of course, the movie. What did you think I was talking about?"

"The movie, yes! No, nothing! Sorry. Just for a moment..." Like a retriever sprung from its leash in pursuit of a squirrel, he was barely able to contain himself. "*The Girl in Number 29*! Of course I remember! The movie where the girl pretends she's going to shoot herself and there's a man in another apartment looking at her. He's a writer, right? But he won't write—I've forgotten why—and so he won't write, but he saves her from killing herself, and then she leads him on a...what would you call it? An—an adventure, yes, a mystery adventure. And, and he shoots someone to protect her and it's all just a trick to get him back to writing," he exhaled triumphantly. "*The Girl in Number 29*!"

Willa just stared at him. "Well?" she asked expectantly.

"Um..." Lucas searched Willa's face for a clue. After a few more moments, he gave up. "Willa, I'm sorry. My mind wandered off and I was thinking about Cracker Jack prizes and Zach and mirrors and faces with scars and—what was your question?"

Willa let out an exasperated sigh. "Do you want to see it again? The movie? I know we saw it just a few weeks ago, but I really enjoyed it, and I thought you did too, and...well, I know you're so busy right now. I just want to be with you all the time, and..."

Lucas gathered her up in his arms and kissed her and promised they would most definitely go to see *The Girl in Number 29* again. By the time they'd finished reminding each other of all the scenes in the movie and how the plot had unfolded, they were standing outside Willa's apartment.

"What's that?" Willa suddenly said, looking over Lucas's shoulder.

Lucas turned to see what had caught her eye.

"Is that a bird?" said Willa, rushing up the steps to the porch and picking up a small metal cage. "Lucas, look, it's a...well, a canary, I think."

The bird chirped its affirmation and jumped to a second perch.

Lucas hurried up the steps and took the cage from Willa's hands, looking anxiously about the stone steps.

"Lucas, what's the matter?" asked Willa, retrieving the cage from him, her voice as melodic as the bird's. "Someone's left this beautiful little thing here in the middle of the night. Who would do that?" She turned the cage around, the bird flitting about inside as if to deny her a view from a second angle.

"I was wondering the same thing," said Lucas, still looking about. "Was there a note or anything with it?"

"I don't see anything," said Willa, turning the cage around without taking her eyes off the bird. "Oh, it's so lovely. Let's go show Aleta!"

Lucas looked down both ends of the street. There was nothing that he hadn't seen dozens of times before. "Let's not wake Aleta," he said quietly. "It's late, and I...well, I just don't know about this," he said, pointing to the cage, his entire face now furrowed with concern.

"Oh, stop being such a worrywart, Lucas! It's just a bird. Haven't you ever seen a canary before?"

He had.

Lying dead at the bottom of its cage in a tunnel in Belgium.

Chapter 16

The smell of stale beer, sour sweat, and day-old cigarette butts saturated the room. Having gotten past the doorman, Zach had minded his promise and bought both men a beer. And a whiskey. Sensing that was as much bounty as they were going to collect, they'd reluctantly trundled off into the shadowed recesses of the bar while Zach had retreated to a dimly lit corner in the opposite direction. Within minutes of sitting down, he'd spotted Miller sitting with another man whose back was turned toward Zach. There was nothing unusual about the second man other than his clothes. Dressed in what looked to be an expensive and impeccably tailored two-piece light beige linen suit with hickory colored stripes, he projected an air not so much of prestige as precision. Military precision. His dark hair was neatly and perfectly parted straight down the middle. Sitting on the table at his elbow, an elegant telescope-crowned, cream-colored panama hat with a dark-brown grosgrain ribbon hat band. On his feet, carefully polished two-toned wingtips.

The clothes suited the man, but the man didn't suit the scene.

Unable to see his face, Zach decided just to nurse his beer and wait for the two of them to get up and leave, at which time he hoped he would be able to get a better look.

Miller sat across from the well-dressed stranger, occasionally nodding but otherwise listening intently to what the man had to say. When he did speak, his face alternated between looking angry and looking smug, a practiced cockiness that no longer needed a workout. Most of the time, he remained silent.

As far as Zach was concerned, both the room and the beer suffered from lack of interest. After fifteen minutes and feeling restless, he decided to do something more decisive. He was about to get up when he sensed someone directly behind him.

"You looked about to leave without sayin' *Slán* to yer new friends...friend!" a voice reeking of stale beer breathed close to his ear, a second voice behind it chuckling.

The barrel of a pistol pressed into Zach's neck. The voice was familiar. One of the men who'd helped Zach gain entrance to the speakeasy. The taller man in the black vest.

Zach's body relaxed, but his brain was urgently calculating the next move. The right move. "Sure, friend. If it's a farewell you're needin', you can count on me, then."

"The only countin' we're countin' on...would be yer wallet—friend!"

Zach thought the man's use of the word *friend* had a particularly unfriendly sound to it. He reached up slowly and scratched his ear.

"I'm sure I can help with that—friend."

With a sudden sweep of his arm, Zach grabbed the pistol in his left hand and shoved it to face upward. The gun exploded into the ceiling as Zach turned and jumped up from his chair. He recognized the gun as an old Remington double-barrelled Model 95 pocket pistol and quickly ripped it from the man's hand. At the same time, with his right hand, he grabbed the man at the back of his neck and smashed him face first into the table. The man bounced up a few inches and Zach smashed him down again, then dropped him to the floor.

The second man held a chair over his head, about to bring it down on Zach, when Zach turned to face him. Reassessing his chances of a successful encounter, the man set the chair down on the floor without a sound and started inching backwards. Zach took two powerful strides and grabbed the man by his shirt front, lifted him off the ground, and kneed him in his groin, then dropped him to the ground. Both men lay writhing on the floor, showing no inclination that they were going to get up anytime soon.

At the first sign of disturbance, the other patrons had stood and instinctively moved away from where Zach had been seated.

All except one.

"Very impressive, Mr. Tucker," said a voice behind him.

Zach turned as the man in the beige linen suit, his panama hat discreetly tilted in front of his face, limped gingerly around the two writhing bodies on the floor and headed toward the door.

It took a moment for Zach to register who had spoken. When he realized who it was, he took a step and called after him. "Hey, you! Fella!"

But before he could take another step, a wooden bat slammed into Zach's stomach, knocking the wind out of him, and he staggered backwards, almost falling to the floor.

"And where'd you think you was goin'?" sneered a burly man holding the baseball bat.

Clutching his gut, Zach ignored the newcomer and quickly looked around.

Both Miller and the man in the beige linen suit were gone.

AUGUST 21, 1920

Chapter 17

Lucas left his apartment early with the intention of getting to the ballpark before anyone could buttonhole him about his team's prospects going into the final month of play. He desperately needed some time to think.

No further thoughts about the mysterious man with the mirror had presented themselves for consideration, and nothing of any note had happened since that strange and irritating encounter the day before. Despite giving it considerable thought, he'd been unable to make any connection between the shovel, the mirror, and the cat. He felt they should somehow be related.

The message in the telegram, at least, was now clear. LOOK FOR ME AT BALLPARK. STOP. YOU WON'T SEE ME. Of course he couldn't see who was behind it all. The flashes of sunlight had obscured any possibility of identification.

There was one thing, though. The man had a tattoo. On the back of his left wrist. What it meant, if anything, Lucas had no idea.

The cool, early morning air was acting like a vacuum on his cluttered brain, clearing out the noise that had been masquerading as thought. And despite the frustration of not being able to figure out what all the mysterious occurrences meant, his mood was slowly improving. As usual, he passed by Zaslaw's newsstand to pick up his morning paper. As usual, Zaslaw needed to share some observation he had about some worldly issue.

"Bloody Russians!"

"Good morning to you, Zaslaw! Another beautiful day in New York City!" Lucas offered, hoping he might be able to dodge the current events lesson. "I'll take a *Times*, if that's okay with you," he said, picking a copy up off the stack.

"Of course, is beautiful day. No bloody Russians invading into your backyard. Not like war in my country!" he scoffed.

Lucas knew a little about the Polish-Russian war. Zaslaw had made sure of that, keeping him posted at least once a week with events from his homeland. It had been raging for over a year now, with the advantage flipping back and forth between the two countries like a ping-pong ball. But Lucas hadn't really been paying much attention to the details. There was so much happening right across America, he didn't much care about what was happening four thousand miles away. Besides, he'd had enough war, and thought the last one would have sated anyone's need for further death and destruction.

"I thought America was your country now, Zaslaw."

"Is my country, beautiful country. I come here ten years now. No invasion from Russia."

"Yeah, well—I don't think we have to worry about Russia. They're too far away. Besides, they were allies in the war. They're on our side now. More or less."

"Not so in Poland. There, they invade and make war with Polish people. But—we are too smart! Look at headline."

He grabbed the paper from Lucas's hands and silently mouthed the headline before looking back at him. "Forty thousand Russian prisoners! Yesterday, ten thousand more! They will not take Poland! Not ever! You can be sure!"

"Well, if you're sure, then I'm sure," winked Lucas. "Just the *Times*, please," he added, reaching back over the counter to retrieve his paper.

"Okay, you don't care. This is not your worry. I can see this." He thrust a finger into Lucas's face for added emphasis. "This is how things happen! Nobody cares until is too late! Believe me, Russians are coming!"

Lucas couldn't imagine any scenario where the Russians would want to come to the United States, let alone how they would get here. Devastated in the Great War barely two years prior and embroiled in their own civil war, Russia was now a mere sliver of its imperial past. Lucas doubted it would pose a threat to anyone else ever again.

"I promise you, Zaslaw, I care. I really do. I just need to get going. I'm late for work."

"Baseball is work? And selling newspapers? This is what?" he said, pointing to the stacks of papers on all sides. "Picnic?"

He looked at Lucas, his face etched in resignation and disappointment.

"Two cents," he finally muttered. "Not a penny more. Same as yesterday. Same tomorrow—"

"—unless the government gets its hands on it," Lucas said, butting in. "Don't worry about that, Zaslaw," he added, handing over the two pennies and turning to leave. "We have a Constitution to protect us!"

Sticking the paper under his arm, Lucas headed off down the street. He hadn't heard anything from Zach yet, although it was still early. He figured they'd catch up later at the clubhouse. And although his heart really wanted him to drop in and say good morning to Willa, he decided to skip going to Aleta Jean's and instead headed straight for the subway.

Rounding the corner, he slipped down the entrance stairs, handed his ticket to the waiting attendant, and walked out onto the platform. He half-expected to see fragments of broken mirror lying about, jagged reflections of his shocked self staring back at him. But it was just a typical day, with people rushing in all directions trying to get to places they mostly didn't want to go to but had no real choice if they wanted to eat again. He settled into his seat and browsed through the first few pages of the newspaper, promising himself that he'd make time later to catch up on the Yankees.

When the train reached his station, he merged his way into the departing crowd and headed toward the exit, thinking he'd grab a quick pretzel from the street vendor who normally stationed his cart a few blocks from the clubhouse. Head down, he raced up the steps and out of the subway, colliding with a uniformed attendant busy sweeping up the early morning rubble. The man didn't seem bothered enough even to turn around and see what clumsy oaf had bowled into him. Mumbling an apology, Lucas kept going, but something gnawed at the edge of his consciousness, and he turned back around to try and determine what it was. He could see it in his mind's eye. Something. Like a memory. Distant but familiar. A shape, or maybe a design. A blue something. On the man's hand. Or his arm maybe; Lucas wasn't sure. Was it a tattoo? But in the few seconds it had taken him to assess the incident and turn fully around to face the attendant, the man was already at the bottom of the stairs. The morning crush of people coming out of the subway blocked Lucas's view, preventing any potential communication, though it didn't seem as though the man was interested anyway; so, Lucas shrugged and continued on his way.

He had just about reached the clubhouse door when his hopes for an uneventful day vanished, and he stopped dead in his tracks. Even from twenty feet away it was clear that the clubhouse door was slightly ajar. The padlock dangled open from the hasp. But it didn't look broken or like anyone had tampered with it. It was still too early for Tommy Marshall to be here, yet he was the only one that Lucas could think of outside of Zach who had a key and could gain access without breaking the lock. Considering the hour, Zach would almost certainly still be at the coffee shop.

Lucas stood still, listening, wondering. Was this another prank, compliments of his as-yet-unidentified mystery man? Or was this something more sinister? He didn't want to be the last one to know. Before making another move, he looked down both sides of the clubhouse and over both shoulders for something, some clue that might explain what was going on. Nothing caught his eye.

Cautiously, he pushed open the door and peered inside. Sunlight streamed in through the upper windows, illuminating the million dust motes that floated about in the stillness.

The door to his office was partially open, and the light that hung over his desk was lit. Not how he'd left it. Probability told him someone was inside. Wanting to keep the odds of surprise in his favor, he elected not to call out. Instead, he took a careful step forward. The floorboards had no intention of cooperating and loudly creaked their objection. He instantly stopped, all senses primed.

Once it became clear that he wasn't going to surprise anyone, he looked around for another advantage. A bat that should have been in the cupboard lay on the floor nearby and he picked it up, grateful to have a new friend. At the same time, he cursed Tommy Marshall for not taking proper care of the equipment.

Reaching the office door, he stopped once more, his ears begging for a clue. Breathing, shuffling, anything that would alert him to some barely perceptible sign that might otherwise go unnoticed. Something that would make the difference between leaving the building in triumph and...what? Leaving in a coffin?

He brushed the thought away.

Using the head of the bat to push the door open further, he yanked it back into a swinging position.

Still nothing. Other than a jolt of tension that raced up his spine.

He could now see clearly into the room.

His jaw fell open.

Propped upright in the middle of his desk was an unopened box of Cracker Jack.

Chapter 18

"Well, go ahead. Open it! It's not going to bite!"

Lucas could hardly believe his ears. He slammed the door open wide to look behind the desk, practically tripping into the room.

"Parker?"

"Well, of course, brother dear. Who were you expecting?"

Parker Blaine, Lucas's older, more flamboyant brother, was seated behind the desk reading a newspaper as if it was the most predictable thing in the world for him to be doing right then. Dressed in an impeccably cut, gray, two-piece suit with a beige checked vest and black bowtie, Parker looked like he'd just come from an early morning meeting at one of New York's more distinguished social clubs. Which might be believable, except that no self-respecting New York socialite would entertain the idea of rising before ten. As it wasn't yet seven-thirty, an alternative explanation was in order. The most likely scenario was that he'd come from some late-night gambling session that almost certainly included some of the city's more suspect business tycoons.

Most everything about Parker was dodgy and, Lucas suspected at times, possibly even illegal. But conviviality oozed from every pore, and he had the uncanny ability of giving people the feeling that a party could break out at any moment. Like his idol, James Buchanan Brady, whom the newspapers called "Diamond Jim," Parker had built his first fortune from a very young age providing industrial supplies to help sate the country's burgeoning commercial appetite. His second fortune had materialized when he'd divined how to fulfill the vast need for war materiel on behalf of a desperate and unprepared government. The fact that that same government cared less about cost and more about speed gave Parker the kind of flexibility he relished when it came time to negotiate. Having amassed a small fortune, he now lived to spend with unmitigated abandon.

"Seriously," Parker admonished, "you look like you were expecting some…some Prohibition agent!" He raised his eyebrows as he pulled a silver engraved flask from his inside jacket pocket and tipped it to his lips. "Mm?" he added, holding the flask out toward Lucas, who shook his head.

"And please, could you just set that bat down? It conveys an unnecessary air of thuggery." He made a face to convey his disapproval with the situation. Pointing toward the bat that Lucas was still holding over his shoulder, he added with a self-satisfied smile, "Look, I'm sorry! I retrieved that from your cupboard to show Claire my home run swing. I really should have put it back."

Claire was Parker's wife. His third wife to be precise, the first two having been generously paid off to find a hobby other than

Parker. Claire was a tall, striking brunette, as svelte as popular fashion was just beginning to dictate, as glittering as a Christmas ornament, and as overindulged as a kid at a carnival with two bucks in his pocket. Having spent the previous two years in Paris, she'd become enamored with the newest fashions emerging from the Lanvin boutique on the rue du Faubourg Saint-Honoré and could be counted on ever since never to appear in anything less.

When it came to Claire, she expected everything. Gift-wrapped. And when it came to Parker, he was only too happy to oblige.

Lucas lowered the bat and exhaled away some nervous energy. "What are you doing here?" he growled, again looking around the room just to double-check that he wasn't letting down his guard too soon, since almost anything untoward was possible when it involved his older brother. "And how did you get in?"

"With this key you gave me last year," Parker replied, holding it up for Lucas to see. "Don't you remember? 'For emergencies,' you said." He cast a disdainful look around the room. "Though other than that ridiculous thing you call an icebox, I can't for the life of me imagine what kind of an emergency might befall you. I just came by to offer my best wishes for the remainder of the sporting season. Here," he said, holding up the box of Cracker Jack. "Have some of this, why don't you? 'The more you eat, the more you want!' It says so right on the box!" His face beamed. "Go on, it's quite...distinctive. One might even say...tasty!" He abruptly pulled the box back in order to examine it closely. "Though I doubt it will show up on the menu at Delmonico's anytime soon!" He dropped the box onto Lucas's desk. "But then, you're all about baseball, so I expect you've already encountered this gooey little confection. Oh," he added with a tight little smile, "if you don't mind, the prize inside is mine."

Never one to give anything away without an attached condition, thought Lucas. Until he'd extracted the last iota of value from something, Parker was tighter than a Gordian knot.

"Always good to see you, Parker," Lucas managed, having worked the surprise out of his nervous system. *Briefly, anyways.* "Are you the one that's been leaving me little gifts on my desk the last week or so? Say, like, a Cracker Jack prize? Or maybe, pulling a little stunt? Like, like flashing a mirror in my face at the ballpark?" The notion that Parker might have resorted to these kinds of childish pranks was not totally out of the question.

"Leaving you toys? Why on earth would I do that, Lucas? You know I don't like giving things away! Besides," he sniffed, "Cracker Jack isn't my regular thing. Today was an exception due to the fact that last night was exceptional!"

Lucas guessed that meant Parker had had a good night at the gaming tables.

"Parker, why are you here?"

"I told you, brother dear, I came to wish you well." He glanced around the room. "I know how much one of those dusty little pennants would mean to you. And how much it would brighten up this...dreary little office of yours." A sad sort of frown wrinkled his brow, punctuating just how pathetic he imagined Lucas's life to be.

The clubhouse door opened, followed by the rhythmic click-clacking of high heels crossing the floor. Within seconds, Claire was standing in the office doorway, two large, warm pretzels in hand.

"Honestly, I cannot understand how he does it," she said,

holding the pretzels aloft. "Two for a penny! How on earth can he pay the rent?"

"Good morning to you, too, Claire. Always a pleasure," said Lucas, with a bare minimum of enthusiasm. He still managed a peck on each cheek, mimicking the French habit that he had picked up while overseas.

As usual, she ignored his greeting and carried on in her own little world. "I'm not really certain that these are edible, Parker dear. Who knows what that horrid little man uses to make them. I only consummated the purchase because you insisted, darling." Holding the salted coils by her fingertips, she dangled the pretzels toward Parker as if they might suddenly spring to life and crawl up her arms.

Parker reached out across the desk to take one. "Don't you just love these, Lucas? So..." Parker struggled to find the right word. "...ethnic!" he concluded with a satisfied smile.

"Look," interjected Lucas, wanting to get on with his day, "this is wonderful that you two would come by to wish me good luck—"

"Good luck?" Claire butted in between bites of her pretzel, having overcome her concerns about sanitation. "Are you getting married? Not to that dreadful waitress, I hope. Really, Lucas, she can be a bit of a flat tire."

"Claire, Lucas is contending for a baseball championship. Remember? We're here to offer our sincerest wishes for a desirable outcome. Oh, and before I forget, also to ask you if you could please, please look after Goodwill while we're gone." Parker tacked on a broad smile, hoping to neutralize Lucas's expected opposition. Goodwill, their yappy, over-groomed, defiant Pekingese wanted nothing to do with Lucas. To say the feeling was mutual was an understatement.

"We're off to Saratoga tomorrow for some fun. I've got a horse running. Exceptional beast. Could be the next Big Red!" he enthused, making an unlikely comparison to the current crowd favorite, Man o' War.

"Goodwill is out of the question," Lucas replied, the irony not lost on at least one of them. "I've got a baseball club to run."

"Lucas, how could you be so selfish?" Claire chimed in. "You know we'd do absolutely anything for you."

"Never mind," Parker interjected. "Louise can take care of him." He looked away, feigning irreconcilable concern. "Though how she's going to keep the house clean and look after poor little Goodwill, I just don't know. He really does suffer under her care, poor thing." He sighed, looking dejected in the hopes he might sway his brother's resistance. Guilt was about the only gift that Parker could offer without reservation.

"As I was saying, I've got a baseball club to manage and a lot of work to do. So, if it's all right with you two..."

"Understood completely, brother dear," Parker said, his face suggesting he really didn't understand at all. Then brightening, he stood up and added, "Come see my new motorcar! It's absolutely outrageous! A Packard Twin Six Roadster—ninety horsepower! Four hundred and twenty-four cubic inches! Goes like the goddamned wind!"

"Parker!" blushed Claire, feigning unease at the sudden devolution into near profanity.

"Sorry, darling." Turning back to Lucas, he added, "Goes like the devil! Come, Lucas, let me show you." Parker came around the edge of the desk and, taking Claire's arm, headed out the door, all the while continuing to list off the vehicle's mechanical specifications.

His description of the car was mostly lost on Lucas, but curiosity melted his resistance, and he followed the two of them out to the street. Sitting barely thirty feet from the front of the clubhouse, Lucas wondered how he could have missed the stunning two-seater that commanded attention from all who passed.

"What do you think?" enthused Parker.

"I gotta give it to you, Parker," said Lucas. "She is a beauty."

"Jump in the rumble seat. Let's go for a jaunt." Parker couldn't pry his eyes off the gleaming red and black vehicle.

In truth, neither could Lucas. From the wooden spoke wheels to the rear-mounted dual spare tire, the car looked the epitome of mechanical excellence and luxury. After the frustration and confusion of the last two weeks, it felt good to have something to smile about, even if it had nothing to do with him.

"It is quite magnificent, Parker. But as I said, I've got work to do. Let's postpone the ride 'til later."

"Pity," Parker replied. "Oh, listen, just between you and I, brother, this horse I'm running—would you like me to place a bet for you? I rather think you'll be pleased. Very good odds. Very good, really. He has a bit of an edge, if you get my meaning."

Lucas wasn't sure that he did, but where Parker was involved, it almost certainly meant something sneaky. "I think I'll stick to baseball, thanks."

"Well, suit yourself, brother dear. Although you really should *not* look this particular gift horse in the mouth." With that, he slid around to the passenger side of the car and opened the door. "Come along, darling," he said to Claire, "we really must be going."

Claire eased herself into the car and Parker shut the door behind her. He strode around behind the vehicle and made his way to the driver side door. "What a beautiful summer's day," he mused, looking up at the cloudless blue sky, then back at Lucas. "You'd almost think we were entitled!" Grinning, he got in and shut the door. "We'll be back in a week or so. Good luck with your pennant race!"

As they drove off up the road, oblivious to any and all, Lucas had to admit that just for a moment, he felt a pang of envy.

It wasn't the money. Lots of people had that. No, his brother possessed something else, something so many people struggled for, prayed for, even killed for. Not the money. It was that sense of carefree abandon. The sense that no matter what, things would work out.

Lucas wondered for a moment what that was like.

The moment wouldn't last.

Chapter 19

"This here fuckin' thing's leakin'!"

Mullan kneeled in front of the clubhouse icebox, sleeves rolled to the elbows, chipping the edges off a block of ice so that it would fit inside. His gigantic head bobbed from side to side as he worked, sweat glistening under his short-cropped black hair, all 250 pounds of him looking like he'd rather just rip the box open than work to make the ice fit.

"Some leaks don't matter," he snickered, "but this one's drippin' like a whore in heat!"

Lucas glanced up from his desk and over to where the man was working and raised his eyebrows. "That so?"

"Sure, and that's a fact. Look it here," he said, pointing to the puddle that had crept out from under the box since the last time Tommy Marshall had emptied the overflowing drip pan. "You sure I'm to put another block in? Won't keep too good, that's for sure."

Lucas tried to remember if he'd seen the man before. Most days, the ice came during game time, so he rarely saw who made the delivery. Today, it had arrived much earlier. Truth be told, Lucas didn't much care when it came or who brought it as long as it got done. He'd just send Tommy in from the field with a quarter to look after the payment. "Well, she keeps good enough, so, yeah, put another block in. Gotta make her last 'til the end of the season." On top of everything else, Lucas wasn't ready to spend the twenty dollars it would cost to get a new one.

"I'd get rid of 'er, t'was mine. Can't make a pig squeal if she ain't got any breath left to squeeze out!"

Lucas tried again to ignore him, but something made him look over. He noticed the man's puffy face, a deep scar running diagonally across his right cheek. Sweat ran down his stretched forearms as he turned the block of ice around to get at the other side. His left wrist was home to a tattoo, but Lucas couldn't make out what it was.

Damn! Scars and tattoos. Seems like everyone's got 'em.

"Thing of it is, she's not gettin' any younger, you know?" Mullan piped in again. "Stinks some, too, yeah? Like a fuckin' shithouse!" he added, slamming the ice pick into the now dripping cube.

A sliver of ice flew off and hit Lucas in the side of his face. He leaned back and drew in a long, deep breath, struggling not to rise to the provocation. "I'd appreciate you just being done with it," he said finally, mustering all his patience.

Mullan turned and gave him a long look, then pointed his ice pick at Lucas. "And I'd appreciate yer lettin' me do it," he said, less than a smile crossing his face. After a pause, he turned back to the waiting block of ice.

Lucas stood up and was about to say something when Zach stepped into the office.

"I got up with Marty Majors," Zach started, tossing his hat down on the chair and glancing over at Mullan. The iceman never looked up, so Zach just ignored him. "He said Miller'd played with him and the Hornets for a coupla weeks, but he had to let him go on accounta he was always mixin' it up with the other players. Never saw a squabble he couldn't turn into a full-fledged brawl."

"Yeah, well, he was like that around here, too."

"He was, yeah. But it never went further than that. So, here's the thing. Majors said he'd heard Miller talkin' with some guy about maybe he could get back at you for lettin' him go, how he'd like that, how he'd like to make you pay."

Lucas thought about that for a few moments.

Get back at me? What makes me so special?

There were several teams that had dispensed with Miller's services and were worthy of vengeance.

"Why me in particular? Did he say?"

"Majors didn't know anything more. That's what he heard, and he couldn't be bothered to mention it to you 'cause it all sounded like crap, like Miller talkin' big as usual. Besides, not like Majors is goin' to go out of his way to be doin' you any favors."

"Hmm. I get your drift." Knowing what Miller had been thinking made even less sense than not knowing. It seemed like every other day now something unusual was happening, something that somehow seemed to involve Lucas. And yet, he couldn't see how.

"So, I went lookin' for Miller," continued Zach, "and caught up with him at this speakeasy Majors mentioned. He met some guy there I didn't get a chance to recognize. Smart lookin'—from the back, at least. I'd say the conversation was on the serious side. Couldn't hear none of it, though."

"You didn't get a look at the guy from the front?"

"I was preoccupied. Coupla wharf rats decided I was easy pickins'." He snorted. "Don't know how they got that idea. Anyhow, when I was done with 'em, the bartender took a dislike to the way I'd treated his customers. Wanted to show me his new baseball bat."

Lucas had a feeling the bartender had struck out.

"Yeah, okay. And so, after you politely explained the situation to the bartender?"

"I gave him back his bat."

"But you're sure it was Miller?"

"No question. Followed him all the way from the 58th Street station. Scar and all on that same cocky face of his. It was Miller, all right."

Lucas looked over at the iceman again, the scar standing out like a fastball down the center of the plate. Tommy had said the man who'd confronted him had had a scar. Now there were two men with scars. Or was it three?

"Two more goons jumped me before I could say my farewells. Coppers came, so I ended up having to spend the night with Sergeant Sheehan and the boys." Zach was referring to one of the more notorious police constables in the city, an easygoing Irishman with a quick wit, an open palm, an untroubled conscience, and a reliable thirst for whiskey. "Told the bartender and his goons he'd look after lockin' me up."

"How'd that turn out?"

"Me and the sergeant spent a few hours sharin' tall tales and a bottle of Kilvannon. When he fell asleep, I let myself out."

"How'd you manage that?"

"The sergeant was kind enough to leave the keys in the lock." Zach grinned. "Wouldn't be a stretch to say he meant to. Left a sawbuck on his desk to show my appreciation"

The iceman slammed the icebox shut and turned to face Lucas. "Fuckin' thing's done. Two bits. And like I said, if I was you, I'd get rid of 'er," he added, jerking his thumb at the leaky appliance.

Lucas pulled a quarter from his pocket and handed it to the man. "Yeah. You mentioned that."

The workman stood staring at Lucas for a few seconds, tapping his ice pick against his leg. Then he turned his attention to Zach for a few more moments before finally grabbing his tongs and shuffling out the door.

When he had gone, Zach asked, "Who's the 'two bits' guy?"

"New guy, I guess. Never seen him. Can't say I like him much. Thinks we need a new icebox."

August 22, 1920

Chapter 20

Rain had been falling steadily all day and into the evening and didn't look like it would be letting up anytime soon. The figure sheltering under the eaves of the Bulldogs' clubhouse didn't much mind, figuring it would provide extra cover for what he had been hired to do. And for what he had schemed to do afterwards.

Looking around once more and seeing only one lonely car on the roadway, he waited until it had passed and then slid around the corner of the building to the clubhouse door. Pulling an icepick from the leather pouch that he was carrying, he inserted it into the lock and gave a couple of sharp raps to the butt of the wooden handle. The lock popped and the door creaked open. The man grabbed the door handle to prevent the door from opening too wide too quickly, then looked over both shoulders to ensure he was still alone.

He wasn't.

Already it was looking like his plan might have to be abandoned as two strangers rounded the corner of the clubhouse and walked in his direction, heads down to avoid the rain. He eased the door shut, slid the icepick up his sleeve in case it was needed, and fiddled with the lock, pretending that it was stuck.

"Miserable night to have to be fightin' your door shut," said one of the men in passing.

"Tis that, and not the first time," replied the man at the door, keeping his voice friendly and calm. "Just needs a little persuasion."

"You want us to hold 'er shut whilst you pull?" said a much younger voice.

"I can manage. She's like this most nights. Worse in the damp."

"Well, damn this damp and suit yerself. I'm lookin' to be out of this, anyway!"

"And I," pitched in the younger man. "Let's get along to someplace dry."

"Dry as the taxman's eye and wet as a nursemaid's nipple, lord be willin'!"

Both strangers roared their approval and headed off up the road, their willingness to help the man at the door a quickly fading moment.

Letting out a sigh of relief, the man immediately pushed into the clubhouse. He stood without moving just inside the entrance door, the rain beating down on the pavement outside. He didn't expect to hear anything or see anybody, but his nerves wanted him to make sure. Satisfied that he was alone, he eased the door shut and took a deep breath. Shafts of pale yellow streetlight struggled in through the four small windows high up along the outer wall, barely illuminating the room. Though he had been here before, he still needed to give his eyes time to adjust to the dark. He could make out the shapes of several familiar objects scattered about. Benches, cupboards, several small wooden footstools the players used for tying their cleats. Things he needed to dodge around between where he was and where he was going.

Carefully moving forward, he arrived at Lucas's office door and reached for the handle. It opened easily, and he slipped into the room. Without any windows, the room offered nothing but total darkness, save for a feeble band of light leaking in from the clubhouse locker room. He'd expected as much and had taken the time to prepare for what would be needed.

Pulling a small candle from his vest pocket, he searched deeper to locate a match. His fingers found several, and he plucked one out. With outstretched hands, he searched for the metal surface he knew to be nearby so that he could use it to ignite the match. A small metal safe obliged, and he gave the match a quick swipe along the top. The match flared and the room revealed its contents. Along with the safe, he could make out a desk and chair, filing cabinet, two visitor chairs, an icebox, some large wooden crates that gave no indication what they held or why they were there, a telephone, two well-used baseball bats leaning against the wall, and an assortment of other knickknacks.

He lit the candle and then moved to go behind the desk, stepping into the ever-present pool of water seeping from the icebox as he went. Lowering the candle to the floor, he examined the water beneath his boot, grunted, then continued on his way, leaving behind a trail of wet footprints as he went.

"Still ain't fixed," he whispered aloud to himself.

Reaching the far side of the desk, he dripped some hot wax onto the surface so that he could set the candle down and have both hands free. Again reaching into his vest pocket, he pulled out the small cardboard curio the man had paid him to deliver and propped it up against the telephone, where he was sure it would be seen. Having completed his assigned task, he turned to what he hoped would be far more lucrative.

Retrieving the icepick from his sleeve, he turned his attention to the center desk drawer, jamming the pick into the lock and wiggling it back and forth until the drawer popped open. Setting the pick down on the desk, he rummaged through the contents, but decided there was nothing of interest and turned his attention to the three unlocked drawers that made up the right-hand side of the desk. Opening each in sequence and poking through the contents yielded the same unsatisfying result.

Turning his attention to the left-hand side of the desk, he abruptly stopped at a sound coming from the other room. He waited several seconds, but hearing nothing further, turned back to what he was doing. Pulling open the top left-hand drawer, he immediately spotted the Colt Pocket Hammerless lying on top of a pile of papers. He reached in and pulled the gun out, turning it over in his hands and rubbing the smooth, short barrel. He hadn't held a gun since his days in the service, and the feel of the weapon had a hypnotic effect on him. Right until he heard the front door to the clubhouse scrape open, snapping him back to attention.

"Damn this lock."

The voice from the other room froze him in place. Someone had definitely come in. He slid the gun into his pants pocket, blew out the candle, and crouched down behind the first few crates he could reach.

The sound of a match being struck suggested that the new arrival was here to stay. The flare of a gas lamp lighting up the exterior room guaranteed it.

Holding his breath, the man wondered who this new arrival was and if he would be coming into Lucas's office. He didn't have to wait long.

Footsteps worked their way across the clubhouse floor right up to the door of the office and stopped.

"Hmph."

Crouching lower behind the boxes, he realized he hadn't shut the office door, and the voice seemed to realize it, too. He eased the gun from his pocket, silently cursing his lack of attention to the small but revealing detail.

"Tommy?"

It was Lucas.

The door opened a bit further, and the voice entered the office and called again. "Tommy, is that you?"

With the light now flooding in from the other room, the man peeked out from behind the crates. He could see Blaine standing just inside the office searching for the light switch, his back toward him, the door partially blocking his view.

This wasn't at all what he was expecting, and a feeling of panic quickly seized him. He knew he had only moments before he would be discovered.

Without further thought, he stood up, aimed, and pulled the trigger.

Chapter 21

The sudden explosion of sound vanished almost as quickly as it had arrived, just as it did every fifteen or so minutes. Maddocks had grown oblivious to the noise, having spent so much of his life working in situations where unexpected noises were a regular occurrence. The rush of a subway car passing by raised no eyebrow.

He set down the box of Cracker Jack he'd been absently picking at and looked about the compact utility room. It was by no means sumptuous. But bearable. Comfort would come later. More importantly, it afforded him the privacy needed to assemble and prepare all the many elements needed for his plan. The plan that God had so meticulously outlined for him. And he was confident that God would continue to steer him through to a final moment of glory.

Stretched out on the lumpy pile of blankets that served as a mattress, he reached out to the side and picked up the Bible that lay there. He thumbed through the well-worn pages, searching for a passage.

A favorite passage.

God would guide him. Hadn't He done so all these past three years? God had saved him in the war. God had sent him to sea so that he would have time to formulate the plan. And God had provided the means to pay for the plan when a distant aunt had passed away, making him the main beneficiary of her estate.

Now he had the money for most anything he wanted. And what he wanted most was revenge. Beautiful, bountiful, deserving revenge. He'd waited a long, long time for it. Plotted with great care over many months. Agonized over how and when to inflict just the right amount of pain, timing it all so carefully. And now it was within his grasp.

Lucas Blaine would come to know it, too, but be powerless to stop it. He would experience the terror of knowing death was creeping ever closer, and at the same time, feel the raging frustration of knowing with certainty that he could do nothing, absolutely nothing, about it.

It was a good plan. The perfect plan, really. Unfolding exactly as he'd imagined. Everything lining up like proverbial stars across a beneficent universe. And soon, very soon, he'd be ready to spring the jaws on his final trap. Revenge would be his.

Setting the Bible back down, he returned his attention to the box of Cracker Jack. His fingers groped for the prize, but then, frowning, he abruptly stopped himself. He needed to force himself to wait. To take charge of his urges, maintain some self-control. Without self-control, people made mistakes. He couldn't afford to be one of those people.

Patience, he reminded himself. Patience, perseverance, concentration. Those were the qualities that had saved him on that fateful day three years previous. The day when everyone had left him for dead in that tunnel on the Western Front.

His mind drifted off and settled for reflecting on his latest accomplishments. Everything had gone without a hitch.

First, at that cafe. That one had made him smile, almost laugh. He'd taken a seat in what he knew to be Lucas's regular booth in the coffee shop, giving his quarry just enough time to notice him but not enough time to start assembling a picture. Closely watching him at the front of the cafe talking to someone else, he could sense Lucas struggling, wanting to turn and have another look, but feeling obligated to listen to the man who had just come in behind him. Before Lucas could resolve his dilemma, Maddocks had slipped out through the kitchen and into the alley amidst the startled looks of the cook and dishwasher.

And then there was the telegram. That was a lovely stroke of genius. LOOK FOR ME AT BALLPARK. STOP. YOU WON'T SEE ME. *Of course you won't see me,* he had thought. *I'll be busy blinding you with a mirror!* A perfectly frustrating stunt. A stunt to raise suspicion but reveal nothing.

Now, that had taken some planning. Using mirrors was something he'd seen the heliograph operators do during the war. Of course, they'd used mirrors to signal one another, not to play games. But it had given him the idea. He'd studied the ballpark for several days, checking and re-checking the angle of the sun to ensure that he would be in the perfect seat to get the perfect reflection. He was. And he did.

And then watching Lucas stumble through the stands, trying to catch up with him. Pure vaudeville! When he'd dropped the mirror out the conductor's window right in front of Lucas...that had been the icing on the cupcake! It couldn't have gone any better.

Distractedly, his fingers once again probed for the reward that lay deep within the Cracker Jack box. And once again, he caught himself, scolded himself for not having sufficient patience to finish the treat before treating himself to the prize.

All in good time. Finish what you've started before claiming a reward.

He grabbed another handful of the sticky mixture and stuffed it into his mouth.

Of course, there was also that second envelope, the one he'd put on Lucas's desk during the game, just before he'd gone out into the grandstand with his mirror. He'd almost been discovered by that young boy—that bat boy, what was his name? Ah, yes. Tommy. Tommy and his ridiculous rabbit, Bear. Right. How could he forget Bear? Tommy had run into the clubhouse only seconds after Maddocks had slipped into Lucas's office, grabbed Bear, and run back out to the field. Well, a lucky day for Tommy, he thought. Tomorrow? Who knew? Tommy didn't figure into his plans, but that didn't mean his plan wouldn't figure out a way to work Tommy in.

He was getting tired. Much had been accomplished, but there was still much to do. Even as he lay on his mattress, events were unfolding that would bring his puzzle closer to completion.

Enough.

Revenge will be mine.

Just like this prize will be mine.

Suddenly, no longer able to control his urges, he stuffed his fingers into the box, grasping for the prize that he knew was there. A pleasurable warmth suffused his face and a groan of satisfaction escaped his lips as he felt the outline of the long, flat piece of tin. He tried to imagine what it could be.

Closing his eyes, he extracted the prize.

"Whatever I find herein," he declared aloud, "it shall be, from this moment on...my good luck charm!"

He seized the prize between two immaculately groomed fingers and pulled it from the carton.

As he opened his eyes, a smile wormed its way across his face. He held the little toy between thumb and index finger, twisting it slowly so that he could appreciate not just its modest detail but the divine irony of its existence.

"Of course," he acknowledged, as if the prize he'd just plucked from the box could hear. "What else would you be?"

Chapter 22

"Boss? Lucas? You okay?"

Lucas's head swam and ached in equal proportions, but he could tell that the voice hovering over him belonged to Zach.

"Boss, what happened? You look like you just went ten with Dempsey."

"Feels more like two tens," replied Lucas, raising himself up on one elbow and rubbing his head with the other hand. "Christ, that hurts!"

Zach reached down to the floor and came back up with a baseball bat in hand. "This what did the damage?"

Lucas stared at the bat, his memory starting to recover. "Yeah, that was it. I managed to get an arm up to break the swing, but he was definitely a power hitter!" He sat upright and looked about the office, spotting his pistol lying in the corner where the intruder must have tossed it.

"He tried that first," Lucas said, pointing to the gun. "Luckily for me, it wasn't loaded." The intruder had had the drop on Lucas, plain and simple. Except for the fact that Lucas never chambered his gun without a purpose, he realized he could be on his way to the morgue right about now.

"Did you make out who it was?"

"No, too dark. And I had my back to him. He must have been hiding over behind those crates."

"What do you think he was after? I mean, he couldn't have been countin' on you showin' up."

"Agreed. I only came back just by chance, wanted to go over some things. I dunno, maybe…"

"Payroll?" suggested Zach.

"Maybe. I didn't get a chance to look. You mind?"

Teams paid their players once a week, and payday was no secret, so plenty of people could have guessed that the money was on hand. Presumably locked up safely in the safe. The most logical place to keep it. Indeed, where most people kept it.

But Lucas had always considered a safe to be the least safe place to keep money. It was like hanging out a map and a welcome sign all in one place. Instead, he concealed it where he felt people would be least likely to look.

Zach reached down and pulled out the bottom left-hand drawer, lifted up the false bottom, and opened the cigar box to reveal a stack of bills wrapped in a rubber band.

"Still here," he said, closing the drawer before standing up again and reaching over to pick something up off the desk. "He left his calling card, though."

Still sitting on the floor, Lucas couldn't see what Zach had noticed.

It was an icepick.

"Someone we know?" asked Zach, handing Lucas the weapon.

Lucas took it without a word. There was nothing about this icepick that distinguished it from the hundreds of others that would have been serving a variety of purposes in New York that night. Still, Lucas wondered how it fit into what was shaping up to seem like a series of not-so-random events. The man killed in the subway. Done with an icepick. Was there a connection? He couldn't see it. Then there was the guy who delivered the ice. He'd definitely had a pick. As far as Lucas knew, though, they had no quarrel. Other than maybe a disagreement over the icebox. The guy with the mirror? Now that was strange. There was no icepick involved, but still. Did he have anything to do with this? At the very least, it was quirky, just like the envelope that Tommy Marshall had delivered. A toy shovel. Was it linked in any way to the toy rooster found on the dead man in the subway? Or the black cat? They all looked like prizes you might find in a box of Cracker Jack. But they could have come from anywhere. And meant anything. Or nothing at all.

Lucas's brain didn't want to sort through it all, but his instinct pressed on. Frankie Miller. Another loose end. He had a short fuse and could at times be reckless, but Lucas couldn't see where an icepick came in. At least, not anymore. Not since Miller had given up gangs for baseball.

Or had he? What exactly would he be doing here anyway? Thinking he'd go for a little bit of revenge? Maybe get his hands on the payroll?

Okay. So payroll *was* a possibility.

Frankie Miller.

Lucas wasn't ready to count him out. But he was having a hard time counting him in.

Zach was about to change the count.

"Ten to one, it's Miller, Lucas. Remember, he's got the background. No question he could put a gun to your head if he wanted to."

"Maybe," said Lucas, still not convinced. He wasn't at all certain that guns were Miller's thing. "The fact that he didn't use the pick tells me whoever it was, he wasn't expectin' trouble. That would've been his first choice."

Zach walked around the desk and picked up the discarded gun from the floor. "The fact that he pulled a gun on you says he wasn't lookin' to get found out, either!"

Lucas grunted acknowledgement, grabbed the edge of the desk, and pulled himself up off the floor. "Whoever it was, I definitely surprised him. And not in a good way."

"Think we should call someone? Cops, maybe?" Zach suggested, pointing to the phone.

Which is when Lucas spotted it.

Sitting propped up at the base of the telephone, a round piece of cardboard with some printing on it. Lucas picked it up. The words CRACKER JACK FORTUNE TELLER ran around the outside edge. The point of the break-in was now crystal clear.

Lucas lifted it up to get a better look, recognizing it right away.

A spinner toy. Exactly like the ones he'd seen kids playing with. Spinning them on the end of a knitting needle or toothpick, hoping the toy would prophesize a favorable future. Ecstatic to discover they might one day become a lawyer or banker or in some other way escape a more probable lifetime of backbreaking work and limited horizons. He could readily imagine a child's sticky hand eagerly pulling it from the depths of a box of the candied treat.

Or an adult's hand. He'd seen a few of the players fool around with the toys now and again, wondering if there might be some truth to such predictions as YOU WILL TRAVEL FAR or YOU WILL BE WEALTHY.

But this one was different.

Because all of the fortunes had been neatly crossed out.

Except for one.

A SURPRISE AWAITS YOU.

"Hm. Interesting," Zach muttered.

Lucas thought he must be talking about the newly discovered fortune-telling toy and its ominous message, but Zach's eyes remained fixed on the floor.

"What do you make of it?" asked Lucas, holding the spinner out to Zach so that he could get a better look.

Zach peered over at Lucas and then back at the floor, distracted by what he'd discovered.

"Nothing yet. But maybe that and this are linked somehow."

Lucas leaned over to try and get a glimpse of what Zach was staring at, but couldn't reach far enough over the desk.

"What d'you got?"

"Footprint. Couple of 'em. Guy musta stepped in the water here. You can thank your refrigerator for that!" Zach said, crouching down to get a better look.

Pushing off the desk and shunting around to where Zach now squatted, Lucas could see the watery traces that a footprint had left behind. The August heat had been doing its job, so the prints were disappearing fast, yet there was just enough of a trace left to make out a very distinct V-shaped cut in the heel of one of the boots.

"Another ten minutes, that would've been gone," Lucas mused.

"I'm guessing whoever left these didn't even notice. All we need now is to find the owner."

Lucas knew Zach was right, but had no idea how to go about that. It's not like they could just line everyone up and check their boots. Besides, except for Miller and the ice delivery guy, Lucas didn't even know who "everyone" was.

Zach picked the icepick up off the desk. "Maybe I ought to look into this new ice guy a bit."

"Yeah. Maybe you could. You never know."

"Works for O'Farrell?"

"Far as I know."

"Yeah, I'll see what I can find out. Head all right now?"

Lucas had almost forgotten about the blow to his head and reached up to give it a gentle rub. "No worse than a foul ball," he said, wincing slightly at the touch.

"Good. See you in the morning, then," said Zach as he turned and left.

Lucas watched as Zach exited the office, then listened to his footsteps retreating across the clubhouse floor and out the front door. He knew Zach was a lot more interested than he was letting on and wouldn't let things simply fade away.

But he was beginning to get that feeling. That feeling he'd had in the trenches in Belgium during the war. The feeling that predicted everything but revealed nothing. Until it was too late.

A SURPRISE AWAITS YOU.

What's the surprise? Lucas wondered. As if there hadn't been enough already.

It was time to start putting two and two together. Time to come up with something better than zero.

AUGUST 24, 1920
Saratoga Springs, New York

Chapter 23

Little puffs of creamy white clouds meandered across an azure-blue sky, making for a perfect summer day at the Saratoga Race Course. A light breeze bearing the scent of freshly turned dirt, sweating horseflesh, and steaming manure wafted over the usual holiday crowd of bankers, brokers, barkers, and bettors, and the heat of competition stoked the passions of both horses and humans alike.

It had been just over a year since the unlikely Upset had beaten the indomitable Man o' War in the Sanford Memorial Stakes race at Saratoga Springs, and rumors were still being jockeyed about that the big chestnut had been turned backwards, sideways, or some other way that left him confused and ill-positioned when the starter's pistol had gone off. The result was, to say the least, unexpected.

With Man o' War having since won this year's prestigious Belmont Stakes earlier in the summer by twenty lengths, horse lovers and gamblers alike were satisfied that the world of racing had been righted once again.

Wealthy businessmen and celebrities, many of whom were staying at the distinguished Grand Union Hotel, had arrived in their Packards, Cadillacs, and the occasional Rolls-Royce, alive with the excitement of illegal gambling and flirtatious gamboling. Less well-heeled visitors, having taken up residence at Riley's Lake House or the Arrowhead Inn a short distance out of town, made their way to the track in their horse-drawn traps and carriages, as well as via a noisy parade of Ford Model Ts. Regardless of their chosen accommodation, most everyone could depend on satisfying their betting urges day or night at a wide range of gaming tables.

Men in straw boaters and women in cloche hats and sunbonnets roamed about the clubhouse and grandstand, waiting for the groomers to finish dragging the track in preparation for the next race. Regulars sought out their favorite bookie, while newcomers milled about, nervously looking for a reliable someone with whom to place a bet in order to avoid the local scalawags, of which there were many.

Parker and Claire sat at their usual table in the clubhouse, sipping Martinis that had been discreetly delivered in teacups, chatting amiably with various acquaintances who wandered by.

Once they were alone, Parker stood up. "Darling, I'm…going to go see a man about a horse."

Claire looked confused. "But…I've already got something, darling," she replied, hoisting her teacup to show him.

"I mean…literally, a horse. Our horse. And our man," he winked. "I want to catch him before he leaves the paddock. Just so we're sure…well, you know. Make sure all is in order."

Claire shook her head, unclear as to what Parker was talking about.

"Just a little business thing, that's all." He shrugged, hoping to avoid further questioning. "After that, if you don't mind, I think I'll go down to the rail to watch the race. I love being right on the track when they dash by the finish!"

"Suit yourself, Parker dear. It's too dreadfully hot down there for me," harrumphed Claire, brushing away a speck of dust from her latest Lanvin ensemble. "And too dirty. I'm just going to stay here and have some more…tea." She lifted her cup with a conspiratorial smile.

"Very well, then. I'll see you here after the race." He leaned down and brushed his lips to her cheek, then turned and left.

The first two races had gone off with the usual amount of fanfare, and the crowd was starting to buzz with excitement in anticipation of the next one. Within a short while, the horses and their jockeys emerged onto the track and cantered or jogged toward the starting barrier. As one flustered horse was finally edged into position, the caller brought the crowd to attention.

"They're at the gate," he announced, his voice as flat as a Kansas wheat field.

In unison, the crowd leaned imperceptibly forward, and the barrier sprang open.

"And…they're off."

Dirt flew in all directions as the six thoroughbreds broke from the barrier and pounded up the track. Eyes blinkered, nostrils flaring, they did what they were born to do. Run. Fast. As fast as they could, guided only by the yank on two thin strips of leather and an occasional not-so-gentle whip to the flank.

Tattery, the number three horse, its jockey in green and white silks, quickly moved to the rail and was soon a full two lengths out in front of the rest of the field, making the other horses look outclassed. Quickly swallowing up most of the backstretch, it galloped along the track with a cocky confidence that appeared to blossom with every stride. Neither horse nor rider looked ready to give up ground to the field in pursuit.

Leaning over the rail, Parker focused his binoculars on the frenzied smear, trying to visually untangle the mass of horseflesh straining to overtake the leader. A voice close to his right ear cut through the noise.

"Which one you got, pal?"

"The winning one," Parker said dryly, his eyes never leaving the track.

"Yeah," cackled the man. "Yeah, we all got that one!"

If you only knew, thought Parker.

Coming into the far turn, Whispering Lips, the number six horse, a sturdy dark bay with white pasterns and a white star on its muzzle, started to inch forward. Its jockey, in red and white triangles, rode far forward in the stirrups.

"At the far turn," came the call, "it's Tattery in front by two, Whispering Lips second, Carraway in third, I'm Your Favorite is fourth, Nellie's Necklace in fifth, and Artemis, sixth."

Sweat gleaming from their hides, their muscular flanks straining to eke out an extra inch or two.

As they began to emerge from the far turn, people in the grandstand stood to get a better look, their voices a growing murmur of constrained excitement and frantic urgency cheering on individual favorites as the blur of horsehide and colored silk pounded up the track, an iridescent wave of uninhibited intensity.

A sunburned man in a slim-fitting seersucker suit and thin

navy-blue tie that ended about six inches above his navel stood shouting for one of the horses to "Go, go, go!" The woman next to him in a wide-brimmed sunbonnet, adorned with a five-inch, rose-colored silk gardenia, nearly lost her hat as she tugged at the man's sleeve, silently imploring their chosen horse to go faster.

The announcer's voice echoed across the racetrack, stark and passionless in a sea of emotion.

"Tattery has the lead on the rail, Whispering Lips in pursuit. Carraway and I'm Your Favorite are neck and neck close behind, Nellie's Necklace is in fifth, and Artemis is bringing up the rear."

Parker pressed harder against the rail, beating the wooden barrier with his paper program, his lips silently moving.

C'mon! C'mon! C'mon!

Coming out of the clubhouse turn, red and white triangles sensed his moment. As did his horse. It might have been the way green and white silks pulled back slightly on the reins. Or the slight push forward on the stirrups. Whatever the sign, it wasn't lost on his pursuer. Responding to the slash at his flanks, Whispering Lips found a hidden burst of energy and ploughed forward.

"They're in the stretch," the announcer called out. "Tattery in the lead, Whispering Lips is second, and challenging."

The entire grandstand was on its feet. Men were shouting through cupped hands, women with hands pressed together at their lips as if in prayer.

"It's Tattery and Whispering Lips, neck and neck. Tattery and Whispering Lips."

Moments later, the six great beasts roared past the finish and a great chorus of mixed groans and cheers went up from the crowd. Paper programs flew into the air as the loudspeaker squawked, went silent, then crackled out indecipherable results.

The man in the seersucker suit stamped a foot, then turned to the woman in the wide-brimmed sunbonnet, his face a mixture of confusion and hope. "Goddamn! I couldn't hear what he said! Could you? Was it six?" He turned to look back out over the track. "Or three?"

The woman's gaze remained fixed on the horses as their jockeys trotted them about, cooling them down. "I'm not really sure," she replied, her face filled with awe. "They're just so marvellous to watch, aren't they?"

"Yeah, yeah, marvellous!" he replied, staring out at the exhausted animals. "But who won, goddammit?"

Parker stood with his back to the rail, his fingers drumming the binoculars that dangled from his neck. The loudspeaker hissed and popped, then screeched and went silent. A few moments later, a voice ladled out the results, loud and clear.

"Shit and goddamn!" said the man standing to Parker's right before stomping off toward the clubhouse. "I thought I had that one for sure!"

A broad smile broke across Parker's face as he turned back to watch the horses leave the track.

"That's my boy!" he purred.

AUGUST 24, 1920
Bronx, New York

Chapter 24

It hadn't been the best of afternoons for the Bulldogs. Going into the top of the ninth, they'd had a 4-1 lead over the Fishers and had the look of a pennant winner. By the middle of the ninth, they were behind 5-4 and shared a collective look of stunned disbelief. The pitcher whom Lucas had slated to close out the game had been sidelined that very afternoon with shoulder soreness, and after huddling with Zach over who should step into the role, Lucas had decided on Harry Asher, a rookie pitcher with a blinding fastball, a cocky disposition, and apparent nerves of steel. Unfortunately for the Bulldogs, Asher's calm, composed demeanor fled the park after the first pitch, never to return. The Fishers went on to score four runs, leaving the Bulldogs scrambling in the bottom of the ninth to manufacture a run to tie. It wasn't to be.

Lucas had remained in the dugout for a good ten minutes after the field had cleared, second-guessing his decision before he finally concluded it wasn't the end of the world. In fact, he thought, it might actually help that dazed, young pitcher to manage his overconfident attitude as well as his faltering curveball.

By the time he'd reached the clubhouse, the players had already put the game behind them and were imitating the home plate umpire, who carried around his waist such an excess of flesh, he was routinely unable to get in position to see pitches properly. While teams on the wrong side of decisions frequently complained, everyone knew that the man's misjudgments all seemed to even out over time.

Lucas headed into his office and threw his cap down on his overloaded desk, sending what at first looked like a snip of paper flying into the air. As it settled onto the floor, he rounded the corner of the desk and bent down, picking the object up between his thumb and index finger. He lifted it to the light coming in from the window, his heart drumming a beat usually reserved for late-inning playoff games.

It was a tiny, delicate feather. A canary feather, bright yellow, impossibly light. A potent, silent message squeezed tight between his fingers.

Without shifting his gaze or setting the feather down, he eased himself around the edge of his desk and dropped into his chair. Whomever had placed the feather on his desk had known. Known that despite its diminutive size and miniscule weight, the feather would be found as soon as Lucas returned to his office, and the message would be crystal clear: *You were right about the canary.*

As he sat staring at the feather, Tommy Marshall tentatively stepped into the doorway. Lucas eased his hand down to the desk, unwilling to let go of the feather, and turned to face Tommy.

The boy shuffled in the doorway, setting a canvas bag down

on the floor almost on top of his foot, looking considerably more shaken than Lucas had ever seen him. His eyes were red and swollen, and he was having trouble looking up at Lucas.

Reluctantly, Lucas put the feather down on the desk. "Look, kid, I'm kinda busy right now. You got something that can wait?"

Tommy stood silent. Finally, he ventured, "No, sir. No. Something can't wait." Tommy trembled, his face devoid of any meaningful color. *Any paler, that kid's gonna disappear altogether.*

"Okay, all right. C'mon, then." Lucas strained to give the boy the attention he was seeking, but the shock of finding the feather was so alarming, and the need to interpret its message so strong, he couldn't help turning back to where it sat on his desk.

"It's too late!" Tommy finally blurted out, his face a picture of agony.

The fear in Tommy's voice snapped Lucas out of his trance. He could see now that Tommy was shaking.

"Okay, kid. Look," Lucas said, his tone much softer now, "I've got a game to think about. You need to tell me what this something is, yeah?"

Tommy's eyes went straight to the ground.

After a moment's hesitation, Tommy whispered, "It was that man."

"Man? What man?"

Tommy tried to rally his courage. "That man what came to try and pet Bear."

With that, Tommy now had Lucas's full attention.

"Okay, so Tommy, just hold on. When did this happen? This man, when did he show up?"

"When you was managin' the game. I came into the clubhouse here to pay for the ice, and he was just standin' here."

Lucas felt like his head was about to explode. Nothing was making sense. For a second time, a man whom the boy didn't know and no one else had seen had come to the clubhouse and intimidated Tommy for no palpable purpose. Was it the man who delivered the ice? The new guy? Was it anyone Lucas knew?

Tommy looked to be on the verge of disintegration. "And he said he'd bash my brains in with a bat if I went outside to tell you he were here." The words tumbled out in a rush as Tommy collapsed to the floor, wailing.

Lucas rushed out from behind his desk and grabbed Tommy by the shoulders. "Whoa! Tommy! Hold on, just—hold on!" Lucas shook the boy hard several times to get his attention. "Tommy, listen to me now, okay? That's just—nope. That's just not going to happen, you see."

"Yes, sir, it could," replied Tommy, sobbing. "I just know it could."

"Tommy, that's—why are you thinking that?"

"'Cause…'cause that's what he done to Bear!" And with no further reserves, tears gushed from his eyes.

Lucas's mouth dropped open. Bear was Tommy's most prized possession. Pretty much his only possession. A mascot for the mascot. A good luck charm that players stroked before stroking their bats on the way to the plate. Lucas knew a lot of words, but couldn't think of how to package any that might relieve Tommy's pain. And Tommy couldn't stop crying.

"Tommy…" *Jesus and Mary*, thought Lucas, *who would do that? And why? A pet rabbit? Makes no sense at all.* "Tommy, listen, okay? Listen now. Where's Bear?" It was then that Lucas remembered the bag Tommy had brought with him into the room. Still lying by the door, the bag was saturated in mahogany-colored stains, now revealing the horrible truth. "Is he..." Lucas could barely bring himself to say it. "Is he...in the bag?"

A near imperceptible nod as Tommy broke free of Lucas's hands and fell down on his knees next to the bag. The tears had stopped, replaced with loud choking gasps as he yanked the laces loose. Reaching in, he pulled out a thick handful of caramel-covered fur, a bloodied mound of furry pulp at one end. Cradling the remains to his chest, he collapsed to the floor, and the tears started all over again.

Kneeling down next to the boy, Lucas tried to extinguish the persistent images that had plagued him ever since his return from France, images of soldiers lying on the battlefield next to him, heads crushed, limbs splintered. Even now, right here in his office, the smell of rotting flesh seemed to permeate the air. He knew it wasn't coming from Bear's crushed corpse, but from the memory of a pointless, tragic war that had decimated not just those who had fought, but the mothers and brothers, grandmothers and lovers, families, neighbors, sisters, and all the others who were left clutching a life that no longer made sense because no sense could be made of it.

And now Bear.

What's going on? Lucas wondered. Who was this man? Lucas wrestled with it, but no amount of willing could persuade his brain to yield any clues.

One thing is for certain, thought Lucas. *This man, this clever, stealthy, cruel enigma—if it's war he wants, it's war he's going to get.*

Just as soon as I can figure out who he is.

WESTERN FRONT
November 1917

Chapter 25

Lieutenant Blaine looked over at his men. They'd all heard the Fullerphone ring and knew exactly what came next. No one was sending a signal that he wouldn't leave the trench, allowing Blaine a brief sigh of relief.

Without announcement, the shelling stopped. He jabbed the whistle to his lips and blew a steady stream of air through the hole in the top. Men clambered up the ladder one after the other, almost on top of one another.

Blaine had wanted to lead his men out of the trench, but had been ordered to pass that honor to Sergeant Gilmore, who promptly took a bullet through the middle of his forehead for his efforts. The men behind pushed his body out of the way and fanned out, struggling to find traction on the still slippery ground. Scuttling more than running, they carried their rifles low, trying to minimize their profile.

With the trench now empty of all but the wounded, the rats, and the empty Maconochie ration tins, Blaine flipped the safety on his

Springfield, releasing the bolt action, then with one hand grabbed hold of the nearest ladder. Pulling himself out of the pit that had been home for the past two weeks, he raced toward the first shell crater he could see through the retreating smoke, sliding in next to two other soldiers.

"G'day, sir! Glad you could make it!" shouted Corporal Thompson, a blustering dairy farmer's son from Plattsburg, New York. "Quite a party going on over there!" Nothing seemed to faze the man, and he never stopped grinning. "Don't know about you, but I figure I can make it under that barbed wire up ahead," he said. He raised his head up out of the crater, and bobbed back down. "Yep, that's where I'm headed!"

With that, he was up and out of the crater, disappearing in and out of the smoke before sliding into the next shell hole.

Blaine watched as Thompson rolled down into the pit. He again checked the bolt on his own rifle, subconsciously aware it made little sense at this point. Just like a lot of things about this war. He glanced at his bayonet, took one last breath, and headed out over the edge. The enemy was pouring out of their trenches, and he raised his rifle and fired. He could see one of the German soldiers fall to the ground, but had no idea whether it was the result of his shot or that of the man behind him. Or some frightened Hun accidentally shooting his comrade in the back. There was no time to think about it. The sound of an enemy machine gun ripping up the ground to his left sent him scurrying into another shell crater.

With so much smoke still drifting across the open field, it was impossible to make out exactly where the machine gunner was, but Blaine was determined to try. Peeking up over the edge of the shell hole was all a German sniper needed, and a near-miss pinged off his helmet. He wasn't sure if it was the machine gunner or someone else, but either way, it was too damned close. The helmet was never going to protect him from a direct hit. Its job was to protect him from flying stones, dirt, and bits of metal from exploding ordnance. Thankfully, it had done a little bit more.

He lifted his rifle up above the edge of the crater and took aim at the throng of enemy soldiers coming in his direction. He fired and then fired again, the first shot hitting his target in the leg, the second squarely in the chest. The man fell face first to the ground, but Blaine barely had time to notice.

Moving up and out of the crater, he ran toward those moving forward in front of him, trying to add to the front line numbers. He tried shooting from a crouched position as he ran, careful not to aim too close to where his own troops were zigzagging. It was impossible to tell if he was achieving anything before once again sliding into a shell hole so that he could reload. A dead soldier lay on the ground next to where he landed, the man's left shoulder and arm blown away.

It was Corporal Thompson.

Still grinning.

Lying on his back, Blaine slammed another five-round clip into the gun. He turned over onto his stomach, ready to peer up over the lip of his latest refuge, when his gut told him to move. Now!

Before he could react, his rifle was violently slapped sideways and nearly out of his hands. But he held on tightly, then rolled onto his back so he was once again facing forward. The big German standing above him pulled the trigger on his Gewehr 88, but the gun jammed. Without further hesitation, the man jumped into the shell hole and thrust his bayonet directly at Blaine, who spun to the side, reflexively holding up his hand to ward off the blow. With a wrenching tear, the bayonet sliced cleanly through the middle of his left palm, and both men momentarily froze, their respective brains trying to determine what to do next.

Blood gushed from the wound as the German yanked the bayonet out of Blaine's hand and readied himself for another thrust. But before his brain could instruct his arm to move, the back of his skull exploded into the dense gray sky, and the man crumpled down on top of Blaine. Trapped beneath the fallen body, rifle still in one hand, Blaine could feel himself slipping into unconsciousness.

"No, you don't! Stay here!" he screamed to himself. "Stay right here, damn you!"

His strength fading, he dropped his rifle and shoved the fallen soldier off, when suddenly another huge body loomed overhead. A shell burst nearby, and the man fell on top of him.

It was the last thing Lucas Blaine would remember before passing out.

AUGUST 26, 1920
Bronx, New York

Chapter 26

The clattering noise from the ammonia compressor and brine pumps was making Cian's headache worse. Each time a block of ice thundered down the conveyor and hit the post at the end, it felt like a sledgehammer to his skull. He sat huddled in a corner, one swollen hand pushing his long, greasy blond hair off his pinched face, the other holding a large chunk of melting ice wrapped in a dirty cloth pressed against his forehead. Every ounce of his scrawny body throbbed in pain. He knew Mullan would track him down before the day was over. The big, ugly Irishman had already come looking for him twice, his huge, hulking body seeming to take up the whole room. Only the booming footsteps had given Cian enough warning to temporarily hide so as to evade the wrath he was certain he was about to experience.

There was really no place to hide, and no point in it either. One way or the other, he would have to accept the blame for his poor decision not to place the bet as Mullan had instructed.

No, not poor decision. Stupid, impulsive, foolhardy decision to listen to Chester and change his bet. Mullan's bet. Now he was out not just his own ten dollars, he was out all the money Mullan would have won: $322.48.

What was he thinking? He hadn't been. He realized that now, and regret wasn't going to save him from a predictable response with an unpredictable outcome. He expected a beating. The question was…would Mullan kill him? One way or the other, he knew it was going to hurt.

When he'd gone to collect his winnings, he'd been in a buoyant mood. A spectacular mood really, entertaining himself with thoughts of how he might spend the money. Sixty dollars, sixty-five maybe—he didn't really know what the amount would be, but it felt like free money. Like making money from nothing. More than a week's pay. And now it was all his. So, when he'd knocked on the door of Queen Rosie's five-story apartment building, he could barely contain his excitement.

But when Chester answered, he started right in saying something about another horse, the number six horse, and how that horse had won. Not number three. Number six. But Cian couldn't make any sense of the words, and they just tumbled to the ground like so much confetti.

So he asked Chester to repeat it. And Chester looked at him like why did he need to be told again. Like Cian was dimwitted. But then he did explain it again. The horse that Cian had bet on, number three, had very nearly won. Just like it was supposed to. Just like Chester had told him it would. But then he started saying it had fallen off in the final seconds and was beaten out by another horse. Number six. The horse Mullan had told him to bet on. Insisted that he bet on.

"Three hundred and twenty-two dollars?" Cian asked, stunned.

"And forty-eight cents," Chester reminded him.

It was like a punch to the gut, and Cian jerked back on the stoop and nearly careened down the steps, staring in disbelief at Chester slamming the door in his face.

"No, no, no!"

He'd actually said it out loud, standing there all alone on Queen Rosie's doorstep, wishing he were dead and then expecting that he would be.

Without thinking, he left the remaining blocks of ice in his cart to melt while he rushed down the street to buy a newspaper and check to see if what Chester had said was true, knowing all along that it was. The newspaper confirmed it. When the full impact of what he had done hit him, when the shock changed to despair, his bowels released, and he fell to the ground in shame and terror.

Now, a full day later, still terrified, he was at least able to start thinking. He needed a plan; he knew that much. And one was starting to take shape. It hadn't fully emerged yet, but it was starting to show promise. *If I could just get rid of this headache.*

Several fifty-pound blocks of dripping ice were now waiting for Cian to forward them down the conveyor that led to the street below. The man at the cart had already shouted up to him twice, wondering what the holdup was. The longer the delay, the more the ice in the cart melted. And the longer it would be before customers got their ice. Which meant more complaints.

He forced himself onto his knees and then onto his feet. Slapping his tongs around the first block of ice, he swung it around ninety degrees onto the rumbling conveyor that would take it to the street below. He was just about to send the second block flying down the conveyor when he heard the sound of heavy boots rounding the corner from the next room. He knew it had to be Mullan. It was too late to hide.

Mullan strolled into the room, his arms thrust out wide. "Cian, my boy, what a wondrous day, is it not? A truly beautiful, magical, fruitful day!" He grabbed Cian by the shoulders and gave him a thorough shake. "Oh, yes, it is, now that we're all a lot richer! Ha! Are we not, Ciany boy? Oh, indeed we are!" He let go of Cian's shoulders and clapped his hands together, rubbing them gleefully.

Cian stood mute, calculating his best moment to weigh in. There didn't seem to be one.

Mullan paused. "Y'er quiet when you should be cheerin' me, lad." He looked straight at Cian. "So maybe you didn't place yer own bet, is that it?" He cocked his head and squinted at Cian. "Ah, that's it, then—you chose to wait aside. Ha! And now there's regret, I can see it in yer little weasel eyes!"

There's plenty of regret, thought Cian. Of that he was certain.

"Okay, lad, no more lollygagging. Give me my money. What is it? Three hundred? Three-twenty? Don't try and cheat me now—them bookies'll tell me everything, don't'cha know."

Cian swallowed and tried his best to make his voice sound clear and confident, neither of which he was able to do. "Well, it's like this, you see. You know that fella that Rosie has take her bets? Chester's his name. Well, I give him the money—and the bet, I told him, like you told me, 'Put that on number… Put that on number…'" Cian hesitated for just a split second, then coughed. He couldn't remember the horse or the race, and he didn't dare commit to either, feeling so confused.

Mullan sensed something was wrong and threw Cian up against the wall, the vein in his neck pulsing like an outboard motor. "Number six in the third, Ciany boy! Six in the third! You got it right, didn't you? You remembered what I told you, yeah? Because I said it twice to ya. Twice."

"That's right, twice. You did, I remember. It's just that…just that…"

Mullan reached down and grabbed the icepick that was stuck in the barrel at the end of the conveyor line. In one swift move, he slammed the icepick into the wall not one inch from Cian's right ear. Cian let out a yelp.

"Tell me you didn't forget, ya festering little sack o' stale oats!"

Suddenly, the plan tumbled into place.

"Jesus Christ, Mullan, listen to me for a moment! Just listen! I didn't forget, I swear I didn't. It's like I was just about to say, I gave that fella yer bet, fifty dollars it was, right? Fifty?"

"Aye. Fifty."

"So, I gives him the money, and I tells him, I tells him, put that on…on…"

"Six in the third."

"Six in the third, I said, just like you told me, and so…and so…when I goes back to collect, this fella, this Chester, he says to me, 'No, no, no, that's not what you said—you said *three* in the third.' Yeah, that's what he said. Three in the third." Cian furrowed his brow. He couldn't gauge how Mullan was responding to the story he was spinning, so he rushed on. "That's what he said: three in the third. Doesn't sound anything like six in the third, nothing like that at all. But I didn't say that! No, no, no, I said six in the third, is what I said. And so, and so, well, he had this big goddamned revolver stuck in his waistband, and then, and then, I saw him reach for it and so—so, what could I do? He was going to blow my brains to kingdom come, that's what he was going to do, Mullan!"

Mullan stared hard at Cian for twenty seconds, his breathing loud, his hand still on the icepick. Then, with a grunt, he backed right off, leaving the icepick still stuck in the wall and Cian trying desperately to hide his fear.

"Goddamn it!" Mullan exploded. "What do I say, yeah? What do I *always* say? You cannot trust them niggers!" He shuffled about, mumbling to himself, giving Cian a chance to think about what to do next. Nothing seemed the best course of action.

Slowly, Mullan turned back to Cian. "But...t'was you that put that bet with them in the first place, Cian," he said, a malevolent twinkle in his eye. "You." He put his face within three inches of Cian's, pulled the icepick out of the wall, and thrust it to where it just nicked the skin under his chin. A small trickle of blood appeared.

"Now, my boy, it's up to you to get it back. You hear? You get me my winnings. Or this icepick is going to slide right through to the back of yer neck!"

Chapter 27

High above the Bulldogs' right-field grandstand, numerous red and white triangular pennants flapped lazily in what was not so much a breeze as a current of air that craved recognition but lacked a mandate. Beyond the pennants, a cornflower-blue sky melted away to the horizon, dotted here and there with billowy splotches of white clouds, giving the afternoon complete authority to be decreed a lazy summer's day. The smell of freshly mowed grass mingled with the tantalizing aromas of peanuts, popcorn, and candy floss, then collided with the unique and disparate pheromones of hundreds of heat-exhausted and rowdy ticketholders, all tinged with just the barest whiff of cow leather and horsehide to produce a fragrance that was distinctly baseball.

The man in the light-tan knickerbockers, sitting alone high up in the grandstand, looked around nervously. His white cotton shirt, which had entered the ballpark spotless, was now stained at the armpits with great circles of gray-wet. The bowtie that had once been attached at the neck to convey an image of respectability now carelessly peeked out from his vest pocket. Atop his head, a working man's flat cap was pulled down low over his forehead, the scar on his right cheek a bright vermillion against his tanned, angry face. He longed to be strutting about on the playing field and shuffled from one side of his uncomfortably compact seat to the other, every muscle in his athletic body tense, ready to react. *If it hadn't been for Blaine*, he thought.

"You don't listen, Mr. Miller," said the voice over his shoulder.

Startled, Miller jumped half out of his seat. Behind him in a spotless, pale-blue seersucker suit and a crisp white skimmer with a two-inch felt band that encircled the crown stood Maddocks, poking into a box of Cracker Jack.

"*End*—of the row, I said," Maddocks added with precision. Without waiting for a response, he turned and walked to the end of the row and sat in the aisle seat.

Miller shuffled after him, assuming a less-than-convincing air of self-confidence. When he had caught up, he said, "What difference does it make? I'm here."

"Ah!" said Maddocks, rubbing his bad leg. "You're wondering what possible difference it could make, is that what you're wondering?" asked Maddocks, popping a piece of the chewy popcorn into his mouth. "Let me see then if I can provide an explanation. Or better yet, an example." He cocked his head to one side and thought for a moment. "Two men. Equally strong, equally brave. Each driving a cart pulled by a horse, and each horse, equally capable. Each cart is filled to the brim with watermelon."

"Wait a second," interrupted Miller. "Must be summer, right?" He raised his eyebrows expectantly.

"I beg your pardon?"

"It's the summertime, right? Because they got watermelons. Must be summertime," Miller added, a smug smile lifting the scar on his cheek.

Maddocks stared at him. "Against all wisdom and common sense, I will continue."

Miller looked confused. "What's that mean?"

Clearing his throat, Maddocks began again. "As I was saying, each cart is filled to the brim with watermelon. The two men find themselves at a railroad crossing. A powerful locomotive is charging down the tracks toward them. Neither man is certain if there is enough time to get through the crossing without being dashed to smithereens. But they are in a race, you see, and only the first to arrive at the finish line will get paid. Handsomely, I might add." Maddocks paused, trying to discern whether Miller was absorbing the essence of his story. "Do you follow me so far, Mr. Miller?"

"Yeah, yeah. Two carts with watermelons."

"In a race. But only the first man to the finish line will take home the prize. Make a dash for it, and succeed…," Maddocks hesitated for effect, "…you win, the other man loses. Make a dash for it and fail—well, then, the other man wins. And so, these two men, one makes a dash through the crossing, the other one elects not to. Which one are you, Mr. Miller?"

"I dunno. It's just watermelon. Does it matter?"

Maddocks stared at Frankie Miller, his eyes narrowing. Then he took a deep breath and let it out slowly. "Certainty, Mr. Miller. It's about certainty. I need to be certain that I can trust you with the responsibility that I have charged you with. Your last outing did not accomplish the outcome I was seeking."

"You mean that little kid's toy? I put it right on Blaine's desk, just like you said. Right by the telephone."

"And then proceeded to club Mr. Blaine on the head. After—and I add with a resounding sense of relief that nothing came of it—after the gun you took from his desk misfired. You had one job, Mr. Miller. What was that job?"

"He took me by surprise! I had to do something."

"And had that something worked, all that I have been planning on…for months…do you hear me? Months…would have been for nothing. And that, Mr. Miller, is why certainty is so important."

Miller grumbled to himself and looked away. Then he turned back to Maddocks and exploded, "I had to do something!"

"What were you doing in his desk, Mr. Miller?"

"Lookin' for somethin'," Miller replied half to himself.

"I do not recall asking you to look for anything. I asked you merely to deliver an item. In the future, I must have certainty that you will do exactly as I tell you. Is that understood?"

A thunderous roar erupted from the crowd, and both Miller and Maddocks turned back to face the playing field. A foul ball came whistling toward them and, without a moment's hesitation, Frankie Miller reached up and caught the ball bare-fisted, just as if he were out on the field and wearing a mitt. The crowd gave a brief appreciative applause and returned their attention to the man at the plate.

Maddocks had pulled his hat down low over his face in the hopes of avoiding any attention.

Miller looked at him and smiled, tossing the ball a few inches into the air and snatching it again with authority as it fell back down. "Certainty!" He held the ball too close to Maddocks's face, flicked his eyebrows, and snorted out a laugh. "Right, Mr. Maddocks?"

Maddocks looked out from behind his hat and stared. "Mr. Miller, I have another job for you. I need to know that I can depend on you…"

"A hundred percent."

"…depend on you to carry it out exactly as I explain it. Is that clear?"

"You talk to me like I'm some kind of dummy."

Maddocks took his time, carefully weighing the odds of Miller following his instructions precisely. Should somebody else be carrying out his next assignment? Somebody who would do precisely what he was told, efficiently, thoroughly? There were others he could call on, others who would do his bidding, had already done his bidding. For a price. In the end, he relished the exquisite irony of Miller's involvement too much. "Here's what I need you to do. It involves a very—"

"So, which one?" Miller butted in.

A quizzical look came over Maddocks's face. "Which one? Which one what? I don't understand."

"Yeah, which one? Which guy? With the carts and the watermelons. What was the right answer? The one who went over the tracks? Or the one who didn't?"

Maddocks blinked twice.

AUGUST 28, 1920

Chapter 28

The big oak door to the Carriage Club stood to the left of a weathered wooden sign that hosted a barely decipherable street number, which, since Prohibition had come into effect, was all that remained to identify the place. The location was now known simply as the Sixty-Six.

Lucas hadn't been here in quite some time and had promised Willa a special night out. Tonight was that night. The Volstead Act had ensured that every cellar, speakeasy, club, saloon, restaurant, pharmacy, or grocery store offering illegal, and occasionally lethal, alcohol for sale would need to rely on some uncomplicated but unique password in order for patrons to gain access. Some also required a specific sequence of knocking. The Sixty-Six was one of them. And despite Lucas's lengthy absence, he had no trouble remembering the sequence.

He rapped on the door.

A voice from the other side: "We're closed."

"Highbridge," Lucas replied in his most clandestine voice.

The password was enough to prompt action from the other side of the door, and a small Judas window slid open, eyes peered out, and the window slammed shut. As the door opened, music sashayed out into the alleyway. Lucas stepped in and the door closed behind him. He tipped his hat to acknowledge the entrance.

"Evenin', Egan."

Egan Arthur, the club's doorman, stood to one side. In his thin, dark suit, hair parted cleanly in the middle and slicked flat to the sides, hands clasped together in front of him at waist-height, and mirror-shine shoes, he looked more like an undertaker than a gatekeeper.

"Ah. Mr. Blaine. I thought we might see you here tonight. To what do we owe the pleasure?"

"I got thirsty. And I missed your smiling face."

"Always eager to please," said the doorman, with a slight nod of his head.

The Sixty-Six was unlike many of the city's illicit watering holes, featuring a splashy bar and an extensive range of alcoholic beverages that gave one a decent chance of waking up in the morning. A distinction Lucas appreciated. It also had a small but frequented dance floor, and live music several nights of the week, all of which helped keep customers drinking.

"Successful today?" asked Egan.

"Eleven to four, Bulldogs," Lucas replied, appreciating the man's interest in his team. "That bastard Peterson crushed my boy Walsh's ankle, though. He's probably out for a few." He peered into the room. "Willa here yet?"

"She's here," Egan nodded. "Over there." He pointed toward a small two-seater in the far corner. "Came in maybe half an hour ago. None of my business, Mr. Blaine, but she seemed a bit...aggrieved."

Lucas looked over to where Egan had pointed. Willa was sitting legs crossed, a six-inch-long cigarette holder in one hand, a glass with what remained of some ice cubes in the other, staring off at the far wall. She was wearing a black and silver chiffon sheath, highlighted by a double row of silver sequins around the neckline and each wrist. She tossed her head back, her shiny, bobbed blonde hair barely moving. Lucas wanted to rush over to her, but instinct forced him to scan the rest of the room before leaving the entranceway.

Far in the back corner and deep in the shadows, a young man, early twenties, sat by himself jotting down something in a small notebook. In his two-toned brown suit, tea-colored silk shirt with green and dark tan stripes, and detachable white club collar, the man didn't look out of place.

Except for one thing.

His skin color.

Newcomers to the club might find his presence upsetting, even venturing a complaint to management. Other than musicians, Negroes weren't allowed in places like the Sixty Six. But Lucas recognized the man to be the regular house bookie. Tubby, he was called. Six-foot-two, 145 pounds, a lively smile and welcoming eyes, Tubby Lewis looked like a cheerful string bean on a starvation diet.

Ever since gambling had been made illegal in New York, people wanted easy, discreet access to placing a wager on any sport they fancied. And bookmakers had learned that customers would place lots more losing bets if, once in a while, their bets paid off. Despite what the actual results were. This occasional generous interpretation meant exceptions could be made and discrepancies overlooked. And Tubby Lewis was an expert at knowing when and to whom those exceptions should be extended. It ensured him continued access to the Sixty-Six, and a whole lot of other places as well.

"New band?" asked Lucas. "Sounds pretty swell."

"Some boys up from New Orleans. Been here about a week. Patrons seem to like what they have. You know. That jazz sound that people have started going crazy for."

And people had been going crazy for it. Ever since the end of the war, music had begun to take on a new shape. A heady concoction of ragtime, marching bands, and African drumbeats, jazz produced a lively, improvised, more exciting sound. One that vibrated with optimism and a growing belief that the war to end all wars had been just that. One where people could entertain hope and envision a brighter future.

"It's got some pep, that's for sure," agreed Lucas. "I'd better get over there. See you later, yeah?" Lucas smiled and headed over to Willa's table. She looked up as Lucas leaned down to kiss her offered cheek.

"I was beginning to think you might not come," she said, her face deadpan. "I was expecting a better welcome."

"Hey, yeah, sorry about that," he said, sitting down. "I really am. I needed to get a few things done. You know. End of the season and all." He turned on his best smile, eager to prevent the evening from sledding downhill. For the first time in two weeks, he wanted to enjoy himself without first having to clear his mind of all thoughts of silly toys. And worse.

"How are you?"

"I'm fine, darling," Willa said, softening. "I missed you, is all. Want to dance?"

Lucas turned his attention to the music.

Bright, brassy, rhythmic. Seeps into your soul.

"I'd like to, but I'm pretty worn out just getting this far," he chuckled, hoping to avoid the embarrassment of stumbling all over himself. "Maybe later. What do you think of the band?"

Willa tipped her head back, half-thinking, half-listening. All smiling. "They've got—what do you call it? Sass! Makes you want to dance!"

"Makes some want to," agreed Lucas. "Makes others just want to listen. My feet gotta get used to this first." He turned to look at the band. "I like that trumpet."

"He's up from New Orleans." A waitress in a short, sequined dress that ended way before it should have cruised over and rested her hip far too close to Lucas's shoulder. Willa lifted a disapproving eyebrow.

"They call that Dixieland," said the waitress. "Dixieland jazz. What will you be having, sir?" She gave him a wink and her most practiced smile.

Lucas eyed the waitress for what must have been just a little too long as Willa shot him a look that said he'd be heading straight to the locker room if he wasn't careful. He knew the look and quickly stepped back into the batter's box.

"A good time, if my lady friend agrees. Make it a Gin Rickey. Willa?"

Willa eyed the waitress's skirt and offered a poisonous smile. "Well, I was having the Bee's Knees. Up until a moment ago."

The waitress returned an unapologetic smile. "One Bee's Knees, one Gin Rickey. Coming up."

She trotted off and Lucas managed not to stare too long as she went. He turned back to Willa. "Darling, she was just trying to be—"

"Helpful?" Willa said, leaning across the table. "The only thing she was going to be helpful with was getting you to open your wallet." She huffed back into her seat. "And possibly her legs," she mumbled under her breath.

Lucas eased back into his own seat, wondering how he could rescue the situation before the evening was ruined.

The band finished their number, and the cornet player was saying something about taking a short break. Over by the entrance, voices were growing louder. Two men were trying to push past a flustered-looking Egan without alerting the club bouncers. The bigger man stood six-four, his dark hair covered in a workman's flat cap. Lucas guessed he easily weighted two-fifty, dark hair, a face like an acorn squash covered in two days of beard, short, bristly black hair and a tattoo on his left wrist, but he was too far away to make out the design. Maybe a crab. Or a bird. The other man was shorter, skinny, and a little older. *Face like a ferret*, thought Lucas.

The bigger man looked familiar, and Lucas slid his chair back, about to go over, when two club enforcers grabbed the bigger man and, with considerable effort, hustled him out the door. The smaller man hesitated, looking like he might try to intercede, then stepped back and edged his way out through the passageway, just as the two club men were pushing their way back in.

Definitely, thought Lucas.
I've seen that guy before.

"Seems my flower has gone from spring to fall," sighed Willa.

Lucas spun back around to face her. Her elbow rested on the table, her chin perched in the cup of her hand, the cigarette holder pinched between her fingers. Calling up his most desperate smile, Lucas went into rescue mode. "How about a dance?"

"Uh-huh. Now that the music's stopped?" Willa rolled her eyes. "How romantic."

Four of the six band members had already put their instruments away and were headed for the exit. The other two were sharing what must have been a joke, their laughter erupting above the noise in the room.

"Seriously, let's dance," Lucas tried again. "I've got connections. Watch. Hey!" he yelled over to the apparent band leader as the other players drifted toward the door. "Over here."

A short, stocky black man stood at the edge of the stage and peered out into the room, trying to locate where the voice was coming from. Spotting Lucas's waving arm, a shy smile slid across his face. Still clutching his instrument, he headed over to where Willa and Lucas were sitting.

"How long you been playing that trumpet?" Lucas said, admiring the brightly polished metal.

"Cornet. This here's a cornet."

Lucas cocked his head and looked closer. "Looks like a trumpet. What's the difference?"

"Mainly, dis here's in da tubin'. Kinda flares a bit. See? Right here. It's on accounta I seen dis fella down in New Orlins when I's growin' up. Name o' Buddy Bolden. He played cornet like nobody's business." The man's smile spread wider. "A whole different kinda way o' playin'. Mixin' different kinds o' music. You know what I'm sayin'? And I just sorta took to it. He made music sassy, and I liked dat!"

"Sassy?" Seemed like the word was going around. "How do you mean?"

"Well, he kinda liked to joke around a bit wit some o' his tunes. You know, kinda unmannerly like. Dere was one he called 'Funky Butt.'" His smile was now accompanied by a chuckle.

"'Funky But?' But—what?" Lucas asked.

"Well, dat's just da ting. T'wasn't dat kinda 'but.'" The smile disappeared quickly as he looked around to see if he was drawing any attention. Satisfied that all was clear, the smile returned, and he lowered his voice to a loud whisper. "It was about dis kinda butt back here!" he said, pointing to his backside, a secret shared with only the closest tables. "And maybe about da air dat comes out when you's had a big plate o' beans!" An explosion of laughter brought back his room-size smile, until he glanced at Willa. Immediately, the laughter died. "Ma'am, I am sorry, I maybe wasn't tinkin' too good, and—"

"Oh, I'm much more modern than that," interrupted Willa, suppressing a giggle. "Please, tell us more about the music."

Satisfied that he hadn't crossed any lines, the musician grinned, nodded a few times, and then continued. "'Course, he didn't gen'ally play dose tunes with da white folks. Lessen it was one o' dem ruff kinda places. You know what I mean."

Lucas kind of thought he did. "So, what's your name?" he asked.

"William is my name. William Clayton, sir."

"Okay, William. And you're from New Orleans?"

"Not now, I ain't. I come up norf to be wif my Aunt Rosie affa da war."

"Rosie? You talkin' about Queen Rosie? Up in Harlem?"

"Yeah, I guess some folks do call her dat."

Queen Rosie was somewhat of a legend, having come to New York from New Orleans, where she'd worked as a domestic and petty thief from the time she was a little girl. It hadn't been an easy childhood. She'd been raped repeatedly by her employer from the age of thirteen until, one day, she took a fireplace poker and split his skull neatly in half. Reckoning on an unfavorable dismissal, she slipped out of the house before anyone could discover the corpse and began an arduous and clandestine journey north, facing rapes and beatings from more than one would-be savior. Arriving in New York with barely the clothes on her back and a ferocious determination to climb out of her miserable circumstances, she fell in with a few of the locals who were muscling in on a numbers racket that had been carelessly administered by several part-time crooks and would-be gangsters in the growing black neighborhood of Harlem.

Smarter than most, and learning to be as ruthless as the best of them, she'd built her own gang and took out the competition in less than nine months. Having won the hearts of several distraught locals with gifts of rent payments and food packages, as well as providing a talented few with paying jobs as book runners and collectors, she'd soon enjoyed a protection that few with her background could ever hope to experience.

"My daddy, he done died when I's just a baby," William continued. "And my mama weren't around much, and so Aunt Rosie, she says, now, you gonna come an' live wif me 'cause dis here world's a whole heap o' trouble. 'Course, I don' stay wif her no more, I gotta place o' my own now. And a job. Couple of dese other boys, dey's from Orlins. Dat's where da music's comin' from dese days. But she's just Aunt Rosie to me. On accounta—"

"On accounta she's your aunt."

"Well, now, I don' rightly know dat fo' sho', but dat's what I calls her ever since I was a little boy. Aunt Rosie."

"Well, tell your Aunt Rosie that Mr. Blaine sends his regards."

"You knows my Aunt Rosie?"

"I know *Queen* Rosie, and I'm pretty sure we're talkin' about the same person."

In fact, Lucas knew Queen Rosie well. Ballplayers were notorious gamblers, and he'd more than once had to use his considerable powers of persuasion, along with a great deal of financial enticement, to rescue a few who'd gotten in too deep. It was all just "proper business," according to Rosie.

"Now, I owe this lady a dance, so I'd appreciate it if you and the rest of the band could get back to playin' real soon."

"Yeah, we gonna do dat, for sho'. Dey jest gone inta dat alley for a quick…for a rest. An' I's gonna say hello to Aunt Rosie for you, for sho'."

Lucas and Willa watched William as he headed back to the stage to stow his cornet just as the waitress returned and placed the drinks down on the table.

"Gin Rickey for you, handsome," the waitress interrupted, her eyes all over Lucas, "and a Bee's Knees for…" She gave Willa a dismissive smile. "Here you go, darlin'." She then quickly turned back to Lucas. "You let me know if you need anything else, okay? I'm around *all* evening!" She dragged the word "all" halfway to the next table in case Lucas might miss her intention, then lowered her voice. "And afterwards too, darlin'!" Without a moment's hesitation, she spun on her heel and was off.

Willa nearly flew out of her seat, but Lucas grabbed her by the arm before she could round the table. "Sweetheart," he said, "let's…let's enjoy our drinks."

With a great deal of reluctance, Willa sat down, an angry scowl on her face. "That one is looking for it," she huffed.

Lucas was pretty sure she was right. He made a few more attempts at conversation, hoping he could settle things down until the music started up again, but it was clear that Willa wasn't listening, so he gave up in favor of glancing around the room. He noticed that Tubby Lewis had left his seat and spotted him talking with the cornet player over by the entrance. The two men were laughing, and William nodded enthusiastically, then pointed to the door and left.

Tubby then turned to the doorman. A quick conversation followed, and Lucas watched as Egan slipped Tubby an envelope, which immediately disappeared into the bookie's pocket. Tubby then pulled out a small black notebook from inside his jacket and made a quick note. Slipping the notebook back into his jacket, he gave the doorman a quick nod and headed out the door.

Lucas let his eyes wander the room, allowing both brain and body to absorb the sensation of finally being carefree. For the moment, anyway.

It's going to be a great evening.

Chapter 29

"I don't hear anything."
"Neither do I."
"I think he's stopped."

Willa stood in the doorway to Lucas's bedroom, straining to hear if the downstairs neighbor was still at his piano. Her blue eyes and blonde hair stole what little light there was in the room and sparkled in the darkness, and her dimpled cheeks and chin looked more provocative than ever. The curves of her ivory-colored silk negligee were a collage of light and shadow, barely covering her own curves as she shifted ever so slowly from one hip to the other, her nipples eager to break free of the fabric. The ivory silk robe she wore over the top of her negligee hung loosely open, its silky white-lace trim adorning the neck and sleeves like a delicate, orchestrated tangle of unspoken invitation. Projecting out from under the hem of her robe were cream-colored, low-heeled shoes, embellished with tiny twists of bright red ribbon perched atop the toes. The seductive smile on her face mirrored the excitement that stirred inside.

Lucas thought she was trembling a bit. He knew he was. But it wasn't just the anticipation. They'd explored each other's bodies thoroughly over the many months since they'd first met and were mostly past the point of inhibition. Yet there was something coy about the way she'd fled from the parlor into the bedroom. Something tentative and unexpected. Any other night, he wouldn't have been at all surprised if this wonderfully modern woman, this woman he adored, was the one to initiate and embrace lustful intimacy, but tonight there was definitely something else. Hesitation. Ambiguity. Mystery. She'd hinted at something new, something not shared before. He wasn't at all sure what that could be, but he was more than keen to find out.

The evening at the Sixty-Six had started off on an awkward note. With extraordinary luck, Lucas had managed to turn things around, and they'd laughed and danced long past midnight. Returning to his apartment, his thoughts had briefly turned somber, with Lucas mulling over the canary feather and Bear's brutal demise. It didn't help that the neighbor downstairs was still wringing out pain from his piano. Little by little, though, they'd managed to bury the gloom and emerged into the present. At which point things had become more playful, full of teasing banter and gentle caresses. Then Willa had suddenly disappeared into the bedroom, ordering Lucas to stay put.

Almost too many minutes later, she called to him from her hiding place behind the door. The lights were off when he entered the bedroom, a single candle flickering with anticipation in the darkness, her voice bidding him to sit on the edge of the bed. Unbuttoning his shirt as he went, he now sat in his undershirt, awaiting just what, he didn't know. And she, all silk and curves, stood in the doorway.

"Yes," she said, tipping her head to one side, her voice decidedly huskier than when she was serving customers at Aleta Jean's. "I do believe he's stopped."

"Definitely stopped," Lucas agreed. Admiring her from all real and imagined angles, he struggled to find the perfect compliment, but the words he was looking for could not be coaxed to make an appearance. Infinitely aware that his words of endearment too often came across to Willa as matter-of-fact, he was desperate not to spoil the moment.

Before he could stumble over another ill-chosen word, Willa's robe slipped to the floor with barely a swoosh.

"I hope it's not too—" she murmured, her eyes cast down to the garment at her feet.

"No!" Lucas blurted out, a little too energetically. He paused, then tried again. "No, it's not! It's..."

"I didn't want it to come across as…you know…"

"It doesn't!" he exclaimed, jumping up off the bed and hurrying around to where Willa was standing. "No, that's for sure, it does not, believe me, it's…"

"Because I've never worn anything like this before, you know."

He reached out with both hands and ran them down the silky sides of her negligee. "Oh, I know. I mean, I don't know, but—you know."

"I just wanted to wear something pretty for you."

"It's—so pretty!" The words weren't at all what he was aiming for.

"And I didn't want to look…"

Lucas rushed in. "You don't! You know? I mean, gosh, you look..." His brain seized entirely while the rest of his body surged with electricity. "It looks swell!" he exclaimed, instantly realizing how he'd managed to trample the opportunity for splendor, magic, and magnificence into a wasteland of banality.

Willa didn't seem to notice. The fingers of her right hand ran up the edge of her negligee. She turned and looked directly at Lucas, her smile shifting to determination. "I didn't want it to look trampy," she said decisively, then quickly looked away. She peeked back warily. "I've never worn anything like this before, and I wanted so much for you to like it, but, not like I was trying to look like, well, you know. Not like I was trying to look like one of those foolish women in a girlie magazine!" Her eyes began to glisten. "Or that waitress!" she added.

So that's what this is all about, thought Lucas. The mystery, the awkwardness. She simply didn't want him thinking that somehow her basic moral values had become perverted. She just wanted to look pretty. And sexy. For him. A crooked smile crossed his face and he led her gently to the edge of the bed. All the confidence, all the self-determination, even her boldness in the bedroom, it was all in danger of being crushed in a single instance of humiliation. All he knew was he'd never seen anything more beautiful.

For an instant, the ugly mystery that had been unfolding over the past two weeks tried to intrude on the moment. The obscurity behind the Cracker Jack toys, the implied threat behind the canary feather, and Bear's horrendous death all sought to sabotage the passion that had been building over the past half hour. He wanted to know who, wanted to dive deep into his memory to try and figure out if there was someone he knew, someone who could... But he fought the blackness, choking out all images besides the one that was standing in front of him, suffocating the intrusion that wanted analysis, explanation, interpretation, conclusion. Every intrusion but the one that suffused his body with the warm and welcome glow of impending pleasure.

Apprehension receded. Tenderly, he took her by the elbow and kissed her on the forehead.

It was then that the Willa he'd been expecting, the Willa he'd been lusting for re-emerged, every trace of doubt and coyness vanishing like a firefly into the night. She threw her arm around Lucas's neck and jerked him passionately into her own aching body. Her tongue slipped into his waiting mouth and they kissed deeply, the world around banished to a distant galaxy.

Abruptly stepping away from the embrace, Willa raised her arms up over her head, her smile summoning him forward. Lucas understood perfectly and reached out, taking her negligee and pulling it up and over her outstretched arms, his damaged hand inexplicably discovering a dexterity he thought he'd lost forever. But there was no time to wonder about his newfound ability. She stood before him completely naked, completely willing, completely ready. Ready to receive his eager body. Not at all ready to wait.

She pushed him down onto the bed and slid his pants down over his feet as he pulled his undershirt up and over his head. Even in the shadowy light that filtered in from the other room, there was no mistaking the hunger that was surging through his body, and she crawled on top of him, together kissing, stroking, and shuffling their way further onto the bed.

Lucas reached around behind her, grabbing her deep below the waist and pulling her onto him so that they were no longer two, just one. One heartbeat, one movement, one breath. Their hands grappled for each other's bodies, gliding over a familiar contour, a favorite curve, losing the topography and then eagerly recapturing the familiar and welcoming landscape. Lucas cupped her left breast in his good hand, his tongue seeking and encircling the straining nipple, his heart pounding with expectation. He took her breast into his mouth, almost as if to swallow it and be swallowed at the same time. Their glistening bodies thrust and released in perfect unison, eager to release the desire that had built up inside.

As if drawn like a bow, Willa's back arched, her eyes fluttered, and she silently screamed aloud something to the universe that only the heavens could hear. The energy rippled through their bodies and they kissed and caressed, until with one last thrust, they collapsed into each other's arms, laying bathed in a delirium of exhaustion.

The candle on the dresser flickered its approval.

AUGUST 30, 1920

Chapter 30

Cian couldn't remember the last time he'd felt in control of his life. Every day was like a punishment for living, without any hope of a reprieve. Every step forward seemed to quickly reverse and lead two steps back. Even as he sat slumped in the richly brocaded chair, willing the fortune teller to conjure some magical solution to his problems, something that would whisk away all his troubles, an overwhelming sense of despair gnawed at what was left of his deeply diminished confidence like a ravenous jackal.

He'd been able to postpone what he believed would be his ultimate demise by shifting the blame for his betting blunder onto Rosie's bookmaking operation. That had seemed brilliant for several minutes. Up until Mullan shifted the responsibility right back onto Cian. Now he needed—well, he needed a miracle. Or something close to it.

He sat up and stared glumly at the small white teacup sitting on the far side of the table immediately in front of the fortune teller. Sitting on the saucer next to it lay the still damp tea leaves that awaited Madame Sophia's celestial interpretation.

Madame Sophia Maricella Navarro. The sign outside The Gypsy Tea Garden had stopped him dead in his tracks. He hadn't gone looking for a fortune teller, wasn't even sure he believed in fortune tellers. His first instinct had been to go see his priest, but in the end decided that he couldn't face the humiliation of sitting in a confessional, lying to Father Whelan.

When he'd unexpectedly stumbled across Madame Sophia's shop, it seemed a sign. In fact, the actual sign that hung from a nail out front confirmed it. *Futures Divined For All Those Seeking Love, Wealth, or Health.* He'd ended up staring at the sign for a good ten minutes, wondering if this could be the answer he was so desperately seeking, the solution he so desperately needed.

Overwhelmed by indecision, and knowing that he couldn't evade a reckoning much longer, his fear of Mullan made the decision for him. He'd pushed past his doubt and in through the doorway.

He stared hard now at the tea leaves, begging them to reveal a way forward. If not directly to him, then at least to Madame Sophia, whose flowing robes, fringed headscarf, and bejeweled fingers promised a revelation that Cian couldn't hope for on his own.

He looked over to where she sat, seemingly lost in her own world of mysterious divinations. "I was thinkin'," he said, "you'd have a—what ya call it? You know. A crystal ball."

Madame Sophia had said very little since Cian had peeled back the heavy maroon velvet drapes at the door and peered in through the glass bead curtains that separated the outer hallway from her parlor. Her brow furrowed into even deeper wrinkles as she looked up at Cian. "I am tea leaf reader," she said. "You want fortune or to look at clouds?"

Cian slunk back into the overstuffed chair and looked away to the side, concerned that he hadn't gotten off to a very good start. Without turning back, he mumbled, "It's, it's..." What exactly should he be asking for? He leaned forward again. "I need a reading," he tried.

Madame Sophia looked up once again. "Good. We have started."

"What I mean is, I need an idea. I'm in a wee bit of trouble, yeah? And so, I, I don't need no fortune is all. I just need, well, I need an idea," he explained hopefully, nodding his head to add emphasis. "A plan, really. Yeah, I need to know, I need to know what's going to happen and—and what I can do about it. How I can do something about it."

Madame Sophia cocked her head. "That is called reading."

"Okay, yeah, a reading then, I need a reading, I'm..." He let out a long sigh. "Is that something you...something you can help with?"

Madame Sophia's arms spread wide in a welcoming gesture. "This is what I do! Give you reading! It is here," she said, gesturing to the tea leaves. "This is why you come, yes?"

Cian raised his eyebrows, wondering if they were ever really going to get started.

"You have love problem," she ventured.

Cian's eyes darted about the room, his forehead screwed up in confusion.

"No, not love. That's not..." He winced, wondering if this had all been a huge mistake. "It's money's the problem."

Madame Sophia was silent, never wavering from Cian's gaze. After several seconds, her head tipped to one side and she raised her eyebrows. "Of course is money problem. But is love problem, too. Someone does not love you, and so," she shrugged, "you have money problem."

Cian was taken aback. *Hold on,* he thought. *Is that right?* There was certainly no love between him and Mullan. Or himself and Chester. So, yeah, you could say that he had a love problem. Having no love was causing the money problem. That made sense. Sort of.

"Yeah, that's right," he confirmed, "it's a love problem. And money, too. Both, you might say."

"I do say!" she said with a smile befitting a movie star. "So." Madame Sophia glanced back at the moist pile of vegetation in front of her. "You need money, so she will love you again."

Cian scowled. "Jesus Christ Almighty!" he bellowed. "I need money to pay back a gambling debt! Not money for some woman!"

Madame Sophia never blinked but waited patiently for inspiration. The kind of inspiration she knew she could rely on to concoct an interpretation that would convince her client she had delivered a divine prophecy, when all the time they themselves had exposed their own secret needs.

At last, it came. Shrugging her shoulders again, she explained. "Money is always 'she.' So, not about woman. Money is woman. So you need 'she.'" She gestured with open palms. "Money, you need money, so money will love you again. When this money loves you, you pay debt."

Cian tried to unscramble what the fortune teller was telling him. "So, you're sayin' money is like a woman. Yeah? But I don't need money *for* a woman. I just need money to love me, to make somebody else love me again!"

The fortune teller's face remained immobile. "Correct."

"I need it to pay back my debt before someone decides to kill me, right?"

"This is what I say," confirmed Madame Sophia, suppressing a smile as she picked up the saucer and peered closely at the leaves once again.

Cian ran his fingers through his hair and down the back of his neck. "Okay, so. Can you see my fortune? Some way out of this mess?"

"This is what I do," Madame Sophia replied as if she were explaining to a school child.

"Jesus, we're right back at the beginning," Cian grumbled, making a move to stand up.

"Not so. I see money. Please. Sit. You will get money."

Cian eased back into the chair. *Now we're getting somewhere.* "Tell me about that, yeah? The money? Where do I get it?"

Turning and tilting the saucer around, the fortune teller studied the contents. "I see house."

"A house? Why a house?"

Madame Sophia flicked her eyes at Cian, picking up on the disconnect.

"No, not house. I look again." Once more her eyes peered deep into the mound of soggy remnants, a delicate finger prodding them gently. "Maybe…book."

Cian thought about this for a moment. A book. What kind of book? He didn't own any books, didn't even read, except for a newspaper once in a while. A book?

"A book…and some numbers," she continued. "And a man!" She slapped the table to add emphasis to her discovery.

A book and some numbers. What kind of book had numbers?

And a man? Wait! Maybe not a book. Maybe a bookie. Could that be it? A bookie? Like Chester? He had a book with numbers. Cian thought this might be going someplace. He leaned forward, excitement now beginning to fuel his imagination.

"Yeah, okay, a book with numbers. And this man, is this a black man?"

The fortune teller kept her eyes fixed on the saucer, willing herself to keep from laughing out loud. "Yes. This book with numbers. And black man. You know such a man?"

"As sure as Saint Patty chases snakes!" enthused Cian. He jumped to his feet and paced back and forth in front of the table. This was making some sense now. Chester. He was a black man with a book that had numbers. Of course! But how would he get the money from Chester? Not a loan. A loan meant paying back. With interest. And that would mean more money. No, he'd have to steal the money.

"So, you are going to get this book?"

"I couldn't give a dead rat about the book," said Cian. No, not the book. Just the money. And Chester would have that. He would figure out a way to steal the money from Chester. Wait, wait, wait! No, not Chester. Chester was dangerous. And going to see Chester would mean trying to get the money at Rosie's, and that wouldn't work. Too many people, too many of her men there. Too many nosy people about. No, it would need to be someplace else, someplace where a bookie was on his own.

"This book and this money—I mean, the book with the numbers." Cian pointed to the tea leaves that Madame Sophia held in her hands. "Does it say in there where I could find that?"

"Very difficult. I need think."

Go ahead, thought Cian. *Think. I need to think, too.*

A book, and a black man with money. By himself. Where would he find that?

And then he knew.

"So," said Cian, getting to his feet, "how much for this fortune, then?"

Madame Sophia looked up in surprise. Things didn't usually end so quickly. People wanted more for their money. More detail, more reassurance. She smiled, feigning lack of interest. "Is illegal to take money for fortune."

Cian looked at her blankly. And then he remembered. The law prohibited fortune tellers from charging for their services. They could, however, accept tips. Which is how they expected to get paid. "Well, then," he said, "I'll be off."

No charge. He couldn't believe his luck.

As he took a step toward the doorway, Madame Sophia called out. "But tip not illegal."

He turned back, planning on laughing it off. But he found himself staring right at a derringer she had pointed at him.

"Tip is required," she said firmly.

Cian tried to calculate whether or not it was worth going for the gun. It might not even be loaded. Or, she might just miss. Or, she might blow a hole the size of an apple in the middle of his chest. Deciding against chancing it, he reached into his pocket and pulled out a quarter and threw it on the table.

"One dollar."

"What!" exclaimed Cian. "Why, you cunt! I—"

"One dollar," Madame Sophia repeated. She tipped her head and smiled. "I am thanking you."

Cian decided negotiation was not going to work. He pulled out a silver dollar and dropped it on the table in front of her.

When he had disappeared out through the velvet drapes, Madame Sophia picked up the coin, lifted her skirt, and stuffed it into a little purse that was laced around her thigh. "Bastard," she spat, all pretense of an accent disappearing. "Get your book and your black man somewhere else next time!"

Chapter 31

It hadn't been a particularly good day. In fact, it was all Clarissa Rose Washington could do to keep from pulling the trigger on her double-barrelled 12-gauge Fox Sterlingworth and blowing Tubby Lewis' brains clear across Harlem. And Lewis knew it. His scrawny, bruised body trembled in terror, and the one bulging eye that wasn't swollen shut flicked about the room, hopelessly seeking a way out. Sweat had soaked right through his new tea-colored silk shirt with the green and dark tan stripes and detachable white club collar, fear and shame collaborating to expose his incompetence. If Percy Russell, one of Queen Rosie's enforcers, hadn't been holding the man's arms tight behind him, leaving himself exposed as a secondary recipient to a face full of buckshot, she would have likely pulled the trigger. She'd done it before.

"You are one dumb muthafucka," she said through a haze of smoke drifting up from the cigarette dangling from her lower lip. "You come out of that blind pig, pockets full of howdy-do money, and some guys, they what? They invite you for a drink? A drink? And where's this drink gonna happen? In the alley, where nobody else can see what's goin' on? And you goin' on with 'em? And so, then what? You get your ass whipped good and tidy! And that money—*my* money—gets stole away! What'd you think was gonna happen?"

Having been woken from her fitful sleep and advised that one of her bookies had been beaten and robbed, she'd thrown on her favorite cranberry-colored satin housecoat and ankle-high fur slippers, lit a cigarette, grabbed her shotgun, and marched out into the foyer of her third-floor 131st Street apartment, ready to teach someone a lesson. With a slim diamond tiara trying bravely to cling to her thinning, dark-burgundy-colored hair bundled loosely atop her head, shotgun at her shoulder, her delicate, guarded face a montage of seasoned fatigue and unbridled anger, Queen Rosie looked like a cross between a bantamweight ballerina and a Hollywood hitman.

Lewis struggled to think of a viable explanation. It had all seemed so innocent at the time. He'd gone to several of the regular places, including the Sixty-Six, picked up bets from his regular customers, laughed with a couple of guys in the band, and was getting ready to head back uptown with the numbers take when those same couple guys asked how'd he like a taste of some homemade southern whiskey. "Better'n dat shit dis joint's got," they'd said. "Come all da way from New O'Leans!" And while he knew to be attentive when collecting bets for Miss Rosie, caution sometimes gave way to more pressing needs. Like having a drink. And these guys seemed like—well, they seemed regular. Besides, he'd wanted to hear more about New Orleans, where all that new music was coming from. Instead, he'd woken under a pile of rubbish in the alley behind the speakeasy, his right arm nearly broken, his faced battered to a pulp, his pockets empty except for the one hidden in the back of his jacket where he kept his betting log.

"Miss Rosie, I—"

"*Queen* Rosie, you dumb muthafucka! Can't you see this crown on my head?" Each word sharp as a razor clam. Her stare never wavered, searing right through Lewis.

"'Course, Miss—I mean..." Lewis shook his head and looked to the floor. He'd gone from terror to paralysis to resignation, certain that nothing he could say would assuage the anger pulsing out of Queen Rosie's body. "It's just, you see, dere was dese guys, and dey was from Orlins, and I just wanted...I just wanted—"

"You just wanted to suck up some godawful white piss and show that you was a somebody. I seen it a hundred times. And instead? Look what you done! Maybe six, seven hundred dollars that you are now *not* turning over to Queen Rosie. How are you going to find that money, plus interest, to reconstitute my pocketbook? I'll tell you how. You ain't. Which means, I got no choice but to shoot you right between the eyes to teach you a goddam lesson!" Her finger tightened on the trigger.

"Wait, wait—Miss Rosie, I can get you dat money, sho I can! You, you, you—you just gotta gimme a coupla, coupla days. Maybe a week, but no mo', no 'mo den dat! Just a coupla days. I get you dat money!" Lewis's eyes looked ready to pop straight out of his face.

"And just how are you going to do that?" The shotgun drooped ever so slightly.

"Why, Miss Rosie, I's just gonna steal it back," he said, looking bewildered at how the solution could not be obvious.

Queen Rosie looked on silently, not certain whether to laugh or pull both triggers. Opting for another option, she set the gun down hard on the side table and picked up the worn black leather notebook that was sitting there. "I cannot abide stupidity. And you are one stupid muthafucka! If those boys had taken this book too, you would be lyin' on that floor, dead as a fuckin' sewer rat." She looked at the book, then back at Lewis, her anger turning to disgust. "I should just shoot your ass anyway, being as how stupid you are."

Tubby squeezed his eyes tight, expecting the shotgun to roar disdain at any moment.

"But I ain't gonna do that," said Rosie.

"Oh, my Lord, Miss Rosie," cried Tubby in relief. "Heaven thanks and praise—."

"Shut up, you fool! I ain't done yet!"

Tubby Lewis jerked himself to attention, his eyes blinking furiously as he tried to figure out what it all meant.

No, I ain't gonna kill you. Not yet, anyway. And maybe not at all, thought Rosie. No doubt, the man was stupid. But he was loyal. And when it came to gambling, loyalty was your ace in the hole. You could buy it for a while. But if a person didn't deliver it of their own accord, it could just as easily be bought by the next highest bidder who would ante up with a bullet in the back of your head.

"Now I got to cover these bets," she said. *Or I'll be taking up residence under a crate down at the wharf.* "So, you better pray to God Almighty that none of these here wagers turns up a big winner," she said, waving the notebook in Tubby's face.

"In the meantime, here's what you going to do. When I'm ready, I'm sending you back to that drinkin' hole with a coupla my boys that got some sense in their heads." *Maybe Percy,* she thought. *And Chester. Maybe Skinny, too. Them boys is all mean muthafuckas, and that's what I need.* "You gonna show my boys who them drinkin' boys was, and they's gonna see to the rest."

"But Miss Rosie—"

Rosie held up her hand to silence him. "Then you going to go steal me that money, just like you said you gonna. From where, I do not care. You got just one week, you understand? Percy here's going to take your book and make your calls until you get me that money back. With interest."

"But Miss Rosie, I—"

"Shut the *fuck* up!" She turned and spoke to Percy. "Now get him the fuck outta here!" She watched as he dragged Tubby from the room.

The door slammed shut. "Why, Miss Rosie," she mimicked aloud. "I's just gonna..." She took the cigarette from her mouth and set it down on the edge of the side table, then picked up the shotgun.

Good God, she thought, *there sure ain't nothin' common about common sense.*

Pushing the breach lever to the side and breaking open the gun, she pulled out the shells and set them down on the table.

Then she looked at the gun and let out a little sigh.

"Sorry, baby. Not tonight."

AUGUST 31, 1920

Chapter 32

Lucas looked at his watch. Again. Zach still wasn't back. He'd gone into the clubhouse about fifteen minutes earlier to try and spy on the iceman. Neither Lucas nor Zach trusted the man. After Bear's death, nobody was totally beyond suspicion. And finding the icepick on his desk after the clubhouse had been broken into convinced Lucas he needed to get a firmer grip on any and all possibilities. Although clearly not the man who had threatened Tommy, it couldn't be ruled out that he wasn't somehow involved.

Still just the third inning, the Bulldogs were nicely ahead by six runs, but Lucas was having trouble keeping his mind on the game. Too many situations and too many unconnected dots, with no pattern in sight. Just him as the target. This was no longer a clever little game, an amusing diversion for someone with an eccentric sense of humor. This had become serious. And deadly. And Lucas needed answers. But so far, all he had were questions. Who would plot something like this? And to what purpose? Devoid of any real ideas, he forced his attention back to the game.

Thornton Bramwell, the Bulldogs' center fielder, stood patiently waiting at the plate. As the opposing pitcher argued with the home plate umpire over whether or not the ball was still fit for play, a second umpire crept in closer, wanting to worm his way into the conversation. Having done most of the arguing, the pitcher resorted to staring the ump into submission, and after a few more moments, succeeded. The umpire, sensing the crowd's growing displeasure at the delay, took the dirt- and tobacco-stained ball, gave it a long, last irritated look, and stuffed it into his pouch, then retrieved a fresh one from the same bag. Both umpires strode back to their respective positions, and the pitcher, spewing a long stream of chewing tobacco into the air, returned to the pitching rubber, a triumphant smile sneaking out from under his ball cap. With the debate finally settled, the other players also resumed their positions as the crowd clapped, cheered, laughed, and taunted, depending on their team allegiance.

In a tone intended to re-establish his authority, the umpire yelled, "Play ball!"

Bramwell returned to the batter's box, and the Bulldogs fans, blood running high, rowdily broadcast their expectations. At six-foot-three, 215 pounds, the big center fielder had home run power that could easily knock the ball right out of the park. Which was pretty much what Bulldogs fans wanted right now, chanting his name over and over.

Marty Walsh, the Bulldogs' first baseman, who'd managed to overcome his ankle injury in record time, shouted words of encouragement from the on-deck circle while at the same time swinging his bat in slow motion as he envisaged the ball soaring across the plate, dead center, belt high. Stretching an insignificant few steps off of second base into a base-stealing lead to third, Eddy Briggs, the team's right fielder, kept one eye on the pitcher and one eye on the dancing second baseman who threatened to come running back to the base to apply the tag, should the pitcher decide to try and pick him off.

None of this was lost on Lucas. He mentally tabulated the options open to each player and the odds of any one of those options occurring, as well as the potential consequence of each result.

The pitcher went into his windup and sent the ball speeding toward the batter. As the ball crossed the plate for a strike, Lucas quickly glanced over to see if there was any sign of Zach. Still nothing.

The catcher tossed the ball back to the pitcher and Lucas looked back into the dugout. Tommy Marshall was guarding the equipment box, but it was obvious his heart wasn't in it. The players, who all season long had made Tommy and Bear a required stop on their way to the plate, now avoided him as though he was spreading Spanish flu.

With one eye on the pitcher, Lucas yelled out, "Tommy!"

Tommy's head snapped up, and with barely a moment's hesitation ran over to where Lucas sat.

"Tommy, I want you to go into the clubhouse and see if you can find Zach. If he's there, come back straightaway. If he isn't, I want you to have a careful look around everywhere. In my office, in the equipment room, everywhere. Then come back here. You see anybody else, you come back here on the run. Got it?"

With a nod, Tommy spun and ran inside.

Lucas turned back to the game in time to see Bramwell foul a ball off into the left side of the grandstand. An alert fan reached up with conviction, intending to grab the ball as it retreated back to earth, then lost his nerve at the last moment. The ball ricocheted off the wooden flooring and bounced off into the crowd. Several fans scurried about the seats in search of the souvenir, and moments later, a victorious hand held the retrieved reward aloft. A small group of boisterous fans cheered the effort, before everyone settled back into their seats as the umpire threw the pitcher a new ball.

With growing concern, Lucas peeked over to the clubhouse door at every pause in the game. What was taking Zach so long? Had there been an encounter with the iceman? He thought about running in to see for himself, but decided he'd better wait until the inning was over. Leaving the ballpark right now would certainly unsettle the team.

Tommy came running back outside. "I don't see 'im."

"You're sure, kid?"

"Yes, sir, I'm sure. He's not there anywhere."

"And no one else was in there?"

"No, sir. It was empty."

Lucas stood up, trying to decide what to do. Before he could formulate an idea, there was a loud crack from the batter's box. Bramwell was speeding up the first base line. The ball was soaring way into the sky, tumbling in slow motion high above the grandstand, until it finally reached the end of its arc and began slowly falling back to earth.

"Son of a bitch," smiled Lucas, as he watched the ball descend.

It was headed out of the park.

Chapter 33

Zacharia raced out the clubhouse door, took a few steps to his left, then hesitated. Quickly turning back the other way, he peered down the street to the next intersection. The man he'd caught sneaking out of the clubhouse, the one improbably dressed in a suit more suited to a yacht than a ballpark, had narrowly escaped and was nowhere to be seen.

Suddenly, not a dozen feet away, a loud *thunk* made Zach turn around. A baseball ricocheted off the cobblestones and rolled off down the street. Within seconds, three boys in bare feet who had been lingering outside the ballpark were in hot pursuit.

Zach peered up over his shoulder at the wall of the grandstand, realizing where the ball must have come from. "Son of a bitch!"

With no time to wonder who might have slugged the ball out of the park or what it might mean to the score, he immediately turned back, hoping to spot his quarry, determined not to let him escape.

Neither side of the street appeared to be harboring anyone who acted like they didn't want to be seen. In fact, everywhere he looked, it was business as usual. Street vendors rearranging their wares, wagon drivers tending to their horses, pedestrians toting parcels of varying sizes, shopkeepers sweeping away the day's debris, two men struggling to erect a sign over a shop window while a third looked on in amusement, kids playing tag and hopscotch…everyone was right where they should be, doing what they should be doing.

Except for one person.

Far down the opposite side of the street, all alone, his back to Zacharia, stood a man reading a newspaper. Which, by itself, was not unusual. What was unusual was the way he was dressed. Unlike the working-class inhabitants of the neighborhood, this man was impeccably outfitted in a blue, pinstriped blazer, spotless white slacks, and equally unsullied white boater with navy blue and orange headband, looking just like the man Zach had minutes ago seen leaving the clubhouse. It reminded him of the man he'd seen in the bar talking to Frankie Miller. The clothes suited the man, but the man didn't suit the scene.

Zach stepped out into the street, tagging along behind a passing horse-drawn freight wagon, then darted ninety degrees away from his target, hoping not to spook him. He shuffled along casually until he got to the far side of the road, then strode up to a shop window and stared in. After waiting a couple of seconds in an effort to appear disinterested in most everything, he snuck a look to where his quarry had been standing. He was still there, still reading his paper.

About to continue his pursuit, Zach stepped away from the window and collided with a powerfully built man in a t-shirt and overalls, a beaten-up flat cap pulled down low over his brow. The man thrust a large bunch of carrots into Zach's face, partially obscuring his own.

"Hello, mister gentleman. Very good vegetables, yes?"

"Yeah, sure," replied Zach, giving the man a cursory glance before looking down the street again, trying not to lose sight of the man in the pinstriped blazer. He pushed past the shopkeeper, who quickly grabbed his arm and tried to drag him back to his cart.

"These I grow myself, please! I pick for you!"

Zach shook his arm loose and once again forced a look down the street to where he'd last seen his target. The man was still there, still reading his newspaper. Or, at least, pretending to.

"Yeah, look, maybe tomorrow," he said, irritation growing. Again he tried to step away, and again the shopkeeper took his arm.

"Tomatoes? Beautiful! Look! Very fresh! " said the man, picking a large specimen from the pile on his cart and thrusting it into Zach's face.

Zach pushed the man's hand away, never losing sight of his objective. "No tomatoes!" he replied sternly, then headed off down the street.

Over his shoulder, he could hear the man yell, "I have lettuce also!"

Ignoring him, Zach sped up and headed straight for his quarry, who still had his back toward him, still reading his paper. He made no attempt to abandon his spot on the corner.

With one final burst of speed, Zach leapt at the man and grabbed him by the shoulder, spinning him around and knocking the paper out of his hand.

"Ho!" said the man, flustered and angry at the same time. *"Et tu, Brute?"*

Eyes wide, his mouth hanging open in confusion, it took Zach several seconds to gather his wits. It wasn't at all who he'd expected to find. While the clothes did indeed fit the man, they didn't suit him much at all. He had to be in his late fifties; hadn't shaved in two or three days; bloodshot eyes from too much alcohol, too little sleep, or both; and leathered skin that had enjoyed far too much sunshine. Zach shook his head, trying to untangle what his eyes were seeing from what his brain was saying. Finally, he mumbled, "But you're not—son of a bitch! Who are you?"

The man smiled and thrust his arms wide by way of introduction. "Phideas P. Crowley, thespian at large!" he declared, adding in his best stage whisper, "Or, might I just say, thespian for hire!" His voice rose so as to include the several onlookers. "Two hundred and eleven performances of *Julius Caesar*! One hundred and fourteen performances of *Twelfth Night*! A proud founding member of the Fourteenth Street Touring Company!" He quickly looked around to see if he was having the desired effect. A young girl of about eight looked up at him, mouth agape, eyes bulging. "Where's your mother?" he demanded, and the girl scurried off. He then turned back to Zach. "As is likely apparent, we're not touring just at the moment, which is why you find me here," his voice rising once again. "Phideas P. Crowley, *histrio cum laude*!" The "*laude*" stretched out louder and longer than the rest.

Momentarily stunned at finding his quarry to be not at all whom he'd expected, Zach glared at the man in silence. But he quickly recovered, his mind gathering and analyzing, calculating, and concluding, until he arrived at what he realized was the obvious explanation. He'd been set up.

"Okay, just hold it right there. You came into our clubhouse, yeah? You were the one I chased out here." He nodded to himself.

"I was indeed. Phideas P...." He stopped abruptly. "Ah, so you must be..." The actor stopped again, this time staring at Zach, his face scrunched up, searching for a clue.

"Zacharia."

The actor smiled. "Of course you are. Of course." He stared at Zach as if he'd just spotted a rare species of gazelle. "In which case," he said, reaching into his blazer pocket and pulling out an envelope, "and before I forget, may I present to you—by the way, speaking of forgetting, I don't ever forget my lines, never, not once, not a single line ever, and that—"

Zach snatched the envelope out of the man's hand and turned it over to examine both sides but found nothing written on it.

"Okay, look. Someone put you up to this," Zach said angrily, waving the envelope in the man's face. "Who was it? What did he look like? Well dressed? Like yourself?"

"Oh, no! Not like this at all. More like a…well, dare I say it? Like a peasant!" he sniffed. "Or maybe a street vendor." He studied Zach's face, his own mildly amused. "He said it was just a joke. I assumed it must be. An old joke between friends."

Zach's eyes narrowed to such a degree, a passerby could have mistaken him for having fallen asleep standing up.

"A street vendor?"

The actor shrugged. "Could have been. You know, overalls and such. And a large, dark mustache, curled up the side of his face, almost like sideburns. Oh, and he had an accent. Italian maybe. Personally, I thought the accent was a bit much. A bit fake, really." He leaned in for another stage whisper. "Never would have made the Fourteenth Street Touring Company!"

Looking once more at the envelope, Zach half turned and looked back up the street. Looking directly back at him, his face all smile, was the vegetable seller.

In an instant, Zach was racing up the street toward the man who had tried to sell him tomatoes, powerful strides cutting the distance down quickly. For his part, the street vendor stood for a few more moments, taunting his pursuer with inaction. Then, having enjoyed his little game as long as he dared, he ran around the side of the cart and up the street. A dozen steps later, and one more look over his shoulder, made him realize he might have hesitated too long, and his face registered the concern.

Zach sensed his own athleticism would put him within reach before another block had disappeared under his feet. The man he was chasing didn't have the speed. Adrenaline pumping through his own body, Zach urged his legs harder, every step telling him that this time he would succeed. This time he would discover once and for all who was behind the messages, the mystery, the threats that had begun to paralyze Lucas. This time he would make him pay.

And he would have. But the workmen who'd been hanging the sign above the store slipped, and the sign, instantly responding to the call of gravity, came crashing down into Zach's path, sending him hurtling head over heels until he tumbled hard onto the pavement, rolling twice before coming to a painful stop.

Wincing with pain, he looked up to see the street vendor standing just thirty feet away.

The man smiled at Zach, then snickered loudly and ran off up the street.

Chapter 34

Only after reaching the entrance to the subway did Maddocks feel safe enough to abandon all pretence of being a helpful, cheerful pushcart vendor. Peeling off his fake mustache, street-seller's apron, and workman's flat cap, he looked over his shoulder one last time, just to make sure Zach hadn't somehow found his footing and caught up with him. With no traces of his pursuer in sight, he let out a mighty laugh and collapsed at the top of the stairs. *That had been close,* he thought to himself. *Too close.* He'd let vanity play a card, and he'd nearly lost the pot. He couldn't take a risk like that again.

Still trying to catch his breath, he reached into the pocket of his overalls and pulled out the Cracker Jack prize that a few days earlier he'd designated his good luck charm. The dull metal figure lay tucked away deep in his cupped hand, hidden from any idly snooping eyes.

"That was quite exciting for a moment, wouldn't you agree?"

he offered to the inanimate object. "In any event, I do appreciate you stepping in at that critical moment. Now," he said, getting to his feet, "if it's all the same to you, I'm going to return to our little hideaway and get ready for our next adventure. Just a few more days, and we'll be closing the book on our friend Mr. Blaine. For good."

With that, he popped the toy back into his overalls pocket and casually strolled down the subway steps. As he neared the bottom step, he once again reached into his overalls pocket, this time pulling out his official-looking subway credentials badge. Nearing the ticket window, he held the badge up, and with a nod to the ticket-taker, walked past the gate and down to the end of the platform.

Moments later, the train rushed into the station, screeching loudly as it came to a stop. As the doors whooshed open, the conductor stuck his head out a tiny window and shouted out the station stop, and a crowd of passengers stepped off and moved toward the stairs. The waiting crowd on the platform then climbed aboard, and the train creaked its way out of the station.

When it had disappeared down the tracks, Maddocks checked around him, then stepped down off the platform onto the rail bed and disappeared the other way up the tunnel, his footsteps echoing as he went.

Chapter 35

The Sun's Up Coffee Shop smelled of bleach and vinegar and looked ready for opening. Which it would do. At 6 a.m. next morning, same as always. Right now, though, it was ready to close.

"I'll finish up, Aleta," Willa called out into the empty coffee shop. "You go home." Busy refilling the last of the ivory-colored sugar bowls, she stopped and looked up, realizing she'd gotten no answer.

"Aleta?"

Still no answer.

Unconcerned but curious, she put the sugar bowl down and came out of the kitchen. Her aunt was sitting in a booth at the back of the coffee shop, head resting in one hand, gazing out the window at nothing. The long, gray braid that was normally curled in a bun atop her head had been released from bondage, and her hair now hung loosely down about her shoulders. She sat perfectly upright, her whole presence one of pride and determination, but her fifty-six years were clearly evident in the wrinkles on her face and the bags under her eyes.

"Hey…you okay?" Willa called across the room.

Aleta looked up and gave her a half-smile. "Mm hmm," she mumbled by way of reply.

Willa wiped her hands on her apron and strolled over to where her aunt was sitting. "Well, that's quite a disguise you've got for 'okay,'" she said, sitting down across from her in the booth. "What's on your mind? You're worried about money, right?" Despite having been left a very sizable inheritance from her late husband, and despite the coffee shop having a steady clientele and being reliably busy, Aleta fretted constantly about money, as if worrying would guard her from a sudden collapse of fortune.

"No, no, nothing like that, dear. I've just…" She turned and stared out the window at the fading daylight. She frowned and turned back to face Willa.

"It's a friend."

"Aleta! A man friend?"

"Don't be ridiculous!" her aunt scoffed. "Why on earth would I want one of those? Lazy, unemployed leeches, most of 'em. And drunk, often as not."

Sensing an opportunity to poke some fun at her aunt, Willa's face transformed into one of mock seriousness. "Absolutely. And don't forget stupid and inconsiderate. Would it be a stretch to say most of them are uncontrollable sex fiends to boot?"

"Willa May, the things that come out of your mouth!"

Willa laughed. "Aunt Aleta, not all men are like that. Uncle Cliff was none of those things."

Willa had only known her uncle, Clifton Neville Hastings, for a few years, but his quick wit and incisive mind had made him her favorite. He had met Willa's aunt at an autumn social when she was already forty-three, and after a scandalously short courtship, had asked her to become his bride. It didn't hurt that he was a successful New York lawyer and as handsome as any Hollywood star.

Having been contentedly widowed for thirteen years, but growing tired of the solitude, she'd accepted his proposal faster than a rainbow trout snatching a Jamison Coaxer Fly. But not before warning him repeatedly that she was just a "simple shopkeeper's daughter" and might not be suitable to those in his social circle. He, in turn, had replied, "My social circle is about the size of a pecan and nearly as interesting," and dismissed her concerns as "ridiculous." Indeed, recognizing and appreciating his immense good fortune in wooing Aleta, he'd treated her like a queen, doting on her endlessly.

When war broke out five years later, Clifton insisted on signing up, but was rejected due to his age. Persistent to the point of annoying, he lobbied the right people for long enough that he was finally allowed to enlist. He shipped overseas in October 1917, and never came back.

"Well, of course, he *may* have been a sex fiend. I really couldn't say," Willa added, grabbing Aleta's hands in her own and giving them a joyful squeeze.

"Willa!" Aleta turned again to stare out the window. Half to herself, she added, "Good gracious, if Mr. Hastings could hear the way young women talk these days...well, I just don't know!" She turned back to face Willa again, her eyes filling with tears. "The old fool," she said wistfully.

"Aunt Aleta, Uncle Cliff was kind, thoughtful, intelligent. And brave, too. How many men his age volunteered to give up everything and go fight for their country in that stupid, bloody war? He was a hero. And a patriot."

"And too old, and too foolish, and too stubborn, and I miss him and that magnificent flowing mustache of his every day," she wept, pulling a handkerchief from her apron pocket.

"I know you do. Is that what you were mulling over back here? You looked very far away."

"No, no, something else," Aleta replied, wiping away her tears and stuffing the handkerchief back into her apron. "It's my friend, Megan. I think her nephew is in trouble."

"What kind of trouble?"

"She said he's gotten himself mixed up with the wrong people. Really wrong people. And he owes them money, or something like that. I'm not quite sure, and I'm not sure she's even sure. Just that it's bad." She scrunched up her face, trying to remember if there was anything else she knew.

"Let's talk to Lucas," suggested Willa. "He's just the person for these sorts of things. He loves solving problems like this."

"Hasn't he got enough problems to solve? What with all those mysterious things going on? And that baseball team he has to manage? I give him such a hard time when he's in here, I'm not sure he'd even—"

"Enough. Lucas adores you, you know that." She gave Aleta a wink. "Generally speaking. So let's talk to him tomorrow when he's in for breakfast. Whatever it is, I'm sure he can help. Now, scoot on out of here and let me finish getting this place closed down." Without waiting for an answer, Willa got up and headed back to the kitchen.

Aleta pursed her lips together, about to say something, then decided to let it go. She edged her way out of the booth and started toward the door.

"And here," Willa called from the kitchen, "take your purse with you."

Taking her purse from Willa's outstretched arm, she smiled. "You're a dear. Sorry to be such a burden. It's just that Megan...she's such a good friend, and—"

"And tomorrow we're going to ask Lucas for his help. You'll see. You just offer him a piece of your gooseberry pie—he'll jump at the chance. Now, please, my feet are killing me, and I'd like to get on home, too!"

Aleta did her best to smile, then turned and headed out the door. The bell over the door jingled as she left, and Willa heard the door click shut.

"So," she said to herself, "at least it's somebody else's money problems." She went back into the kitchen and went to retrieve her own purse when she heard the doorbell ring once again.

"What did you forget?" she called out, continuing to tidy up. She stuck her head out into the restaurant but couldn't see anyone. *Huh. That's strange. I'm sure I heard the bell ring.*

"Hello? Aleta?" No noise of any kind came from the restaurant. Shrugging, she went back into the kitchen and reached down under the butcher counter for her purse when she heard a noise in the other room.

"We're closed!" she shouted, her body starting to tense. "Open tomorrow at six, same as always." She cocked an ear but couldn't hear anything more. *Darn,* she thought, noticing some pots still sitting on the counter. *I'd better do wash those before I go, or the cook will have a fit.* She reached for the pots, but before she could touch them, a hand slipped around from behind her and jammed a cloth over her mouth. She jerked back into what was clearly a man's torso. A second hand, the left one, skimmed around her waist and slipped into the pocket in the front of her apron, rubbing briefly between her legs before retreating up to her waist and grabbing tight what minimal flesh was there. The cloth over her mouth, reeking of chloroform, leather, and tobacco, made Willa want to retch. She knew that sooner or later the chloroform would win the day and she would be swallowed up into a whirlpool of ever-decreasing consciousness.

Frantic for any idea that would give her some leverage, she reached up and grabbed the hand that covered her mouth and tried to pull it away, but the man held on tight. For a brief moment, she noticed a tattoo on the man's wrist, but couldn't make out what it was. He pushed her down hard onto the butcher's counter, sending the pots flying onto the floor. She could feel the unyielding strength of the man's body against her back. Every time she pushed backwards, he would push forward, and the dizziness kept growing. She slammed her foot down hard on the toes of his left shoe, and he let out a yelp but didn't let go.

Nausea, fear, confusion, anger, her brain was signalling panic. She tried to bite him, but couldn't get her mouth open wide enough to do it.

She could feel his hand reach down into her apron pocket.

"Here's a message for you—and your baseball boyfriend," the voice whispered. It was as cold as ice. Willa didn't recognize it and knew there was no time trying to make it make sense.

Willing her hand to reach down and into the counter drawer, she grabbed the first thing she could put her hand on. A three-inch paring knife. With one swift move, she slammed it into the man's right thigh, and the hand and cloth fell away from her mouth.

"Bitch!" he screamed, stumbling backwards and falling to the floor. "You bitch! Fuck!"

Tumbling backwards in a heap, Willa scrambled to her knees and scratched her way to the far side of the kitchen without turning around. She could hear the man moving, maybe getting up. Yes, getting up. And scuffling toward the door.

She stayed kneeling on the floor, gasping for breath and trying to get a look at her attacker, but the counter stood between them, blocking her view. The dizziness started to recede. *Where's the knife? What have I done with it?*

The bell over the door rang its now terrifying melody, and footsteps fled into the shadows of the night.

Trembling, she looked down at her hand and realized she was still clutching the bloody paring knife. She started to cry.

Chapter 36

"Maybe it's all connected somehow?"

Lucas continued pacing the floor, desperately wishing that he hadn't stopped to chat with Zaslaw at the newsstand. That he'd arrived at the Sun's Up Coffee Shop just a few minutes earlier. While he knew it was irrational, he blamed himself for not being there to protect Willa, for somehow not appreciating how much more serious things had become, how much more threatening. And yet, what exactly was the threat, and who was it targeting?

"Lucas?"

He knew Willa was right; there must be a strand that connected it all. He just couldn't see it. "That's what I'm trying to figure out," he answered. "How it's all connected."

With Bear's death, things had taken a very ominous turn. But it all seemed so unrelated to the Cracker Jack prizes that he didn't know where to start.

Willa sat perched on a chair in the coffee shop, where Lucas had carried her after finding her crying on the floor in the kitchen shortly after the attack. Her arms wrapped about her middle, she bobbed a little in place, and Lucas thought she might be about to burst into tears again. But suddenly, she sat bolt upright and started listing off the various strange events as if the attack had never even happened.

"First, there was that shovel, right? That toy that looked like it might have come from a Cracker Jack box? And then, what? There was that tiny tin cat? Can you see a connection there?"

As surprised as he was by Willa's near-instant recovery, he decided not to question it and just go wherever the conversation might lead.

"No. I can't. Not yet, anyway. But even before the cat, there was that telegram that came addressed to me, care of the coffee shop. Remember? The one with the strange message?"

"I do. And that strange man sitting in your booth that morning."

"What makes you say strange? You didn't say that at the time. Was there something about him that made him strange?"

"I don't know. There was just something about the way he acted. Like he knew that booth was exactly where he shouldn't sit. I never really thought about it at the time, but yes, there was something strange about him, now that I think about it."

"Did he ask about me? Mention my name? Or Zach's name?"

Willa thought about it for a second. "No. Nothing like that. It was just..." She stopped again, her lips pressed together. "I dunno. He didn't say much at all. It was just a feeling I had about him. Like he knew someone was coming...that you were coming...and that he could sit there until you arrived. But he never actually said anything like that."

"No distinguishing marks? Like a scar?"

"Sorry, Lucas, I don't remember." Willa looked like she'd run out of details, when suddenly she got a sparkle in her eyes. "Wait. I do remember something. He had very clean hands." She stopped, reconsidering. "No, not just clean. Manicured. He was sitting there, his face cupped in his hand, just smiling. I do remember now thinking how nice his hands looked. Most men don't bother. The funny thing was, his actual hands were all swollen. And it looked like he'd scratched them or cut them or something—or at least worked with them his whole life. You know. Manual labor. But otherwise, they were spotless and perfectly manicured."

Lucas stole a glance at his own contorted hand and wondered if a manicure could do anything to help restore his lost sense of pride.

"Do you think he could have had something to do with that telegram?" she added.

"Could have."

"Well, in any event, what's that got to do with a shovel? Or a cat, for that matter?"

"Maybe nothing. Maybe everything. I don't know. But I do know that telegram had something to do with the guy in the ballpark with the mirror. Maybe not the guy in the restaurant, but definitely the guy in the ballpark. And he most definitely wanted my attention. And yet..." Lucas paused to think about it. "He went to a lot of trouble to make sure I didn't get close enough to see him."

"Because you'd recognize him?"

"Maybe." Lucas ran a hand through his hair and sat down next to Willa. "Okay, so let's say those things are all connected. What's the point? And who's behind it? It's gotta be the same guy."

"Or a guy with an accomplice," Willa suggested.

"Or a guy with an accomplice," Lucas acknowledged. "But then there's the canary. How does that fit in? I don't think that was a, a gift, you know? That was something else, I just don't know what yet."

"But it's so pretty, Lucas. You have to admit, it would make a pretty nice gift, wouldn't it? And it's doing fine, just sitting in the window at Aleta's apartment."

Maybe, thought Lucas. *For now, anyway.*

"What about the robbery at the clubhouse?" he asked. "How do you see that fitting in?"

"Maybe it doesn't," Willa replied. "I mean, nothing was taken, right? And you getting hit with the bat—maybe that was just because you interrupted the intruder's plan. That could have been, well, anybody."

"Except for that spinner toy he left behind. That wasn't just anybody. He came to deliver that spinner."

"That's right. I'd forgotten about that."

Lucas stood up again and walked over to the counter. He stood looking into the kitchen for a few moments and then turned back to Willa.

"So, the guy that came here tonight, the guy that attacked you. Even if it was just anybody…I mean, somebody not connected to any of the other things. I just can't reconcile any of it with Bear getting killed. Or with you being attacked. Neither of those things seems to have anything to do with Cracker Jack toys. Or mirrors, or telegrams, or…" Lucas wandered about, ideas and assumptions morphing into speculations and theories about what, if anything, meant something.

Willa stood up and idly stepped away, lost in her own world

of confusion and emotion. For the moment, it seemed as if neither could offer a workable proposition. Suddenly, she whirled about. "Lucas!"

Startled, Lucas snapped to attention. "What is it?"

"I remember something else."

"About the man in the restaurant?"

"Yes. He had a tattoo!" she said excitedly, as if that solved the entire conundrum.

"What kind of tattoo? A bird, a face, a—"

"No, no. Let me think. No, it was, it was…oh, Lucas, I'm not sure," she said, her momentary enthusiasm draining into a pool of uncertainty. "It was just a quick glimpse when he reached for his coffee. You know, his sleeve pulled up a bit, and I just remember seeing a tattoo on his wrist. It's not like I was looking for anything, or anything like that. I just remember seeing the tattoo and thinking how nicely dressed he was and his manicured hands and everything, and the tattoo just didn't seem to fit, and I guess that's why I even noticed it in the first place." She let out a little sigh. "Oh, Lucas, I'm so sorry. I just wanted to help, and now that hasn't helped at all."

It didn't take Lucas more than three seconds to reach out and wrap his arms around her and pull her close. "Darling, it has helped. I promise you, it has. More than you know." He backed away slightly but still held her in his arms. "Do you remember which wrist? Right? Left?"

Willa thought for a moment. "Left. He reached out to pick up his cup with his left hand because he was resting his head in his right hand, like this." She demonstrated, cupping her face in her hand.

"Left. Okay, good. That's good." In the struggle to make sense of everything Lucas had almost forgotten that Willa had been attacked by a stranger not even an hour earlier. Tenderly, he pulled her tight once again. "How 'bout we say enough for tonight."

It was all the prompting Willa needed as she collapsed into his arms and started to quietly sob. The fear and pain that had receded once Lucas has arrived to comfort her now came flooding back. Her mind filled with possibilities that might have occurred had she not gotten her hand on the knife in the drawer.

"It was such an awful feeling when he had his arms around me, Lucas. And he was holding that cloth over my face, and I thought I would pass out, and I could feel his hands reach down the front of me, and, and, and…" And the tears poured down her face.

Lucas just held on, wondering as always if anything he might say would help.

Within a few minutes, the sobbing slowed, sputtered briefly, then stopped. Willa lifted her head up, to find Lucas's smile waiting for her.

"I seem to have gotten you mixed up in something that I don't even understand myself," he said, half to himself.

"No, Lucas, I'm sure that's not so. It's just…" She pulled herself gently out of his arms, straightened up, and attempted a smile. "It's just not right," she said firmly. "And I know that you'll figure it all out," she added, thrusting her hands into her bloodstained apron pocket.

The smile that had been bravely trying to set Willa's face alight disappeared instantly, and the color drained from her face.

Lucas caught the change right away and his brow furrowed in response.

"What? What is it, Willa?"

Hesitating for an agonizing few seconds, Willa slowly eased her hand out of the apron and held it up in front of Lucas's face. Dangling from her fingers as if it were some poisonous insect was a tiny imitation pocket watch. A toy. Like something a child might enjoy while pretending to play grown-up. A toy just like the others.

Instead of numbers, though, the eleven letters in C-R-A-C-K-E-R J-A-C-K ran around the perimeter of the watch face where the hours would have been, skipping the number six, which had forfeited its spot to a miniature dial that looked like it might count the passing seconds.

"What does it mean, Lucas? Why a pocket watch?"

Lucas struggled to make a guess. Pocket watches were as common as shoelaces. And it certainly looked harmless enough.

But there was something about it that Lucas knew was more than just a toy. Something about the whole day that had put

Lucas on edge, an edge that was carving his imagination into a million pieces.

Tick tock.

Lucas sensed that time was running out.

SEPTEMBER 1, 1920

Chapter 37

Alex Conway had been hitting balls into the outfield while Eddy Briggs, Thornton Bramwell, and Rudy Suarton raced to every corner of the field, assiduously running them down. One spectacular fly ball had sailed high into the centerfield grandstand, and a half-dozen young boys who had snuck into the ballpark early ran over, under, and around the seats, chasing the souvenir down. Bert Morrissey, one of the Bulldogs' pitchers, was loosening up along the first base line, lobbing soft pitches into Chip Mavers's well-worn catcher's mitt, which in turn coughed up a cloud of dust each time the ball found its home. Frosty Stevens, Geoff Canwell, and Marty Walsh rehearsed double-play routines, and the rest of the team, whether scheduled to be part of the lineup or slated to warm the bench that day, were tossing the ball around the field in an effort to get limbered up.

Lucas and Zach both stared out at the field, but neither could concentrate on what any of the players were doing.

"But she wasn't hurt otherwise, was she?" asked Zach, having already peppered Lucas with a dozen questions about the attack on Willa.

"No, but she was plenty shook up. Though I gotta tell ya, all in all, I'm surprised how well she's managing."

"Brave woman, that's all I can say," replied Zach as he looked at the imitation pocket watch that Willa had found in her apron. "Not sure what to make of it, but if it's supposed to predict something, I guess you could say that something is meant to happen at a quarter to noon."

Lucas peered over Zach's shoulder. Sure enough, if there had been numbers on the face of the pocket watch, the minute hand would have been resting right on the number nine, which on the little toy had been replaced by the first letter "C" in the word "Cracker." The hour hand pointed directly at the second letter "C" in the word "Cracker," where the number twelve would have been.

Lucas pulled out his own watch from his pants pocket. The timepiece said 12:45 p.m. If something was going to happen just short of noontime, it wasn't going to happen today. "Or a quarter to midnight," Lucas replied, holding his watch up for Zach to see.

Zach grunted acknowledgement and peered out again at the players running their drills.

"How's the leg?" asked Lucas.

Looking down at his foot, Zach screwed up his face. "Son of a bitch," he mumbled.

Lucas wasn't sure if Zach was talking about his foot or about the man he'd been chasing who'd gotten away.

"Thousand-to-one shot that sign would fall right where I was runnin'. Another ten seconds, I woulda had 'im! Son of a bitch!"

Zach clenched his teeth. "I had 'im, Lucas! Right in my hands! I had that son of a bitch!"

Lucas wasn't so sure who had who. "Did you recognize him? This street vendor? I mean, after you realized it was him, did he look like anyone you know?"

"No one."

"What about that guy you saw in the bar talking with Frankie Miller?"

"Boss, it happened so fast. I wasn't even payin' attention to that vendor. When I realized what had happened, he was too far away for me to be sure. Maybe there was somethin' familiar about him, I dunno."

"How about that guy that delivers the ice?"

Zach struggled with the idea. "I dunno. Maybe it coulda been." Zach rubbed his face. "Son of a bitch, maybe it coulda."

"You checked with O'Farrell?"

"Yeah, he delivers ice for him, all right. Name's Mullan. Fergal Mullan. Didn't know too much about him otherwise."

Okay, so just go over it for me again. You chased this guy out of the clubhouse..."

"Out the clubhouse and across the street," answered Zach. "He was wearin' a fancy striped blazer and a skimmer. At least, I thought he was our guy. Turns out he's some actor hired to impersonate our guy. But before I could figure that out, I bump into this street vendor fella—"

"Hold on, just a second. A minute ago you said the street vendor bumped into you."

Zach thought for a moment, replaying the incident in his mind. "Yeah, I guess that's how it happened. He bumped into me." Again, he paused to think. "Son of a bitch, that takes guts," he added, realizing the significance of the man's intentional obstruction.

Lucas had come to the same conclusion. No longer satisfied with secretly delivering obscure messages, this guy, whoever he was, purposely wanted to be part of the moment. And he wanted Lucas and Zach to know that he was completely in charge.

"So, you chase after this actor, yeah? Who's not going anywhere, just standing around reading a newspaper?"

"Readin' a newspaper, and he says…" Zach's shoulders slumped and his eyes rolled upward. "Son of a bitch," he announced yet again. Reaching into his jacket pocket, he pulled out the envelope the actor had given him. "Boss, I'm sorry. I just—I just totally forgot about this," he said, handing the envelope over to Lucas, a look of chagrin crossing his face. "That actor fella gave me this."

Lucas stared at the envelope. Finally, he took it out of Zach's outstretched hand and turned it over to look at the back, and then over once again, checking carefully to see if there was anything at all written on it. It was blank on both sides.

"No name on it." *But the mail must go through,* Lucas thought to himself. "Did he say this was for me?"

"He didn't specifically say that, boss. I just assumed, you know, because of the others."

"Yeah. Probably." Lucas continued staring at the envelope, not wanting to open it but knowing that he must. Knowing that it contained yet another mystery, another clue, another…another what?

Lucas ripped the envelope open at the end and tipped it down to release its contents.

Both men stared at the object now in Lucas's hand for longer than they needed to before coming to a conclusion.

"You don't even own a car, boss."

Zach's right, thought Lucas. *And besides, this thing looks more like a truck.* "Doesn't even look like a car. Looks more like one of those trolley buses. Except without the wires."

"Maybe. Kind of stubby, though," replied Zach.

Car. Truck. Trolleybus, maybe?

Whatever it is, mused Lucas, *it's another mystery. And it's driving me crazy.*

September 2, 1920

Chapter 38

High atop the O'Farrell Ice Making Company, the building's work whistle shrieked loudly, announcing the end of a work shift and adding to the late afternoon cacophony that signalled a busy city shifting gears. The alley behind the factory was empty, as Cian had expected it to be. He paced back and forth, repeatedly pushing his lank, greasy blonde hair off his narrow, twitching face, keeping an eye on both ends of the alley, hoping that no one would decide to use it as a shortcut. He needed privacy for when he and Mullan would be splitting the money.

All had gone according to plan, just as they had discussed it. Well, maybe not exactly. Mullan had beaten the bookie outside that speakeasy pretty badly, and that most definitely had *not* been part of the plan. But they'd gotten the money, and in the end, that was all that mattered. That meant Mullan would get his money back, and all would be as before. No debt, no threat, no hard feelings. And Cian could get his life back.

Maybe even better than that, he now thought. The bookie had had more than seven hundred dollars in his pocket, according to Mullan. And Cian's debt to Mullan was, what? Three hundred and twenty-two dollars? Ah, yes. And forty-eight cents. He smiled to himself. It all seemed so unimportant now.

The way Cian figured it, there was almost an extra 378 dollars to split. Okay, so even if Mullan took an extra ten, no, say, an extra twenty dollars to compensate for his troubles, or more accurately, for Cian's foolishness, that still left nearly 360 dollars to share between them.

The fortune teller had divined the solution from a bunch of randomly spread tea leaves. Cian grimaced when he thought about his time with her, but he had to admit, it was a dollar well spent. The money would come, she'd said, from a black man with a book. A bookie. Chester had come to mind, but Cian had dismissed the idea almost right away. Chester could not be the target. He was always at Rosie's, and it would be suicide trying to steal money right at Rosie's front door. Besides, he was a mean son of a bitch with a quick temper. Not to mention that big goddamned pistol he always had tucked in his waistband. It had to be one of Rosie's other men, someone who worked far from where Rosie's gang called home.

When Cian had disclosed his plan to Mullan, all he'd gotten was a look of derision. "It's your problem," Mullan had sneered, sticking a giant fist into Cian's face. "You fix it. And do it fast. I wants me money." But when Cian suggested there might be a lot more money than just what Mullan was owed, he began to warm to the idea. In the end, it was Mullan who'd suggested they make Tubby Lewis their target. Tubby made book for Rosie at a number of places, a couple where Mullan was a regular. He reckoned Tubby wouldn't put up much of a fight.

Cian desperately needed Mullan's muscle for his plan to work. He had proposed they catch Tubby at Sixty-Six, reasoning there might be more money to grab there than some of the other speakeasies because that's where the bigger-money clientele went. Eventually, Mullan had come around. They'd gone to the club, stepping inside just to ensure that Tubby was there, but had been quickly hustled outside by the club's bouncers. Then they'd stood out in the alley waiting for their chance. Cian had insisted it be after dark and that they wear disguises, as Tubby might recognize Cian from when he delivered ice to Rosie's. When Tubby had come out with the band members and proceeded to get good and drunk, they couldn't believe their luck. They didn't even bother with the disguises. They waited until the band had gone back in to play, gave Tubby a few more minutes with the bottle, and then jumped him. He'd never even seen them coming and was in no shape to do anything about it.

Mullan had gone a bit overboard, smashing Tubby again and again. "Just to be sure," he'd said. Cian was upset about that and had begged him not to kill the man, but in the end he'd decided to keep his mouth shut. He couldn't take a chance on further upsetting Mullan. With Tubby lying crumpled in a pool of blood, they grabbed his money pouch and took off.

When the plan had first gelled, Cian hadn't counted on getting any money out of it himself. He'd have been happy just to set things square with Mullan. But afterwards, it occurred to him that he had taken some risk, too. Shouldn't he be entitled to some money? If there was any extra? Well, there had been. More than seven hundred dollars, all told, Mullan had said. So why shouldn't Cian have a bit of it, too?

The factory door swung open with a loud creak and Mullen stepped out, snapping Cian out of his reverie.

"Well, Ciany boy, didn't that work out, yeah? Seven hundred and four dollars, it come to. Just enough to clear your debt."

Cian looked confused for a minute, then found his bearings.

"Hold on...just a minute, Mullan. This all was my idea, no? I'm the one what came up with the plan to get that money. And your debt...your debt was just 322 dollars, okay?"

"Oh, my debt, was it? My debt?" Mullan had cocked his head to one side and drawn himself up straight. "Now, let me remind you whose debt it was, Cian. You was the fool that took my money and gave it to them black crooks. You was the fool what didn't even check to see that my bet was placed right. And you was the fool what fucked it all up, so then ya come to me for help? No, no, Ciany boy! My bet. My money. You lost it. I got it back!"

"But I got it back for you!"

"Aye, with my help. Otherwise, you might be resting down at the end of some fuckin' dark alley with a pick through yer throat. So, I'm not seein' how you fit into this, this money part."

Cian grabbed Mullan by the front of his shirt. "There was seven hundred dollars, we got. Seven hundred! More than enough for you and, and some for me too. I took the risk, too!"

Mullan pushed him away, eyeing him with disdain. "Y'er a snivelin' weasel, Cian. Count yer blessings and be gone with ya. You've done yer bit and paid yer debt, and there's not a penny that's got yer name on it."

Turning away, Mullan started to walk down the alley. Cian tried to form some words but could manage little more than to call after him, his voice catching in his throat. Mullan ignored him and kept walking.

Cian turned to one side, then the other, looking for something without really knowing what or even why. A rough wooden pole lay off to the right in a heap of trash. In a rush, Cian bent down and picked it up and chased up the alley after Mullan. Within steps of reaching him, he lifted the pole up over his shoulders and with all his strength brought it crashing down on Mullan's head. Mullan collapsed on the ground.

Cian stood panting, still holding the pole, trying to grasp what he'd just done.

"Oh, no. Oh, good God," he whispered, kneeling down next to Mullan, unsure of what he could or should do. He couldn't tell if the man was breathing and wasn't even sure if he knew how to tell. Quickly tossing the pole to one side, he shot a glance down both ends of the alley to see if there had been any witnesses. There were people crossing the alley where it met the street at either end, but no one was paying Cian any attention. A yellow tabby with one eye stared warily at Cian, blinked once, then eased off the crate it was resting on and quickly snuck away. Mullan's head had a nasty gash, and blood seemed to be oozing out in all directions.

Another quick glance down the alley, and then Cian reached into Mullan's right-side pocket. He felt sure the man would have the money on him, but there was nothing there. Wincing, he rolled Mullan over on his other side and checked his other pocket. Nothing. Both vest pockets were also empty. Without knowing why, Cian reached for the icepick that was stuffed into the carrying pouch that hung from Mullan's belt, hesitated, then let it drop. Slowly, he inched his way to his feet and stood up straight. He tried to think, his heart pounding in double time.

Three seconds later, he was gone.

Chapter 39

Light from the blacksmith's forge flickered and danced, creating an endless array of constantly changing silhouettes against the far wall. A smell of fresh straw and manure filled the air, though no animals were present. Two kerosene lanterns hung on wooden beams at the other end of the crowded barn, casting a pale-amber cloak of light on a small group of men. A battered cornet lay on the floor, close to where one man dangled by his wrists from an overhead beam, his toes begging to reach the floor. Off to one side, a second man lay on his stomach, the rope that had stretched his arms taut to the beam above just moments ago now a flaccid coil of hemp draped over his body. He was still breathing. Barely. Queen Rosie's enforcer, Percy Russell, dragged his brass knuckles across the dangling man's face, then dropped his hand to his side before delivering a punch to the man's midsection, eliciting yet another agonized scream.

THE MAN IN THE BLEACHERS

Two more men stood behind Percy, pistols hanging loosely by their sides.

Percy delivered a kick to the man's groin. "Now, you niggas betta tell me soon what you done wif dat money, or dey ain't gonna be no niggas left to be no Yankee Doodle, let alone play dat tune. You hear me? 'Cause if you ain't dead when Queen Rosie gits here, you sho' gonna be before she leaves if dat money don't come here soon!"

"What money?" the man hanging tried to cough out. Blood stuck to each word. "We ain'…we ain't got no money!"

That prompted a blow to the man's solar plexus, the brass knuckles digging deep into his flesh.

At that moment, the door to the stable opened and Queen Rosie entered, shotgun in hand. Two men were pulling Tubby Wilson in after her, his face still bruised from the beating. Tubby kept his face to the floor, wishing he were anyplace else.

"These them boys what took Tubby's take?" asked Rosie.

"Dey ain't said so, but dey's da band what was playin' dat night at that place he was at."

Rosie looked up at the man hanging by his wrists from the beam. "You're in a heap of trouble, boy. You thought New Orleans was rough? Well, how you likin' it here in Harlem? This is gonna make Orleans look like some kind of rest and recuperation home. You catch my meaning? That dimwit muthafucka' you stole from—that was *my* dimwit and *my* money. Now you don' look like a bad fool, but you sure as hell are a stupid one." Rosie's face wrinkled, trying to better assess the man hanging in front of her. "Look at you. Time ain't on your side, and I ain't so young that it's doin' me much favor either. So, let's get this over with. You tell me where my goddam money is, and I'll think about waylayin' your funeral."

The man tried to say something, but the words stayed stuck in his mouth.

"Yeah, well, Percy, that there guy ain't gonna be sayin' much anytime soon or maybe never, so cut him down and pour some water on him. I don't want him expirin' 'til I find out where they put that money. Then kill him. What about that other guy there? He tell you anything useful?"

"Just kept saying' how's he don' know nothin' too."

"Turn him over. Let me look at him."

The men turned the prostrate body over.

Rosie squinted into the gloom, then jerked her head back suddenly, not quite sure she was seeing straight. She bent down again to take a second look.

"William?"

Chapter 40

The Bulldogs had played poorly and lost painfully. With one out in the ninth and the winning run on third, Eddy Briggs had tried to run a bunt up the first base line, sacrificing himself so that Rudy Suarton could score from third. Unfortunately, the bunt had gone straight back to the pitcher, making Suarton, who had taken a huge lead off third base, easy pickings. He got caught in a squeeze play and was eventually tagged out. The inning ended without further fireworks when the pitcher struck out. Once into extra innings, the visiting team had popped a ball over the fence for a home run, and the Bulldogs were unable to answer in their turn at bat.

Lucas struggled to replay the game in his mind, wondering if another play at another time would have made any difference. The bunt had been his idea, as he had tapped his cap twice with his left hand and then rubbed his right arm twice to signal to Briggs what he wanted him to do. But, as is not uncommon with ideas, the imagined outcome, initially just plausible, had in the space of seconds grown to become probable and within another few seconds deemed absolutely certain, and all thoughts of alternatively predictable and undesirable outcomes dismissed to the gambler's graveyard. Life had other ideas.

Strolling along in the twilight on his way to meet Willa at the coffee shop, Lucas allowed thoughts of the game to wander away on their own and turned his attention back to all the mysterious events that had preoccupied most of his day. A Ford Model TT truck, sagging under a load of freshly cut hay, wheezed past, honking a greeting or a warning—it wasn't clear which—momentarily interrupting Lucas's thoughts. He stopped to watch it sputter up the street, absentmindedly sliding his hand into his vest pocket. His fingers found the miniature tin truck that had fallen from the envelope that Zach had been given by the actor, and he pulled it out. Once again, he tried to imagine what the meaning could be, but nothing revealed itself. A truck? A trolley? Neither? Whatever it was, it sent a shiver up his back.

Sliding the toy back into his pocket, he continued on his way. Willa had asked him to help Aleta with something, and he thought if he was going to remain in either or both their good graces, he'd better make it a priority. As he reached the front door to the coffee shop, he cast a quick glance at his reflection in the window. A man in a striped blazer and crushed skimmer brandishing a hatchet stared back.

Lucas flinched and reflexively stepped back. He shook his head and stared back in through the window once again.

Willa stood immediately on the other side of the glass, a smile on her face, her left hand thrust into the front of her perfectly pressed striped apron, her hair covered in a scarf, her right hand holding a long-handled wooden spoon that she was waving at Lucas. She cocked her head to one side as if to question what Lucas was doing.

He relaxed, tried to smile as he tipped his hat and carried on in through the front door, cursing his overactive imagination.

The bell over the front door welcomed him into the coffee shop.

"You look like you'd seen a ghost out there!"

"Well, I saw something, for sure, but I realize now it was just the prettiest girl on the street," Lucas replied, trying to recover.

"Just the prettiest girl, Lucas? Any man might have imagined that!" she teased.

Once again, Lucas realized his words hadn't captured his intention. "The absolute prettiest!" he beamed, throwing his arms wide to depict an all-encompassing assessment.

Willa waved the spoon at Lucas. "You've still got some work to do, mister!" Then she threw her arms around his neck and squeezed him tight.

He was stunned at how cheerful she sounded. Only two nights ago she'd been attacked by an unknown assailant, and tonight she was acting like it was ancient history.

She's a whole hell of a lot tougher than I give her credit for.

"How'd the game go today?" she asked.

"It wasn't the prettiest. Unlike the girl I'm holding right now."

"All right," she laughed. "Enough of that." She took his good hand and pulled him into the restaurant. "Aleta needs a word with you."

"Uh-oh. What'd I do?"

"Nothing. Don't be silly! I think she needs your help."

"She needs *my* help? Well, that's a first."

"First or not," chimed in Aleta, coming out of the kitchen, "it's true. And I'll thank you not to think that it's going to become a habit."

Lucas raised his eyebrows in surprise, but couldn't think of anything to say.

"I'm going to go finish cleaning while you two get reacquainted." Willa smiled, adding, "With the idea of being civil to each other, that is." And with that, she headed off to the kitchen.

Neither said a word until Willa was out of sight. Aleta broke the awkward silence. "She's right, Lucas. I haven't been entirely civil with you. But not because I don't like you. It's because Willa's all I've got and, well, I just need to be sure she's taken care of. Properly, I mean."

"I do know what you mean, Aleta. And I will. So, how about you tell me what it is you need help with, yeah?"

The two moved over to one of the booths where Aleta explained how her friend Megan's nephew had gotten mixed up with some dangerous people and was now in danger of being seriously hurt.

"Okay, so you don't actually know who he's in trouble with. You just know that it was serious, yeah?"

"Serious enough that Megan's nephew thinks he might be killed. She said...that is, Cian, her nephew, he said something about racing. Horseracing. That was about all she knew, other than that Cian owed some people quite a bit of money."

"You know his name?"

"Cian. Cian Nolan."

Lucas thought about it for a few moments but didn't recognize the name.

"He works over at O'Farrell's, over near the wharf," added Aleta.

"The ice-making factory?"

"Yes, that's the place. Is that helpful?"

"Might be," said Lucas, trying to get some traction on an idea. "Aleta, I need to meet this fella and hear it directly from him. Find out exactly what kind of trouble he's in and with who. Get your friend to tell her nephew we need to meet. Then I'll know what I can do to help." *If anything,* Lucas thought to himself.

Tears started to well up in Aleta's eyes. "Thank you, Lucas." She stared at him for another ten seconds, and then with an exhausted sigh, stood up and announced aloud, "Well, this place isn't going to clean itself," and she walked off toward the back of the restaurant.

Chapter 41

"William, what the hell are you doin' here?" Queen Rosie bent over William, trying to make sense of why her nephew would be lying crumpled on the floor in this blacksmith's shop instead of washing up at the restaurant where he worked. Or at the very least, practicing his cornet like he usually did when he had time to spare. She'd been expecting some musician from New Orleans who had stolen her bookie's money. That was what Tubby had said.

William struggled to say something, a thin thread of spittle emerging from his lips.

Rosie turned to the two men standing behind her. "Could one of you dumbass bring me some water? This here's my nephew!"

Rosie set the Fox Sterlingworth down on the ground and lowered herself onto the dirt. One of the men grabbed a bucket of water that lay nearby, pulled out the ladle, and thrust it toward her.

"I don't need water, you dumb muthafucka. This here boy needs it!"

The man with the water bucket quickly stepped around Rosie to where William lay and held the ladle up to William's lips, promptly spilling half of it down his shirtfront.

"He ain't lookin' for a bath, you fool," she said, grabbing the ladle from the man's hands. "Lemme do it! Lord mercy," she added over her shoulder, "you got the brains of a catfish." She turned back to William, then looked over to where Percy was standing.

"Percy, cut that other one down!" she yelled. "'Til we find out what the hell this is all about," she added, mostly to herself.

Percy pulled a switchblade from his pocket, flicked it open, and sliced through the rope, dropping the man to the floor.

Tubby Wilson had come up about ten feet behind Rosie. He'd heard her say something about her nephew but couldn't quite make out what was happening. Something was wrong, that much was clear.

Little by little, Rosie managed to ladle a bit of water into William's mouth. His left eye was swollen and closed tight, the other barely open, and blood had crusted across his lower lip, which had been split open. The front of his suit coat was stained with blood, and his right arm rested at an unusual angle by his side. He peered up at Rosie and managed a weak smile.

"William, what are you *doin'* here?" she repeated, now in a voice just above a whisper.

"I—I don't know, Aunt Rosie. I was with some fellas, jes sittin' around practicin' our music, and then some guys, they jumped me and brung me here. And they brought Bernard here too. Aunt Rosie, please tell 'em, we ain't done nothin'!"

Tubby inched a bit closer, certain that he recognized the muffled voice that was sneaking out from Rosie's embrace.

"All right, now," said Rosie, "let's just try and see what happened here. You and this other guy over there, this what's-is-name, Bernard or somethin', you was playin' at the Sixty-Six t'other night, right? I mean, that's what my man here told me," she said, yanking a thumb over her shoulder at Tubby.

William frowned, tried to make sense of what his aunt was saying.

"Playin' Sixty-Six? What night was that?"

"Don't you mind what night, William. Was you and that other beat-up fella playing at the Sixty-Six?"

Again, William struggled to remember. Then something clicked.

"Oh—oh, yeah," he said, licking his blood-caked lips. He screwed up his face as a jolt of pain shot through his body. "Yeah, I was, Aunt Rosie. I played the Sixty-Six all last week. Me and Bernard and a coupla other fellas. Dey's all from New Orlins." A frail smile crossed his face. "We played real good."

"Well, hell," Rosie managed, looking away and trying to think of what she should do or say next.

By this time, Tubby had managed to get within five feet of where Rosie was crouched.

"Miss Rosie?"

"Shut up, or I'll start havin' second thoughts about lettin' you off, you goddamned cockroach!"

Tubby did a quick double-step backwards.

Rosie turned back to William. "William, when you was at the Sixty-Six, did you see Tubby Wilson in there? You know Tubby, right?"

For a few seconds, William couldn't quite make the connection. Then he smiled as wide as the pain would let him. "Tubby? Sho, I knows him good, Aunt Rosie. He was at that club. Me 'n him, we went to have a, have a...we went outside for a smoke."

Tubby had braved a few steps closer, certain that the voice he could now hear was Rosie's nephew. "Miss Rosie? I mean, Queen Rosie—"

Rosie stood up and stuck the shotgun right into Tubby Wilson's face, finger on the trigger. Tubby squeezed his eyes shut and hoped he'd have time to explain.

"I don't think I can take a whole lot more of you, boy. So, what I want to know is, what the *fuck* do you want, interruptin' me?"

"It ain't him, Miss Rosie. It ain't William!"

"What ain't him? You don't think I don't know my own goddamned nephew?"

Tubby rubbed his hands together, then held them straight out in front of him, palms forward, trying to make a shield between him and the shotgun. He needed to find just the right words to explain before Rosie ran out of patience. "No, ma'am. That ain't what I mean. What I means is, he ain't the one what attacked me."

Rosie cocked her head and lowered the shotgun an inch, trying to decipher what Tubby was telling her.

"So, now you changin' yer story? Is that it? Now that you can't get it co-roborated?"

"No, that's not it, not it at all." He squirmed in front of her. "It's just that, it weren't William what attacked me."

"You said it was the band, and now here we are, two of them band right here in front of us. And William is one of 'em. And

281

he done said, he remembers you. And remembers you being at that speakeasy. So, what is it you mean that you don't mean?"

Tubby licked his lips and quickly nodded his head several times. "Yes, ma'am. And I knows William, I surely do. And I don't know that other fella layin' in that hay there, but I sure do recognize him. Him part of that band too. But it wasn't them fellas, Miss Rosie."

With a look of contempt, Rosie lowered the shotgun.

"So, how come all of a sudden you knows it wasn't them? You said it was the band what attacked you out behind that blind pig."

"No, ma'am, I didn't says the band attacked me. I says I went out to have a *drink* with 'em in the alley."

Frustrated to the point of exasperation, Rosie yelled, "Then who the hell did attack you?"

Tubby paused for a moment, his shoulders drooping, his face studying the floor. The words that came out were almost a whisper. "I tried to explain, Miss Rosie, surely I did. You just didn't—"

"What did I just didn't do, Tubby Wilson?" The words came out like shots from a pistol. "You gonna tell me? Or stand there all night blubberin'?"

"Yes, Miss Rosie. What I sez was…I *was* drinkin' wif the band. Surely I was, and I knows that was wrong. But what I tried to explain that night was, it weren't the band what done the beatin'."

"Well, then," said Rosie, rolling her eyes in disgust, "who the hell was it?"

"It was some white guys."

SEPTEMBER 3, 1920

Chapter 42

A wave of sunlight streamed in through the windows of Queen Rosie's third-floor parlor, trying valiantly to lift the atmosphere that pervaded the room. William sat slumped in his aunt's imitation maroon-upholstered Louis XV fauteuil, his left elbow sinking deep into the padded chair arm. His right arm rested in a sling flat across his chest, his right eye discolored and swollen. The top of his head was wrapped several times with a blood-stained bandage that had turned a rusty brown since leaving the blacksmith's forge. The fingers of his left hand, battered and bruised, clutched the stem of a delicately etched Italian crystal tumbler, half-filled with apple brandy. Despite the summer heat, and the dark-gray and white patterned throw that had been placed around his shoulders, he involuntarily shivered every few minutes.

Rosie had ordered William and Bernard be brought back to her apartment on 131st Street, cursing at anyone who dared get in her way or speak out of turn, directing her most vitriolic invective at Tubby. By the time they reached her apartment, her temper had subsided to the level of mere irritation, and she was more interested in what Tubby might be able to tell her now than in what he hadn't told her before.

White guys? she thought to herself.

Who were these white guys? Irish? Italian? Trying to muscle in on my territory? Sending a message? And why Tubby? I got plenty of other runners on my payroll.

She needed answers, and she needed them fast. Though she wasn't going to admit it, she knew that her own impatience had prevented Tubby from giving her the whole story the night he had come to admit his foolishness. And now William was beaten near half to death.

Arriving at the apartment, William had been carried up to the third floor. Rosie's private sanctuary. Bernard was put in a bed on the second floor, unconscious or asleep, no one seemed quite sure. With Rosie not knowing what to do with Tubby, he'd ended up in the parlor with William.

Sitting on the far side of the parlor in a chair matching the one in which William sat, Tubby tentatively hung onto an icy glass of lemonade, looking like he might bolt the room at any moment. His head ached and various bruises still throbbed from the beating he'd taken in the alley out behind the Sixty-Six. He could barely take his eyes off Rosie's twelve-gauge resting on the table by the window. For an apartment normally alive with a multitude of voices and noises of infinite description, barely a sound could be heard. Even the street racket that usually drifted up from outside seemed to have taken refuge. Only the repeated *tick-tock* of the grandfather clock in the hallway disturbed the quiet.

Snatching a quick a look at William, Tubby decided to take a chance and break the silence.

"William, I never sez it was you. You knows that, right?"

William's left eye fluttered open and he looked across the room at Tubby, a faint smile trying to force a presence.

"Hey, Tubby," he whispered hoarsely.

"William, you knows what I sez was right, don' you? I never told your Aunt Rosie it was you."

"And you never told me it wasn't, neither," snapped Rosie as she strode into the room, surrounded by a cloud of cigarette smoke. In the few minutes that they'd been back in the apartment, she'd changed into her favorite cranberry-colored satin housecoat and ankle-high fur slippers. Though her anger had waned, her ferocity remained intact. "Why you didn't tell me that night it was some white guys?"

Tubby thought about defending himself but chose to remain silent. He'd already tried that. Nothing was going to exonerate him from what had become a much more complicated issue.

Rosie took the cigarette out of her mouth and sat down in another one of the Louis XV style fauteuils. "So now the problem is," she said, dangling the cigarette from her right hand, "who is these guys?" She looked back and forth between the two men sitting in front of her. "William, you was out in that alley that night, right?"

"Yes, ma'am."

"And you was with the band?"

"Yes, ma'am. Me, Bernard, and, uh, well, two other guys." William sounded confused. "I don' remember their names right now."

"Yeah, never mind that. Was you in the alley when these white guys come around?"

"No, ma'am."

"So, you an' the band, y'all what? Went back inside?"

"Yes, ma'am. We done finished our break and went back inside to play."

Rosie continued to study William for several more seconds, trying to decide how much more help he could be. Deciding not much, she turned to Tubby. "But you was out there when these fellas showed up?"

"Yes, ma'am. Well, what I means is, I was in the alley when they jumped me. But I didn't see 'em 'cause they snuck up on me. No, ma'am, I didn' see 'em…at all! Not really."

Rosie cocked her head like she'd heard a twig snap. "When you say 'not really,' what exactly do you mean? You seen 'em? Or you didn't seen 'em?"

Tubby paused, trying to check his own memory. "What I means is, I didn' seen 'em comin', but when they was beatin' on me, I seen somethin'."

"And what exactly did this 'somethin' look like?"

"Well, there was two of 'em. White guys." Tubby stopped to consider. He couldn't afford to lead Rosie and her gang down some dead-end alley. "Yeah, two. One real big guy, and t'other guy was just kinda regular-like."

"Uh-huh. Go on."

Tubby strained to think of something. Something that would help identify the two thieves as well as take the focus off him. If he could just think of something, something at all, Miss Rosie might even forgive him and give him his old job back.

Suddenly, he remembered.

"The big guy, he had a—a tattoo. Uh-huh, a tattoo. Down here on his arm, like…," said Tubby, grasping his left wrist.

Rosie sat forward in her chair. "Now maybe we gettin' someplace. Okay, Tubby, you tell me now 'bout this tattoo. What kinda tattoo?"

Struggling to remember, Tubby closed his eyes. He could feel the punches all over again, and he could feel the bigger man grab him around the chest to turn him over. That's when he'd seen the tattoo. An image of something, just a blur now.

"I think maybe it was a animal of some sort. Or a bird, maybe. It's kinda blurry in my mind right now, Miss Rosie. That is, Queen Rosie, I mean," he added, head lowered, remembering in the moment how he was supposed to address her.

"But you don' remember for sure? Whether it was a seagull, or a—a what do you call it? A hippo-*pot*amus?" she said.

"I knows it weren't no hippopotamus," Tubby giggled. "I seen a picture of one of them once!"

Rosie's face remained set in stone. "Oh. You seen a picture once, huh? So how come you can't remember what the fuck picture was on this guy's wrist?"

"Please, Queen Rosie, I just don' remember. It was dark in that alley, and they grabbed me when I wasn' lookin', and then they punched me a bunch, and I only saw that tattoo for jus' a second, tha's all. I jes kinda remember it was maybe a bird or a animal."

Realizing he wasn't going to remember something he couldn't, she settled back into her chair, thinking.

Okay. A bird or an animal. At least that's something.

"And that tattoo, it was on his left wrist, like you showed me?"

"Yes, ma'am. On this wrist here," he said, once again grabbing his left arm.

"What about the other guy? The guy you said was more regular. Anything about him you remember? He have a tattoo?"

"I didn' get a real good look at him, Miss Rosie," he said, forgetting once again to use her preferred title. Fortunately, she seemed to have lost interest in that detail. "But I didn' see no tattoo. I jes hear him say, 'Don' kill 'im, yeah?'"

Rosie slumped back. This wasn't going to be easy with so little to go on.

"But I think I recognized his voice," Tubby added.

Once again, Rosie jerked forward. "You recognized his voice? Why you didn't say that before? Whose voice was that?"

"Well, now, you know I ain't a hun'rd percent positive, but…" Tubby replayed the voice over again in his mind. He hadn't even thought about it until right now, but sure enough, that was the voice he recognized.

"It was dat iceman," he said.

"That iceman? What iceman you talkin' about?"

"Dat iceman! Dat guy what delivers ice here! I seen him sometimes when I's here to deliver yer money. And now I remembers…dat's his voice I heard that night! Dat's a Irish voice, yes, ma'am!"

Rosie jumped out of her chair. "How's that gonna help, you fool? Half this fuckin' city's Irish!"

"Well—well—well, now hold on…dat not all!" Tubby squeaked. "No ma'am, dere's sompin' else. Sompin' else, uh-huh."

"Out with it, boy! Was is this 'sompin' else?'"

Tubby thought for a moment, trying to get it just right. "It's a sound he makes when he talks. Kinda like he got gravel or sompin' in his throat."

Rosie looked hard at Tubby. The iceman. She never even took notice when the man came around. She was pretty sure she couldn't pick him out of a group. Besides, lots of people had a throaty voice. Lots of people. It was hardly conclusive. On the other hand, it might be a start.

"Chester!" she suddenly yelled. "I know you out there. Get in here now!"

William and Tubby both jumped when Rosie yelled out, surprised at her abrupt change of focus.

Looking sheepish at having been caught listening, Chester slunk into the room from where he'd been eavesdropping out in the hallway. "I was just makin' sure you were all right, Queen Rosie."

Rosie's eyebrows went up in mock surprise. "You think I need help with my nephew and this fool?" she asked, pointing at Tubby.

"No ma'am," Chester promptly replied.

Rosie ignored him and continued on. "Now listen to what I'm sayin'. You here a lot when this iceman comes. You talk to him, right?"

"Yes, ma'am, I do sometimes."

"And is what Tubby sayin' about this guy—you know, about the way he talks, all gravelly and all—is that so?"

"The guy what comes regular, yeah, he got that way of talkin'," Chester nodded. "Kind of a—a gravelly sounding voice."

"Dat's him!" blurted Tubby. "He got that kinda gravelly voice, like Chester says! You know, like he got sompin' caught in his throat, or sompin'."

"Yeah, that's right. He brung some ice round just a couple of days ago," Chester added. "Made a bet on some horse, too. Name o' Keane...."

"Dat's him!" Tubby yelled out again, bursting with relief. "No one else got dat name, Miss Rosie! Dat's da man! 'Cause when he says…when he says, 'Don' kill 'im, yeah?'…den dat other guy, dat guy wit da tattoo, he says, 'You shut up, Keane!'"

"'Cept he don't spell it regular-like," Chester cut in. "Spells it kinda funny. Says it's Irish. I got it in my book." Chester pulled the notebook out of his pants pocket and thumbed through the pages. "Here. C-I-A-N. But when he says it, sounds like 'Keane.'"

Rosie looked around the room. Everyone waited for her to declare what would happen next.

Finally, she spoke.

"Chester, you go get Percy, Mason, Leonard, and Clinton. And that dumb fuck, Skinny Taylor, get him too. Get them into the kitchen in half an hour. We're gonna get ourselves a plan." She hesitated, calculating what to do next. "First things first, we're gonna find Mr. Gravel Voice. Then, he's gonna show us where to find the guy what done the beatin' on Tubby."

She stood up and walked to the parlor door.

"Then we're gonna kill both them muthafuckas."

SEPTEMBER 5, 1920

Chapter 43

The light rain that had slicked the cobblestones earlier that morning and made walking tricky had disappeared now that the sun had finally broken through the overhead blanket of gray. Still, Frankie Miller had to gauge each step carefully to avoid slipping and further injuring his right thigh—the thigh that Willa May had stabbed with a three-inch paring knife, sending him screaming in agony out the door of the coffee shop and into the night. He hadn't expected that. Hadn't expected any resistance at all.

As he hobbled along, his leg throbbed with every step, and he reached into his pants pocket for the bottle of Mrs. Winslow's Soothing Syrup the doctor had given him after stitchinup his wound. It was the same doctor he'd gone to when he'd needed something to enhance his baseball performance and outplay his teammates when his own natural talent wasn't enough. The same doctor who had botched so many abortions that he'd finally lost his license.

Stopping to ease his leg, Miller tipped the bottle of painkiller into his mouth and felt the warm, slightly sweet liquid trickle down his throat. He was well aware of its unfortunate reputation for killing babies due to an overly generous percentage of morphine. But the doctor had assured him not to worry. He wasn't a baby, after all. And it worked. It worked well.

Miller could feel the effects of the medicine right away, a satisfying blanket of comfort and calm lulling him into a state of dreamy consciousness. Not enough to make him pass out or too dizzy to walk, but more than enough to numb the nerve endings that were shuttling pain signals between his leg and his brain. He slid the bottle back into his pants and carried on down the street.

As he approached the address Maddocks had given him, he went over the excuse he had worked on over the past couple of days, hoping that it was enough. Ever since he'd agreed to help the man with his plan in exchange for some much-needed cash and a chance at revenge, he hadn't quite been able to fulfill his end of the arrangement. The break-in at the clubhouse had been botched when Lucas arrived unexpectedly. Fortunately, the revolver he'd pulled in panic from Lucas's desk drawer hadn't been loaded. Though he loathed the man for kicking him off the Bulldogs and humiliating him in front of the other players, murder was one step beyond his willing capacity. In the end, he'd had to club him with a bat to keep him from learning his identity.

And then there was that cunt in the coffee shop. Bitch! How had she done that? Stabbed him in the leg? He'd had both her arms pinned, he was sure of it. Or maybe he'd let one go. He wasn't sure. But where'd that knife come from? He hadn't seen anything on the counter except a bunch of pots. And then a searing pain in his right thigh. Goddamn it! That bitch was going to pay!

Still, that unfortunate mistake hadn't prevented him from slipping the little metal toy into her apron. Or, from sliding his hand down between her legs while he was there. A perk of the job, right? Hopefully, Maddocks would appreciate what he'd accomplished and ignore the fact that he might have made the whole episode a bigger issue than it was supposed to be. The man had promised him quite a bit of money for delivering that toy truck into her apron, money that he needed.

Checking to be sure he had the right address, he took one last mouthful of the syrupy medication before knocking on the door. Slipping the bottle back into his pocket, he pulled out his pocket watch and checked the time. Maddock had told him on no account should he arrive, or even be in the neighborhood, before 7:30. And on no account should he be later than 9:00. He had no idea why the time was so important and didn't dare ask. It had been nearly a week since his failed attack on that bitch in the coffee shop, and he couldn't afford to irritate Maddocks any further. The watch read 8:22, which Miller took to be just about perfect, so he knocked on the door.

Thirty seconds passed. Then forty.

A full minute passed. He was just about to knock again, when the door swung back to reveal Maddocks standing there in a plain white t-shirt under an ordinary pair of workman's overalls, both covered in dirt. Miller had never seen the man in anything but proper and immaculate dress clothes and couldn't grasp why he'd be dressed the way he was.

Neither of them said anything for several seconds, putting Miller on edge. When he could stand the awkwardness no longer, he decided to initiate the conversation.

"I figured this was okay. You know. The time?" It wasn't much, but it gave him a tiny sense of control, even as his head was now starting to register the effects of Mrs. Winslow's potion. He pulled out his watch again and held it out for Maddocks to verify. "You said not before—"

"Yes," Maddocks broke in, "not on any account before 7:30, and no later than 9:00. Exactly. Why? To be sure Mr. Blaine would not be at home." Maddocks offered no further explanation. "And so here you are. Right on time." He limped aside, gesturing Miller into the house.

"There's some things didn't work out right, but I know what to do," said Miller, stepping into the hallway. "I know how to fix it. If you just—."

Maddocks held up his hand to stop Miller from offering any further explanation. "I had expected a more—let's call it a more professional approach to the task I had assigned."

"I can explain—"

"Please do not. It would most certainly extinguish what little respect for you I still possess or trust that I have in your ability to competently complete the most modest of tasks."

"Let me just tell you—" Miller tried.

Maddocks again held up his hand to interrupt Miller's renewed attempt to explain. "We are now at a crossroads, Mr. Miller. My plan is at a crossroads. From here on, everything must unfold like clockwork. Not a single thing can go wrong, not a single detail can be sacrificed or substituted. Timing is everything, and everything must be precise. Do you hear me, Mr. Miller? Precise!"

Maddocks turned away briefly, then turned back, his anger rising, all pretense at civility flooding away. "This is not some game I'm playing, Mr. Miller! Some silly little joke! That man Blaine left me to die! Do you understand? Die! He left me under a tunnel full of dirt and rock and never gave it a second thought! Not once! And do you know what he left me with?" He pointed to the scar on his face. "This! And this!" he added, pointing to his twisted leg. "This is what he left me with! When it came time to make a choice, he *chose* to let me die! Yes! Die! But —" he said, stabbing a finger into Miller's chest, "I didn't *want* to die, Mr. Miller. I wanted to live! I wanted to live so that I could make my own choice, make Blaine pay, pay for the choice *he* made! And, so I struggled! Oh, yes, I struggled! I clawed, I scratched and scraped, and I made my way out of that godforsaken hell hole! I got out with just one thing in mind! Revenge! I would get revenge if it was the last thing I ever did! I would get revenge and Lucas Blaine would die!" The words came out of Maddocks's mouth in a torrent of spittle. "I want revenge, Mr. Miller! I *need* revenge! And I will have it! Do you understand? I will have it!"

Maddocks stopped abruptly, eyes bulging, his breath coming hard, then looked away. Miller had barely been able to make out what the man was talking about and desperately wanted another swallow of syrup to persuade his heart to stop racing. He opened his mouth to say something, but then decided just to be still and see where Maddocks's fury would go.

Nearly a minute passed. Then, mostly composed once again, Maddocks took one final deep breath and looked back at Miller. "I have waited long and suffered greatly in my efforts to deliver to Mr. Blaine what he so justly deserves, and I will not be denied, Mr. Miller. *Everything. Must. Be. Just. So.* Am I making myself clear?"

Miller could think of nothing to say and so just nodded his head.

"So," Maddocks continued, "it is not in my nature to provide opportunity where lack of ability appears to reign supreme. But, these are extraordinary times. Requiring extraordinary efforts. So," said Maddocks, "I have one further surprise for Mr. Blaine in which you…can play a part. One final message that you, and you alone, can deliver." He swung open the doors to the parlor, and with a broad sweep of his arm, gestured Miller into the room.

Miller smiled, relieved that he was being given yet another chance to prove himself. *I'll get it right this time. One hundred percent right.* He stepped into the room and looked about. Slowly, the smile bled from his face. His muddled brain tried to make sense of what his eyes were seeing, tried to formulate why the room looked the way it did.

There was no furniture anywhere. Not a single piece.

Just piles and piles of dirt.

Suddenly, feeling like a rat trapped in a maze, Frankie Miller came to a simple, inescapable conclusion.

Something was terribly wrong.

SEPTEMBER 11, 1920

Chapter 44

With Peekskill and Poughkeepsie in the rearview mirror, and multiple wins to salve the bumps and bruises of overland travel, both Lucas and Zacharia were feeling pretty content. The seven games away from their own ballpark had provided not only a change of scenery, but an opportunity to refocus on the club's pennant race, which had taken a back seat in importance to all the strange happenings that had been going on over the past couple of weeks. Now on their way home, Lucas felt ready once again to try and decipher the mystery that had wormed its way into every corner of his life. *With a little luck,* he thought, *I might even crack this mystery.*

Rather than take the train to their out-of-town games as they normally did, Lucas had opted to try out one of the new motorbuses that had started to appear on city streets. The New York Suburban Coach Company had offered to accommodate the team in exchange afterwards for a good word to other ball clubs about the convenience and comfort of luxury bus travel. The convenience factor had lived up to the claim, allowing them to drive right up to the ballpark. *Comfort* was a different matter altogether.

"Goddamn it!"

The driver, Carl, shouted aloud after every major bump, and muttered under his breath to accommodate the minor ones. "What the hell…," he said, yanking the steering wheel first left, then right, trying to avoid yet another major depression in the road.

Zach's newspaper bounced up and down in his hands as he tried to analyze the latest baseball results, while Lucas tried to assemble the upcoming afternoon's lineup. Phil Dooley sat at the back of the roof deck, pouting. He'd been so insistent that his ankle was only minutes away from healing that Lucas had decided he'd be more dangerous talking to newspapermen back at the clubhouse than travelling with the team on the road.

After another hour, Lucas thought the team probably needed a stretch, and even though they were only a few miles from being back in the city, he shouted down to Carl to pull over.

Carl edged off the road. As the bus came to a stop, the left rear wheel emitted a great withering gasp. Carl shifted the gears into neutral and shut down the engine.

"Goddamn! I think she's gone flat," he growled. "It's these damn roads, and never mind that I told you so," he said to no one in particular. He climbed down the stairs, opened the door, and stepped out into the still-settling cloud of dust.

Lucas pulled out his pocket watch. *Just about 11:30 a.m.,* he noted. *We'll still be home well before dark.*

"Okay, boys, let's get some stretch into those legs. Looks like we bivouac here for a while."

A mixture of grousing and jesting ensued as the players stepped around Lucas to climb down to the lower level and out the door. Absorbed in his paper, Zach was holding it up to the sky to block the sunlight from his face. A dozen or so errant beams managed to peek through some tiny holes sprinkled about the page.

"Looks like some moths got to that paper before you did, Zach," said Lucas.

"Yeah. Coulda been." Zach turned the page. "Son of a bitch. Babe hit his forty-eighth yesterday." He read a bit more. "Right in the first inning, over the right-field fence."

Carl called up from the back of the bus. "She's flat, all right. Flatter'n a flapjack. It's gonna take me...maybe an hour or so to fix 'er."

Carl's voice trailed off as he climbed around to the back of the bus to where the toolbox was stored.

Phil still hadn't moved from his seat.

"Phil, go take a walk. Give that foot some exercise."

Phil looked up, the same sullen expression on his face since Lucas had first told him he was benched. "I'm stayin' put. She's sore as hell, and I ain't gonna move if I don't have to." He shuffled in his seat and turned to stare off into the woods.

"Zach, c'mon," Lucas said. "Let's you and me look over the lineup together. I think we should sub Harrington for Briggs in right."

"Sure," Zach offered, folding his paper and tucking it under his arm.

They climbed down out of the bus and meandered over to a couple of stumps that had at one time supported a pair of majestic oaks.

Sitting down, Zach started. "Boss, as soon as we're back from bein' on the road, I'm gonna chase down that Mullan guy."

Lucas had to think for a moment. "Mullan? You mean the guy that delivers the ice?"

"That's him. This whole icepick thing's been botherin' me. I think it's pointin' his way. Time we find out for sure."

Right now, I'd like to know anything for sure, thought Lucas. "Yeah, okay. You do that. But right now, let's concentrate on the next game."

"Sure," said Zach, and the two of them huddled over the lineup card. When they'd finished, Zach went back to his newspaper.

"Chicago's facing a grand jury next week," he said. "Serves 'em right, though. Throwin' the World Series and all. Here, look," he said, holding the paper up for Lucas to read. Sunlight streamed through the back side of the previous page.

"Zach, let me see that a second." Lucas took the paper from him and held it up to the sky. The holes appeared in no particular order, but they weren't just a flaw either. They were perfect little round circles.

Same kind of thing our intelligence unit did during the war.

He could remember painstakingly sticking a pin under individual letters in a newspaper to spell out a coded message. He turned the page over, running his fingers over it to see if he could find where the first letter might be.

"What is it, boss?"

"Not sure. Might be nothing. Maybe a message. These holes? If I'm right, each one corresponds to a letter. You know. Put the letters together, you make a word. Put some words together, you got a message. Just like we used to send secret messages during the war. But why are they in your paper is what I'm wondering. You picked this up this morning?"

"In the hotel. Some kid handed it to me."

"What do you mean?"

"We was gettin' ready to leave, and some kid runs up and hands it to me. Says you gave it to him to give to me."

"Some kid did that?"

"Never thought anything about it. 'Cept what were *you* gonna read on the bus?" Zach grinned.

Lucas looked at Zach, puzzled. "You never told me."

"Figured you must know. Since yer the one what gave it to me."

"This kid. He say anything else?"

"Nope. Just handed it to me, said you told him to give it to me and then took off."

Lucas stared at Zacharia for a moment, his mind churning. "I need to find where this message or whatever it is starts," he said, running his fingers over the page again. "Copy this down, yeah?"

Zach took a pencil out of his pocket and turned the lineup card over. "Sure. Go ahead."

"Here. I think it starts here." Lucas peered closely at the first pinhole. "'L.'"

"'L.' Got it."

"Hold on a minute. There's an 'I' before the 'L.'"

Zach made the correction and sat waiting for the next letter.

Continuing to work his fingers across the page, Lucas tried to make sense of why there would be a coded message in Zach's newspaper. A joke, maybe? One of the other players? Or maybe it wasn't a message at all. Maybe no connection at all to Zach, to the bus, the players, or anything connected to the team. "'C,'" added Lucas, having already called out a half a dozen or so other letters.

"I need a bit of help," Carl shouted. He had emerged from around the back of the bus, looking dirty and frustrated. "Get me one of those mittheads back here, would ya?"

Lucas didn't want to put the paper down and just shouted back, "Find someone, Carl, I'm kinda pinned down here."

When he couldn't find any more holes, he turned to Zach. "What have we got?"

Zach showed him the letters he'd written down: IILL-RINRNINGCOLS. "Looks like...looks like shit, boss! I can't really make anything out." Zach screwed up his face. "If that's a message...I dunno. Doesn't make any sense to me."

Lucas felt rusty. He'd probably gone too fast, been too sloppy. "I must have missed some letters." He handed the card back to Zach and returned to the newspaper, steadying his search. "Hold it, here's another one." Within a couple of minutes, he'd found three more letters.

"What have we got now?"

Zach showed him the card. It now read: ITWILLRAINRN-INGCOLS.

"I think it's tryin' to say it's gonna rain." Zach looked up at the dazzling blue sky, shielding his face from the sun. "Beats the hell out of me."

Lucas looked at the letters and agreed. "Yeah, something. But rain what?" He scanned the newspaper once more, spotted another letter where the pinhole had been less precise and the ink above it was faded just a bit. "I think I've got a 'B.'"

"Where? At the end?"

"No, right after 'rain.'"

Zach inserted the letter and turned the notecard back over to Lucas.

And there it was.

"Son of a bitch," mumbled Lucas.

Zach looked at it too. "Son of a bitch," he agreed.

Chapter 45

"Everybody, move away! Move away from the bus now! Zach, get those guys back! Way back!"

Lucas ran in the opposite direction from Zach, pushing players farther away from the hobbled vehicle. He wasn't sure why he was doing this, but when his gut spoke, he listened, just as he had all through the war. All except once. And that singular omission was the one he would regret forever, having left him with a lifelong token of another country's ungratefulness for Lucas having entered the war.

"Carl!" Lucas shouted. "Get away from the bus!"

Carl, still occupied with changing the tire, had either not heard or had decided to ignore Lucas. Lucas ran up and grabbed the man's arm and started to drag him away.

"What the hell!" Carl shouted, pulling his arm free. "That tire ain't fixed yet. Lemme go!"

"I'm going to do that, Carl, but for now," Lucas added, grabbing Carl's arm once again, "I need you to move back from this bus. Fast! That tire's just going to have to stay unfixed until I figure out what's going on."

Carl continued to grumble, but Lucas ignored him and turned away to make sure that everyone was now well clear of the bus.

Zach darted over next to him, pointing to the lineup card in Lucas's hand that held the cryptic message that he'd written down. "You think that really means something, boss?"

Lucas looked at the letters that Zach had written down: IT-WILLRAINBRNINGCOLS. Even with two letters still missing, it was clear the message was an omen. But an omen about what, Lucas had no idea.

"I don't know. But I need time to think. I need time..." Lucas turned back to the bus. "Where's Phil?"

Zach looked at Lucas, then back at the bus. Still sitting atop the upper deck, Phil had fallen asleep. And now Carl was on his way back to the bus, still holding the tire wrench.

"Jesus. Get Carl! I'll get Phil!"

But before either could move, a thunderous roar erupted across the field, knocking them instantly to the ground. An angry cloud of metal fragments, glass shards, and horsehair-filled seating engulfed in flames exploded in all directions around them.

Lucas blinked up at the smoke-filled sky, struggling to understand how, moments ago, he was forty miles from Manhattan and now he lay shocked and confused on a battlefield in Belgium. Instinct kicked in, and his fingers clawed the ground, desperately trying to locate his M1917 Enfield. Instead, he found a hand with no arm.

It took him a few moments to realize he'd plunged into one of his wartime hallucinations again, and that the hand was Carl's, the driver's bloody fingers still grasping a large, twisted wrench. He propped himself up on one arm and looked around. Most of the players lay on the ground, struggling to get up and wiping away bits of debris. Zach was stumbling to his feet, hands holding his head, but aside from a few bloody scrapes, no obvious sign of a critical injury. Smoke from the explosion wafted over the field and little fires burned the dry summer grass in a dozen different spots.

Struggling to his feet, Lucas could see Carl's body about twenty feet away. No arm attached.

The back of the bus had been blown right off, leaving an ugly gash where the last two rows of seats had been. There was no trace of Phil, and Lucas realized that looking for one made no sense at all. Anything left would be unrecognizable.

The other players were now mostly clambering back up onto their feet, smothering the remaining fires or helping other players to get up.

Lucas looked down at his hand. The lineup card on which Zach had written down the fateful letters was still clutched tightly between his fingers. He lifted the card to his face. ITWILLRAINRNINGCOLS. The message was now clear. IT WILL RAIN BURNING COALS. He hadn't needed the missing letters to interpret the essence of the message. His gut had done the rest.

Burning coals had indeed rained down on him. And everyone else.

But why? And who? Nothing made any sense.

Except that this was now war.

And if it was war that this person, this threat, this enigma wanted, it was war he was going to get.

Just as soon as Lucas could determine who *he* was.

Western Front
November 1917

Chapter 46

"How are we doing today, Lieutenant Blaine?"

Lucas pulled at his right foot with all his might but couldn't free it from the knee-deep muddy quagmire that was determined to swallow him up forever. His left foot was stuck just as quick. The harder he struggled, the firmer the mud tugged, insisting it was in charge. Repeated shell bursts kept up a dull, repetitive thumping sound, as constant as a heartbeat. Twenty yards in front of him, ten—no, it had to be more, many more, maybe thirty of even fifty German soldiers, he couldn't really say—were charging directly at him, bayonets fixed and ready, the sun glinting off them, and, and...pretty...very pretty. Like candlesticks. No, not candlesticks. More like icicles. Yes, that was it. Icicles. Sharp as a tiger's tooth, pointing right at him. And sparkling like—like jewels, and...

"Come now, Lieutenant, you can't sleep forever," said a second voice, this time a male. "We've got a war to fight after all. Nurse Cairns here needs to change that dressing."

The big German infantryman with the wide toothy grin was looking straight at Lucas and clearly speaking English, but no words were coming from his mouth, and he wasn't carrying any candlesticks or icicles or bayonets or anything else.

Lucas tugged on his right leg with all his might, suddenly popping it free of the enveloping mud.

"That's better," said the nurse. "Now try and get your other eye open for us," she added, as she continued tucking in the sheets tight around both of Lucas's knees.

His left eye pulsed about under the lid, finally managing to pry itself open. A female figure in blue, her face completely surrounded by swirling white clouds, smiled back at him. Lucas guessed it to be an angel.

"There we are!" said the angel. "All ready to join us again? I'm Nursing Sister Cairns."

Lucas's lips pried themselves apart. "I was expecting red," he managed to mumble.

"What? Ah, yes! Of course! The Red Cross. But I'm with the Canadian contingent, you see, and we're called Nursing Sisters. Or Bluebirds, if you like. Because of the uniform."

Lucas could see now that his angel was quite mortal, neatly dressed in a bright-blue uniform covered in a long white tunic, a starched white veil flowing down over her hair onto her shoulders, encircling her face.

"Nasty little cut, Lieutenant," said the male voice that Lucas now realized belonged to a doctor, "but nothing that will keep the ladies from enjoying the bits that still work, if you catch my drift!" The doctor held a large hypodermic needle up to the light. He leaned in close to Lucas's face. "You do catch my drift, Lieutenant?" he prompted, then winked and offered a conspiratorial smile to Nursing

Sister Cairns, who smiled politely, then turned and rolled her eyes as she went back to her job. "We'll have you back at the front in no time!"

The doctor leaned over Lucas and seemed to be adjusting the sheets when he abruptly rolled Lucas onto his side and jabbed him in the right buttock. Lucas winced and watched as the doctor withdrew the now empty hypodermic.

Nursing Sister Cairns pulled the sheet up over Lucas's chest and arranged his arms over the top.

Realizing he'd just been given an injection of some sort, Lucas began to decipher where he was and how he'd gotten there. Though he thought he could hear the sound of mortars far off in the distance, he realized that he was now most likely at a casualty clearing station safely away from the front lines.

His head ached in rhythmic thumps, which he guessed was the result of the chloroform they would have used to anesthetize him. He could hear the doctor rattle on, but his mind begged to wander back to what had happened. Slowly, his memory clicked into gear, his eyes drooped shut, and the events of the previous morning came back to life.

The company had successfully advanced out of their trench, and he could see himself dashing across the choppy ground toward the enemy line. Far ahead, through the smoke and detritus of previous engagements, he could see the Germans coming out of their trenches, the two sides irrevocably headed for collision. There was a shell hole and some other men, he remembered that. But they were his men. And they were all okay. Except for Thompson. He'd had half his body blown away.

Then he'd left that shell hole and fallen into another. And then…and then…

"I think we're on top of the infection, Lieutenant, but we'll have to leave any further treatment to those at base hospital. I'm afraid we've got a full house here to deal with."

The doctor's words registered, but Lucas couldn't hang on to them.

There was a second shell hole.

Yes, he remembered it now.

He was trying to reload when a German soldier had knocked his rifle out of his hands and then aimed his own gun at Lucas. But it hadn't fired, and he'd... What had happened next?

"I'm afraid that hand is no longer going to be of any use, Lieutenant. Though the good news is, we won't have to amputate."

His hand.

Lucas opened his eyes and peered down to where his left hand lay wrapped in a massive swath of bandage. He blinked, and his left hand glided over the bass keys of a piano, adding depth and nuance to a piano concerto by Chopin. He raised his hand from the keyboard, admiring the way the skin wrapped smoothly over his strong, supple bones as a razor-sharp sword neatly skewered the hand through the middle of his palm. Blood gushed as if from a fountain, the hand crumbling and disintegrating into a squirming ball of worms before finally erupting into a fiery ball of flames.

Lucas snapped out of the reverie and stared down at this hand. Not bleeding. Bandaged. Still.

The German's gun had misfired, and he'd immediately thrust his saw-bladed bayonet toward Lucas's chest.

Instinctively, Lucas had thrown up his left hand to block it, but it was no match for the finely honed edge of the bayonet, which slid neatly through his palm like butter. The German had tried for a second stab, but something had stopped him. What was it that had stopped him?

"I said, 'your head,' Lieutenant. How's your head?" Nursing Sister Cairns hovered just slightly above his face, an island of calm in a sea of madness.

That was it.

The German's head had exploded, shattered into a hundred pieces, and his body had fallen on top of Lucas.

"I expect it hurts like hell," said the doctor.

"Like hell," mumbled Lucas. He could remember pushing the dead soldier off, but then there was a second man looming over him. And then—nothing. His memory came to a dead end.

"Right. So, listen, old boy, you won't be carrying a rifle or anything much for a while, but this bloody war is a long way from being over. They'll find something for you to do, you may depend on it," he said, writing something on what Lucas thought must be his medical chart. "I've got to move on now, but they'll ship you out to the base hospital soon. Once you've recovered sufficiently, it's back to the front, I expect. In the meantime, Nursing Sister Cairns will be making rounds. You call her if the pain gets too unbearable."

He tapped his pencil once to his forehead by way of salute and headed off down the row of cots, stopping here and there to have a word with one or another of the newly wounded.

"How did I get here?" Lucas asked the nurse.

"I couldn't really say, sir, but most likely the same way everyone does. Field ambulance to a dressing station and then here."

"No, I mean—what happened out there? I thought I was done for. There was a man…"

"Oh, yes, that. The one who saved you." Nurse Cairns started to blush. "A very nice gentlemen. Very…"

The nurse blushed again, realizing she was straying too far.

"He was somewhere about earlier. I'll go see if he's still here, *though I expect he's had to go back to the front." She left the bedside and wandered out through the front of the tent.*

Lucas closed his eyes again and tried to conjure a picture of the man who had stood over him in that shell hole. Nothing came to him. Despite the throbbing pain in his head, he felt like he might just slip under again, when he heard someone very close by clear his throat. Lucas opened his eyes. Standing at attention within arm's reach was a very large man with neatly cropped, reddish-brown hair, dressed in a Canadian Expeditionary Force uniform.

"Sir."

It took a few moments before Lucas found the words. "At ease, soldier."

"Yes, sir. Thank you, sir."

"You're the one who saved me from that Bosch wanting to slice my head off."

"I was, sir."

"Well, I'm truly grateful." Lucas closed his eyes. "Truly grateful."

"Very good, sir."

"What's your name, soldier?"

"Tucker, sir. Corporal Zacharia V. Tucker."

SEPTEMBER 12, 1920
Bronx, New York

Chapter 47

Hurrying along the street, Cian kept his head down, making eye contact with no one. Light from the streetlamps was ample enough, as long as he stayed on a main thoroughfare, but he knew that once he reached Mullan's flat, he'd have to negotiate the fire escape that was down the alley and in near total darkness in order to reach the tiny room that Mullan rented on the third floor.

Thoughts of his confrontation with Mullan came flooding back. He'd left him lying in the alley behind O'Farrell's Ice Making Company, bleeding profusely from the head. He'd wondered if he'd killed him. Early the next morning, more panicky still, he'd grabbed a copy of the *New York Tribune* and scoured all twenty pages for any article suggesting that Mullan's body had been recovered. Nothing. Desperately wanting to make everything look as normal as possible, he'd gone back to work, sneaking a quick look into the alley before clocking in. Mullan's body was no longer there. Whether or not it was in the morgue or somewhere else, Cian had no idea. He'd spent all day looking over his shoulder, listening for bootsteps, evading O'Farrell's enquiries about Mullan's whereabouts, while catastrophic imaginings shredded his nerves into tiny remnants of uselessness. Still nothing materialized. He'd spent the afternoon delivering ice and evading shadows—Mullan's face in every doorway, every window.

More than a week had passed, and Cian felt that he could finally make his move.

Mullan hadn't had the money from the robbery on him when Cian checked his pockets in the alley after smashing him on the head with that wooden pole. So, where was it? Mullan lived in a very limited world. He worked. He slept in a tiny room that had been carved out of a larger apartment in a tenement. He drank. Usually at the same two spots. The most logical place for him to hide something was in his apartment, which was where Cian was now headed. While he regretted having attacked Mullan, maybe even killed him, the fact remained that 704 dollars was still lying around somewhere. And as far as Cian knew, besides Mullan, he was the only one who knew that it was out there. And he very much intended to be the one to retrieve it.

As he approached the tenement, he slowed his pace so as not to draw any attention. He turned down the alley and headed in the general direction of the fire escape. Several oil lanterns shed more light along the narrow passageway than Cian had been expecting, but cast no moving shadows other than his own. Reaching the foot of the dangling metal stairs, he was about to take a step up when he heard a noise. He stood completely still, trying to determine from which direction the noise had come.

A scratchy voice called out. "'For all have sinned and fall short of the Glory of God!'"

Cian swung around and spotted a pair of legs sprawled out from behind one of the many empty crates that were stacked near the wall of the building. He took a step in that direction and stopped. Another man sat propped against a second crate about six feet away, eyes closed, an empty bottle that had recently held some form of bootleg spirits resting against his torn boot.

The first man sat up and wagged a dirty, crooked finger vaguely in Cian's direction. "'I warn you, those that live like this will not inherit the kingdom of God!'" he crowed, then broke into spasms of irregular laughter.

Cian relaxed. Neither man seemed conscious of his presence.

He was about to turn back to the fire escape when the second man shook himself awake. "'Whoever conceals their sins does not prosper,'" he blurted out to no one in particular. "'But the one who confesses and renounces them finds...finds mercy!'"

Eying first one and then the other, Cian shook his head, concluding they were no threat to his undertaking. He turned back toward the fire escape, once again ready to continue his task.

"'He who is tormented by the guilt of *murder*...will seek refuge in the grave!'"

Through the gloom, Cian could see that the first man was now suddenly looking directly at him, and the man's use of the word *murder* rattled him.

Am I now a murderer as well as a thief? How has my life suddenly gone so wrong?

The second man, having rolled onto his knees, now also looked straight at Cian. "Proverbs 28:17. And may God be our witness, we have surely murdered this bottle," he cackled, holding up the empty flask before tossing it to the ground. His smile revealed a mouth of black, broken, and missing teeth. "Can you spare…," he started, then frowned, appearing to have to have lost what track his train of thought had been running on. He tried again. "Friend, can you spare a few miserable cents for two of God's children?"

"From the looks of it, friend, God's not lookin' to spare you," mumbled Cian. Once again, he started toward the fire escape.

"'Can the blind lead the blind? Will they not both fall into a pit?'" yelled the first man, rising shakily to his feet. "'If your enemy is hungry, feed him; if he is thirsty, give him something to drink!'" he screeched, his voice gaining strength with every word echoing off the surrounding walls.

Cian hastily stepped toward the man, one hand trying to shush him quiet, the other frantically scrounging around in his pants pocket for a coin. "Keep quiet, old man! You're waking the dead." *Which might be me if you keep up this bloody noise.* "Here," he said, "be at peace," and he threw a nickel onto the ground in front of the man.

Unsure of what had just come his way, the man looked down at the coin on the ground but made no attempt to retrieve it. "Praise be to the God and Father of our Lord Jesus Christ!" And with that, he crumbled back down onto his knees, and then fell face first into the dirt.

The second man stumbled over and picked up the coin, then stumbled away toward the street, chattering to himself.

Cian waited a few tense moments to see if the commotion had roused any onlookers, but as was so often the case, people were not inclined to get involved. He could hear voices in the apartments above him calling to one another, but none seemed to register the slightest interest in Cian or his new companions.

Satisfied that nobody was watching, Cian grabbed onto the fire escape handrail and pulled himself up the two and a half feet to the first step. As he climbed higher, the light from the oil lanterns faded away.

Arriving at the landing outside what he knew to be Mullan's window, he took a few moments to catch his breath. Still nothing below that rattled Cian's relative sense of safety. His plan was starting to feel like it would all work out. Placing his hands underneath the wooden crossbar, he urged the window upward. Offering only the barest resistance, it creaked open. A draft of foul air immediately drifted out, and Cian instinctively drew back, waving it away from the front of his face. Clearly, Mullan had not emptied the chamber pot for a day or two. Cian turned his head to breathe in some fresh air, and after a few more seconds, he poked his head tentatively in through the window. He wasn't expecting anyone to be there, but at the same time, he wasn't at all sure where Mullan was.

Glancing around, and allowing his eyes to adjust to the darkness, Cian felt confident that there was no one within. Nerves taut, he pushed his body in through the window and collapsed on the floor inside. Breathing heavily, more from anxiety than exertion, he did a quick survey of the room. A shred of what was once an oriental carpet lay prisoner under a small table and chair on one side of the room, a tired and stained mattress partially covered in a dirty and well-used bed sheet on the other. In the center sat a wheezy-looking bergère-style chair that had once been overstuffed and now sprang tufts of horsehair from multiple rips in the fabric. And in another corner rested several wooden boxes that appeared to hold Mullan's few personal possessions.

The table offered no hiding spot that Cian could imagine. But not wanting to assume himself out of finding the money, he crawled underneath to see if it had somehow been tucked away there. The room was so dark he could barely see anything and had to resort to feeling his way along the undersides and down the legs. Nothing came of it except a handful of dust.

He moved over to the mattress and yanked the bedsheet off, tossing it in a pile in the corner. He then lifted the mattress completely off the floor and ran his hand underneath. Nothing.

As he shuffled over to the chair, he inadvertently knocked over the chamber pot, sending the contents pouring out into the room. "Shit!" he spat, louder than he intended. Heart pounding, he stood perfectly still to determine if the noise had alerted any nearby resident. Babies cried, spouses yelled, lovers groaned, and children laughed, but no alarms were raised.

Avoiding the spilled contents from the chamber pot, Cian knelt down onto the floor and began probing the various rips in the fabric with his fingers. On the third try, he found what he'd been expecting.

What he wasn't expecting was the knock at the door.

Cian's head snapped upright, his brain sifting through every possible meaning for this totally incongruous occurrence. He cocked his head, imploring his ears to work harder, but there were no further sounds.

Until the second knock.

Without thinking, Cian jammed the money back into the chair as quickly and as quietly as he could. Then, stepping gingerly over the spilled chamber pot contents, he tiptoed toward the window, the fear making his legs feel like they were plunging through a vat of molasses. On the third step, the floorboard let out a resentful creak, and Cian froze. For about three seconds. Right up until two bullets from a Smith & Wesson .38 special exploded through the door, sending a shower of slivers across the room, narrowly missing him.

The door clattered loudly, then swung open, and three men pushed their way inside. Which Cian didn't witness, as he was already out the window and sprinting down the fire escape.

Climbing and slipping, Cian fled down the fire escape as fast as he could. Above, he could hear the three men trying to clamber out the window.

With only feet to go and freedom beckoning, Cian fell to the ground. He picked himself up and took one hopeful stride before two pair of arms wrapped around his neck and waist and threw him face-first to the ground.

He tried to lift his face to see who it was, but a heavy hand ground his face into the dirt.

From behind the crates, he heard a shuffling. And then a voice.

"'Do not take revenge, my dear friends,'" shouted the familiar voice, loud and clear, "'but leave room for God's wrath, for it is written…'" The man sputtered, searching for the next line. "What? Um…oh, yes…God's wrath…'for it is written,'" Another pause. Then a self-conscious chuckle. "Damnation! What was it? Oh…oh, yes! 'For it is written,'" and then the man was mute.

Cian felt his own lips move. "'Vengeance is mine…'"

A punch to the back of his head knocked Cian unconsciousness.

September 13, 1920

Chapter 48

The last thing Cian could remember before he passed out was having his face squashed hard into the dirt in the alley behind Mullan's rooming house. How different that dirt smelled from the freshly tilled soil on his parents' small farm back in Ireland. No smell of sheep or cattle. No smell of the horses he used to ride down by the creek that ran through the back of the property. No smell of carrots or potatoes or turnips that grew every summer in the carefully tilled garden out by the barn. Or of the gorse- and reed-filled meadows where Cian loved to play. Where he would lie on his back and pretend he could make the clouds change shape just by pointing up to the sky. No comforting smells at all. Just dirt. Dirt laced with urine and boot leather and tobacco and coal dust and cheap bathtub gin and a hundred other odors that made up the city's essence.

And now, with his brain struggling to emerge into consciousness, there was a new dirt smell. Damp, fetid, menacing. A smell of intangible danger. A smell he hadn't yet been able to fully absorb.

He tried to open the one eye that seemed willing to respond. A single oil lantern dangling from a nail cast shapes and shadows across the room, triggering sensations of terror and splintered memories of being dragged down a flight of stairs, stripped naked, tied to a chair, and beaten senseless. And then beaten again. And maybe again, he couldn't remember.

His was still sitting in that chair, still naked. Still bound with heavy sisal rope that dug into his skin whenever he tried to move. Risking another rope burn, Cian twisted his head away from the light and closed his good eye, trying to mask the images conjured up by his brain. The momentary squint about the room had confirmed his worst fears.

He now did remember where he was. Exactly. And why he didn't want to be there.

But before...

What had happened before?

He was at Mullan's, he remembered that much. And then... what? Some part of his brain begged for serenity. Tranquility. Anonymity. But he forced himself to remain focused, his memory sneaking out from somewhere deep within his brain like a cat stalking a wounded sparrow. Mullan. Why had he gone there? He hadn't been looking for Mullan, didn't want to bump into Mullan. Ah. Of course. The money. He had guessed that Mullan had left the money in his room, the only realistic place it could be. It certainly wasn't on him when Cian had hit him with the...

He didn't want to think about it.

Okay. What then? The money. Yes, yes, the money. He'd found it. But where had he put it?

A thunderous explosion, and a hurricane of splinters hitting him in the calves and buttocks, practically heaving him out the window headfirst. He could remember that. Then he was on the ground in the alley and someone was on top of him. Or two someones. And a voice. There was a voice calling to him. And he had called back. What was it? Something about vengeance.

Then there was a blow to his head, and he was out cold, waking up in this dark, dank room and trying to remember the rest of it. And now he mostly could.

Four of Rosie's men had put him into a truck and driven him here. He had recognized Chester and that other guy, the big guy who always scared him when he delivered ice to Rosie's place. Then they had dragged him down into this room, this basement with the dirt walls. He remembered them stripping him naked and tying him to the very chair he was now sitting in, taking turns beating him, peppering him with questions and then beating him again until he fell unconscious.

He hadn't told them anything except Mullan's name. They kept asking about the money. And at first, Cian didn't know what they were even talking about. But then it came to him. It was the money he and Mullan had stolen from that bookie out back of the Sixty-Six, and they wanted that money back. Mullan had beaten the bookie pretty badly, and Cian had tried to get him to stop, pleaded with him to stop, but he'd never had the chance to explain that to Rosie's men before they'd beaten him unconscious. And they still wanted the money.

Despite his halting awareness, Cian knew if he told them where the money was, he wouldn't be getting out of the basement alive. He had one card to play, and he needed it to deliver a winning hand.

Several voices filtered down through the ceiling. Cian wriggled against the ropes, which only served to force them deeper into his skin. At the top of the stairs, a door opened, and footsteps started weaving their way down to where Cian sat. With no other plan presenting itself, Cian closed his eyes and tried to appear unconscious.

"Damn fool," said one of the voices. "Gimme that."

Within seconds, a cascade of icy-cold water slammed into Cian's face, and despite his best efforts to appear lifeless, he gasped, spit, and choked himself into full wakefulness.

"Sit up," barked one of the voices. Cian recognized it as Chester's, but couldn't quite imagine how much more sitting up he could do. He shuffled in the chair so as to give the impression of cooperation.

"Where is *my* money?" The female voice startled Cian, and he forced open both eyes to see Queen Rosie standing directly in front of him. She looked calm but determined.

"I—I..." Cian shook his head, trying to think of what to say.

Rosie shifted her shotgun so that it rested in the crook of her left arm. "Now, whatever you is about to say, don't make it, 'I don't got your money, Queen Rosie.' 'Cause I know you do got it."

Cian started to whimper. "I don't got it, Queen Rosie, and that's sure. But—but, I do know whereabouts it be! You take me outta here, and I'll show you, I'll show you exactly where it is."

"Why don't I shoot you right here?"

"Well, that—that's—I know that's what you might want to do, but if you just untie me here and, please, don't shoot me, Queen Rosie, because then I can't show you where your money is, but if you let me show you, I can show you, sure."

Rosie thought about it for a few seconds and then lifted her shotgun and aimed it right at Cian's head.

Cian squeezed his eyes closed. "No, no, no, please, please, I can show you, I can show you where the money is!" He willed himself to think harder, to think of some way to get Rosie to put her gun away and lead him out of the basement where he might be able to think of a way to escape. "And, and, and there might even be some other money there! I mean, yeah, uh-huh, I remember him sayin' so. Sayin' there's some other money there, he told me that. There's some other money, a lot of money, and, and you could have it all!"

Once again, Rosie lowered her Fox Sterlingworth. She took a step closer to Cian, tipping her head first to one side, then to the other, like she was examining a spider inching up the wall, trying to decide whether or not to squash it.

Sensing an opening, Cian hurried on. "A lot of money, as I remember it, and that's for sure. But I'll have to show you. You can't find it on your own. It's hid pretty good, yeah?"

"Where you say this money's at?" squinted Rosie.

"Well, it's where yer boys was at, where they come across me, but—but—it's hid real good, and I can show you, but you got to take me there, 'cause you ain't gonna find it on yer own."

"So, y'er sayin'…it's back where Percy caught you sneakin' out the window?"

"Yes, ma'am, that's the place. That's the very place," Cian nodded vigorously.

"That little bitty place?" said Percy, secretly fingering the roll of bills wedged deep within his pocket that he'd pulled from Mullan's overstuffed chair. "We could take that apart inside out in about five minutes, Queen Rosie. We don't need this fool."

"Sure, yeah, the place, it's small," agreed Cian, jumping in. "I know that, but you see, the hidin' place where this money's at, well, it's hid real good, you won't find it on yer own. And if Mullan gets back there before I gets it for ya…then that's gone, for sure. But I know where it is, I can—"

"Mullan?" said Rosie, jumping in. "That the other guy's name? Mullan?"

"That other guy?" said Cian, suddenly lost in his own story.

"That guy what beat up my boy, Tubby, out behind that blind pig. Name of Mullan?"

"That's what he called him," Chester nodded.

It took barely a second for Cian to get back on track. "That's him!" he yelped. "He beat up yer boy real bad, and I tol' him to stop, I tol' him ten times, don't beat that colored man no more, le's just take the money and go. But Mullan, he just keeps beatin' and beatin'—"

"Let me just do some beatin' right now, Queen Rosie," interrupted Percy. "We don't need this fool anymore."

"Maybe." Rosie chewed at her lower lip for a few seconds. "Hmph," she decided finally and turned to Percy. "You just beatin' him 'til he's dead ain't gonna get my money back." Deep wrinkles crept across her brow as she struggled to decide on the right course of action. "Percy, you, Chester, me, and this fool gonna go back to that room and get my money. An' if it ain't there, I'm gonna shoot this guy right on the spot." *Which I might do anyway*. "Go get the truck. Let's see what's hid back at that roomin' house."

Rosie shot Cian a final look of disgust.

"And why he's all naked and all? That little white thing sneakin' out between his legs? That ain't no way to treat a lady! Git him dressed, you hear, and let's get on with this."

And with that, she turned on her heel and strode up the stairs.

Cian's muscles eased into the ropes that threatened to cut him to pieces.

His plan to delay the threat on his life had worked.

Now all he needed was a plan to postpone it indefinitely.

Chapter 49

A new moon provided Rosie and her men the comfort of darkness as they waited in the alley behind Mullan's rooming house. Satisfied that all was quiet, they made their way around to the front door.

"Chester, wait yourself here by the truck while we look upstairs," Rosie ordered. "And," she added, pointing to Cian, "you see this bastard come down these steps without us, you shoot him dead. I ain't done with him."

"Yes, ma'am," Chester replied.

"And, you hear anything not right, you come up on the double."

"I will do that, yes, ma'am," he nodded.

"Percy, you got that gun of yours?"

"I do, Queen Rosie," he said, pulling the Smith & Wesson .38 from his waistband to prove his readiness.

"Good. Now grab that oil lamp, too. These old buildings ain't generally lit up like the Fourth of July. Now," she said, turning to Cian, "we gonna take those cuffs off you here, and we gonna go get us that money."

"Yes, ma'am. Third floor. Right up on the third floor," he said, holding out his hands so that Percy could remove the cuffs.

Together, they started up the stone steps.

"Hold on just a second!" interjected Rosie. "There ain't no one gonna be there, right? You sure about that?"

Cian hesitated. He had no idea if Mullan would be there. He didn't even know if the man was still alive. He hadn't seen him since the afternoon he'd clubbed him on the back of the head out behind O'Farrell's Ice Making Company. "Well, no…that is, I can't say for certain. But I'm pretty sure he's long gone somewhere." Silently, Cian prayed it was true.

"You and him both better hope so. We gonna be sure, though, so we gonna go in quiet. And don't get any ideas about runnin' off, 'cause 'ol Foxy here got a mean way of showin' her disapproval." She gave the gun an appreciative tap on the breach.

Once again, Cian headed toward the entrance. The front door offered no opposition, producing barely a sound as it swung open smoothly. Light from a single gas lamp tried valiantly to brighten the hallway inside the main entrance but struggled to reach the corners, leaving a good portion of the room in shadow. A large, bearded man in torn, dirty overalls over an even dirtier undershirt lay snoring against the wall at the foot of the stairs, sticky drool hanging from his lower lip, an amber bottle that had once contained some sort of spirits overturned by his side. The three of them eased their way past and started upward, Percy and the oil lamp leading the way, the scraped wooden stairs loudly announcing every other step.

On the third-floor landing, Rosie reached out and grabbed Cian by the shoulder.

"Percy gonna take it from here," she whispered. "You take the lamp, so he got his hands free. Stand right over there to the side."

Cian took the lamp from Percy and moved out of the way.

With his pistol held out in front of him, Percy nudged the still-splintered door open just a bit. A quick flick of the eyebrows from Rosie was all the permission he needed to kick it open the rest of the way. He caught the rebounding door with his left foot, and all three of them stood on the edge of silence. A few indistinct noises from around the building drifted into the spaces between them, but no sound or movement could be detected from within the room.

Percy took a small tentative step forward, then turned back once again to check with Rosie. She nodded her approval. About to take a second step, a silvery glint of metal shrieked an emergency warning to Percy's brain. Just half a second too late. An icepick slammed through the front of his skull, killing him instantly. His gun clattered to the floor.

Rosie's face knitted up in surprise. "What the—?"

She rushed forward, her shotgun straight out in front of her. A hand from nowhere reached out and grabbed the barrel, pointing it upward. Instinctively, she pulled the trigger. The gun erupted with a thunderous boom, buckshot smashing into the ceiling, sending a cascade of shattered plaster scattering in every direction. The same hand yanked the shotgun out of Rosie's grasp and sent both her and her prized weapon sprawling to the floor.

Face bruised and still flecked with bits of dried blood, Mullan reached out into the hallway and yanked Cian into the room, violently flinging him into the overstuffed chair that had previously held the stolen money. The oil lamp sailed out of Cian's hand and off into the corner, smashing against the wall and releasing a stream of fiery liquid across the floor.

The distraction caught Mullan off guard. Sensing opportunity, Rosie grabbed for the Fox Sterlingworth, but Mullan slammed one foot down hard on the barrel, trapping Rosie's fingers beneath. Then he brought his other foot down on her ankle. A painful howl flooded from her mouth.

"Ah, so that's no fuckin' way to earn a welcome, now, is it, missy?" he sneered. "You just slide on back across the floor and sit yerself in that chair by the table."

"I can't move," winced Rosie. "I think you broke my ankle." She grabbed her foot and gave it a rub.

"Did I now?" Mullan slammed his foot down on her other leg.

Rosie shrieked in agony. "You mutha—!"

"Fuckin' move!" Mullan barked.

Rosie glared at him, her outrage barely contained as she shuffled awkwardly across the room, and with effort, hauled herself up into a chair, the fire rapidly spreading out behind her.

Mullan grunted. He pushed the door closed, then looked at Cian. "So, Ciany boy, you thought you could go crook on me, did ya? It's the devil who'll make a ladder of yer backbone, you backstabbin' bastard!" Mullan glanced again at the fire and then back to Cian.

"Now listen good, my little ice-makin' friend. We haven't got a lot of time here. Not that I'll miss the place," he added with a scowl as his eyes roamed about the room. "I wants me money back."

"I haven't got it, Mullan, I swear it! It was right here," he cried, pointing to the side of the armchair. "Stuck right in one of those holes there like where you must've put it!"

"Ah, so, 'twas you what broke in here! Ya made a tidy mess of me door, Cian. If we had the time, I'd be makin' ya make it whole."

"No, no, 't'weren't me, Mullan. 'T'was him," said Cian, pointing to the prostrate Percy, the icepick still sticking out of his forehead, a small pool of blood forming under his chin.

"And so now y'er hangin' about good with them muthafuckas, are ya? I shoulda known you was in it together."

"I'm not, no, I—I came to see if you was okay, and—and..."

"Y'er a fuckin' *bréagadóir*," said Mullan.

"No, no! I ain't lyin', Mullan!"

Flames licked up the far wall, feasting on the delicately patterned wallpaper and inching out further from the corner.

"It's right here," coughed Cian, the smoke now beginning to thicken. "I left it right here, I swear! I never took a penny!" he added, fruitlessly poking his fingers into the torn fabric.

"You're a fool and a liar, Cian, but there's nothin' that'd please me more than to blow yer fuckin' brains out. Which is what I'm gonna do if you don't give me that fuckin' money!" he screamed.

A floorboard outside the room creaked. Any other time, it would have raised no eyebrow. But it stood out like a thunderclap, loud and menacing, even amidst the crackle of the fire now threatening to overtake the room. Mullan fell to the floor and grabbed Percy's pistol, then swung around to face the door.

The splintered door burst open. Chester stood, arm outstretched, clutching his pistol chest-high, the smoke now so thick there was nothing but vague shapes in front of him.

"Chester, get back!" screamed Rosie.

But it was too late. He chose to roll the dice and fired two shots where no chest was.

Mullan returned fire with three shots of his own, and Chester collapsed to the ground. Mullan scrambled over to make sure he wasn't getting up.

When he turned back around, Rosie was waiting for him, the shotgun aimed directly at his face. His look of smug satisfaction quickly turned to one of confusion. Then realization. Then terror. Just before she pulled the trigger.

The shotgun roared, and Mullan's body burst open as he blew out the door, a deep red spume of blood tracking his flight.

"Bastard!" she screamed, struggling to locate another round tucked into the front pocket of her dress. But the smoke was now so thick she started to cough, dropping the gun to one side so she could cover her face.

Having now reached the top of the back wall, the fire threatened to bring down the ceiling. Sensing a sliver of opportunity, Cian jumped up from his chair, coughed his way to the door, and turned back to face Rosie.

"Don't leave me here!" she screamed. "My ankle's busted good!" She reached out, grasping for her gun, trying to get up, but quickly collapsed back down. "I can't walk, you hear me? Don't you leave me!"

Cian hesitated, bobbing on unsteady feet, trying to untangle this sudden change of fortune. With a final cough, he turned and ran out the door.

"Muthafucka!" screamed Rosie, lapsing into a coughing fit as the smoke finally began to win out. "You mutha…you…!" But she couldn't find the strength to finish.

She struggled to keep her eyes open, willed them to see. Begged her legs to move. But her body shut down the effort. "Where are you, Foxy?" she whispered, her fingers creeping across the floor, desperately searching for her shotgun. "Come to Rosie, girl! You come on here now!"

With one final effort, she managed to squeeze an eye open. Through the billowing smoke, she thought she could see a large but amorphous figure standing in the doorway. Maybe a man, she couldn't tell. Maybe an angel. *An angel come to get me.* She smiled at the thought as it trickled away.

Seconds later, she felt herself being lifted up and carried, gently and effortlessly, out of the room, the steady, lilting sound of what she was sure were church bells tolling in the distance.

"Wait!" she whispered, her voice choking from the smoke. "Don't leave my Foxy here!"

Then everything went dark.

Chapter 50

The cobblestones crackled and popped like a string of fireworks under the wobbling wheels of the calèche as the pair of dappled grays trotted their way up Tenth Avenue. Every few seconds the coachman, jacket open and flapping in the breeze, cracked his whip over the horses' backs, urging them forward but being careful not to actually hit his prized ponies.

In the carriage, Rosie lay on her back, pressing hard into Zacharia's side. Unnerved by the closeness, he squeezed hard into the far corner, looking like he might push his way right through the side wall. The harder he pushed, the closer Rosie snuggled back. Far behind them, the urgent clanging of a fire engine's warning bells were quickly fading away.

The evening breeze was cool and sweet, slowly diluting the smell of smoke that had permeated their clothes, allowing Zach to mentally rerun the last couple of harrowing hours.

Having tracked down Mullan to his rooming house, Zach

had waited patiently in the front hall, waiting for his chance to search the iceman's room. When Rosie and her entourage had arrived with some white guy in tow, he'd stepped into the hallway shadows and peeked outside through the glass in the front door, trying to better understand what was going on.

While he recognized Rosie as someone Lucas knew, he wasn't at all clear who the white guy was. Or, how he fit into the overall picture. He'd strained to hear what they were talking about but couldn't make it out. When they'd started up the front steps, Zach had grabbed an empty bottle that had been flung into a corner and quickly laid down against the wall at the bottom of the stairs, spitting into his beard and messing his hair and clothes as best he could, hoping he'd be mistaken for just another unlucky victim of the city's illegal liquor business.

Rosie, one of her men, and their captive had stepped right over him. They were up a couple of flights when Zach had heard the gunshot. He was about to race upstairs when another of Rosie's men had come barreling up the front steps, so he'd immediately laid back down. The new guy had leapt over Zach's body and raced up the stairs without even a second glance. Once he'd disappeared around the first turn in the stairwell, Zach had jumped to his feet and started up the stairs, but stopped instantly when he'd heard the shotgun blast.

With the smell of smoke drifting down, he didn't know what to make of the situation but decided he wouldn't find out by standing still. Nearing the third-floor landing, the man who had been Rosie's captive stumbled past Zach, coughing and shouting that somebody needed help. Between the smoke and wanting to know what had happened to Mullan, Zach opted to let the man pass and continued on up to the now blazing room. One look and he could pretty well guess what had happened to both Rosie's bodyguards and Mullan. He also guessed that the body writhing on the floor next to the shotgun must be Rosie. Covering his face with his jacket, he ignored the smoke and flames, dashed into the room, and picked her up, then grabbed the shotgun and carried them both downstairs. As he emerged onto the front doorstep, Rosie lying unconscious in his arms, he spotted and hailed an oversized hackney cab that happened to be passing by. The Negro driver said he knew just where to take her.

The cab took off at a trot, and Zach let out a sigh of relief.

He wasn't sure what to do next, but at least she'd stopped moaning, he thought.

As if on cue, Rosie opened her eyes and looked up at Zach. "Praise the Lord! An angel come to git me!" she murmured, and then lapsed again into unconsciousness.

Zach stared down at her for a few moments, then turned away. "Yeah," he mumbled. "That's me."

A crack of the whip brought Zach back to attention, and he yelled up to the driver. "You sure you know where this place is? This doc? The one that treats coloreds?"

"Yes, sir, I do!" yelled the coachman over his shoulder. "Like my mammy's lap, I do!"

The cab rounded the corner at 126th Street. Dim pools of lamplight opened up the darkness, but shadows still held much of the road hostage, ensuring the cab would find its share of potholes in the uneven cobblestones. Each time the wheels hit a cavity, the driver would bounce up out of his seat and land back down with a thud, while Zach and Rosie were slammed about from side to side in the back. Inevitably, the cab found a hollow that should have been avoided but wasn't. The right front wheel fell in heavily and bounced awkwardly back out. The back wheel then slammed into the hole, cracking apart in two places before collapsing out the other side. The horses, yanked up short, frantically pawed the air and whinnied their fright as the driver was jettisoned onto the backs of both.

Rosie jerked awake as she and Zach were thrown violently into the rear-facing seat in front of them and then off to the side. Each desperately clutched for something that would keep them from falling out of the shattered vehicle, which was now leaning precariously toward the gutter.

"What the hell? Percy? Chester?"

As the cab thudded back down into a more or less upright position, the driver, stunned, shook his head and slid off the backs of the confused and panicked animals, wrestling with the reins to get them under control.

"Whoa up, Sammy! Finster! Settle! Settle down! Easy now! Easy!" he shouted as he brought the two horses under control.

"What the devil is goin'—?" moaned Rosie, looking around. "Where's my shotgun? Where's Foxy?" She groped about on the floor, then realized she wasn't alone. "What the—who the hell are you?" she said, looking at Zach.

"Zacharia V. Tucker, ma'am," Zach replied, as he started to clamber out of the cab. "You took in a little smoke a while back. And I think ya may have hurt your ankle. Maybe both of 'em. I'm trying to get you to a doc. And this man here," he said, pointing to the coachman, "he said he knows where we could go."

"That doc is just two blocks up around the corner," the coachman pitched in. "He'll fix ya right," he added and went back to calming his horses.

"I don't need no doctor," Rosie replied. "I'm just fine," she added,

THE MAN IN THE BLEACHERS

gathering her coat around her. She went to get up and fell back down with a yelp. "Ow! My ankles! I think they's both broke!"

Stepping to the pavement, Zach turned back to Rosie. "Why don't we see what the doc has to say? Won't take but a few minutes."

"I told you, I don't need no doc. I just need…I just…" Rosie slumped back into the seat. Shaking her head, she let out an exhausted sigh. "I suppose a glass of brandy wouldn't hurt."

Zach yanked her out from the cab and slung her over one shoulder, then grabbed the shotgun and slung it over the other.

"What the hell! You put me down, you hear! Put me down right now! This ain't no way to treat a lady!"

Zach ignored her. "Where's this doc at exactly?" he said to the coachman.

The driver sketched out instructions, and within minutes Zach stood at the top of a stairway leading down to a basement apartment. Still holding Rosie, again unconscious, and the gun, he eased his way down the steps and knocked on the door. He could hear shuffling inside, and a man's voice called out, but Zach couldn't make out what he was saying.

Several locks of varying degrees of complexity were snapped and twisted undone until the door finally swung open. A tall, thin, balding colored man of about fifty in a faded yellow cardigan stared out at Zach.

The man looked startled, but finally summoned enough courage to speak. "Uh…yes, sir. Were you looking for someone? I mean, someone you know?"

"If you're the doc, then I'm lookin' for you."

"Well, I am, but…," he said, trying to make out who it was that was draped over Zach's shoulder, "…but I'm—well, that is—it's usually just colored folk that come to call."

"Well," said Zach, wheeling around so that Rosie's unconscious face was now visible, "that's what I got here."

The doctor's eyes widened, and he took an involuntary step backwards, then leaned forward again to get a closer look.

"Do you—I mean…do you know who that is?" the doctor stammered.

Zach hesitated, then turned back around to face the doctor. "Like my mammy's lap, I do."

Chapter 51

When the mantel clock in the living room struck three, Lucas finally gave up trying to fall asleep and sat up on the edge of the bed. Ever since returning from the road trip, he'd been trying to forget about the bomb on the bus, obliterate the memory of the explosion, and deny that Phil Dooley and Carl the bus driver were no longer alive. He'd reasoned with, then urged, then begged his mind to erase all traces of the strange and troubling events that had taken place over the last couple of weeks. But his brain refused to play along, nagging him relentlessly with the growing ugliness of a puzzle that he simply couldn't put together.

He pulled a cigarette from the package on the night table, lit it, then stubbed it out and started pacing.

The bomb on the bus had changed the situation dramatically. Given it an entirely different significance. One of helplessness and terror. Yet, what exactly did it mean? Who would have put it there? When? How? It had to be someone with an extensive knowledge of explosives. Was the intent to kill the entire team? Or just send yet another message? Either way, it had been a risky venture. How could the person be so sure of the outcome? The timing? Or did that person even care? If the bus hadn't stopped for a break, half the team might have been killed.

The mantel clock ticked louder, hounding Lucas to figure it all out. He desperately wanted to, forced himself to think more methodically.

What about the other clues? The telegram, the cat, the spinner toy. Those had all been warnings. He could see that now. All had been sent to alert him to some imminent event. And yet, he hadn't been able to decipher what the warnings foreshadowed. Was that the idea? Had they just been meant as a tease, a private joke that only the sender understood? Or, had Lucas simply not tried hard enough? Did his intelligence training count for nothing? Had his skills become numb, seduced by a lifestyle of comfort and safety? Had they all been exhausted by a world of batting averages, player lineups, and fielding strategies? Suffocated by his all-consuming world of baseball?

He wasn't sure. Willa had told him he was being too hard on himself. That the clues or whatever they were weren't obvious enough. That he needed...what did she say? That he needed to understand what they related to before he'd be able to figure out what they meant. It made sense...of everything he couldn't make sense of.

He clenched his fists, twisted his neck around to work out the knots. He wanted to scream and unleash the frustration that had been building. To spring the trap that was suffocating his reasoning.

He couldn't do it.

Take control of your thinking. Don't let it take control of you.

It all came down to that first clue, he thought. The shovel. That was the most troubling. It didn't seem to relate to anything else. And yet, why was it the first? Shouldn't that have been the key to all the other clues? A shovel was for digging, not much else. But digging what? A garden? Coal? A grave?

Then the canary. Lucas had known immediately it was a message. But what was it trying to convey? And who was it for? Him? Willa? Both?

Thoughts whirled furiously around in his head, like the hands of a clock that had gone out of control.

A clock.

Something about time.

In time? On time? Out of time?

Suddenly, Lucas stopped pacing. What was the time on the toy pocket watch Willa had found in her apron? Twelve-something. No, not twelve. Almost twelve. Yes, that was it. Eleven forty-five.

"Shit!" Lucas muttered angrily.

Just about the exact time the bus had exploded.

The pocket watch and the strange-looking truck that Lucas and Zach thought looked more like a trolley were linked. That much was now clear. But how on earth was he supposed to have figured it out? Figured it out in time?

Lucas chided himself for not seeing it, not making the connection. It was clearly meant as a warning.

No, not a warning. That would only have been obvious to the person who'd sent it. A test of Lucas's skills. A way for the sender to show how clever he was. How much *more* clever than Lucas.

Damn it!

He is cleverer!

Lucas snatched up the clock from the mantel and stared at it, his brain starting to register the fatigue. The strain.

The numbers running around the face sagged into an awkward, penitent smile, the face of a child caught sneaking an extra cookie from the pantry.

Lucas shook the clock, trying to make it behave, but it just ticked louder, the smile morphing into an ugly, mocking, wordless sneer, underlining his inadequacies and punctuating his failures.

The sneer became a laugh.

Muted at first.

Then louder. Much louder.

Lucas shook his head, tried to clear it. But the hands of the clock stretched out, like some Halloween goblin come to life, suddenly grabbing him by the lapels of his pajamas and shaking him. Shaking him and laughing and mocking his pathetic little attempt to understand it all. And not understanding it *at all* and making a charade of his ability to protect the people around him. Willa, Tommy, the team, even Zach. Something he'd done had put them all in peril.

But what was it? What had he done? What?

He tried to put the clock down, but it clung to his hands, refusing to be ignored. He shook it once. Twice. But still it clung tight, the hideous, derisive laugh turning maniacal.

He squeezed the clock as hard as he could, trying to strangle it into submission.

But the clock refused to obey.

In one last frantic attempt to quiet the nightmare, he raised the clock over his head, and with every ounce of strength, smashed it to the floor.

He stood shaking above the shattered pile of time. Time that he no longer had. Time no longer on his side.

The ticking now silent, he stumbled back to his bed and collapsed, exhausted.

Time, he thought.

I need more time.

Time to make the connection.

Time to make it all fit.

Because everything does fit.

He could feel it.

Smell it.

Taste it.

He just couldn't *see* it.

September 14, 1920

Chapter 52

Zach led Lucas down the steps to the doctor's door, but before he could knock, Lucas grabbed his arm.

"So, you're saying she shot this guy, Mullan? This new guy, the one who was delivering our ice?"

"There was a lot of smoke, Lucas. And whoever he was, he was missing a lot of what used to be him. So, I'm not a hundred percent sure, but—yeah, it looked like it could be him. And if he was the one causing all the trouble, you won't be seein' him anymore. Or them mysteries."

"I'd be happy to hear it. But something tells me he isn't our guy. Doesn't sound like he coulda thought all these things up. You know what I mean? The bomb and all? That took planning. That was somebody who could plan. I don't think Mullan was a planner. Frankie Miller fits better."

Zach grunted agreement.

"And what about this other guy? This...this white fella? The one you said Rosie had in handcuffs. He runs out from the same room and passes you going down the stairs, yeah?"

"Faster'n a rabbit through a hedgerow."

Lucas frowned. None of what Zach had told him added up. What business did Queen Rosie have with Mullan? Some sort of gambling debt? What was worth killing him over? And who was this white guy she supposedly had captive? How did he fit in? "I'm not sure this has anything to do with us," said Lucas, "but let's find out what we can."

Zach nodded in agreement and rapped on the door.

Within a few moments, the doctor appeared. He seemed surprised. "Ah, Mr. Tucker, you are here once again. When you left, I wasn't sure...well, you *did* say you would be back, and so...yes, here you are."

"And this here's Lucas Blaine," said Zach. "He knows Miss Rosie and he needs to talk to her about last night."

"Welcome, Mr. Blaine. Please, do come in," said the doctor, leading both men into the house. "I will take you forthwith to see the Queen. She's not—how might I say—not terribly convivial this morning," he added over his shoulder.

They worked their way down a darkened hall over a well-trod runner that led to a door at the far end. The doctor gently knocked and spoke just above a whisper. "Uh, Queen Rosie? Are you awake in there? Some gentlemen here to see you."

From behind the door, a woman's voice called out. "Don't you open that door, Jenkins. I ain't fit for strangers!"

"Well, these gentlemen ain't exactly strangers, Queen Rosie. That is to mean, you are acquainted with them both, it seems."

"I don't care if they is President Wilson himself, I ain't receivin'!"

Zach pushed passed the doctor and flung the door open. "Kind of in a rush today, Miss Rosie."

Laying in a four-poster bed with the covers pulled up over her head and one bandaged foot sticking out from under the sheet at the end, Rosie cried out, "I told you, Jenkins, no visitors. I don't—"

But before she could finish, Zach spoke up again. "Miss Rosie, Lucas needs to speak with you."

Upon hearing his voice a second time, Rosie immediately peered out from under the covers at Zach, her face breaking into a radiant smile. "My angel!" she exclaimed. "Come to save me again!"

Before Zach could answer, Lucas strode forward and stepped to the edge of the bed.

"Good day, Rosie. I'm very glad to see that you're recovering so well."

"Lucas Blaine," she said, her words tinged with curiosity. Turning to Zach, she added softly, "You know this man, Zacharia?"

"I do, and you do. And he needs some answers that maybe you can provide."

Looking directly at Lucas, Rosie reached out and took his hand. "We done business together, ain't that so, Mr. Blaine?"

"We have, Miss Rosie. Proper business, where we both had a stake."

"Uh-huh. And so, this proper business, Mr. Blaine, you know there's got to be something in it for me?"

"I do. And if I can make it good with you, you know I will. But right now, I've got a mystery on my hands that needs untangling. And every long straw I can pull out and throw away gets me closer to finding the one short straw that could be a fuse ready to blow. And I'd sure like to snuff that fuse out before it's too late, Miss Rosie. So, please, tell me about the man you shot last night."

Rosie crossed her arms, looked away, and huffed. "I didn't shoot no man last night." She paused for a moment, then turned back to look at Lucas. "But if I did, he had it comin'."

"I believe you. I just need you to tell me, best as you can, how did you know that guy that you didn't shoot."

Rosie uncrossed her arms and smoothed out the sheet around her. "Then you'd better set yourself down, 'cause this ain't no short story." She proceeded to tell Lucas and Zach how she came to be chasing down the two men who'd attacked Tubby out in the alley behind the speakeasy. She left out the part about William and Bernard being beaten half to death.

When she'd finished, Lucas thought about it for a few moments. Suddenly, it hit him. "What was the name of that blind pig where Tubby got robbed?"

"The Sixty-Six," replied Rosie. "Use to be some kinda club."

Now it was starting to make sense. The man at the Sixty-Six that night, the one at the door hassling Egan. Lucas hadn't been able to tell from where he was sitting who it was, but he knew the man looked familiar. That was Mullan. Mullan and this other guy, the one with the gravelly voice. By some strange coincidence, they had come to the Sixty-Six the same night Lucas was there, and they ended up beating and robbing Tubby.

Mullan was now dead. But the other guy...where was he? And who was he? Lucas had a strange feeling he might already know. "Okay, so the guy who didn't beat up Tubby, he took you to the guy who *did* beat up Tubby? Why would he do that?"

Rosie rolled her eyes and looked out the window, then turned back to Lucas. "We had a little chat with that ice boy and he got real clear on why he should do that. He took us to that rooming house so we could get the money he stole from Tubby. Which is the same thing as stealin' from me!"

At this point, Zach interrupted. "She means the rooming house where Mullan lived. Rosie took the other guy, the one she had in handcuffs, upstairs. And then the fire starts, and he come down the stairs past me when I was goin' up."

Satisfied that he now understood the story, Lucas needed to know just one more thing, hoping he didn't already have the answer. "Rosie, what was this guy's name? The guy that you took upstairs at Mullan's? The guy with the gravelly voice who delivers your ice and says he didn't want to beat up Tubby? You said Irish, maybe?"

Rosie closed her eyes, straining to find an answer. Without opening them, she murmured, "Zacharia, all this talk about ice got me thirsty. Would you be my angel and get me a glass of water?"

Stunned, Zach's mouth dropped open as he started to bluster a reply when Lucas broke in.

"He'd be delighted to, Rosie." He shot a quick glance over to Zach, silently urging him to let it go.

"Water," was all Zach could manage to mumble as he left the room.

Once he was out the door, Lucas asked again. "Rosie, do you recall the man's name?"

Rosie scrunched up her face as if the exertion would help her recall. "I dunno. Not for sure. Maybe—maybe John?"

"It's important, Rosie. Really important."

"Oh, I get that, Lucas. Otherwise, you wouldn't be here. So, why do you care so much about these two guys?"

"Some strange things have been going on that I need explaining. The guy you shot, or didn't shoot, or whatever, that guy might be behind some of those things. If he was, I can forget about it all, 'cause he's no longer my problem. If not, then I gotta keep lookin'. And it feels like time isn't takin' my side. But this other guy, he's a whole different problem. 'Cause I promised a friend I'd help get this guy out of trouble. And if it's the same guy that got away from you last night…I just might need you to keep *lettin'* him get away."

"He may not be your problem, Lucas, but he sure is causing me a whole mess of trouble. No way I can just let this go."

The door opened and Zach came in with Rosie's glass of water. Handing it to her, he was about to say something, but one look from Lucas and he changed his mind, huffing his way into the corner of the room.

Rosie never missed a beat. "Why thank you, Zacharia. You *are* an angel—and a gentleman!"

A weak smile crossed Zach's face before he quickly looked away.

Not wanting to lose the momentum, or any possible memories attached to it, Lucas forged on. "Rosie, this iceman, the one that tried to stop the other guy beatin' on Tubby, please, think hard for me. What was his name? You said John?"

Rosie frowned. "That weren't it." Looking directly at Lucas, she added, "You hear what I'm sayin', Lucas? We talkin' *proper* business here or not? 'Cause at the moment, I'm out a whole lotta money."

"Good and proper, Rosie. I'll see you get your money back."

"And somethin' for gettin' it took in the first place. Because now I got no Chester, and no Percy, and—"

"And for all those things too," Lucas broke in. "Just the name. Please."

Again, Rosie smoothed the sheets around her, then looked up at Lucas, her face revealing no emotion. Then she looked over at Zach. "That angel, Zacharia, he saved me…and Foxy," she said, reaching over to the dressing table to give her gun a little pat. "And I do appreciate that." Then she looked back at Lucas, as if her duty was now clear. "If my memory serves me, his name was Keane. But it don't look like it sounds, 'cause he spells it funny."

"Spells it funny? How do you mean?"

"Makes no sense to me, Lucas. Spells it, C-I-A-N. Least that's what Chester said. How you get Keane from that beats the hell out of me!"

Lucas didn't know whether to be happy or devastated. He went over the pieces of the story in his mind, trying to think about what to do next. This had to be the same Cian that Aleta had asked him to protect. And Cian, this Cian, had lost a bet and then tried to get the money back by robbing Tubby. And this other guy, Mullan, the one who was now dead, had gone along to help. Or maybe it was his idea. Either way, he wouldn't be causing Lucas any more trouble. But Lucas now had to find a way to get Rosie her money back in order to protect Cian. And he still had no answer for who was behind all the mysteries.

"Rosie, I've got to think about this. But I need you to leave this guy Cian be. I'll get you your money back."

"And some for Percy and Chester," Rosie insisted.

"And some for Percy and Chester," agreed Lucas. "But you need to give me your word, you'll leave Cian be."

"Your word and my word's the same, Lucas. That's all we got to work with."

Lucas nodded and turned aside, grateful that, for the moment at least, it looked like he might be able to help Aleta's friend Megan get her nephew out of debt, a debt he'd incurred when he and Mullan had robbed Tubby Lewis out behind the Sixty-Six He had no idea how he was going to get Rosie her money, but he'd worry about that later. For now, he needed to focus all his mental energy on uncovering who was behind the many bizarre events that had happened over the past two weeks. Events that were getting more confusing...and more threatening...every day.

With Mullan dead, that's one less suspect I need to think about, he concluded.

But it wasn't enough. Not nearly enough. The toys, the mirror, the bomb on the bus. His brain kept triggering messages that simply refused to harden.

Rosie studied Lucas's tortured face. "You look like a rabbit, Lucas, 'bout ready to break for a tunnel."

"I feel like a rabbit," he said. "Trying to break *out* of a tunnel."

And in that one instant, everything started to fall into place.

WESTERN FRONT
March 1918

Chapter 53

Recently promoted Captain Lucas Blaine and three of his men entered the Restaurante des Amis separately over a span of about thirty minutes. Variously dressed in unremarkable outfits, two of them sporting berets, one a Homburg, the other a workman's flat cap, they were careful not to draw attention to themselves. Moving as unobtrusively as they could past the chattering crowd of mostly old men, one by one they slipped first into the kitchen and then into the pantry at the very back of the building. Once there, Lucas breathed a sigh of relief, grateful he hadn't had to muster anything more than a friendly smile, as there was nothing he could say in French that would convince even a six-year-old that he was a native.

An anxious waiter in a smudged white shirt, black pants, black bowtie, and baggy, waist-length black jacket helped the men move several large crates. The stencilling on the top read: "Attention: Contenu Lourd," but the crates weren't heavy at all and slid easily out of *the way. Once they were pushed aside, the waiter pulled up the hidden trap door, and the four men quickly stepped onto the waiting ladder and disappeared underground. As the last head cleared the opening, the trap door closed quickly, and Lucas could hear the crates being pushed back into place overhead.*

As they stepped off the ladder, a lantern lit up the walls of a massive souterraine—an underground maze of corridors and tunnels originally dug out as a hiding place some 2,500 years earlier.

"Evening, Captain. Any trouble?" Sergeant Thomas Nelson stood at the ready.

"Nothing noticed, Sergeant. All quiet here?" asked Lucas in a hushed voice, as the new arrivals slid out of their civilian clothes, revealing their uniforms underneath.

"Ain't heard a peep, sir. 'Course, we ain't exactly close to the action. It's a mile and a bit 'til we meet the tunneling unit."

"Then we'd better get going."

"You'd best take one of these, sir," Sergeant Nelson offered, as he handed each of the men a well-used Lee-Enfield. "Never know when Fritz might pop his 'ed in to say hello." A broad smile revealed a mouthful of broken, blackened teeth.

Patting his holstered Colt Hammerless, Lucas deferred. "I've got this, Corporal." Then, holding up his damaged left hand, added, "I'm afraid this no longer works."

"Very good, sir."

With that, Lucas and his three men, led by Sergeant Nelson and his two men, headed off into the depths of the underground passageway.

Ever since his run-in with a German bayonet on the battlefield, Lucas had been eager to get back to the business of winning the war. After two months of recuperation, his hand was as good as it was going to get. Which wasn't very good at all. Certainly not good enough to hold a rifle. But there was nothing at all wrong with his mind. And after wading through and filling out the usual reams of paperwork, he'd been placed with a British intelligence corps and undergone a crash course in looking for, listening to, analyzing, and assembling tidbits of information that might make the crucial difference in a war that seemed stuck between trenches. Ultimately, he'd been promoted to captain and assigned to one of the many British tunneling companies. And today would be a first going underground.

Moving through the cave at a measured clip, talking was kept to a minimum. Even though they were still under their own lines, everyone knew the importance of staying quiet. It was critical under No Man's Land, mandatory once under enemy trenches.

Eventually, the cave narrowed into a long, low neck that emptied into the tunnel proper, and the men had to duck their heads to get through the opening. Emerging out into the first gallery, they were met by a bedraggled and exhausted group of men who were sitting quietly on the earthen floor. They looked like they hadn't seen daylight for a month.

Lucas wondered how these men could do it. Many, he knew, had been coal miners in Wales before the war. Others had worked digging the London Underground. Claykickers they were called, and each had been intentionally recruited for their skill and experience in being able to quickly and silently "kick" what looked like an over-sized tin can into the chalky clay soil, tunnelling their way with agonizing caution under enemy lines where explosive experts could then lay devastating charges. It was foul, dangerous, backbreaking work in treacherous conditions, and Lucas knew that many of these men ultimately fell victim to poison gas or ill-placed or defective explosives, or even came face-to-face with the enemy tunneling in the opposite direction.

On the far side of the gallery, a canary flitted about inside a small iron cage, an advance warning for at least one of the many threats.

"As you were," said Sergeant Nelson before a single man even attempted to stand up. "This 'ere's Captain Blaine, come over from America to see if we're needin' anything."

"'Ow 'bout a nice 'ot shower," said one of the men in a low voice, and the others chuckled softly in response.

"Men, I know you've been putting your backs into it," said Lucas quietly, not wanting to elevate the level of tension they were all under. "Perhaps one of you could just fill me in on where we now stand. I don't pretend to know much about this."

"I can do that, Captain," said one of the tunnellers. "We four here come out of that tunnel over there about an hour ago and that's the last of 'us. Diggers, that is. Sappers is in there now, layin' charges."

"How long's that shaft?"

"She's about twelve hundred feet, sir."

"And we're, what, about sixty feet underground?"

"Not quite a hundred, sir."

Lucas couldn't stop being amazed at the logistics the tunnelling companies faced. Hours upon hours in the damp, stinking air, never knowing what the next kick might bring.

"Any signs of Fritz in here?"

"I 'ad me teeth clamped to a stake for a while. Couldn't feel nothin', sir."

Good, *thought Lucas.* No vibrations through a stake that had been hammered into the floor or wall of a shaft meant no Germans tunnelling nearby. Checking his watch, he wondered why the men hadn't retreated to the safety of the cave or taken one of the shafts up *and into one of their own trenches. "My timetable says fifty minutes," he said. "How's that looking?"*

"Right on time, sir. Should see them two sappers any minute."

"Why are you still here?"

"Just to make sure all's done."

Added another, "Once they show, we'll be gone. You can be sure of that, sir!"

Lucas looked into the six-foot by three-foot opening. It had been dug favoring a slight incline in order to prevent water from seeping back to where the men were digging.

Just then, he heard soft footsteps approaching, and he reached for his sidearm as Sergeant Nelson lifted his Lee-Enfield up to his waist. A head popped out of the tunnel and a lone man stepped out into the gallery.

"Came across somethin' we didn't like, me 'n Maddocks," he said, by way of introduction. Noticing Lucas, he attempted to stand straight up to salute, but the roof of the shaft prevented it, the overall effort making him look a little clownish. "Lance Corporal Netty, sir. Royal Engineers."

"At ease, Lance Corporal," said Lucas. "Where's the other sapper? Maddocks, you said?"

"Yes, sir. Well, as I was sayin', we came across somethin' we didn't like, Maddocks and me, and Maddocks, he says he's going to set a small camouflet and—"

"Hold on," interrupted Lucas. "A camouflet?"

"Yes, sir, it's what we use to blow up enemy tunnels. You know, small-like, so it don't break through the ground up above."

"Or into our own bloody shaft!" said one of the others.

"Wait a minute," said Lucas, looking toward the men sitting on the ground. "Didn't you just say with that stake trick you hadn't felt any signs of enemy tunneling?"

"Yeah, that's right, sir. But, it's no guarantee. Tunnelling starts and stops, and Fritz, well, sometimes...wham!" The man clapped his hands and threw them out over his head to depict an explosion, triggering the other men to laugh along with him, as if it were all just a child's game.

Suddenly, a muffled roar shot out the end of the shaft and into the gallery where Lucas and the others sat. Instinctively, they all ducked and covered their heads as a small cloud of dust and dirt followed.

When the sound had mostly faded away, Lance Corporal Netty lifted his head, and with a smile said, "That would be our camouflet."

"Where's—what's his name? Maddocks, yeah? Why isn't he here?"

"Oh, don't worry 'bout 'im, sir," said one of the tunnellers. "That's Arthur Trystan Maddocks! King Arthur, we call 'im!"

The other tunnellers chimed in with an agreeable chuckle.

"E's plenty smart," the first man added. "Smarter'n all us put together, I reckon!"

"'N proper, too! Talks real good, he does," said another.

"E'll be tucked into a cutout somewhere in there along the way. I expect 'e'll be out 'ere presently."

The other men nodded in harmony.

The words were barely out of his mouth when an earth-thundering explosion shattered the air, sending everyone catapulting to the floor as an enormous wave of dirt, dust, and rock roared out of the tunnel.

The man called Maddocks didn't come with it.

September 16, 1920

Chapter 54

"The shovel and the mirror," Zach repeated.

"Yes," said Lucas as they hurried along the street to the clubhouse. "Exactly! The shovel and the mirror!" Having uttered the words for the third time that morning, they were no longer just some vague reference to a perplexing mystery. Lucas had spoken them with a new energy, a new life, and Zach sensed that the frustration and despair that had been plaguing his friend for the past weeks had suddenly vanished, opening the door on a vast expanse of clarity and comprehension. Tentative, incomplete…but tantalizing. And now within reach. It was the same transformation that Lucas would undergo when a ballgame looked all but lost. Suddenly, some unexplainable insight would materialize and turn desperation into a plan.

"You think they're connected somehow?" prodded Zach once again.

"I know they are," enthused Lucas. *I just can't figure out how exactly.*

Ever since his conversation with Rosie, Lucas couldn't get the image of a tunnel out of his mind. Not one that he was going into, but one he was trying to get out of. Urgently. There was something about a tunnel that could tie everything together. But what was it?

He'd been in plenty of tunnels. But the one that sat at the periphery of his consciousness was different. It wasn't dark like a tunnel should be. There was light. But where was it coming from? He could feel the roof of the tunnel collapsing slowly, a steady rain of chalky dirt falling all around him, and yet...not on him. He wanted to escape, wanted to burst out into the daylight that he was certain was just around the next turn. But his legs refused to move. Because of the voices. The voices telling him he needed to help, he needed to do something. But he couldn't make out what that something was.

"You were sayin', boss," Zach interrupted, trying to break into the labyrinth in which Lucas seemed to be trapped. "The shovel and mirror?"

Oblivious to Zach's efforts, Lucas ploughed on. "This guy, he's spent a lot of time working things through, working out how he was going to get to me, how he was going to...I don't know. Get some...revenge, maybe." Abruptly, Lucas stopped, a hint of recognition spreading across his face. "Hold on." It was just a word, one word. But for Lucas, it was the one word that had been blocking the door to understanding everything. The door to *why*. And now, as that door swung open, he suddenly had the other answer he'd been blinded to for so long. The answer to who was behind it all. "Must be!" he said, excitement creeping into his voice. "It absolutely must be!" And just as abruptly as he had stopped, Lucas shot forward.

Zach was left two steps behind but quickly caught up.

"My God, Zach! That's it! Oh, he's been clever, all right, I'll give him that. Daring. Reckless at times. But definitely clever. It took some careful planning, you can be sure of that. And he needed help, yeah? He couldn't have done all those things by himself. He couldn't have! And money too."

"I'm followin'...but I'm not followin'," Zach said.

As if noticing Zach for the first time since leaving the coffee shop that morning, Lucas stopped and turned to look at his friend. He reached out and put his hand on Zach's shoulder. "Zach. You've been trying..." He studied the look of anxiety on his friend's face. He knew it well. That look of wanting to help and not knowing what to do.

"You couldn't make it make sense, Zach. You weren't there." Lucas smiled as if to suggest that that explained everything. "Don't you see? You weren't even there! Otherwise, you'd be stitching this all together like the cover of a shiny, new baseball. I know you would! You would have figured it out long ago!" And then, without another word, Lucas sped off toward the Bulldogs' clubhouse, Zach once again a step behind.

"The cat, for example," Lucas blurted out, carrying on as if Zach had been privy to his whole inner conversation, "now that was cunning. You see...the cat wasn't a clue. Not like the shovel or the mirror. Uh-uh, the cat was something else. I shoulda seen it, but I didn't."

"Yeah, okay, the cat," said Zach, trying to re-establish a connection before they reached the clubhouse door, knowing that once there Lucas would be trading thoughts of winning pennants for thoughts of solving mysteries.

"The cat was a nudge, a warning. I don't know, a threat, a tease. A black cat, remember? We knew it at the time but couldn't see it clearly. Bad luck and all. Everybody knows that. And that's what it was meant to be. A bad luck warning. It wasn't specifically a clue. Just a way of saying...more to come. I think it was just this guy's way of laughing at us." Lucas stopped abruptly, steps away from the clubhouse door. "Unless it was something else. Something we haven't figured out yet."

Zach didn't feel like he'd figured anything out. "Not crazy about cats, boss. Especially black ones that cross in front of ya. Which that one surely did."

Lucas looked up at Zach, his mind still struggling to get out of a tunnel. "Could a black cat mean something else?"

Before Lucas could reach for the handle of the clubhouse door, Zach tried once again to find a starting point to the puzzle that Lucas seemed to be completing.

"Boss, before you go in, can you just tell me...the shovel and the mirror. What did you figure?"

Lucas looked back at Zach and took a deep breath. "It all goes back to the war, Zach. There was this guy." *A guy I never met, who now wants revenge. Could that really be it? After all this time?* "Damn it, what was his name?" And with that, Lucas turned, opened the clubhouse door, and hurried inside.

"Jesus, Mary, and Joseph!" he exclaimed, quickly covering his face with his arm as he entered the clubhouse.

Zach, one step behind, yanked his handkerchief from his pocket and thrust it over his own nose and mouth as soon as he'd stepped inside, the wave of noxious air escaping from the room quickly filling his nostrils.

"Son of a bitch! That icebox has got to go, boss! It ain't goin' to make the season."

"Maybe it just needs some ice," said Lucas hopefully as he looked around the clubhouse, forcing down the wave of nausea at the same time. Given the early hour, no players were about. "Tommy?" he shouted, but no answer came. "Kid's usually here by now," he mumbled, closing the clubhouse door. "Looks like just you and me," he added as he headed for his office.

"Boss, let's take 'er outside. Team's gonna quit with this stink."

"Yeah, maybe," said Lucas as he reached the office door. "We can't afford to have them..." The words stopped suddenly as Lucas stared into his office.

Zach stopped as well. "What is it, boss? Thing's leakin' out everywhere, right? Bound to happen, just a matter of time. But the smell! Like somebody died in here!"

Lucas hadn't moved. "Does smell like that, Zach."

Zach finally managed to squeeze around Lucas so that he could see into the office. "Son of a bitch," he muttered for the second time since entering the clubhouse.

Neatly placed on top of the icebox was a bird cage.

Just like the cage that Lucas and Willa had found on her porch the evening she and Lucas had strolled home through their favorite park.

But there was no bird to offer a welcoming chirp.

"Son of a bitch," Zach repeated.

"Yeah, Zach. Son of a bitch," echoed Lucas. "Looks like our guy isn't done yet. Not by a long shot."

"We need to move that thing outta here. Quick."

"We do," acknowledged Lucas as he stepped further into the room. "But there's something—" he said aloud, looking about the office. "Something's different."

"You can say that again, boss. It's that icebox. It's a whole lot different than when we left yesterday, bird cage or no bird cage."

Lucas studied the floor. "There's no water," he mumbled to himself.

"What?" Zach stepped forward to see what Lucas was looking at. "Okay, so the ice musta just melted away and the water evaporated."

"Don't think so, Zach. Even with the heat, every morning there's always been traces of a leak. A little puddle of water, greeting me like some pesky pooch." Lucas moved closer. "It's got something to do with the smell."

"And it ain't gettin' any better, boss!"

Lucas knew Zach was right. The icebox couldn't have rotted so much in a single day that it was now threatening to close the clubhouse down.

Without thinking about it, Lucas reached for the icebox handle and pulled open the door.

Staring out at them was the contorted face of Frankie Miller, an icepick neatly sticking out of his head, the crushed body of a canary stuffed in his mouth.

Lucas and Zach reeled back into opposite corners of the room.

"Son of a bitch," they uttered in unison.

Chapter 55

"Good morning, Mr. Morgan."
"Good morning. Miss...uh...?"
"Pierce. Yes, sir. I'm here about my uncle's estate."
"Oh. Yes. Quite. And...who are you here to see?"

Willa had arrived early at the J. P. Morgan & Company offices at the corner of Broad Street and Wall Street on the morning of September 16th, hoping that her meeting with one of the Morgan partners could be advanced a little bit so that she wouldn't have to leave her Aunt Aleta all alone at the coffee shop during the lunch hour.

What she hadn't hoped for was to run into Junius Spencer Morgan himself.

Not that he was overtly intimidating. Certainly not as intimidating as his father, J. P. Morgan. But Willa, like many people, felt a distinct sense of inferiority when coming face-to-face with the men who actually owned the legendary House of Morgan.

"Yes, sir. I'm here to see Mr. Lamont. Oh, but I have an appointment. And...and one of the clerks...a Mr. Dunn, I think...went to tell him that I was here. But I'm early, you see. My appointment isn't until 11:15. It's just that my aunt...Aleta Jean Hastings...well, as I said, it's my Uncle Clifton's estate, and—"

"So!" interrupted Junius, his cheeks rounding into a smile. "You're in good hands, then! Now," he said, pulling a gold Patek Philippe pocket watch from his vest pocket, "I, too, have an appointment, so...I really must be going." He slid the watch back into his pocket. "A pleasure, Miss...uh..."

"Pierce."

"Yes, of course. Well, good day, Miss Pierce." And he continued on down the hallway to his office.

Willa smiled after him, and once his back was turned, let out a slow sigh of relief.

I really don't know why I was so nervous. He wasn't at all intimidating. After all, he's just another man.

Still a little flustered, she blamed it on the man's handsome looks, then laughingly scolded herself, wondering what Lucas might have to say about her thoughts running away like this.

Clerks were busy hustling armloads of files in all directions, disappearing discreetly into various offices and then moments later reappearing with a brand new stack of papers. The whole building oozed prosperity, a constant current of commerce that accompanied every movement, every handshake, every head nod.

Yet, it was strangely quiet, thought Willa. Almost like a library. None of the noises from outside...the construction, the pushcart vendors, the curb brokers...none of it seemed to penetrate the walls.

It wasn't Willa's first visit to J. P. Morgan & Company. But looking around at all the gleaming marble, glass, oak, and mahogany, she couldn't help but feel a bit in awe. What had only a few years before been a rather modest establishment compared to the great banking institutions of London had emerged from the war the world's preeminent financial institution, having bankrolled an immense quantity of wartime necessities and ultimately financing endless reconstruction efforts into what was now a staggering fortune.

"Miss Pierce?"

Snapping out of her reverie, Willa spun around, coming face to face with one of the clerks. "Yes?"

"Mr. Lamont is running a bit long in his current meeting. Would you care to have a seat over here for a few more minutes." It wasn't a question.

"Oh. Of course. Yes, of course."

"I'll come and get you when he's available." The clerk disappeared before Willa could answer.

Taking a seat, she peeked at her wristwatch. Eleven-twenty. She hoped she wouldn't have to wait too long.

Chapter 56

Before two hours had passed, a coroner from the recently established Office of Chief Medical Examiner of the City of New York had arrived at the Bulldogs' clubhouse and declared Frankie Miller deceased, most probably as a result of a sharp object having been thrust through his brain. While not the most profound conclusion, it was far better than what New Yorkers had become accustomed to from their coroners over the past twenty years, whose various backgrounds featured eight undertakers, six real estate agents, two saloon keepers, two plumbers, a musician, and a butcher, among others.

By the time Detective Florianus Klucznik had finished examining the body and the icebox, and then furthered his investigation with a somewhat cursory inspection of the office, the equipment room, and a seemingly random selection of a few of the players' lockers, it was after 11:00. It was clear to Lucas that the investigation wasn't going to answer any of the questions that he had, let alone yield any usable information about who had murdered Frankie Miller.

"What about the pick?" asked Lucas, in a vain attempt to hurry things along. He still had a game to prepare for. "Thought you might want to give that some consideration."

The detective half looked up from his notepad. "It's of no interest to me, Mr. Blaine," he sniffed. "It's just one of dozens we could undoubtedly uncover in this block alone," he added, wiping his hands clean of some imagined unpleasantness. "Furthermore, as you undoubtedly noticed, it was covered in the victim's blood. No useable fingerprints to be had, I'm afraid. None at all," he concluded, turning his attention back to his notepad. "It's facts we need now, Mr. Blaine, not pointless curiosities." He peered back up from his notebook. "And that's a fact." A smarmy smile crossed his face.

"Indeed," was all Lucas could offer. *I'm in desperate need of a few facts myself.*

"And speaking of facts, Mr. Blaine, let's go over a few of them again."

After going over the known events with both Lucas and Zach one more time, and making a half-hearted effort to interview a handful of Bulldogs players who had arrived early to get in some practice before the game, Detective Klucznik concluded that all could be dismissed to go about preparing for the afternoon.

Not wanting to wait for the detective to make a decision about the icebox, Lucas decided to take action. "You four," said Lucas, pointing to a group of players still gawking about. "Take that icebox outta here and put it 'round back of the clubhouse." Amidst much complaining, the men wasted no time extracting the rotting box from the premises, then quickly retreated to the safety of the playing field.

"So...I've got everything I need. No real clues, no suspects, just a common, everyday gangland murder. Probably them Italians. They love the pick." The detective was about to tuck away his notepad when he casually asked, "No one else...unaccounted for?"

It was then that Lucas realized he hadn't seen Tommy anywhere all morning. He pulled out his pocket watch. Two minutes to noon. "Our bat boy. Mostly he's here before I am, but I haven't seen him yet today. I don't know where he is."

Klucznik cocked his head, squinted, and slowly pulled his notepad out of his pocket, eyes fixed on Lucas as if he had just spied a shoplifter at Macy's. "Your bat boy?" he queried. "That's unusual, isn't it? That he's not here? I'da thought he'd be one of the first to show."

It was more than unusual, thought Lucas. It was unheard of. But how could Tommy possibly be involved with Frankie Miller's death? That made no sense. "Like I said, mostly he is here first thing. Haven't heard from him, so I couldn't say where he could be today. Sick, maybe."

"Gets sick a lot, this kid?"

"Hardly ever," Lucas replied without further explanation.

Klucznik continued to stare hard at Lucas, as if the man's entire being oozed suspicion. And then, flicking his notepad closed, he winked conspiratorially. "You make sure he comes to the station to talk to me when he shows, right?"

And with that, Detective Florianus Klucznik spun on his heel and started for the clubhouse door. That was when a sudden distant booming sound echoed up the street from somewhere far downtown, sped past the clubhouse, and off into the distance, causing the old wooden building to shudder slightly.

"What was that?" chirped up one of the players who was still milling about in the hopes of being first to hear some juicy tidbit about the murder.

No one said a word for ten or more seconds, waiting to hear if there would be another loud boom. When nothing came, Detective Klucznik broke the silence. "Sounded like thunder," he offered from the doorway as he looked up at the brooding gray sky. "Can't ever tell with September. Could be a storm before the day's out." He looked back at Lucas and Zach. "Could be almost anything," he added. "And that's a fact."

Zach watched the detective wander out the door and into the street. "So…that's what a detective does," he said. "Quite impressive."

"Yeah, except for the fact that we don't know who killed Frankie," replied Lucas. *And if he's planning the same thing for me.*

"No loss if you ask me, boss. Miller was always trouble. He left a smell in here when he walked out a year ago, and he left a smell when he got carried out today."

"One thing got cleared up, though," Lucas observed. "You saw it, too, right? When they were pulling him out of the box?"

"You mean the boot? Yeah, I caught that."

The V-shaped cut on the bottom of Miller's boot had meant nothing to Detective Klucznik, but it was a moment of clarity for both Lucas and Zach.

"Same as the imprint that was left in the water on the floor after the robbery," said Lucas. "Definitely Miller."

"Think he was the guy we're looking for?" asked Zach.

"I did for a while. But not anymore. Although he was involved, that's for sure. Left me a personal memento, if you remember," said Lucas, rubbing his head where Frankie Miller had hit him with the baseball bat. "He also left us that...what d'ya call it...a calling card. That fortune teller spinner toy. But, no, he's not our guy. He's just another problem."

"Meaning?" asked Zach.

"Who killed Frankie Miller? And why?"

"Right. Yeah." Zach thought about it for a moment and sensed an opening. "About the connections, boss? The cat? The mirror? You haven't got around to explaining those."

Lucas seemed to drift away for a moment. "Yeah," he said, returning his attention to Zach. "They make sense now. And I will explain it. I will. But right now, we've got a game to play and a pennant to win, and I intend to do both." And with that, Lucas grabbed his cap and headed out to the field as if it were just any other day.

Chapter 57

The afternoon had dragged on, and despite a staggering 13-3 win, Lucas's attention to the game had barely surfaced. He'd noticed something odd when he'd first come out onto the field. Noticed that the crowd was particularly thin. In fact, some people were leaving the ballpark before the game had even started. And throughout the afternoon, his subconscious brain had poked and prodded his conscious brain, trying to tell him the crowd was thinning out even more. Something wasn't right. Fans didn't usually leave a game before all odds of a comeback had virtually vaporized. But he was so absorbed in his own puzzle he hadn't made any effort to wonder why.

Coming up the steps of the subway, people seemed to be chattering all around him, but his brain was singularly focused on putting the pieces of his puzzle together.

"Anarchists!" shouted Zaslaw, thrusting a newspaper out toward Lucas. "They're everywhere!"

"I'm not sure about everywhere, Zaslaw," replied Lucas, pushing his way through a small crowd of people hanging about the old man's newsstand, "but I'm sure they might be somewhere." He took the *Evening World* that Zaslaw was holding out and stared at the headline.

19 Dead, 200 Hurt in Explosion in Wall St;
Exchange Closed; J. P. Morgan's Office Wrecked

"What? When did this...was this today, Zaslaw?" Lucas blurted out as he riffled through the pages hoping to find anything that would further explain what had happened.

"Today. Tomorrow. Any day! Anarchists! This is what I tell you! You will see. This is only beginning!"

Lucas stared at the newspaper in horror, vaguely remembering the odd booming sound that had come echoing up from downtown just after noon. A sound so distinct that everyone in the Bulldogs' clubhouse had simultaneously stopped talking. But a sound so distant that no one had bothered to give it a second thought. "Thunder," Detective Klucznik had concluded, and no one seemed to need a better idea.

But now Lucas understood. He'd simply tuned out because the tune he'd been listening to was trying to find the rhythm that connected tunnels and clues and murders and bombings and everything that was almost making sense.

Now he knew. As the fans had known then.

Zaslaw continued prattling on even as Lucas reran the afternoon scenario, wondering how he could have missed something so obvious. Nearly three-quarters of the fans had been aware that New York was under attack and had left the ballpark out of confusion, curiosity, fear, or a sense of duty that maybe there was something they could do to help. Anything to help. And yet just enough of a crowd had stayed to avoid triggering an awareness.

And he had missed it all.

Silently, he cursed his lack of attention when something else suddenly struck him. Something even more disturbing.

Willa had said she was going downtown that very morning for an appointment at the bank.

Lucas flinched. Was it the same bank? He couldn't remember for sure. Maybe.

He grabbed up the paper and quickly reread the headline, praying that he'd misread the story. But the headline confirmed it: J. P. Morgan Bank.

Yes, that's it! The same bank where Willa had an appointment.

"Ah, so now is clear, yes?" interrupted Zaslaw, nodding his head in satisfaction, believing that his words were finally getting through. "This is here! In America! Not Russia. Not Poland. How is this happening? I am telling you this…"

"Zaslaw, quiet. Please. Just for a moment." The old man snorted in disgust and wandered off to call out to another customer.

But Lucas needed to think. Why again was Willa going all the way downtown to the Morgan bank? All the way down to Wall Street? There were plenty of other choices closer to home.

And then he remembered. Her Aunt Aleta had always hated having to deal with bankers. Pompous, loathsome bloodsuckers, she'd called them, much to Willa's amusement. And so Willa had stepped in to help her aunt manage her late uncle's estate. An estate that Uncle Clifton, on the advice of some of his wealthier clients, had insisted always be kept with J. P. Morgan. That way he could go to his grave knowing his money would be safe.

Anxiously, Lucas scanned the various newspaper columns, trying to discern what time the bomb had gone off. Had Willa been there at that time? How long was her meeting? Was she all right? Why hadn't he heard from her? Why hadn't she sent a message?

"Zaslaw," Lucas called over to the old man, "when...I mean, what time did this happen? Do you know?"

"Ah-ha, so, now I am advise again! You want to know, when did this happen? But I tell you, these anarchists, they don't care about time. Anytime is good time! They just want to kill, and—"

"Yes, right, I understand. Anytime is a good time. But what time was it?"

"Noontime," sniffed Zaslaw, annoyed that his insights were being so summarily dismissed. "Twelve noon. Big crowds everywhere, people coming..."

Zaslaw rambled on, but Lucas couldn't hear what he was saying as he tried fitfully to remember what time it was Willa had said she was going to go downtown. Eleven? Two? Noon? None of those sounded right. And he couldn't decide whether it would be better to head straight home or go directly to the apartment Willa shared with Aleta. Or would the coffee shop make more sense? He pulled out his watch to check the time: 8:30 p.m.

Tucking the paper under his arm, he turned to work his way back out through the milling crowd. For the first time since he'd left the clubhouse, still mired in the muddy complexities of his own personal mystery, the voices around him became more than a blurry, incoherent mumble. Everyone was talking about the bombing.

Before he'd taken two steps, he heard Zaslaw call out, "Is no library, Mr. Manager! Three cents!"

Lucas dug into his pants pocket, pulled out a nickel, and flipped it over the heads of the men who had pushed their way to the counter as Lucas had left.

With barely a glance at the tumbling coin, Zaslaw plucked it out of the air as deftly as any major league shortstop, threw it in the box behind him, and continued lecturing the two men who stood closest to him at the counter.

Free of the cluster of people at the newsstand, Lucas hustled down the street to his own apartment, having decided to go there first, as it was closest. He sped along, dodging other pedestrians as best as he could, distractedly apologizing to those he couldn't.

Minutes later, he was racing up the front steps and opening the front door to his building. No piano music from his neighbor's apartment greeted him. Once inside, he leapt up the steps to his apartment two at a time, fishing into his pocket for his key as he went. He plunged the key into the always reluctant lock, grabbing the door handle at the same time.

Before he could turn the knob, the door flung open.

Standing just inside the door was Willa, her clothes covered in blood, her left arm wrapped in a bandage.

"Good God!" muttered Lucas.

A stunned second later, they crashed into each other's arms.

Chapter 58

"I'm scared."
"Scared? Of what?"
"The dark."
"It's not that dark. Pretend you're an explorer. In a cave."
"I don't like caves."
"It won't be much longer now."
Silence.
"It's very dark."
"Yes...it is."
"What's that sound?"
"A subway train."
"Is it coming this way?"
"No."
"Is it going to hit us?"
"No. Subways have their own tunnels. It's very far away."
"I don't like tunnels."

"That's enough. I need to concentrate."

Silence.

"Where's my rabbit?"

"I'll give it to you when we're finished here."

"You promised me a rabbit."

"You need to be quiet while I set this up. Just another minute or two."

"I really want a rabbit."

Silence.

"What are we doing here?

"Springing a trap."

"What kind of trap?"

"We won't be much longer."

"I want to go now."

"When I'm finished. Right now, I need to concentrate so we can get out of here."

"I want my rabbit."

Silence.

"You said you'd give me a rabbit."

"Here. Hold this for a few moments."

"What is it?"

"It's a rabbit. It'll bring you good luck."

"This isn't a rabbit."

"You don't want it?"

"It's not a real rabbit. This is just a toy. I want a real rabbit."

"Give it back, then. I'd better keep it anyway. I may need that luck."

"I want my rabbit!"

"Stop that! I told you, whispering only! No yelling!"

"I want my rabbit! I want my rabbit! I want my rabbit!"

E. J. BRIDGWATER

Silence.

Chapter 59

"Okay. Slowly. Tell me again. Everything you can remember."

Willa sat trembling in Lucas's arms as they sat on his bed together, the tears just starting to ebb away. For forty-five minutes, she'd been telling him all she could remember about the J. P. Morgan bombing.

"It was horrible, Lucas. I don't know what else I can tell you. I don't...everything was just a blur. Like a dream, in slow motion. Each person, every scream, there was glass and brick and...and...parts of people everywhere! It was just..." She gulped huge mouthfuls of air, and her tears ran anew. "It was horrible."

Lucas had listened without interruption. It sounded too much like what he'd experienced on the battlefield.

At precisely 12:01 p.m., a bomb had exploded immediately in front of the J. P. Morgan Bank at the corner of Broad Street and Wall Street, right across from the New York Stock Exchange.

A huge flash, a tremendous roar, then a pummeling shock wave and a wall of flame ten stories high crashed into the midday crowd and the surrounding buildings, instantly killing more than thirty people and seriously injuring two hundred more, while shattering every window within a hundred yards and sending deadly chunks of wood, brick, stone, and marble in every direction.

The blast had apparently originated from either a nearby touring car, now an unrecognizable pile of twisted metal, or a rust-colored horse-drawn cart that had been standing in front of the bank, the horse now a bloody smear of pulp, the wagon a spent hurricane of splinters. According to witnesses, the cart driver had left the scene long before the explosion.

"That poor horse," whimpered Willa.

Lucas thought it better not to challenge her choice of mourning. Or to try and hurry things along. He knew from experience that shock was intensely personal, and people overcame it in their own time. Or sometimes never.

Suddenly, she pulled away from him. "Everyone was running, Lucas. Up Nassau Street. Over to Broadway. And they were trampling the people who were lying injured on the ground. Just stepping on them. As if they didn't even seem to see them." She turned her face away. "Or care."

Lucas slowly pulled her close again, and she draped her head over his shoulder.

"I ran too, Lucas." Again, she pulled away without leaving his arms. "At first, anyway. For the subway. But then...I don't know. I thought maybe I could help. I didn't even realize that my arm was bleeding. Everything was just so...so...crazy! But then I saw this man, an older man, very distinguished, maybe a...maybe a stockbroker, or a banker. And he had a cane. And I saw him reach down to this man on the ground who was bleeding really badly because his leg was...leg was..." For a moment, her eyes glazed over, but then she hurried on. "I wasn't sure what he was going to do. But then he pulled off his tie and he wrapped it around the man...just here," she said, pointing to her leg, "just above the wound. And then he—he slid his cane in under the tie and twisted it so that it would tighten. You know. Like a tourniquet." She searched Lucas's eyes for understanding. "People were trying to help, Lucas. And so, I thought...I thought maybe I could help, too. So I went back."

"That was very brave."

Willa didn't wait to hear Lucas's words. "At first, I didn't know what to do. I just started to...but then there was a doctor there. And he must have been in one of the buildings nearby because he wasn't hurt at all, and he came right across the street, and the first thing he did was wrap a handkerchief around this man's head. Because it was bleeding. And he tied it under his chin. A Dr. Silvey, I think I heard him say, and he started treating people, so I just started helping him. Oh, Lucas, I can't begin to describe it, it was all so terrible."

She pressed her lips tightly together in an attempt to stifle more tears, but the effort collapsed, and tears once again poured forth.

"Who would've done this, Lucas?" she exclaimed, her anger suppressing her concern. "Who would want to do such a thing?"

Who indeed? wondered Lucas. There had been numerous bombings across the country during the past two decades. Just the previous year, seven of the country's most notable public figures had been the targets of attempted assassinations. Many of the bombings were claimed by, and others blamed on, anarchists. Terrorists. People wanting change and frustrated that they couldn't get it. Frustrated that they were being left behind in a country that was racing ahead into the future.

Maybe Zaslaw was right. Maybe it *had* been anarchists. Or maybe it was yet another message from his tormentor. Could it possibly have been—? But his thoughts were interrupted as Willa continued aloud with her own.

"All those people!" she exclaimed. "Those innocent people! Their lives are a shambles! And for what?"

Lucas took her face gently in his good hand, hoping the gesture would be welcomed for the words he didn't have. "Whoever it was, they'll be punished," he offered. "You can be sure of that."

He wasn't at all sure.

Willa collapsed into the bedcovers, her body giving in to the exhaustion left behind by the excess adrenaline receding from her body. "I'm going to have a bath, Lucas," she said, closing her eyes. And then I need to rest. I need to..." The words drifted away, and Lucas didn't try to catch them. She'd fallen asleep, still dressed in the same bloody clothes she'd arrived in.

Lucas got up, walked around to the other side of the room, and turned off the bedside lamp, then sat down in a side chair and looked over at the open window. A gentle breeze riffled the curtains. Otherwise, all was still. No street noise. No dogs barking. No piano.

His mind slid back to the Wall Street bombing. Once again he wondered, *Was it possible the man behind his own mystery could have been responsible?* But why? Why kill and maim all those innocent victims? Was he trying to kill Willa? Was he simply willing to ignore all the other carnage?

It made no sense. How would he even know that Willa would be there? *No*, thought Lucas, *this is not the same guy.*

The Wall Street bombing was much more treacherous. It was a message, all right, but not to Lucas. It was a message to the city and to the country. To the world. A message that capitalism, the engine that had been grinding out the most prosperous economy ever, was grinding up a great many of its citizens in the process. A message that democracy, where anyone could be a part of shaping the future no matter what their beliefs, was inexorably enslaving a large segment of the population in spite of its declared intentions. Where freedom, having once been imagined, fought for, and won by an implacable faction of patriotic rebels in a Boston harbor nearly 150 years earlier, had become the very template that would spawn and nourish the anarchy that would forever define the future meaning of freedom.

How easy it was to hate something you didn't understand, thought Lucas. How easy it was to rely on violence to try and avenge perceived wrongs. To get revenge.

How easy it was to ignore someone else's pain.

Lucas shook his head. *Enough,* he thought. *This is getting me nowhere.*

He looked over at Willa. Fast asleep, her face exhibited no element of fear, no hatred, no disgust. Just a placid look that could have been mistaken for a smile.

Deciding he'd better get some sleep himself, Lucas got up from the chair and went and sat down on the bed. He'd get into his pajamas in a moment, he thought. Just a cigarette first to settle his nerves.

Before he'd even picked up the pack of Camels, a noise made him sit bolt upright.

A voice. Yelling almost. But muffled. Like it was far away. Or blocked. So quiet that he wouldn't have even noticed had it not been so still in the bedroom.

As subtly as he could, he got up off the bed and crept over to the bedroom door and out into the parlor.

Yes. More yelling. A child's voice?

But where was it coming from? Downstairs? Outside? In the kitchen?

Easing himself over to the doorway, he turned the handle. The apartment door was still locked. He turned the latch and stepped out onto the landing. Nothing. For nearly a minute, he stood perfectly still. But no more sounds came.

Unaware that he'd stopped breathing, he inhaled deeply, then exhaled a long, slow sigh of relief.

Nerves. Playing tricks on me. But I'm not going there.

Careful not to wake Willa, he managed to creep back into the bedroom without disturbing her, plucked the pack of cigarettes from his night table, along with a box of matches, and sat down on the bed.

I'm close, he thought, pulling a cigarette from the pack.

I just need to stay focused. I'm going to get this guy.

He lay down, pulled a match from the box, and then lay back on his pillow.

Holding the match out in front of him, he paused for just a moment and stared closely at it, deep in thought. Then, with one swift movement, he stroked the match head across the red phosphorous striking surface on the box, at the same time whispering a single word.

"Shit."

The room exploded with a brilliant flash, as a bellowing roar shattered the silence, followed by a crushing shock wave that slammed through the room, sending chunks of plaster, wood, and shards of glass splintered in all directions, and threw the bed two feet up toward the ceiling. Two seconds later, gravity took back control, and Lucas, Willa, and the bed crashed through a crumbling, jagged-edged chasm that moments before had been the bedroom floor.

SEPTEMBER 18, 1920

Chapter 60

Except for Lucas, the clubhouse was empty. He sat at his desk, staring at the far wall as the overhead fan sliced the air above him into thin, invisible layers. It had been two days since he and Willa had plummeted through the bedroom floor of his apartment, landing in one terrifying, cacophonous crash directly on what was left of his downstairs neighbor's grand piano. Thanks to its irregular shape, the piano had gotten snagged on the ripped edges of the flooring on which it sat, narrowly avoiding tumbling down into the tunnel beneath. The tunnel where the bomb had been set. If it hadn't been for the mattress and what was left of the piano, both Lucas and Willa would now be dead. As it was, Willa had suffered a broken arm and a handful of other cuts and bruises and had been rushed off to the hospital, where she remained under observation. Lucas had miraculously avoided any serious injury.

The explosion had triggered a flurry of activity, with police, fire trucks, an ambulance, and eventually the press rushing to the scene. Hordes of people filled the surrounding streets, vying to get a closer look at what had happened, delaying initial rescue efforts and damaging some of what would later be deemed evidence. A gaggle of newspapermen, notepads in hand, had encouraged cataclysmic comments from people milling about, most of whom had been asleep at the time of the explosion. Not to be deterred, both parties elected to invent facts and create scenarios that bore no resemblance to what had actually happened.

Due to the explosion coming on the heels of the J. P. Morgan bombing that morning, Attorney General A. Mitchell Palmer decided that it might very well be the work of anarchists and ordered his special assistant, J. Edgar Hoover, to immediately dispatch a pair of agents to the demolished building. They, in turn, deduced that the bomb had been placed in a tunnel underneath Lucas's apartment, and that the tunnel had been dug from the basement of the house directly next door, leading to the conclusion that it was more than likely gangland retaliation and thus the purview of the local constabulary, giving them clearance to abruptly abandon the scene.

Fortunately, acting Fire Chief Hodges, a fervent Bulldogs fan, recognized Lucas and was insistent that this was in no way a gang-related affair but offered no further explanation. While this observation satisfied the police, it didn't put them any closer to imagining who might actually have been responsible.

But it clarified everything for Lucas.

Everything except his tormentor's name.

And what he looked like.

He could be standing right in front of me and I still wouldn't know it was him.

"Falling through a hole in the floor doesn't seem to have troubled you, brother dear!"

Lucas looked up to see Parker standing in the doorway to his office. He'd been so absorbed with his own thoughts, he hadn't even heard him come in.

"I thought you might be over at the police station. You know, helping them solve this dastardly deed."

"If solving it were the hard part, Parker, then the hard part's been done."

"What do you mean?"

"I know who's responsible. Even though we've never met, I know exactly who it is. What I don't know is *where* he is. Or what he looks like. Or what he's got planned next."

And I still can't remember his name.

"But...surely the police can help with something like that," offered Parker. "Or the Federal Bureau of Investigation. I have contacts there. I could put in a word, get things moving."

"This is personal, Parker. He's only after me. And I'm not going to find him. He's far too clever for that. When he's ready, he'll find me."

"Yes, but...ready for what?"

Ready to kill me. "Whatever it is he's got planned."

"That really isn't very clear, Lucas. What about all that intelligence work you did during the war? Surely you learned something there that could be of some help. You know, be a detective! Track this person down!"

Lucas looked up at Parker but said nothing.

"Well, all right then, if that's all you're yielding up today, I think I'll be going. I only stopped in to see that you were...in one piece." Parker's face slid into an impish grin. "We're off to Saratoga again, Claire and I. Later this week is the plan. Got a splendid horse running—"

Abruptly, Lucas sat up in his chair, his thoughts immediately shifting gears. "Parker, the last time you went to Saratoga, you wanted me to place a bet on a horse you were running."

"Yes, I remember. Splendid animal. You really should have trusted me on that one. Turned into a very nice payday!"

Lucas hadn't thought about the race since the day Parker had announced he and Claire were going up to Saratoga. But suddenly, all thoughts of explosions and falling mattresses and Cracker Jack prizes and mystery men vanished.

"Remind me, Parker, what day was that?"

Parker pursed his lips. "Tuesday. The twenty-fourth, if I recall."

"Which race was it? And where was your horse running?" asked Lucas.

"When did you develop such an interest in horseracing? You've always played it so aloof."

"Which race?"

"Really, Lucas, you'd think this was a..." Parker tugged absently on his pocket handkerchief. "Very well, it was the third."

"And you ran…?"

"Six. The number six slot."

Lucas stared at his brother, trying to get his thoughts in order. "I need to ask you something. And I need a one hundred-percent, no-nonsense answer." *If that's even possible,* he wondered silently. "Was that race rigged?"

"Lucas!" laughed Parker, an embarrassed smile spoiling his attempt at indignation. He took his hat off and wiped his brow. "How could you even suggest such a thing?"

"Because a man's life might depend on it. Was that race fixed?"

"Well, it's not like there's a guarantee or anything."

"Fixed?"

"Your persistence is abrasive, brother dear!" sniffed Parker, turning his face to the door.

Lucas waited for a few seconds. "Fixed." It was no longer a question.

Realizing that Lucas was not about to give up, Parker let out a long sigh and turned back to face him. "All right, let's say that..." Parker paused again, searching for just the right words. "Let us say that the odds favored my horse. Perhaps...perhaps even a little more than 'favored.'"

Lucas rubbed his face. Could this possibly have been the race at which Megan's nephew Cian had lost all his money? The race that triggered the robbery of Queen Rosie's bookie and all the other events that followed? Lucas shook his head, trying to make some sense of it all. *Probably not,* he thought. *Probably nothing more than my imagination looking for closure.* But his imagination wasn't yet ready to quit.

He looked over at Parker. What if it was the same race? What if it was the same race where Cian had lost all his money?

Uneasy with his brother's silence, Parker interrupted. "Lucas, you're obviously preoccupied. All this mystery, all these... Look, I'm just going to leave you here to sort things out your own way. If you need me, just...just...well, I don't know," he blurted, jabbing a finger toward the phone. "Just call me."

And at that exact moment, the phone rang.

Chapter 61

Lucas sat staring at the phone.

On the fifth ring, Parker broke the silence. "It's not going to answer itself, you know."

Hesitantly, Lucas reached over and pulled the phone toward him, then lifted the receiver off the hook. "Yes?"

"Ah, Mr. Blaine," the voice on the other end of the line said. "How pleasant to find you available."

Lucas didn't recognize the voice, but he knew who was calling. And in that instant, he remembered the man's name. "Maddocks," he said bluntly.

"Oh, good! You remember me! Or, at least, you remember my name. I wasn't absolutely certain you even knew what it was."

"I wondered how we would finally meet," Lucas said.

"Too bad it hadn't happened earlier. Much earlier, really. All of this could have been avoided."

"Let's talk about this."

"Absolutely, we shall. Exactly as it was meant to be the first time."

Lucas guessed that meant face-to-face. "So...what happens now?"

"Oh, it's all very easy. You simply have to do as I say. If it all goes according to plan, maybe Tommy will even get his rabbit."

Lucas faltered. "Tommy? He's there? With you?"

"Yes, yes, here with me. And he's fine. For now. But his well-being is where you come in. And that means following my instructions. Now, get a pencil and a piece of paper and write this down."

Immobilized, Lucas felt completely at a loss. As if the phone were connected to some distant being on another planet and the voice was speaking to him in a foreign language.

Parker stood helplessly on the other side of the desk, shuffling in place, unable to hear what the caller was saying. He waved his arms, trying to get Lucas's attention. "Lucas? What's going on?"

"Do it now, Mr. Blaine," the voice on the other end demanded. "We haven't got a lot of time."

As though released from a trance, Lucas dropped the receiver and pulled open the top drawer of his desk, scrambling through papers looking for a pencil. Grabbing the first one he could find, he realized the graphite tip had broken and flung it into the corner of the room, then dug further into the drawer for another. Not finding one, he slammed the drawer shut and pulled open the top left-hand-side drawer. His Colt Hammerless sat there, beckoning. Ignoring it, he dug underneath until finally, finding a pencil, he pulled it out along with a sheet of paper and picked up the receiver.

"Yes, okay! Go ahead! I'm ready!" he managed to choke out, struggling to tamp down the alarm he could sense in his voice.

"You need to come see me, Mr. Blaine. It's time we met. In person. And you have exactly forty-five minutes to get to the address I'm about to give you."

As Maddocks continued speaking, Lucas scribbled down the directions and then hung up the phone.

"What is it Lucas? Who was that?"

"Someone I never met. But should have." Pulling out his pocket watch, he gave it a quick glance, and then stuffed it back into his pocket. "A long time ago." Without knowing exactly his next move, he stood up and snatched his skimmer up off the desk.

Parker frowned. "You're not going to wear that, are you, Lucas? It's already the eighteenth of September, after all. You know after the fifteenth, straw hats just aren't—"

"What? Are you…?" Lucas couldn't believe his brother could be so easily distracted. Or so trite. "Look, he's got Tommy. And I don't know if I have enough time to get where I need to go before he takes out his hatred for me on that kid."

Parker looked at him, arms open, palms up, as if the answer were obvious. "We'll take the Packard!" he exclaimed, his eyes lighting up at the possibility of an adventure. "Goes like the goddamned wind!"

For a few moments, Lucas just looked at him, trying to weigh the wisdom of doing anything with Parker. He quickly realized he had limited choices. "Right. Let's go!"

"Where, exactly?" asked Parker.

"Up Broadway. Coliseum Theatre."

"The Coliseum?

"That's what he said, Parker. The Coliseum."

"But it's not even open yet."

"What? How do you know?"

"I've got tickets for the opening on the twenty-third. Invitation only. Should be the berries! Eddie Foy's performing, and Claire and I—"

"Parker, we haven't got time for this!"

"Right, then! Let's go!" As Parker hurried out of the office, he called back over his shoulder. "I'll start her up!"

Lucas dove back into his desk drawer and grabbed his pistol, dug back in a second time for some bullets, and jammed them into the gun. By the time he got out to the car, it was already running, the engine generating a steady, confident growl.

"Here, put these on," Parker shouted over the sound of the revving car as he handed Lucas a pair of driving goggles. "Which way?"

"Take the Macombs Dam Bridge over to St. Nicholas!" Lucas yelled.

Parker grinned like a kid with a newly spun cone of cotton candy, his eyebrows dancing with excitement, completely oblivious to the terror that Lucas was trying to stifle. He jammed the car into gear and the Roadster leapt away from the curb.

As the car sped off from the clubhouse, slipping easily around other cars, pedestrians, and numerous other obstructions, a reluctant smile snuck across Lucas's face as he momentarily allowed himself to marvel at the elegance and strength of the powerful vehicle.

Parker veered hard onto the Grand Concourse and headed toward the bridge. Barely slowing down, the car made a sharp right onto 161st Street and then a sharp left, swerving onto Jerome Avenue and the access road to the bridge. Moments later, it clattered onto the swing bridge, just as the operator was stepping into the control booth at one of the four stone piers.

"Go, Parker!" shouted Lucas. "Before he can open that swing!"

Almost sensing the urgency, the car gave a mighty roar as Parker dropped it down a gear and stuffed his foot hard onto the accelerator. The car bounded onto the bridge just as it started to inch apart from the roadway.

"Faster, Parker! Faster!" Lucas grabbed the top of the windshield and pulled himself almost upright. "We need to get over to the other side before it swings open too far!"

The car raced toward the yawning gap in the roadway. Seconds later, it hurtled into the air, landing with a thud onto the far side, its tires shrieking in anger. Parker yanked the wheel hard to the right, barely avoiding the metal guardrail and narrowly missing a horse-drawn cart with a load of chickens coming the other way, then straightened the wheel and exited the bridge onto 155th Street, south of the Polo Grounds.

"Isn't she a beauty!" yelled Parker.

"Only if I get where I need to go!" Lucas shouted back, fumbling with his pocket watch. "Turn up St. Nicholas and onto Broadway."

Shifting gears once again, Parker sped up until he was almost at the junction of St. Nicholas and Amsterdam Avenues.

"Look out, Parker!"

Just then, a streetcar rumbled into the intersection, and Parker slammed on the brakes, screeching to a halt just inches away from the potentially deadly mass of metal. People sitting by the windows screamed in anticipation of the crash that never came, and the streetcar driver furiously rang his bell to signal his irritation. Parker waved a cheery hello, which only served to make the driver angrier as he yelled out a string of obscenities.

"Back up, back up!" shouted Lucas as he looked back over his shoulder.

Accompanied by the sound of crunching metal gears, Parker put the car into reverse and backed away from the streetcar. Then, another grinding of gears, and the Packard angled its way through the crowded intersection and sped off up Broadway.

A few minutes later, spotting the intersection he was looking for, Lucas leaned forward in his seat. Thrusting an arm out almost into Parker's face, Lucas called out. "There! Over there! Across the street."

Seconds later, the car slid to a stop, and Lucas jumped out, pulled off his goggles, and threw them back onto the seat. He looked across at the building's handsome new marquee, announcing what Parker had already told him: *Opening Soon*. A large vertical sign ran down one side of the building, outlined with hundreds of lightbulbs. *B.S. Moss Coliseum*. A second sign proclaimed B. F. Keith's Vaudeville, adding to the overall cachet.

"Get a message to Zach! Tell him to meet me here!" yelled Lucas.

"Here? Where would I find him?" Parker shouted back, his view now blocked by several cars as Lucas dashed across the roadway. When the cars had cleared, Parker yelled again. "Lucas? Lucas!"

But Lucas was long gone.

Chapter 62

Creeping in through the theater's main doors, Lucas looked about, his senses on high alert. There was no one in the front lobby, and the only sound he could hear was his own breathing. As far as he could tell, the building was empty. Careful not to make any sound, he started to cross through the lobby area. It was impossible not to admire the room's overall aura of opulence, with its ivory-colored walls and rose-striated marble columns, the entirety highlighted with fine gold trim. But he knew there was no time to linger.

Thinking it might provide a better vantage point, he advanced tentatively toward the staircase that led to the upper foyer, then suddenly stopped.

Some other sound had broken the stillness.

Music.

Coming from the auditorium.

He backed off the stairs and crept cautiously toward the

THE MAN IN THE BLEACHERS

auditorium doors. As he entered the cavernous space, the music grew louder, and his eyes grew wider. Although the room was only dimly lit, he could see into the farthest corners, and he was stunned by the enormity of it. At the front, a huge stage framed in swooping yards of red velvet. Below that, an orchestra pit large enough to hold two dozen musicians. High up on one wall was an enormous, built-in organ overlooking what Lucas guessed was enough seating for more than three thousand people. The Coliseum was obviously going to be not only one of New York's largest theaters, but also one of its finest. A place to showcase Hollywood's most dazzling new creations, as well as a stunning setting for vaudeville celebrities to parade their talent.

Methodically, Lucas surveyed the room, his eyes adjusting to the faint lighting, his ears hunting for the origin of the music.

It didn't take him long.

In the back left-hand corner of the orchestra pit was a shiny new Victrola where a kettle drum might normally sit.

I know that tune, Lucas thought to himself.

Whispering.

A Paul Whiteman recording from the Victor Talking Machine Company. The bright tempo, the kind you might whistle along with, was completely incongruous from where Lucas stood. More suited to a dance hall than an empty one.

He stood motionless for another half-minute, surveying the room, trying to glean a hint as to why he had been sent there. Tentatively, he called out.

"Hello?"

No answer came back.

He was about to step forward when suddenly a timid figure emerged from between the curtains at center stage. Lucas grabbed for his gun, but before he could get it even halfway out of his jacket, he could see that the figure was that of a boy. Carrying a sandwich board.

Lucas stepped further down the aisle, checking over his shoulder as he went. The music had stopped, and the only noise was the repetitive *thick-thick-thick* from the now completed recording as it continued to spin about on the Victrola. Within a few steps, he recognized who was carrying the sandwich board.

And what was written on it.

World Premiere: The Death of Lucas Blaine. Invitation Only.

"Tommy? How did you...?" Lucas blurted out, hurrying down the aisle.

Tommy just trembled as Lucas climbed up onto the stage.

"What is this, Tommy? I mean, who did this?" he asked, as he took Tommy's head in his hands. "It was the man who messed with your rabbit, yeah?"

A barely perceptible nod confirmed Lucas's fears.

"Here, let me get this thing off you," he added, and reached down to pull the sign board off the quivering bat boy.

"No! Don't! You can't!" Tommy screamed as he jumped back a foot.

Confused, Lucas let his hands fall to his sides. "Okay, Tommy. Just...just be steady now. I'm not going to hurt you. I just want to get that thing off of you so we can talk."

"No!" Tommy screamed again. "You can't! Please!"

Lucas cocked his head, as if that might help him understand. "Okay, kid," said Lucas, stepping back a bit, hoping to ease the tension, "how 'bout we just relax and you tell me what's going on?"

Tears welled up in Tommy's eyes. "I'm going to explode!" he blurted.

Lucas smiled. "Well, I don't know how that could happen. There's just two of us."

"It's underneath this!" Tommy squeaked, indicating with his eyes the sandwich board that rested on his shoulders.

The smile instantly disappeared from Lucas's face. "Underneath? What's underneath, Tommy?"

The boy tried to form the words but could only manage to gulp down great lungfuls of air. Finally, he managed, "Dynamite." It was almost a whisper.

Lucas took an involuntary step backwards and then, catching himself, eased forward again.

"Dynamite, yeah? You sure about that?"

"He said it was dynamite."

"Who said that?"

"The man what—what killed Bear."

"Okay, so...can I have a look?"

Tommy didn't reply, but his body language screamed against it.

"Listen, Tommy...I won't touch the sign. I'll just have a quick peek beneath, yeah? I won't touch it."

"He said he'd give me a rabbit," Tommy whimpered.

The music had stopped, but the needle continued to scratch out a steady clicking sound.

Stepping forward, Lucas nodded and gave Tommy a weak smile. "A rabbit, huh? Is that what he said? That he'd get you a rabbit?" He wanted to keep Tommy talking, talking about anything so that he could crouch down and see what had the boy so frightened.

But looking under the sandwich board silenced him. Firmly strapped to Tommy's body were three sticks of dynamite. Thin metal wires led to a small alarm clock, two shiny ringers on top with a tiny metal hammer in between. The whole construction was held in place by multiple strands of rope.

Lucas quickly pulled out his pocket watch and felt his whole body freeze. Maddocks had said he had forty-five minutes to get to the address. Now that he was here, he could see where that forty-five minutes was heading. By his reckoning, he had about five minutes before...

He stuffed the watch back into his pocket.

"It was just a toy," Tommy gurgled. "It wasn't a real rabbit at all."

"A toy rabbit, yeah?" Lucas queried, his eyes glued to the wired alarm clock, his ears now registering the steady *tick-tock*. "Well, that wasn't what you wanted at all, was it, Tommy?"

"Not a toy rabbit."

"Tommy...I can see now how this is all set up here, yeah? So, this thing, this sandwich board, it's not connected to anything, and so, and so I'm going to take it off..."

"No, no, no, no, no!" Tommy wailed, backing away, his arms outstretched in front of him, trying to keep Lucas at bay.

"Tommy, wait."

"No! He said no!" He looked about ready to collapse.

"Okay, okay, just...just hold on a second. Just...let me think." Lucas tried to smile, but it wouldn't come. He took off his hat and lowered his head. After a few moments, he crouched down and looked up at Tommy. "Tommy, look up. Look here at me."

Reluctantly, Tommy lifted his chin, his eyes still moist.

"Here's the thing, kid. I need to take that signboard off. 'Cause something's going to happen for sure if I don't. And, well...if something does happen, then it's going to happen to both of us, yeah? So, I'll be right here with you. And then..."

Lucas stopped, not knowing whether he was helping or hurting the situation. "Look, kid, it's going to be all right, okay? We've got to do this...right now!"

Tommy looked as though he might shake the sandwich board right off, but nodded once and then squeezed his eyes shut.

Lucas stepped forward, his right hand grabbing the sandwich board on Tommy's left side, his left hand pressing hard against the other side.

"Okay, so, it's like..." Lucas closed his own eyes, struggling for an idea. "It's like...like the bottom of the ninth, okay, Tommy?" Lucas opened his eyes and took a deep breath. "Bottom of the ninth, bases loaded, and you're up to bat. Game's tied, so it's all up to you. And you can do this, kid. Just one good swing. That's all we need. Just one good swing, right? Just one good—"

And before the boy could object, Lucas yanked the board up and over Tommy's head.

In that one moment of sheer terror, Tommy let out a raging howl. And then, realizing that nothing had changed, he abruptly stopped.

"Home run, kid." Lucas smiled.

Once again, the room was filled with the ticking sound of the alarm clock and the scratching sound of the record.

"Now, there's just one other little thing we've got to do," he said, staring hard at the dynamite, hoping that that one more thing would present itself. But before he could plan another move, he spotted something in Tommy's shirt pocket.

An envelope.

Quickly, Lucas bent down, took the envelope between two fingers, and slid it ever so slowly out of Tommy's pocket. Across the front, in plain block letters, his own name. He could tell by the feel there was something more than just a slip of paper inside. But not much of something. Certainly no Cracker Jack toy. Nothing hard or three-dimensional.

Lucas reached into the envelope and pulled out a handwritten note. And a subway ticket.

As if it might itself explode, he unfolded the note with great care. A neatly scripted message revealed itself.

> *Mr. Blaine. My regrets about Tommy. Your friend Zacharia is presently in the same situation. Meet me on the subway platform at 181st Street by 9:45, or he will surely be blown to pieces.*

Lucas staggered back on his heels, his brain swirling in confusion, disbelief, and anger. Zach? How could he have gotten to Zach? And why Tommy? Why go after Tommy in the first place? Was he really going to let him die?

He stared at the letter again.

Meet me on the subway platform at 181st Street by 9:45...

"The subway? Why would he choose the subway?" Lucas wondered aloud, his voice tinged with desperation.

Yanking his pocket watch out, he quickly calculated. He had less than twenty minutes to get there.

Throwing the paper to the stage floor, Lucas grabbed the still-shaking Tommy.

"Listen carefully, Tommy. You need to keep very still. I'm going to unhook this thing, and you're going to be okay, yeah? Very still now."

Lucas knelt down once again and closely examined the time bomb attached to the quaking boy, trying to remember what he'd learned about dynamite from his service overseas. Nothing useful came to mind. Yet it looked straightforward enough. Dynamite. Wires. Alarm clock. If he just pulled out one wire, would that be enough? Two wires? He had no idea. But there wasn't enough time for another plan.

"Okay, Tommy. Bottom of the ninth—"

"We played that inning," the boy interrupted.

For one brief moment, Lucas wanted to laugh and cry all at the same time. But time was an endangered commodity right now, and Lucas knew it was running out.

"Extra innings, then, yeah? Here we go. One, two…," hands sticky with sweat, "…three!" Lucas yanked all three wires from the red cardboard tubes.

With reflexes stretched to snapping, they both abruptly recoiled at the movement. But when nothing happened, both collapsed on the floor, Tommy weeping and Lucas laughing. Moments later, the clock's ringer went off, clattering loudly in the empty auditorium. They barely noticed.

Lucas shuffled over to where Tommy lay and hurriedly began unravelling the rope tied around his chest.

"Tommy, you're all right now. All right? It's over. Done." He threw the disarmed dynamite onto one side of the stage, the alarm clock to the other. "But I've got to go. And you need to stay here. Wait for… for someone! Just…I don't know. Just wait!" urged Lucas, suddenly aware there was nobody he could hope would show up.

Without another word, he ran up the auditorium aisle and out through the lobby doors.

Chapter 63

Lucas raced out the front door of the Coliseum, his heart pounding. Before he could reach the roadway, a wave of nausea flooded over him, that familiar trigger that told him he was going to lose touch with his surroundings. Grabbing hold of a nearby lamppost, he knew he would be swept up in some momentary nightmare that would shatter all connection with reality.

His head felt like a ball of yarn, a monstrous tangle of fuzzy threads that led nowhere.

And then it started. Scattered clouds of dust choked the air like a dirty veil, half obscuring the endless line of tanks that rattled by in both directions, their combined clatter a deafening blanket of noise that smothered the roadway. A cluster of horse-drawn carts fought for space amidst the muddle of men and machinery, their bottles, boxes, and barrels banging about under dirty canvas tarpaulins. Crisply uniformed bike messengers swirled in and about, their regimental insignia proudly displayed. People shouted, others shouted back, an indecipherable stew of voices, demanding, pleading, questioning, cajoling.

Lucas stood transfixed, the blood in his ears pulsing madly. The blurriness, the soft edges, everything around him melting into a bubbly pool of impenetrable but all too familiar confusion. Once again, he'd been transported back to the mind-numbing horror of the Western Front.

"Hey, pal. You okay?"

Lucas turned to look at a grizzled man in a uniform standing next to him, not comprehending. The man appeared to sneer back, one hand resting threateningly on his sidearm.

"You don't look so good."

"I'm not…sure. I think I'm—"

"Hey! Look out!" yelled the stranger, grabbing Lucas by the arm and yanking him backwards just as a butcher's carriage rambled by, oblivious to anything on two legs. "That cart near run you over!"

Lucas jerked away from the man, but the sudden movement was enough. The cloudy, distorted images began to melt away, and the world around him was, once again, restored to order. Tanks disappeared, morphing back into an orderly column of cars heading up and down Broadway. Carts no longer transported artillery but instead carried on, delivering their loads of lumber, housewares, and various pieces of machinery destined for the surrounding factories. Bike messengers continued to swirl about, their uniforms now clearly indicating their Western Union affiliation.

"That cart just about run you down," the man repeated. "You okay?"

Lucas shook his head. "No," he replied. "But I intend to get there!"

Without another word, Lucas stepped into the traffic and jockeyed his way across the road.

Reaching the other side, he looked around in all directions but couldn't see the subway entrance. Then he remembered. The entrance was not on Broadway, but two blocks further east at St. Nicholas Avenue.

Sensing the minutes tick away but with no time to check his watch, he raced down the street toward the subway entrance, confident that Tommy was no longer in trouble, certain that Zach had more trouble than he could handle.

Coming around the edge of the metal railing to the head of the stairs that led down to the subway, he stopped. A sandwich board, just like the one Tommy had been wearing, stood in his way.

Closed for repairs.

He kicked the sign out of his way and leapt down the stairs two at a time.

At first, he thought the station was empty. No clerk stood beside the ticket chopper, and no passengers stood on the platform. But then he noticed the station attendant, slumped over in a corner of his booth. Snoring loudly.

Lucas pulled out the subway ticket that had been in the envelope he'd taken off Tommy and set it down on the ticket chopper.

"Keep the change," he said to no one, and slipped through the gate.

He pulled his gun from its holster as he stepped gingerly over to the platform. Leaning out over the edge, he peered deep into the tunnel. First one way, then the other. A light down one end of the tunnel was moving toward him. Not fast enough to be a train. But still moving. Still coming his way.

"Hey!" he shouted toward the approaching light. His voice echoed off the tiled walls, but no answer returned.

The light continued to move in his direction.

With a quick glance down the opposite end of the tunnel to ensure nothing was coming his way, he slipped over the edge of the platform and onto the tracks, stepping cautiously toward the light.

"Hey!" he yelled again. "You there!"

With his attention fixed firmly on what was in front of him and far from the ticket booth, he hadn't noticed that the snoring had stopped.

Nor that footsteps were approaching from behind.

He did, however, sense the whoosh of air over his right shoulder just as a heavy iron bar smashed into his hand, knocking the pistol to the ground and then rising back up into his face, knocking him out cold.

Chapter 64

The trembling had stopped, but the sniffling hadn't, even as Tommy had managed to slow his breathing. Still lying on the stage in the Coliseum Theatre where Lucas had left him, he looked around, his eyes coming to rest on the dynamite that only minutes ago he'd been wearing like a vest. An involuntary shudder surged through his body, and he quickly turned away.

Lucas had told him to wait. And the boy was used to doing what he was told, *wanted* to do what he was told. But wait for who? Or what? The auditorium made him nervous. It was dark. Unfriendly. Not at all like a baseball park.

And no one had come. Maybe no one *would* come. It had already been five minutes. How much longer?

Tommy felt scared and lonely.

Where had Lucas gone?

Springing to his knees, the boy scrambled across the floor to where Lucas had dropped the note. He unfolded the paper and looked at the scribbles on the page. The words meant nothing. He'd never learned to read.

But he knew his numbers.

Baseball was all about numbers.

What had Lucas said? Something about a subway.

He stared at the note again. A number stared back. 181.

Tommy looked hopefully toward the auditorium doors, but they hadn't moved since Lucas had gone out.

He rolled back onto his haunches.

He wanted to wait. Do as Mr. Blaine had said.

He just couldn't.

Chapter 65

A reedy consciousness lapped at the shore of Lucas's brain, each wave slightly stronger, reaching slightly deeper, until it finally became a steady tide of what felt like wakefulness. His head throbbed. He wanted to reach up and touch it but couldn't move his arms.

In the distance he could hear a deep rumble rushing closer, then stopping for a few moments before receding again. Beneath him, a dirt floor, cold and rough, pressed hard against his cheek, tickling the lashes of his right eye. Inhaling as deeply as he dared, the sweet smell reminded him of a newly turned springtime garden at dawn, a rich blanket of swollen fertility. A garden of promise, fresh and clean, with big, fat, nightcrawlers stretching and contracting, burrowing their way deep, deep into the ground, turning the soil over as they went about their work, exposing new earth, new smells.

Then a smell that wasn't quite right. And then another. Smells that weren't at all like a garden.

Oil.

And grease.

Lucas inhaled again. *That's not making sense. A garden of oil and grease?*

He willed his brain to clear. To remember what had happened. To decipher where he was.

Above all, one thing was certain. He wasn't in a garden.

Wherever he was, he could sense that there was light in the room, despite his eyes still being shut. Forcing one eye open, he could see a shape a short distance away, also lying on the ground.

It was a man, that much he could tell. And whoever it was, he had a cloth bag over his head. The man's hands were tied behind his back but his feet were untethered. The longer Lucas stared, the more he was convinced. It was Zach. He was either unconscious or…Lucas didn't want to think about the *or*.

Lucas tried to talk, to shout out, but nothing more than a gurgle came out.

"Ah, Mr. Blaine."

The voice sent a shiver up Lucas's spine.

Maddocks.

He knew it right away.

"Let me help you up."

Hands gripped Lucas's shoulder and yanked him up into a sitting position. It was only then that Lucas realized that his own hands were tied behind his back and his feet were tied at the ankles. He quickly surveyed his surroundings, hoping to find something that might be helpful. It was obvious now that he was in a tunnel, and he wondered if his mind was playing tricks on him again. But, it was a much bigger tunnel that the ones he had crawled around in overseas, and Lucas realized that he was firmly in the present. What kind of tunnel, or where it might be, he couldn't tell, though the smell of oil and grease suggested that it had once held machinery.

Two kerosene lanterns lit the space immediately around the three men, but the light was swallowed up rapidly as it tried to reach into the darkness. At the closer end, a door. To freedom? It seemed unlikely, given Lucas's current situation.

"So. We meet." Maddocks smiled at Lucas. "It's taken quite some time. Although, in all truthfulness…we've already met. Several times, in fact. You just didn't realize it." The smile broadened as he turned to work on something that was hidden from Lucas's view. "Let's see now. There was that night at the newsstand. A brief encounter, and in all fairness, you weren't yet aware of what I was engineering, so perhaps that shouldn't count. So…how about…ah…the subway station! I dropped my mirror, don't you remember? You looked like you'd seen a ghost! Which I very nearly was…thanks to you! And then another day, when I was pretending to be cleaning the subway steps. You bumped into me. Or I bumped into you, I can't really say. And, of course, the bomb on the bus! Sheer majesty! How would you have known the attendant at the service station where you stopped that morning was me? Ha! Doesn't matter. The point is, we've met. And I've had quite a bit of fun along the way."

As Maddocks spoke, Lucas looked about, trying to get some measure of his situation.

"You killed Frankie Miller," Lucas said bluntly.

"Mr. Miller was incapable of performing his assigned tasks properly. I released him from his duties."

Lucas looked around, tried to find some avenue of leverage. "Where am I?"

Maddocks ignored him. "And then your friend there, Mr. Zacharia. I don't think he appreciated my portrayal as a pushcart vendor." Maddocks looked back over his shoulder at Lucas and nodded at Zach. "A big man, but...very little imagination."

"Is this some...some sort of subway tunnel?"

"Was," acknowledged Maddocks. "At one time, years ago, it was a subway maintenance tunnel. There are a few of these about town." He waved his hand, as if showing off the space. "Just wide enough for a single car and long enough for about eight of them. Long since abandoned, and the hardware removed. Most of it, anyway. They were kind enough to leave a few things that I'm able to make use of."

The smell of oil and grease now made sense.

"And now, happily, it is my...," Maddocks stopped to consider his choices, "...workshop!" he concluded, a wry smile enveloping his face. A moment later, the smile had vanished. "And, in good time, it will be your tomb, Mr. Blaine." Maddocks turned back to his work.

With Maddocks turned the other way, Lucas quickly surveyed his surroundings. He needed time to think. Time to clear his head and focus on finding a way out. Besides himself and Zach, there wasn't much to see. Two kerosene lanterns. An unmarked wooden crate. Some rope. A small, two-wheeled cart. A crumpled-up tarpaulin, a shovel, and a pickaxe. Maddocks's jacket hung from a nail on one of the wooden beams.

Lucas needed to keep him talking. "Why the Cracker Jack?"

Maddocks looked back over his shoulder. "What? Oh, yes, the toys. Such an inspiration, don't you think? At first, it was really just about the confection. Popcorn, peanuts, molasses. Did you know, Mr. Blaine, that Cracker Jack was invented more than twenty-five years ago? By a German immigrant." Maddocks stopped and looked down at the earthen floor. "A German immigrant," he mused. "Made right here in America by someone whose relatives we recently blew to kingdom come!" Maddocks smiled at the irony. "Isn't it odd," he added, "how someone can be your best friend one moment and your vilest enemy the next?"

When Lucas didn't reply, Maddocks continued.

"Not only did we win the war, we got to keep the prize. Or prizes, as it may be. A prize in every box, yes? Of course, I'd never even tasted Cracker Jack until earlier this year, when I first arrived here in New York, ready to initiate my plan. Didn't really even like it at first. But then...then...a little toy rooster showed me the way. And I started to think how much more fun my plan might be if I worked in a little...mystery. And the more fun I had thinking about it, the more I began to like...Cracker Jack!" Again, Maddocks paused to consider his point. "The popcorn gave me the idea, Mr. Blaine. And I thought about how I would do to you what you almost did to me." Maddocks stared hard at Lucas. "Poof! Like a piece of popcorn! And now...now, you're my prize, Mr. Blaine."

"What do you want, Maddocks?"

"Why...you, of course." He stood up. "I want you, Mr. Blaine. I want you to experience what I did, what I went through. And now you will. I want you to feel the pain, the terror, the darkness everywhere, the hopelessness...the sheer terror of being buried alive. You left me to die in that tunnel in Belgium, covered in tons and tons of earth. You could have helped, Mr. Blaine, but you didn't. You ran away. Left me there to suffocate and die. To rot and fester, to become some maggot's dinner, to become part of the earth before my time. But I didn't do that, Mr. Blaine. I didn't do that. I started digging...no, *not* digging...clawing...clawing my way out of that hellhole. Scraping and scratching, inch by inch, fighting for air, pleading, begging to see the sky once again. *Just one more time, let me smell the air,* I prayed, *and see the sky.* And I swore I wouldn't stop until I did see the sky. Every muscle wanting to give up, hours and hours of frustration and pain, of terror, while you, you and the others just...ran away. You ran away!"

He paused, struggling to control his emotions, but failing. "But...I did see the sky again, Mr. Blaine! Little by little, I dug myself out of there. And when I got out, I swore...I'd get revenge! Yes, Mr. Blaine! Revenge! I want revenge! Vengeance will be mine! And I will...I *will* bring burning coals down on your head!"

Sayeth the Lord. Romans 12: 17-2.

Lucas recognized the verse. But he knew it wasn't the right moment to try and debate its actual intent.

He waited for Maddocks to stop hyperventilating. When it appeared his tormentor had once again gained control of his emotions, Lucas offered, "Some plan you put together. Must have taken a long time."

"And every minute a pleasure," Maddocks replied in disgust, as he wiped the perspiration from his forehead.

"You had some help, yeah? You couldn't have done it all by yourself."

Maddocks studied Lucas for a moment. "I'm glad you appreciate the enormity of it, Mr. Blaine. Yes, I had help. Quite a bit at times. Unsurprisingly, a few dollars here and there buys all the allegiance one needs. Though it doesn't guarantee aptitude, I'm sorry to say. But vigilance, Mr. Blaine. Vigilance is the key to a successful outcome. And immediate retribution when called for." Maddocks smiled. "Now...no further appreciation needed. I've dispensed with my assistants, so that it's just...you and I. And that one also," he said, pointing to Zach. "Though I doubt very much he's in any shape to grasp what's going on."

Maddocks kneeled down, his attention now back on the work in front of him.

"I'm here...you're there...and soon, you'll be under a ton of earth as I was, clawing and scraping and praying and wondering if you'll ever see the beauty of the sky once more." Maddocks looked about the tunnel, a look of admiration crossing his face. "But you won't, Mr. Blaine. You won't. I've made sure of that. Now," he said, removing his vest and hanging it on a nail stuck into one of the wooden beams opposite to where he'd hung his jacket, "I trust you won't object if I leave you for a few moments."

Standing up, Maddocks picked up the wooden crate and placed it into the cart, then grabbed one of the kerosene lanterns that was hanging overhead. As he stepped away from where he'd been squatting, Lucas could see what he'd been working on.

A bright red dynamite detonator stood alone in the middle of the tunnel.

"Oh, don't worry about my little toy, here, Mr. Blaine," he said, reaching down and grasping the plunger handlebar in one hand. "Nothing happens...until I do this!"

And with one swift push, he slammed the handle down into the top of the detonator.

Chapter 66

Maddocks laughed as he held up the ends of the fuse for Lucas to see. It was obvious now that they hadn't been attached to the detonator.

"Just a little joke, Mr. Blaine. Surely you didn't think I was going to blow myself up along with you?"

Lucas hadn't had time to think of anything other than where all of his body parts would end up.

Chuckling to himself, Maddocks grabbed one of the lanterns. "You'll forgive me if I don't wait around for you to recover from your shock. There are some details I need to attend to before we can move ahead with my little plan." With one last mocking smile, he moved off into the tunnel, pulling the cart behind him.

Lucas watched him go. At intervals, Maddocks stopped, picked out one or more sticks of dynamite from the wooden crate, and wedged them into crevices in the tunnel walls. Each wax-coated cylinder was then linked to the main fuse as he went.

The meager light from his kerosene lantern pried open the darkness in front of him, but with each step forward, shadows quickly filled in behind, and within a few short minutes, Maddocks had disappeared from sight.

Only the creaking of the cart betrayed the presence of anyone in the tunnel at all.

A weak voice mumbled, "Son of a bitch!"

Lucas jumped to attention.

"Zach! You're alive!"

"Doesn't feel like it." Zach rolled onto his side and tried to squint the room into focus. "Can't see much. Kind of dark here."

Lucas couldn't help but smile. "You've got a bag over your head!"

"That would account for it. Has he gone?"

"For the moment."

"What about you, Lucas? You okay?"

"If you don't count a cracked skull and smashed hand. He got the jump on me."

"Same," said Zach. "Three guys, maybe four. Night before last. I was in the clubhouse after the game, thinking you might show up. They jumped me when I left. Threw a sack over my head and clubbed me with something."

"Soon as we get out of here, I'll make things right, yeah?"

"Last game's today, Lucas. I'm guessing that pennant's on hold 'til next year."

In all the turmoil of the last few days, Lucas had lost sight of the season's finish. He wondered what the players would be thinking right about now, without either himself or Zach there to explain.

He looked into the tunnel where he'd last seen Maddocks. "We need to think. I expect he'll be back soon."

Zach writhed about, still unable to get up. "Expect so."

The last thing either of them expected was for the door to open. So when it did, just a crack at first, they froze.

A frightened voice called through the opening, "Hello?"

Lucas turned to Zach, who had turned toward the sound of the voice. In unison, they both whispered loudly, "Tommy?"

The door creaked open wide, and Tommy stuck his head in. A look of relief played across his face.

"Tommy, where did you—how did you find me?"

"I got scared. I waited at first. But nobody came, and I got scared." The boy stepped tentatively into the space where Lucas and Zach lay tied up. "So I left. I know you said to stay there, but—. But I heard you say 'subway' when you was readin' that note, so I figured that's where to go. 'Cept I didn't know where that was. I just ran fast down the street, and then I seen the sign with '181' on it, and I knowed that was the subway, and I went down the steps, and I heard that man, the one that killed Bear, the one that tied me up, I heard him talkin' to some other fellas, and then I seen them draggin' you into the tunnel, so I followed. I didn't want to, 'cause it was dark."

Lucas could barely find the words. "But you came anyway."

"Jesus, kid. You got the nerves of a major league shortstop," said Zach.

"I didn't like it. The dark, and all."

Lucas had a hundred questions, but he knew there wasn't enough time for any of them. "Tommy, we need you to help us find a way to get out of here. Look around, everywhere. Look for something that might help, you know, something sharp. A knife, or maybe—I don't know. Something, yeah?"

Tommy rushed into the tunnel, glad to be where there was

light. He looked under the tarpaulin and all around the edges of the tunnel, but found nothing helpful.

"Give me that pickaxe, Tommy," Lucas urged. "Maybe I can make that work."

Lucas managed to get onto his knees while Tommy dragged the pickaxe over to where he sat. "Slide the blade up under my hands, kid. And see if you can pull that hood off of Zach."

As Lucas worked away, trying to fray the ropes that bound his hands, Tommy slid over to Zach and worked the bag so that it finally slid off his head, then stood up and walked over to where Maddocks's jacket was hanging and lifted it up. His eyes widened.

"There's this," Tommy said.

Lucas looked up. Hanging underneath the jacket was Lucas's holster. Inside the holster, his gun.

"Holy smoke, kid!" Lucas exclaimed. "Grab that quick! Before he comes back!"

Tommy reached up and lifted the holster off the nail, then rushed over to where Lucas was sitting, dropped it on the ground, and started to untie his hands.

Before he'd gotten very far, Zach lifted up his head and called over to him. "Lucas, let me have it. He'll think I'm still out cold!"

With the hood off, Lucas could see the large crimson smear down the left side of Zach's face, his left eye a swollen mound of purple flesh.

"What about your eye?"

"Looks better if you don't look. I'll be all right once I get used to the light," Zach replied.

Lucas could tell Zach wasn't seeing much of anything. And he didn't like how that might play out. "No good, Zach. We're only going to get one chance at this. I'll just have to try."

"It'll take a steady hand, Lucas. Didn't sound a minute ago like you had one of those."

Zach was right and Lucas knew it. *Think, Lucas, think!*

"I can do it." Tommy looked straight at Lucas.

Lucas stared straight back. "Tommy...you ever shot a gun?"

Tommy hesitated, then looked down at the ground. "Not a real one," he murmured.

"Listen, kid, this isn't the time—"

"I can do it!" Tommy declared forcefully.

Before Lucas could argue the point, he heard a noise from the tunnel. A noise, and then the slightest flicker of light from a lantern.

"Mr. Blaine?" Maddocks called out from the darkness. "I hope you haven't missed me!"

"Tommy, get under that tarpaulin! Now!"

"What about your hands?" Tommy asked.

"Now!"

Tommy grabbed the gun and, before Lucas could object, scooted beneath the dirty canvas.

Within a few moments, Maddocks's face emerged from the shadows, calling out as he came. "Everything's in order, Mr. Blaine. And soon, we can be done with all of this."

It took Maddocks another minute to fully emerge from the depths of the tunnel. When he'd finally reached where Lucas was sitting, he stopped, kneeled down, took out his handkerchief, and wiped his brow. "So, Mr. Blaine. It's been a tiresome journey. Not without some fun, as I've already elaborated, but tiresome nonetheless. So...here's what we do now. I'm going to untie your feet, then you and I are going to walk down into that tunnel. You...are going to stay. I am not. And that will be the end of it. You and I will be—"

Without warning, the tarpaulin stood up.

Startled, Maddocks jumped to his feet and moved back a quick few steps. The look of shock on his face turned to confusion as a small arm emerged from under the canvas and proceeded to wrestle it off the figure standing beneath. It wasn't until the tarp fell to the ground that he understood what was happening. Just eight feet away, Tommy stood pointing the gun directly at his chest.

Maddocks held out both hands as if welcoming a long-lost friend. "Tommy!" he said, struggling to be believed. "How delightful to see you! I thought you might be...tied up for a while!"

Tommy said nothing but took a step forwards, forcing Maddocks to step back.

Lucas knew he needed to take control of the situation. On the one hand, shooting Maddocks right here, right now, might be the best outcome they could hope for. On the other hand, it might also make Tommy a murderer. And even if he wasn't charged, it was something he would have to deal with for the rest of his life, a fragile kid with an inadequate capacity for nuance.

"Maddocks. It's over. Untie me," said Lucas.

Frowning, Maddocks took a moment to think, his hands still out in front of him as if he thought it would keep Tommy from advancing. "No...no, I don't think that will work, Mr. Blaine. You see, Tommy here is going to give me the gun and then...and then, we'll just go home. Isn't that right, Tommy?"

Tommy shuffled forward another step, again forcing Maddocks back. The gun quivered in his hand. "You killed my rabbit." The words crept out in a venomous whisper.

Lucas could tell that Maddocks was starting to get nervous, starting to lose his patience.

"Maddocks! Untie me! Now!"

"Be still, Blaine! Tommy and I...well, we have things to discuss. Don't we, Tommy?"

Tommy's face tightened, his cheeks reddened, and his voice grew stronger. "You killed my rabbit!"

Maddocks bristled. "That won't do, Tommy! Put down that gun!" He took a step toward the boy, but Tommy raised the gun higher, and Maddocks quickly stepped back.

"Maddocks, you need to stop!" Lucas shouted. "All of this! Right here!"

"No, no, Mr. Blaine," Maddocks replied, trying to recapture some of the calm that had served him so well for so long. "Today is my day. My day! And you are my prize." He turned his attention back to Tommy, once again raising his hands as if to ward off Tommy's anger. "Listen to me, Tommy! You need to put down that gun! Put it down! Then we can—"

Long stifled by fear and shyness, Tommy's words streamed out in a frenzy, drenched in hatred. "You killed my rabbit!"

Maddocks ground his teeth, trying to suppress his own anger, but the dam had burst. "Your stupid rabbit! I don't care about your stupid fucking rabbit! I'm going to—"

No longer able to restrain his anger, Maddocks abruptly sprang into the air, directly at the boy.

There was no time to think. No time to consider alternatives or outcomes. Tommy just pulled the trigger. The gun exploded in a furious roar, hurling both Tommy and the weapon onto the ground.

Chapter 67

Maddocks screamed in pain as he grabbed his bleeding left hand and folded into a ball of fury before slamming into the ground.

"You bastard!" he screamed. "You little fucking bastard!" Blood spurted from his hand as he writhed in agony on the earthen floor, inches away from where Tommy lay, the gun now out of reach. "What have you done? Jesus Christ! You fucking little monster!"

"Tommy," shouted Lucas, "the gun! Grab the gun!"

But before Tommy could react, Maddocks was on top of him, his bloodied hand forgotten, his good hand clutched around Tommy's neck. "You!" he screamed. "You're as dead as your little fucking rabbit! Do you hear me? Dead!" He lay atop Tommy, writhing in pain. "I should have killed you when I killed that fucking little ball of fur! Do you hear me? You bastard! Oh, Jesus!" The words were stifled by the pain as Maddocks rocked back and forth, drawing in great lungfuls of air as more blood oozed from his hand. He mumbled aloud to himself, trying to regain control of his senses and emotions.

Tommy managed a few feeble tugs and kicks, trying to squeeze out from under Maddocks, but the man's good hand was still grasped tight around his neck.

Using his weight to keep Tommy from getting up, Maddocks stretched out his good hand until his fingers found the gun. He yanked it toward his body, grabbing the barrel in his injured hand. The warm metal and familiar shape restored his sense of domination, and he struggled to his knees, commanding his brain to summon the coordination and strength to stand up. He nearly made it.

Amidst the confusion, no one had noticed Zach struggle to his feet. His hands still tied behind his back, he rushed the few feet separating him from Maddocks, and with a mighty roar, plunged headfirst into the now upright man, sending him sprawling to the ground. Zach knew it was never going to be enough, but he hoped it might give Tommy a chance to once again grab the weapon.

"Tommy, the gun!" shouted Lucas, his own hands and feet still bound.

But before Tommy could make a move, Maddocks smashed the gun against the back of Zach's head and pushed his body off to the side. He aimed the gun at Zach and pulled the trigger just as Tommy lunged toward him, pushing his arm aside and sending the bullet into the tunnel wall.

Maddocks screamed as he turned back toward Tommy and swung the pistol at his head, but Tommy fell back out of reach. Immediately, he turned back to aim once again at Zach, but the man lay unconscious at his feet.

Panting furiously, Maddocks turned the gun back on Tommy. "I'm not done with you yet, you little bastard! Now stay...right there!"

For several minutes, no one moved or said anything until Maddocks, nostrils flaring, eyes bulging, finally wobbled to a standing position.

He turned his focus to Lucas. "Seems I was a little too hasty letting my assistants leave," he sputtered. "I should have...should have been more careful."

Keeping the gun fixed on Lucas, he stumbled over to where Tommy lay quivering, grabbed him by the scruff of the neck, and dragged him over to where his jacket was hanging. He dropped the boy to the ground, then unhooked his jacket and awkwardly wrapped it around his injured hand.

"I would end this right now, Mr. Blaine, bring it all to an end," he nodded, smiling, "with a bullet to your brain. That would be easy, efficient...maybe even the smart thing to do. Except for one thing. I must," he screamed, "have revenge! And it shall be on my terms, my timing. It must follow my plan exactly!"

With the clumsy padded bandage in place, he once again grabbed Tommy by the neck and pulled him over to where the dynamite detonator stood, then roughly threw him to the ground and knelt down.

"I hadn't foreseen this, Mr. Blaine," he said, picking up the ends of the fuse and attaching it to the detonator. "I had not foreseen this...at all! But...I can't blame it on you. This was entirely my oversight and I'm discomfited to have to admit it. You can be certain it shall not happen again."

With the fuse firmly attached, Maddocks pointed to Tommy. "You...grab one of those pieces of rope," he said. "You're coming with me."

Tommy shook his head.

Maddocks blinked twice. Then he stood up, took two steps to where Tommy was kneeling, and with one quick move, whipped him across the face with the gun. Tommy let out a shriek, as much from surprise as pain, and fell back onto his heels. A trickle of blood appeared under his lower lip.

Lucas writhed in his rope holds, desperate to be able to do something, anything. "Maddocks! Enough! You want me, you've got me! Let the kid go!"

Maddocks ignored him and pointed the gun at Tommy. "Get the rope." His voice was detached, the careful diction giving way to colorless monotone.

With all resistance in retreat, Tommy scurried over to the pile of ropes and picked up a short length.

"A longer piece, Tommy."

Tommy did as he was told.

"Now," said Maddocks, grabbing one of the kerosene lanterns from where it hung on a beam, "you come with me," and he headed once again into the tunnel.

Tommy, still in shock from being slammed with the gun, didn't move.

His hand throbbing, Maddocks grabbed Tommy and thrust him forward. "Move!"

"But it's dark."

Maddocks pushed him into the tunnel and followed two steps behind. "It's going to get a lot darker, Tommy boy."

Lucas watched helplessly as Maddocks and the boy disappeared into the tunnel. The remaining lantern sputtered and threatened to die completely.

Lucas tugged at the ropes around his wrists, but they wouldn't yield. He looked over at Zach. No movement at all. The sound of Tommy's footfalls were rapidly fading.

Lucas sat staring into the tunnel.

It's going to get a lot darker, for sure.

Chapter 68

"Zach!"

No answer.

"Zach! It's Lucas!"

A slight stirring.

And then, a painful groan.

"C'mon, Zach. We've got work to do!"

More stirring.

"Lucas?"

"Yes! I'm here! C'mon, Zach, slide over here. We've got work to do."

Zach groaned again. "I'm not sure I can do that, Lucas. My head's—"

"You have to, Zach. You have to! And you have to come now! We haven't got much time!"

Zach managed to get onto his knees, but couldn't find his balance and toppled over onto his side.

"Zach, listen! Maddocks has got Tommy, and I'm pretty sure he's planning on tying him up in that tunnel and leaving him there when he blows it up!"

"Lucas, I don't know…"

"Zach! It's the bottom of the ninth! Bottom of the—"

"I know, I know. Bottom of the ninth, the bases are loaded. Okay, but just…just…" And with one mighty heave, Zach managed to hike himself up onto his knees. "Son of a bitch!"

"Okay, good! Now, quick, get over here! I want you to sit your back against my back so you can untie my hands, yeah?"

"Lucas that ain't gonna…"

The lantern sputtered again. "Zach! There's no time for discussion!" *Maybe no time at all.*

Zach crawled over to where Lucas was sitting, and the two worked their bodies around so that they were sitting back to back, their hands fumbling over each other's knots.

"Don't get too friendly, Lucas."

"Just…work the knot, Zach!"

For a full minute, Zach pulled and pushed at various ends and bulges in the knot but couldn't find a way to pry it open.

"No good, Lucas. I can't seem to get…" He stopped talking, his fingers starting to move more intentionally.

Lucas could feel the change. Zach's whole body had stiffened, a new sense of alertness.

"Hold on. Maybe I can…" For another thirty seconds Zach dug his fingers into and around the sisal fibers, working the one strand that seemed to be giving way just a bit.

"What?" urged Lucas. "Do you have something?"

"Yeah. Hold on."

Lucas could feel the strands loosening against his wrists.

"Jesus, Zach, you got it! Keep going! Keep—"

A sudden scream from the tunnel, and both men froze.

"Tommy?" asked Zach.

"Sounded more like Maddocks."

Without another word, Zach grabbed at the rope around Lucas's wrists, pulling and unlooping the strands as fast as his fingers could work them.

Seconds later, the rope fell away.

"Jesus! You did it, Zach!" Lucas yanked his hands back and forth, freeing the last of the knot, then reached around and grabbed at the rope around his ankles.

A second scream from the tunnel and then footsteps. Running.

"Help!" The voice was muffled, but the terror was clear.

"Tommy!" yelled Lucas. "To the light! Run to the light!"

As if mocking him, one of the lanterns flickered and appeared to die, but like a punch-drunk boxer not yet ready to give up, it sprang back to life.

Lucas pulled the rope away from his ankles and stumbled shakily to his feet.

An angry scream from the tunnel, followed by a gunshot.

"Help!"

"Tommy! Run!"

Seconds later Tommy emerged from the shadows, a wobbly light far behind him but coming on fast. Lucas thought he could make out Maddocks's face behind the lantern.

Lucas had no plan. He just wanted Tommy out of that tunnel. But in that instant when all seemed lost, a plan emerged. Crystal-clear. And suddenly, Lucas knew exactly what to do.

Shuffling with stiffness, he stumbled straight toward Tommy.

Nothing between them but the dynamite detonator, a solitary beacon in a sea of hopelessness.

"Tommy! Wait!"

But Tommy didn't, and neither did Lucas. Willing his legs to move, Lucas aimed straight for the detonator.

"Tommy, get down! Get down!"

Another shot rang out. Lucas crouched as Tommy screamed and fell to the ground.

"No!" yelled Lucas, scrambling back to his feet. "No!"

Tommy looked up, his face bristling with rage, a trace of red running down his shirt. Struggling awkwardly to his knees, then to his feet, Tommy stumbled forward, arms leading the way, eyes razor-focused on the detonator.

Two more shots rang out. The lantern splintered into a hundred pieces, pitching the room into total darkness as Tommy and Lucas both lunged forward into the gloom.

For one brief heartbeat, there was nothing. Then, a bellowing cascade of fiery explosions, one after the other, flashed up and down the length of the tunnel, collapsing mountains of dirt, stone, and broken tile into the empty space.

Maddocks's vest flew off the nail where it had been hanging, landing inches from where Tommy lay in the dark.

A small, flat, metallic figurine slid out of the vest pocket.

A rabbit. A toy rabbit.

Like the kind you might find in a box of Cracker Jack.

DECEMBER 15, 1920

Chapter 69

A wind out of the west made the day feel colder than it actually was, and Lucas wasn't the only one standing outside Zaslaw Prusinowski's newsstand with his collar pulled up around his neck.

"Ah, Mr. Manager, you're still here!"

"Still here, Zaslaw." Lucas smiled to himself. Same question every day since the end of the season. It had become a joke between them. "I won't be heading south until after the holidays. Too many social engagements."

"And Mr. Tucker? He is here still, also?"

"Nope. Left last week. He's not a big fan of the city at this time of year. Too many social engagements."

For a moment, Zaslaw looked confused. Then a dawning understanding wrapped his face in a rare smile. "Ah, he is not fond of...how do you say...shenanigans?"

"I think he's just happier on his own. At least, when there's no baseball about."

And after all that we've been through, he needs sand and sunshine more than he needs a couple of cups of eggnog.

"This is good. I am also happiest on my own," Zaslaw said, passing Lucas a copy of the *New York Tribune*. "Look," he said, pointing to the front page. "That man Dempsey wins. Last night, twelve rounds. Just like I say."

Lucas hadn't remembered Zaslaw saying it, but wasn't surprised to hear that the heavyweight champion had beaten yet another ill-qualified challenger. He was, however, surprised that the fight had gone twelve rounds. No one had expected Bill Brennan to take the champ that far.

"So…no Christmas parties for you, Zaslaw?"

"I go to Pennsylvania. Donora. I have cousin there. We will have nice time. And visit new baby."

"Your cousin had a baby?"

"No cousin. A friend. Also Polish. His wife has baby boy. They call him Stanislaw. Nice name, I think."

"Nice name," Lucas agreed.

"Already three weeks old!" the news seller beamed. "Stanisław Franciszek Musial. He is American! They are very proud!"

"They should be," agreed Lucas. "Best country in the world!"

"Hey! Maybe he becomes baseball player. Like you, Mr. Manager."

"I don't play, Zaslaw. I just manage. But…yeah, you never know!" Lucas tucked the paper under his arm, handed Zaslaw the requisite two cents, and headed off down the street.

"See you tomorrow, Zaslaw! There's a lady waiting for me to take her to dinner!"

THE MAN IN THE BLEACHERS

* * *

Murray's Roman Gardens may not have been the city's most distinguished restaurant, but it was certainly among the most opulent. Or garish, depending on your taste. In any event, its lavish embellishments, designed to mimic a luxurious Roman villa, were, at a minimum, overwhelming.

As Lucas and Willa handed over their coats to the cloak room attendant, the *maître d'* rushed forward to greet them.

"Good evening, Mr. Blaine! And...?"

"Miss Pierce," said Lucas.

"And Miss Pierce! How lovely to see you this evening!" he said with a little too much enthusiasm. "Mr. Blaine...that is to say, the *other* Mr. Blaine...asked that I look after everything. And," his eyebrows jumping with excitement, "I can assure you I have." Snapping his fingers like an emperor calling for his palanquin, a waiter in an immaculate black and gold jacket appeared out of nowhere. "Henry here will take you to your table and further attend to your needs. If you require anything at all, anything...please...don't hesitate to request it. Henry!"

With two quick claps of his hands, he was off to greet another guest with the same ebullient welcome.

As they strode up the huge marble staircase to the main dining room, Willa's head spun in all directions, trying to absorb the outlandish ornamentation.

"Good gracious, Lucas, look at all the...the statuary, the vines climbing up those columns, the paintings! It looks just like a Roman garden! How on earth...! Does Parker come here often?" she asked, her voice filled with awe.

"I can only imagine," mumbled Lucas as he gazed about the

room and the many tables filled with men and women in glittering evening wear. "It's definitely his kind of place!"

"Well, it was very gracious of him to plan this evening for us," she said, as Henry the waiter pulled out her chair.

If you only knew, thought Lucas, sitting down himself.

"Oh, look, Lucas! The ceiling is covered in tiny little stars!"

Lucas looked up at the twinkling electric lights overhead and smiled. "Even a silly make-believe moon," he chuckled, pointing a finger at the butter-colored disc that glowed above their heads.

"Lucas, don't ruin it!" she admonished. "Please."

"Sorry, it's just a little...maybe too much."

"Over there!" Willa said, ignoring him. "That looks just like Gloria Swanson!"

"I think that's because it *is* Miss Swanson," Lucas observed, peering over his shoulder.

"Really? Oh, my! And over there, is that...?"

"Yeah, well, if it isn't, she's got a twin," he conceded, confident that the woman Willa was referring to was yet another Hollywood star.

They spent the next few minutes pointing back and forth at the many lavish and exotic decorations in the room when the waiter returned with their menus.

Willa's eyes grew large as she scanned the elaborate *carte du jour*. Blue Point oysters and little neck clams to start. Then a cream of capon soup, followed by a choice of baked sea bass or filet of sole. Next, a mousse of Virginia ham with sweetbreads, and finally a main course of goose and turkey, accompanied by a variety of winter vegetables, rounded off with a Salad Fleurie and cheese tartlet.

"I can't think I'll ever have room for all of this," said Willa, astonished at the sheer volume and variety.

"And that's even before dessert," added Lucas. "Pumpkin pie, mince pie, English plum pudding. Hard to know where to start." He looked up at her, a twinkle in his eye. "But I know where I'd like to finish!"

"Behave yourself!" Willa scolded with a dimpled grin, just as Henry returned.

"Allow me to suggest these as a starting point," said the waiter, placing two delicate crystal flutes down in front of them. "Our very finest," he added. "Compliments of Mr. Parker Blaine."

"A toast then," said Willa, raising her glass and taking a quick sip as the waiter glided away. "Oh, my," she said suddenly, pulling her glass back, a furtive smile sneaking across her lips. "That doesn't taste at all like ginger ale!"

Lucas took a sip and winked. "Did I ever mention how much I like my brother?"

Feasting their way through first one course and then another five, they laughed and talked about this and that, rambling off into everything and nothing.

Just as dessert was being placed in front of them, the band struck up a new tune.

Whispering.

Lucas went white as chalk.

"What? What is it, Lucas?"

It was if he'd been clubbed in the back of the head.

The music, the people, the opulent surroundings all started to swirl about as Lucas was carried back to that day in the tunnel, that horrific day when he and Maddocks had finally met. The day when he and Zach had fought for their lives.

And Tommy. Poor kid. That bullet that nicked him in the shoulder as he dove for the dynamite detonator. That did some damage.

Not sure he'll be back next year. Not sure he'll ever recover. Even with his new rabbit.

For a few long moments, all Lucas could do was stare out into the room, a look of torment twisting his face into an image of misery.

Then, as if every repugnant memory had been instantly and magically swept away, he came back to the present and smiled.

"Nothing, darling," he said, "nothing at all." He leaned forward to close the gap between them, then hesitated. "That music," he confessed. "That was the song that was playing when I...when Tommy..." He closed his eyes. "Whenever I hear it, I just go right back...right back to that day in the tunnel." He leaned back into his chair. "I'm over it now," he smiled without conviction.

Willa studied him for several seconds. "All right, Lucas. Are you ever going to tell me what finally happened? Was it you? Or Tommy?"

Over the past three months, he had spoken with Willa many times about that day. Together, they'd discussed the various clues he'd received. About how the shovel, the mirror, and the canary were all about the war and the tunnels. That they were clues he should have recognized, clues he should have realized involved someone or something from his days overseas.

He'd told her about the tunnel in Belgium, where Maddocks had been trapped, and how he'd had to make sure the others got out until he could figure out what had caused the explosion. Was it theirs? Or was it the Germans? Things had moved so quickly afterwards. He'd presumed Maddocks dead. And the war had moved on, leaving Lucas no chance of ever finding the man he'd never met.

He'd told her, too, about the spinner toy, the cat, and the pocket watch. How they were all just warnings. Teases meant to confuse and alarm Lucas and show him how much cleverer Maddocks was than him.

All just mental torment before Maddocks was ready to deliver his final retribution.

"You couldn't have known what that pocket watch referred to," Willa had reminded him on more than one occasion. "The time that it was set to…that could have referred to anything! Or nothing!"

But it hadn't referred to nothing, and Lucas was haunted by the memory of his irreverent shortstop Phil Dooley and the bus driver Carl being blown sky-high.

Of all the things that had happened in those final moments in the tunnel with Zach and Tommy and Maddocks, the one thing he'd never talked about was who had actually fallen on the dynamite detonator handle. Who had finally ended Maddocks's reign of terror?

He wasn't sure he knew.

Just as the lantern had sputtered and died, both he and Tommy had hurled themselves forward into the darkness. After that…he couldn't say for sure.

What he did know was that Maddocks had been singularly and fanatically focused on one thing: revenge.

And revenge had dealt an unexpected card.

Or had it?

Was it truly unexpected?

Or was it simply a tunnel from which one could never escape?

Leave that to me, sayeth the Lord.

But expect the unexpected.

"Well, then," Lucas said, brightening and refocusing on the present. "Why don't we have some more of that wonderful cham...that ginger ale that Parker procured? No telling how much longer Murray's might be willing to take a chance serving it."

Willa glowered at him. "Lucas." She turned and stared off for a few moments, then turned back. "You're not going to tell me, are you? All right, then...tell me this. How did you manage to help Aleta's friend Megan with her nephew's problem? Cian, was it? My aunt thinks you're the brightest star in the sky right now!"

"And I take it you don't?" he teased.

"Are we talking about the whole universe?" she taunted back.

Lucas couldn't suppress his laugh. But helping Aleta with her friend's problem had been no laughing matter.

As it turned out, Parker had been involved in fixing the very race on which Cian had bet all of Mullan's money. And when Lucas had threatened to reveal that little detail to the Saratoga Racing Commission, Parker had agreed to donate his winnings to a "charitable cause." Once Parker had turned over the proceeds (an alarmingly large sum of money), Lucas had made haste to get it into the hands of one Clarissa Rose Washington. As a result, Queen Rosie had deemed their *proper business* concluded, and Cian was freed of his debt. It hadn't hurt that Cian had left town shortly thereafter, and Aleta's grateful tears had sealed the deal.

"It wasn't all that hard," said Lucas, once again sidestepping Willa's question. "Parker was a big help. Now, how about some more of that ginger ale?"

Realizing that Lucas was never going to tell all, Willa softened. Then giggled. "More ginger ale, huh? Do you really think we should?"

"I think...," he started. "Well, honestly...I think we'd be fools not to!"

Willa burst out laughing as Lucas called out to Henry, who bustled over to take their order. When he turned back around, Willa's beaming face had turned very solemn.

"Darling," he frowned, hoping he hadn't said something to spoil the evening. "What is it?"

"That man. Maddocks. They never found his body, did they?"

Lucas looked back at her, his eyes absent of any connection.

It was true. The tunnel collapse had proven too much for both the IRT and the New York Police Department's budget constraints, and no attempt had been made to clear the debris or find the body of the man called Maddocks. Considering that there were no future plans for the tunnel, it didn't seem likely that that would change anytime soon.

"But it *is* over, isn't it? I mean, you're sure he couldn't have survived the explosion. Could he?"

Lucas picked up his glass and twirled it around twice.

Could he?

The man had done it once before.

"Impossible," he said with threadbare certainty, his voice just above a whisper.

He repeated the word to himself once more.

Impossible.

Damn! Is it?

He wasn't entirely certain.

"How about we dance?" Lucas deflected, pulling back his chair and taking Willa by the arm. "We're not likely to be back here anytime soon!"

As they stepped onto the dance floor, he swept her into his arms.

"I'll tell you one thing I do know for sure," he said, his eyes staring into hers. "I'm the luckiest guy in the world!"

And of that, he was totally certain.

Author's Note

In 1920, the world was ready for change. The Great War had ended barely a year earlier, leaving twenty million dead and another twenty million wounded. The Spanish flu of 1918-19 added to the carnage, killing an estimated fifty million more people worldwide. Yet, amidst this global exhaustion, there was hope. The United States, once a struggling debtor nation, had emerged as the world's leading banker, and American factories that had churned out unprecedented amounts of wartime materiel now turned their attention to producing anything and everything that the country, and the world, needed.

A growing optimism was beginning to pervade the American psyche, and people looked tentatively, trustingly, toward fewer restrictions and greater leisure. Thousands moved from farms to the cities, a mass migration to better-paying jobs and the hope of a better life. Jazz emerged as the new music, lifting spirits and skirts across the country. And baseball recaptured its title as the National Pastime as Babe Ruth put the roar in the Roaring 20s with his longball prowess. Home runs became the new rage, sending Major League Baseball attendance skyrocketing.

But beneath it all, things were amiss. Protectionism was on the rise. Anarchism entered the American labor movement and bombings were not infrequent. Social disparities became more pronounced.

The 1920s were an exciting decade. I was challenged to not overlook the many startling similarities and ironies reflected in contemporary events in the 2020s. Beyond tracking down the dangerous and insidious man in the bleachers, I hope you enjoy that exploration as well.

Acknowledgments

All creative work is forged through a process of inspiration and perseverance, but it ultimately emerges through a belief that the work has value. Sometimes that belief originates with the artist, quickly, in full self-confidence of the effort within. More often, it evolves more slowly, as a result of the careful consideration, firm guidance, and nurturing encouragement of others.

Family members are frequently inveigled into playing a bigger role than imagined, and perhaps no one endures a writer's journey more exhaustively than one's partner. To my wife, Debra, a special thank you for your unwavering support, encouragement, and patience throughout the process. To my sons, Spencer and Jeremy, and my sister, Patti, thank you for listening to my many moments of disentangling ideas and trying to bring order to the impenetrable.

My very deepest appreciation to close friends and first draft readers Kirby Chown, Theresa LeBlanc, and Howard Warren, who invested incalculable hours painstakingly tracking down errors and inconsistencies and providing thoughtful and gracious guidance and feedback.

I am also grateful to wonderful friends Nasim Ansari, Ted Bridge, Jackie DiGiovanni, Charlie Dougall, John MacMillan, Rual Suarez, and Lynn Wilson, who provided unequivocal encouragement without having seen a single word of the manuscript. My thanks as well to friends and classmates Jeanine Caltagirone, Jeff Cannell, Ruth Jackson, Nancy Nelson, Wayne Robertson, and Frances Youssef, who listened appreciatively as I stumbled through a brief reading over Zoom. This is, of course, what friends are for.

For invaluable help with research, my thanks to Desiree Alden-Gonzalez at the New York Transit Museum who explained the essentials of 1920 subway equipment and tunnels, and to Eric van Slander at the National Archives at College Park, MD, who provided information on the Army's WWI Officer Training Camps.

Also, a special thanks to Cassidy Lent, Manager of Reference Services at the National Baseball Hall of Fame and Museum in Cooperstown, NY, who was able to fill in a small, but elusive, detail about Minor League Baseball.

Finally, I would like to acknowledge the skillful and thorough editing performed by David Aretha, who exceeded all my expectations as to what an editor might deliver. Any errors that remain are mine alone, carelessly, but unintentionally, introduced after David's fine work.

About the Author

E.J. BRIDGWATER has over forty years of film and video production experience and has won over fifty national and international awards for writing, directing and videography. He is the author of *Boardroom Director: How To Produce Exceptional Corporate Video*, as well as an award-winning radio play, *A Fisherman No More*. *The Man in the Bleachers* is his first novel. He lives in Toronto with his family. You can reach him at maninthebleachers@gmail.com.

Made in the USA
Columbia, SC
20 November 2020